The Four Gifts of the King

THE FOUR GIFTS OF THE KING

R. SCOTT RODIN

NEW YORK

LONDON • NASHVILLE • MELBOURNE • VANCOUVER

THE FOUR GIFTS OF THE KING

Published in New York, New York, by Morgan James Publishing. Morgan James is a trademark of Morgan James, LLC. www.MorganJamesPublishing.com

The Morgan James Speakers Group can bring authors to your live event. For more information or to book an event visit The Morgan James Speakers Group at www.TheMorganJamesSpeakersGroup.com.

ISBN 9781683509325 paperback
ISBN 9781683509332 eBook
Library of Congress Control Number: 2018930674

Cover Design by:
Megan Whitney
megan@creativeninjadesigns.com

Interior Design by:
Christopher Kirk
www.GFSstudio.com

Illustrations by:
Douglas Whittle

In an effort to support local communities, raise awareness and funds, Morgan James Publishing donates a percentage of all book sales for the life of each book to Habitat for Humanity Peninsula and Greater Williamsburg.

Get involved today! Visit
www.MorganJamesBuilds.com

To Linda.

All I am and all I have to give to others is but a vivid reflection of all you are to me.

A Note from the Author

Two-thousand miles away from the cold, grey winters of Spokane, Washington, a morning awaited us that we had anticipated for months. My wife, Linda, and I started one of our favorite walks from our little one-bedroom condo on Lawaii Beach up to the Spouting Horn, an icon on the south shore of the Hawaiian Island of Kauai. We soaked up the warmth of the morning sun as we walked along the path that led to the major tourist attraction in this area known as Poipu.

This morning was filled with a sense of exhilaration that transcended the tingling of unfiltered sun on the pasty-white cheeks of two Spokanites venturing out in pursuit of much needed vitamin D. My excitement anticipated the moment every writer dreams of and dreads all at the same time.

My dear wife knew that I had something on my mind that would cause me to explode if it were not shared, and so we chose our morning walk as the venue for the controlled detonation. We walked quietly for a while, past sweeping landscapes of green fields dotted by white-feathered cranes and outlined in iron-red clay dirt hillsides on one side and the crashing of waves along the rocky beaches on the other.

Finally, I took a deep breath and slowly introduced her to a land that my mind had occupied for the preceding months. The characters were undeveloped, the story line was somewhat vague, and the most compelling parts of the plot were still months from being formed. Yet in this primitive state I introduced her to the land of my new friends; Adam, Anna, Merideth, Reed and Walter, and from there slowly on to Steward, Astrid, Elopia, Claire, Dunston and the Black Knight. Most all of the names were not yet even known to me, but Steward's journey was taking form as I breathlessly shared with her the geography of the land of the King.

By the time we returned to our room some two hours later, I had told her everything I knew about the story that was emerging in my mind. She was her usual encouraging self, and I was relieved to finally have a fellow traveler on this journey. I pulled out my laptop that morning and from our lanai overlooking the ocean with its humpback whales and daredevil surfers, I typed the hardest words in a writer's vocabulary – 'Chapter One.' I wrote for nearly three hours, and looking back I acknowledge that few if any of the words I penned that morning remain in the pages that follow. But the journey was engaged!

It is my humble and distinct privilege to invite you to join me in the land of Ascenders and Transmitters, of little kings and mighty warriors, of distortion and the quest for truth, of the dark and menacing Phaedra and the tragic and beautiful Claire. I invite you to walk with four people whose own journeys took them far away from a legacy that was almost lost, and to venture into a world created by a brokenhearted father who craved the return of his children to a life and faith that he so dearly desired for them. I invite you to Harvest and to Aiden Glenn, to Marikonia and Petitzaros. I invite you to laugh with Abner the Blacksmith and grieve with a young man named Steward from Aiden Glenn as he seeks to fulfill his destiny and learn the meaning of his name and the purpose of his life.

This is a parable written to inspire a new appreciation for our call to be holistic, godly stewards in our King's rich and abundant world. The journey is hard, the demands are many and the path is narrow and filled with danger. But the calling is sure and the rewards are without measure.

I invite you to immerse yourself in the story and find in it your own calling, your own journey as a child of the King. And as you do, may you know his Deep Peace!

Scott Rodin

March 2018

Prologue

Mel Sidek waded his way through the relentless crowds lining Shanghai's Nanjing Road. Neon signs glared and pulsated like electronic fireworks, and Mel closed his eyes, tugging at the neck of his shirt. The humidity was suffocating, but this was an important client meeting he didn't want to miss. He maneuvered his way into the street through the stalled traffic, barely making it to the other side as a wave of dizziness forced him to grasp a light pole.

Was he going to lose it right here in the street?

He straightened and pushed forward.

Thank heaven. The Ming Khan restaurant, at last. He stopped outside to catch his breath, looking through his reflection in one of its massive windows.

Where would they be seated?

The Ming Khan was more crowded than usual for a Thursday evening. Waitresses in colorful saris sped platters overloaded with steaming food to the one hundred or so patrons seated at ornate, hand-carved mahogany booths. Chinese lanterns, papier mâché dragon heads, and replicas of samurai swords made the Ming Khan one of Mel's favorites, and he always brought visiting colleagues here to taste authentic Chinese cooking while in Shanghai.

He searched the interior. There, at a far booth, Brian and Art sat waiting for him. Mel watched them through the constant parade of servers moving around them with choreographed precision. Phil was probably on his way. He was always late for these things. Mel turned and started for the front door—

The sidewalk spun around him. Sweat dripped over an eyebrow.

What was going on? Not even the Shanghai humidity produced this kind of sweat.

Mel grasped for the side of the building. He looked up just in time to see Phil approaching the restaurant door.

Phil grinned at him. "Hey, Mel. I'm glad you're late. It won't make me look so…" He frowned. "Hey, are you all right? You look terrible."

Mel wanted to answer, but everything was swirling. Phil's words sounded like he was shouting them from a mile away. A searing spike shot through his left side, into his neck, and down his shoulder. He grimaced as his knees gave way.

Phil caught him and eased him to the sidewalk. "Mel, hey, buddy, easy now. Think you just fainted. It's this crazy heat. Sit here and catch your breath. I'll go get the guys. Are you okay?"

The pain eased, and Mel managed a nod. The heat. It had to be the heat.

"Okay then, just stay here, and we'll be right out."

Mel managed not to groan as Phil propped him up against the restaurant wall then disappeared inside.

Mel lifted a hand to wipe some of the streaming sweat from his face, but the searing pain returned. He clutched at his chest…he couldn't breathe…

Not now, not tonight, please, dear God.

He slumped down and lay flat on the sidewalk, hoping to ease the pain. People scurried around him, and a few stopped to stare.

Air…he needed air…he fought to drag it into his lungs, but in his spirit he knew.

This was his time.

Images flooded his mind. The people he would leave behind. The work at the law firm left undone. And then, another face….

Sam Roberts.

I have to make sure, have to be sure before—

Someone grasped his wrist. An elderly Chinese gentleman had knelt beside him and seemed to be checking his pulse. The man felt Mel's chest and looked into his eyes. There was a sense of peace about him that calmed Mel.

"Mel!"

It was Phil. Mel turned his head and saw his three companions bolt out of the restaurant.

"He's over here!" Phil pushed his way through the crowd that had gathered. The three men fell to their knees beside Mel.

Phil cradled Mel's head in his arms. "Mel, Mel, can you hear me?"

Brian closed in beside him. "Did someone call an ambulance?"

"Yeah," Phil replied, "but this is Shanghai. Who knows how long it will take."

The Chinese man looked up at Mel's friends and bowed then spoke to them in broken English. "Your friend will not see the end of day. Say to him what you must. Now!"

Mel grabbed Art's shirt and pulled him down. "Art, you know…." It was so hard to force the words out. "You know…what must be done…for Sam."

Art looked at Brian, and they nodded. Art leaned close. "It will be done, Mel. Just as you wanted. On my word—"

"—and mine!" Brian echoed.

Mel managed a slight smile. So this was where he would die, outside the Ming Khan restaurant, surrounded by his three closest friends.

In one week they would bury him in a meadow near his home in Salem, Oregon.

CHAPTER
One

Walter Graffenberger guided his silver 1999 Cadillac along a narrow, two-lane ribbon of road that cut through the heart of the Palouse, the expansive wheat country in southeastern Washington. Under his command the land yacht sailed across the rolling terrain and endless curves. He knew every feature of this two-hour drive. He made it a couple of times each month, commuting from his law office in Spokane to his weekend retreat in his hometown.

Walter's hands rested on the wheel. His eyes scanned the terrain, moving between the road ahead and the endless landscape of rolling hills, which alternated between the white patches of snow covering shady hillsides, the light green of emerging winter wheat, and the chocolate brown of overturned earth ready to accept the spring planting.

Despite the scenic beauty rolling past him, his mind was lost in the numbness of grief and anxiety. He played over in his mind the challenge that awaited him, and his spirit struggled.

An enormous responsibility now lay on his shoulders.

As the road neared the edge of a long plateau, he passed a sign that read, "Harvest 3 Miles." Drawing a deep breath, he sat up, focusing on the drive as the road crested the brink of a shelf of land then made a wide, sweeping curve. Next came the descent into the deep crevasse that exposed a ribbon of river shimmering from the last rays of a fading winter sun. In the distance Walter could see the silos—steady sentries on the outskirts of his destination.

He slowed his Cadillac to a stop at the flashing red lights of a railroad crossing. As the freight cars rolled past, his mind was forced back to a frost-covered night and the horrific scene of policemen, flares, fire trucks, and flashing ambulance lights—and the sight of that Toyota Corolla on its roof, crumpled almost beyond recognition. He could still hear the cries of anguished onlookers who recognized the vehicle and assumed the worst.

They were proven right.

The polite horn of the car behind him brought him back to the present as the last train car cleared the intersection and the barrier rose. He drove ahead and turned onto Main Street, glad to shed the memory. At least for now.

As he eased his car through Harvest, Walter managed a smile. Anyone who came through this little city would find it hard to remember the next day. It was one of the hundreds of small towns in the western United States that seemed disconnected from the rest of the world.

He was several hours early, so he pulled into Jerry's Big Stop and cruised up to a waiting gas pump. He worked his credit card through the slider, and as he poked the silver gas nozzle into the side of his car he sensed someone was watching him. A set of eyes peered at him from inside the dirty station windows. Then the doors swung open, and a gray-bearded man in a wheelchair propelled himself toward Walter.

"Is that you, Mr. Graffenberger? Hey, it's great to have you back in Harvest." As the man wheeled closer, his countenance changed. "I guess you're here for the funeral. I'm so sorry, Mr. Graffenberger. I mean, we all are. The whole town is pretty torn up by it."

"Thanks, Jerry. It's a tough day for all of us." Walter put his hand on Jerry's shoulder then looked out across the busy intersection and down Main Street. "Still, it's good to be back here. It's been almost a month, way too long. Any big news to share?"

"Naw, not really. Oh, Mayor Stallings may not run again on account of Harvest Drugs needing to move locations—dry rot in the ceiling beams, I think. Let's see, you heard about the fire at the fairgrounds?"

"Just a quick blurb in the Spokane paper. Tell me about it." Walter didn't much care about the fire, but he always looked forward to seeing Jerry and hearing all the latest Harvest news. He remembered when Jerry left for Iraq as a naive young kid fresh off the 3rd Street baseball diamond. He was also there when Jerry returned.

Without his legs.

Walter watched as Jerry rubbed his thighs to fight the pain that never left him. "How's business? Are you keeping your head above water?"

"Oh, yes, absolutely. I work hard, ya know. Gas prices are tough, but lots of people still rolling through town. Mr. Graffenberger, I can't thank you enough—"

Walter waved him off. "No need, Jerry. I'm glad you're doing well. You're important to this town, you know."

Walter had drawn up the papers that helped the young man buy the gas station on the north edge of town. Jerry had become sort of the official greeter for visitors to the area, almost all of whom were in desperate need of gas and a bathroom by the time they arrived.

Jerry talked on about life in Harvest, and Walter got caught up on the latest gossip, a welcome diversion from the main theme of the day. As Walter got ready to drive away, Jerry shouted after him.

"Be sure to stop by the Mill Stone. They have a new shipment of garden and lawn stuff—spring can't be long now."

Walter drove on for a few blocks, passing clothing and shoe stores, insurance and realtor offices, and the small travel agency that did great business each year right after the grain harvest.

Walter loved this place…and these people. The residents of Harvest were heartland people with strong values and a love for small-town life.

He needed time to escape his growing anxiety so he parked halfway down Main Street. He was happy to lose himself as he strolled along the rows of shops and businesses. And to breathe deep. The smell…that might be what Walter missed the most. Wheat land had its own sweet aroma. Main Street boasted no fewer than five farm implement outlets selling everything from combine parts to full-size threshers and repairing every imaginable piece of farming equipment. New Holland, John Deere, and CASE were the leading retailers here. The town's economy flourished or floundered on the Chicago Board of Trade's announcements of wheat futures and the unpredictable Northwest weather patterns.

Walter watched as the electronic marquee at the bank scrolled the latest wheat futures prices, just as it did every hour of every day. No wonder they held parades to celebrate the wheat harvest. How simple life was here. So many things causing controversy in so many other places seemed to be accepted in Harvest without any question. The three bars in town closed on Sunday, as did the car dealerships and most all shops. The local schools had Easter pageants, the Fourth of July parade was opened with a prayer, and the town put up a Nativity scene each year on the courthouse lawn without a protest. Amazing.

He walked on for several blocks and then paused in front of the windows of Harvest's only jewelry store. He liked to survey the modest collection of diamond rings sparkling under the garish array of lighting. As his eyes moved up the display, he caught his reflection.

He started…then frowned.

While the image bore all the features of a successful country lawyer—thinning white hair cut short and combed back from his face, round spectacles, starched white shirt, gold cufflinks, and tailored suit—the features were lost in a somber grayness. Grief inhabited every wrinkle and crease in his sixty-three-year-old face. He had to look away.

Come on, Walter. You need to be strong today.

"Walter, hey, welcome back to Harvest!"

Walter turned at Carter Blake's booming voice. A broad-shouldered man in his fifties, smothered in a gray parka and fur hat, came toward him, accompanied by a smiling Cathy Blake, who stepped ahead of Carter and gave Walter a hug.

"Walter, it's so good to have you here."

"Hi, Cathy, hey, Carter. How are you folks?"

Carter slapped him on the shoulder and laughed. "Cold. Do you have time to grab a cup of coffee? The funeral is a couple of hours off." The three found a quiet table at the Combine Café next to the Mill Stone.

Carter warmed his hands on a large ceramic mug of black drip coffee. He sat back in his chair and shook his head.

"Well, I have to tell you this is a hard day. One sad day."

Walter nodded, not looking up. "I feel the same way, Carter. It's a day that'll impact all of us."

The comment hung in the air, and their silence was transformed into a moment of reverence.

Cathy stirred some lemon into her tea then looked up. "Will you be in Harvest for a few days, or do you have to go back after the funeral?"

"No, I'll be here for a couple of days. There is the disposition of the estate to deal with."

Carter and Cathy glanced at each other as though searching for permission to talk. Carter took a long sip of coffee.

"Walter, we saw Alex this morning. Had a nice chat, well…cordial, I guess. I can't understand what went wrong with him—"

"—with all of them." Cathy raised her hands in frustration. "How can four children of such wonderful parents turn their backs on them like that? I'll just never understand it." She paused, fidgeting with her tea bag and stirring more lemon into her cup. "I assume they'll all be here?"

Walter nodded. He had confirmed with all four Roberts children that they would be there for two days. They couldn't understand what would take so long, but Walter insisted, and they agreed.

"You know how much I liked Alex when he was that little guy growing up around here." Carter sat forward. "I taught him to throw a baseball, you remember. Sam wasn't much for sports. I coached him every year he played. He was one smart and happy kid, so at home at the church and Sunday school. I don't think he missed a week I taught sixth grade at Resurrection. Such a nice kid then off to seminary, and then—what do you think happened, Walt?"

"I'm not sure we'll ever really know. His first three years went fine, according to Sam. But something snapped when Lori died, and I guess he never recovered."

"God rest her soul," Cathy whispered.

Carter put his arm around Cathy and rubbed her shoulder.

"And then there's the rest of them." Carter stared down at his coffee. "Each one seemed to drift away. All I can say is that it should be an interesting funeral."

"Now, dear, these are Sam and Lori's kids, and we need to make them feel welcome here. This is their home after all, regardless of how much they've turned away from it... and us."

Walter reached across and squeezed her arm. "I know they'll appreciate that kind of welcome. I'm sure they're expecting the worst."

Dear Cathy, ever the sensitive one. He sat back and continued.

"Cathy, may I ask you a favor?"

She set her cup down and gave Walter a look of surprise. "Well, yes, Walter. Of course, anything."

"You know those amazing cinnamon rolls you bake?"

Cathy smiled at the compliment.

"Could you bring a batch by the house tomorrow on your way to church? I have a feeling they might be just what we need about then."

"I'm happy to do so."

As the coffee and conversation ended, the three of them rose and stepped out onto the sidewalk that glistened with ice. Walter watched as Carter took Cathy's arm, tenderness and love on display as he tucked it under his, and they ambled away in their half-embrace down the empty brick walkway.

Walter knew he had to watch his time, but he couldn't help but stop in at the Mill Stone.

The barn-like structure had dominated Main Street for more than sixty years. Walter's dad told him stories about when it was a blacksmith and tack shop. In the sixties its flat-front facade had been whitewashed and new lettering added to showcase its transformation into a combination hardware, lawn and garden, appliance, and even clothing store. Walter smiled at the thought of the days he'd spent getting lost among its mountainous racks of goods. A person could find about anything they needed on those soaring, dusty shelves of this Harvest icon.

Time will run out if I'm not careful...just a quick look down a couple of aisles.

By the time he emerged onto the sidewalk, the afternoon was losing its light. Walter walked back to his car under the hiss of old-fashioned gas lamps sparking to life. They were added in the eighties in an attempt to turn Harvest into a tourist town. The tourists never came, but the gaslights remained. Each summer they supported dangling baskets of glorious nasturtiums, petunias, lobelia, alyssum, and ivy. Stripped of their floral glory, the baskets now hung empty and forgotten against the graying February sky, and the dim light of the globes added an eerie luminosity to the scene.

Walter had one last stop before the funeral. He drove past the Harvest Gospel Mission. For the first time in its history it was closed for the day. Just seeing the mission overwhelmed him. His grief welled up, and he struggled to steer his car to a parking spot. He was suffocating in emotion. How could he accept that Sam would never again be at the door with his welcoming smile and deep compassion?

I need to do this. Come on. Pull it together.

For several minutes he sat and prayed and grieved. Then, collecting himself, Walter made his way to the mission.

Carl Martinez was there to greet him. "I am so glad to see you, Mr. Graffenberger."

"It's good to see you too, Carl, and you know you can call me Walt."

"Yes, yes, you have told me. It just doesn't seem…respectful. But, yes, I will call you Walt." A heavy-set Hispanic man in his early forties, Carl wore the one dark blue suit he had for special occasions. Carl was one of the most gracious men Walter had ever met. He'd worked alongside Sam for the past two years, and now he was stepping into the role of director of the mission.

Walter put his hand on Carl's shoulder. "How are you holding up?"

"I have no time to grieve, Mr. Graffen—Walt. You know the wheat prices were down last year. Many farmers lost everything. That sent so many people to us that I started to panic every time I heard the train stop."

Walter shook his head. "I can't believe they still haven't straightened that out, after all the time and money we spent." He'd worked for two years to help the city council correct an old law that required Burlington Northern Railroad trains to come to a full stop at the crossing on the north end of town.

"Unfortunately not. As soon as the train stops they jump out, and more and more it's younger men, women, and even small families. I've stood and watched them. It breaks your heart."

As a kid, Walter would run down to the tracks in the autumn to watch long trains pull hundreds of empty, red wheat cars. They rolled into Harvest, ready to be filled to capacity with the region's golden treasure. He used to cover his ears at the screech of steel train wheels against the tracks. That sound resonated for miles, but no one in Harvest minded. It was the sound of money.

It was so different now.

"I had hoped that the Farm Aid and other programs would help most of them hang on."

"No, they just keep coming. The trains are so dangerous, but still they come to find shelter, food—and hope. They are so scared, so discouraged. Most of them need the basic things: food, a bath, a cot, and a job. They put their trust in us, Walt. They trust the people of Harvest to give them the kind of stability and hope they lost by lousy weather or the dropping wheat prices."

"Or just plain poor farming."

Carl nodded.

"Do you still get the pros?"

"Oh, yes. A few still show up and dupe every kindhearted soul they can find and then move on to the next town. But they're the exception. Most of these folks are just searching for a better life. We do all we can. We have the recovery programs for the addicts, and for others we just try to restore a little dignity. It's a lot to try to do when you're just three blocks from the train stop. I don't know how Mr. Roberts did it all these years."

"Carl, you've done a wonderful job here. I know it can seem overwhelming, but you have a good board, lots of volunteers, and a town to support you. You'll do well. Just trust in the good people you have around you."

Carl's smile was warm. "Thank you. May I say that you almost sounded like Mr. Roberts."

"That's a real compliment. Thank you." Walter shook Carl's hand and hoped it would convey just a small bit of the confidence he had in him. Sam had hand-picked Carl when he was a recovering meth addict. To see him now was testament to the power of God to change lives, a power that Sam relied on for all his thirty-two years at the mission.

Walter looked at his watch. "We'd better be heading to the church. Do you need a ride?"

"No, I will lock up and walk. This is a day for long walks and lots of talking to God."

On the way back to the church, Walter made the short drive to Orchard Street. He eased past the Roberts home. Four cars were parked in the driveway.

Thank God, they're all here. Help me, Lord. I hope I can do this. They all know Sam's secret, and I pray that won't destroy everything we have planned. Help me honor Sam's wishes, Lord. I can't do this without You.

Walter drove on to the church and sat in his car for several minutes. All around, people dressed in their Sunday best were walking toward the Resurrection Christian Church.

The time he'd dreaded had arrived.

He stepped out of the car, put on his suit coat, and joined several others making their pilgrimage on the somber, late-winter day. Two thoughts flooded his mind. That the lives of four people were about to be changed forever.

And that this little town he loved would never be the same.

Two

Alex froze, suitcase in hand, staring up the front sidewalk leading to the expansive, covered front porch of the Roberts family home.

I can't believe I'm the first one here. Where are Merideth and Anna? They should've been here by now.

But it was just him.

I'm not ready for this.

He would be the first to walk into the family home without a mother or father to greet him. The first to fight his way into the heartless silence of a house that, until now, had only known voices and music and life. He took a step back toward his car. He could sit there and wait—

"Alex, is that you? Hey, it's good to have you back here at the house."

Alex turned to find Frank Farquar standing in his yard. He had lived next to the Roberts family for as long as Alex could remember. He lifted his suitcase in a half wave.

"Thanks, Frank. Good to see you."

"Will the other kids be here?"

"Yup, we're all here for, well, you know, Dad's funeral."

Frank shook his head and smacked his forehead with an open palm.

"Of course, of course you are. Stupid question. Beth and I will be there. Four o'clock, right?"

Alex nodded. Then he turned back to face the moment.

C'mon. Let's get this over with.

He walked up the stairs, and they groaned under his weight. He set his suitcase down and slid the lid off the porcelain kettle sitting on a little table next to two rattan lounge chairs. Inside was the front door key. It'd been there forever.

Everyone in the county knew that.

The heavy lock turned with a bit of force, and the large wooden door creaked open. Alex switched on the hall light and closed the door behind him. He was in.

It was so quiet.

As he turned on lights and made his way to the living room, he kept waiting to hear his dad call out from the den or see his mom come around the corner from the kitchen, wiping her hands on her apron, preparing to give him a welcoming embrace.

They were gone. They were really gone.

His breathing grew heavy and his chest began to ache. He grabbed his suitcase and headed upstairs to his old bedroom. Nothing much had changed. He'd been here two years ago when his mom died, and two other times since then. He never thought he'd be back here so soon for another funeral. And burying Dad. This was really happening. He was now the oldest remaining member of the family.

Alex put his suitcase on the bed. He could unpack later. He went downstairs and walked through the house, peering into rooms and looking out windows at the changing view of the lawn and neighborhood. With no one there, the whole place seemed bigger.

Lonelier.

Dad had a lot of days here by himself. How did he do it? I should've come over more often, but work has been so…. Okay, stop. We're not taking this guilt trip.

He checked his watch. 11:30 a.m.

Plenty of time before the funeral.

He made his way back to the kitchen to put on some coffee. He'd left Seattle at 6:00 a.m. to avoid the traffic and give himself a little time before the service. He'd not seen Anna or Merideth in over a year, and it'd been longer than that since he and Reed were together.

With a hot cup of Kona Gold in his favorite old mug, he wandered into his father's study. He paused at the door and studied the room.

Everything had been left the way it was the last time he was here. It was as if Dad had just stepped out for a few minutes.

Even the familiar smells of Old Spice and alder firewood still hung in the air, like an invisible memorial. Alex walked in and examined his dad's desk. He sat in the leather swivel chair and looked around, his hands feeling their way along its well-worn arms. Life through Dad's eyes. The mantel and massive bookshelves were filled with memorabilia that sat like silent talismen bearing witness to a life well lived. Alex walked to the book-shelf marked *Theology*. He ran his fingers along the spines, letting them stop and start again as he read the titles. On the second shelf, halfway across, his hand stopped. He read the spine. Then again.

The Epistle to the Romans. Karl Barth.

He reached on top of the book with his finger and began to pull it out then paused—and pushed it back in its place.

I can't do this. Not yet. Not today.

Anna saw Alex's car in the driveway. Thank heaven. She did *not* want to be the first one to arrive. She pulled her six-year-old Prius in beside the new Lexus. She got out and glanced back at the two cars.

I guess that about says it all.

She dragged her suitcase up the walk and onto the porch. The lights from the hallway shone out through the front door glass, giving warmth to the February gloom, even at noon.

"Hey, Alex, where are you?" She wheeled her suitcase across the wooden hallway floor and into the kitchen.

"I'm in here, Anna. In Dad's study."

She left her suitcase and joined him, stopping at the door of the office and peering in. Alex stood by the bookshelves, examining various titles. He smiled when he saw her.

"It's like Dad never left. I think Walt wanted it that way. How are you? How was the drive?"

Anna pressed against the doorframe, tilting her head to lean into it.

"I was here with Dad just a couple of months ago. It was exactly like it is now. Every-thing is here, in its place…everything but him…." She put her hand to her lips. Alex started across the room, but she halted him with a raised hand.

"I'll be all right. I just need some coffee." She turned to leave then looked back. "Oh, and the drive was fine. Just a couple of hours to Walla Walla with the new bypass."

Alex followed her into the kitchen. "Have you had lunch?"

"I actually brought us all lunch from the restaurant. I figured nobody would have time to stop and eat. It's out in the car. I'll go grab it."

Alex put his coffee down. "Here, let me help."

They walked out together and unloaded three large brown bags from the back of her car. Each one was labeled *The Boat Inn*. Alex set the last one down on the kitchen counter then studied the stenciling. "How many years have you been at the Boat Inn? Ten?"

"Fifteen, ever since I left—well, okay, ever since I dropped out of college. I'd leave it in a second if I knew where else to go or what else I wanted to do."

They unpacked the bags onto the large, rectangular kitchen table and laid out an impressive spread of deli meats, cheeses, breads, salads, and all the trimmings.

Anna waited for Alex's critique.

"What about the next five years from now, or ten? What do you want to do?"

There it was.

My big brother the planner, the strategizer. Always with goals, dreams, and ambitions. Must be nice.

"Dear brother, you know how it is with me. Live a day at a time and try to make the most of it. You wake up from dreams and fall short of goals. I'm just happy to get through each day, and I don't worry about tomorrow until it comes."

"But you can't stay at the restaurant—"

She was *not* going to get into this.

"Alex, I appreciate your concern. But let's just be here for Dad and not do the career counselor bit, okay?"

That was harsh, but she couldn't take the condescension. Not today. This was Dad's day. Anna tried a conciliatory smile. "I'm going to unpack and get changed. Could you give me a hand with my suitcase? My back's been giving me fits lately."

"Sure, and I'm sorry, sis. I just want the best for you."

Anna spun around. "And what *is* that, Alex? What is 'the best for Anna'? Tell me. Do you know? Because I sure as heck don't. I was pretty lost before Mom and Dad died, and now, now…." She threw her hands in the air.

Enough. Now was not the time.

She turned and pounded up the stairs, walked into her room and went over to the window, looking out into the backyard. Alex put her suitcase in her room and left.

Dad, why did you have to leave me? I needed you. I needed Mom.

And they'd both left her. Now all she had left…all she could hold on to…was the secret.

"Look, Jack, either get that contract to FedEx today by six or clean out your desk. Is that clear enough?" Merideth punched the red *end* button on her phone with such force that she broke her nail.

Great, just great. Incompetent jerk. Why couldn't she find any good people? All she ever seemed to do was hire and fire. Why couldn't she find any loyalty anymore?

She sighed and took a moment to look around. She'd pulled up behind the well-worn little Prius that now looked even more out of place than usual between Alex's Lexus and her BMW.

Poor Anna. Would she ever be able to afford a real car?

Merideth collected herself. The sight of the family home calmed her a bit. She pulled out her bag and walked up to the porch. Despite the cold, she sat for a moment on one of the rattan chairs. She could hear voices in the house.

She closed her eyes. A moment…just a moment to prepare.

She breathed in and blew out through pursed lips then got up and walked in the door and down the hallway to the kitchen. "Hey, you two…oh, hi, Alex. Where is Anna?"

He rolled his eyes. "Upstairs. Guess I set her off a bit."

Already? That didn't take long. "Be nice. She's fragile, you know."

"I *was* nice. Geez, sis, all I said was that I wanted the best for her."

"Meaning your best or hers?"

Alex slammed his hands on the counter and looked down at the floor. "Can't I say anything around here without its getting blown out of proportion?" He looked up at Merideth. "I just want her to be happy. Is that so bad?"

Poor brother. You're wound so tight. Well, go ahead and get angry. I'm keeping this smile on my face until I know what Walter has in mind.

"Okay, let's forget it and start over. I'm sure she's fine. And, Alex, it's good to see you."

Merideth gave him a hug, which she could sense he appreciated. She poured herself a cup of coffee while Alex took her suitcase upstairs to her room then wandered down the hall into the family room. She picked up the corner of her favorite comforter and rubbed the soft cotton fabric between her fingers. It had a log cabin pattern made of strips of fabric in deep greens, browns, rusts, and golds. Lori had made it for her sixteenth birthday…

She sat down for a minute and pulled the heavy comforter over her.

How many mornings had she sat here under this quilt, drinking coffee and wondering how soon she could get out of this town?

"There's a familiar sight. Welcome to Harvest, sister."

"Hi, Anna." Merideth looked over as her younger sister entered the room. She was wearing an oversized beige shirt over her jeans to hide her weight. Her hair was a dull brown, and without makeup she looked pale and old.

Oh, Anna, you look terrible.

Anna leaned down and hugged her. "It's good to have you back in the house. Dad would be so pleased to see you here."

"Yes, well, I hope so."

Anna took hold of her arm. "Mer, you know he would be. Look—I know you two drifted apart, but Dad missed you and always wanted you to feel welcome here. He loved you so much. You know that, don't you?"

Sure, he loved *her*—he just hated what she did.

"Yes, sure, I know that. But thanks for the reminder. So are you okay? I guess big brother pushed some old buttons."

Anna dropped her gaze. "That's my fault. I'm too sensitive. I'll apologize. He was just trying to help."

And there she was. Anna, always apologizing and taking the blame. Heaping more weight on her tired shoulders.

Stand up straight, girl. "Hey, don't let him off the hook so easily. He can stew a little. It's good for him."

Anna gave a half smile. "Not today. This is Dad's day, and I want us to be together and get along...for him...and for Mom."

With that, she looked at Merideth, stepped forward, and fell into her arms. "Mer, they're gone. They'll never be back here!"

Merideth consoled her older sister, cringing as Anna's tears soaked into her silk jacket.

I should've worn a blend.

"That's it, the big house on the corner. Just stop in front. It looks like everyone else is here."

Reed paid the cab driver, got his suitcase from the trunk, and started up the front walk. He noted the three cars.

Must be nice to have the time to drive across the state. Still, maybe better than that turboprop, puddle-jumper he'd bounced over in.

As he stood looking up at the old familiar surroundings, the front door opened and Alex came down the stairs. "Reed, hey, welcome home. How was the flight?"

Reed set his suitcase down and shook his brother's hand. "Cramped, slow, and bumpy. Not exactly first-class to London. How was the drive?"

"Not bad, actually. It's been awhile since I've driven across state. Pretty quiet over here. Hey, hold on for a minute and let me grab my cell phone charger." As Alex went to his car, Reed looked at the house. His boyhood sprang to life in front of him.

Over there was where he played Superman on the roof and fell off. His cape—a big beach towel from Seaside, Oregon—caught on the gutter and left him swinging six feet from the ground.

Can't believe I didn't break my neck. Glad old man Farquar found me before Dad.

He noticed the piece of plywood nailed to the side of the front stair risers.

The skunk. He'd forgotten about that.

Alex beeped his car lock and rejoined Reed. "There, thanks. C'mon—the girls are inside."

Reed put out his hand and stopped him. "Hey, Alex, do you remember that skunk that got stuck under the front stairs the day of the prom?"

"Oh…yeah. Dad had a broom and a bed sheet, and you and I each had a pan and a wooden spoon."

Reed started laughing. "Yeah, and some guy…Tommy Mertz, that was him…he was supposed to pick Mer up for the prom any time. And here we are banging on pots and Dad trying not to get sprayed, and the whole front porch smelled like skunk."

Alex was bent over. "And Dad…Dad catches the thing in the sheet and stands there looking at it and says, 'Maybe we can teach him not to spray and keep him as a pet.' And then it sprays him, right through the sheet."

Reed wiped his eyes. "That porch stunk for a week, and poor Mer had to meet her date at the end of the block. She said she could smell it most of the way to the gymnasium."

Alex nodded. "Anna called us the smelly boys that entire summer."

Reed relished the memory and a chance to laugh out loud. He caught his breath. "So…how's Anna doing?"

Alex collected himself. "Oh, not great. We've already had a run-in. She's pretty vulnerable right now."

Right now? He'd never seen her when she wasn't vulnerable. Reed followed Alex inside and found Anna and Merideth in the kitchen. "Hey, ladies, the gang's all here now." He gave them both a hug.

Anna held on for an extra moment. "I'm so glad to have you here, little brother. After what we went through when Mom died, can you believe this? I mean, just two years?"

Reed had spent several days with Anna and his dad going through their mom's things, telling stories, and laughing and crying together. Alex was tied up in a big real estate deal and only came the day of the funeral. Merideth had been overseas on business and nearly missed it altogether.

Theirs wasn't exactly a close-knit family. Reed was surprised everyone was here. Of course, they all knew Dad's secret. "Yeah, I still can't believe he's gone. How is it for you guys? Being back here without Dad…and Mom?

Alex reached in the refrigerator and took out a Pepsi. "I was the first one here, and it was hard. My heart knew they were supposed to be here. I waited for their voices…and nothing."

The four looked at each other, silent.

Finally, Merideth grabbed a cup from a rack on the wall. "Reed, can I get you some coffee? You're just in time for lunch. I'm guessing they didn't feed you on the plane."

"Not hardly. Five stale pretzels won't cut it. Where'd all the food come from?"

Anna raised a hand. "That would be me, from the restaurant."

"Wow, thanks. Can we pay for this?"

Please don't take that the wrong way.

Anna smiled. "No, Allen—he's the owner—he gave it to us no charge. He wanted to pass along his sympathies."

Reed picked up a slice of bread and buttered it. "Tell him thanks from all of us."

The four made lunch and sat around the familiar kitchen table to eat. Reed watched his siblings…

Alex was guarded but grieving.

Anna, of course, was struggling to hold it together.

But Merideth…she acted like she was at a reunion, not their dad's funeral. Didn't she feel anything at all?

Merideth looked at her watch. "What time should we leave?"

"Say, 3:30?" Alex replied. "It starts at four, and then the graveside service."

Anna perked up. "Reverend Frolic asked us to stay afterward and be part of a reception line to greet people. Don't forget that."

Merideth grimaced. "I wish I could. We get to shake hands with a town full of people who wonder why we're even here."

Reed felt the tension fill the room.

Well, the cat was out of the bag now. Leave it to Merideth.

No one dared reply for a moment, so he waded in. "That might be a little unfair, Mer. Although I can't say I'm looking forward to it."

Alex set his sandwich down and wiped his hands with his napkin, pushing with more intensity than necessary. "You all don't have to worry. I'll be the target for most of the daggers."

Anna started toward him. "Alex, that's not—"

"C'mon. Let's be honest. I'm the golden boy of the church who went off to seminary and disappointed God, my parents, the church and, well, the whole blasted town. Left the calling, left the faith, left the community. No, I'll be the target here."

Reed watched Anna and Merideth for a response. Anna stepped in—no surprise there.

"Alex, that all may be true, but there's enough in all our lives for people here to question. I mean, Mom and Dad had views…and values…and expectations—"

Merideth slammed her fork down. "And we let them down. Is that it, Anna? So by following our hearts, moving away, working hard, and being successful, we somehow violated a family vow of—what? Poverty?"

Reed turned sideways in his chair and crossed his legs. "Mer, you have to admit our lives don't exactly reflect our parents' values. I mean, look at me. Dad tried so hard to teach me about being a steward, being generous, and not loving my toys so much. Mom hoped I would stay closer to the faith, find a church, and marry a nice Christian girl. I've missed the mark on about every score. But I know Dad loved us, just like we talked about at Mom's funeral. They may have been disappointed in our decisions, but they loved *us*. And the people here knew that, I think."

Merideth's shoulders lifted, and a scowl spread across her forehead. "Well, I'm sorry, but I'm not going to apologize for success. I know Dad never understood it, but I'm not carrying a load of guilt because I chose a different life from the one he'd hoped I would. And if these people can't deal with it, then to…." She shook her head. "Well, that's their problem. *Not* mine." She stood, looked at each of them, lifted her chin and strolled out.

Reed looked at Anna, and she mouthed a silent "thank you." Alex just sat quietly, staring down at his plate of picked-over food.

Reed drew a sigh. He was hoping they could hold it together long enough to get through this. They had two days.

Two very long days.

Three

𝕱rolic Hastings stood next to his assistant, Molly Flaughtery, as they peered out the window from the east wing of Resurrection Christian Church.

Molly put her hands to her lips. "Look at all the folk, Reverend. I don't think the church will hold 'em. I hear the whole town is closing. I guess he's about the only real hero we've ever had. Dear God in heaven, there's more than we had on Easter." Her airy Irish accent captured the feel of the moment.

Frolic could only nod. *God, please help me shoulder this responsibility.*

"Reverend, you still have some time before the service. Can I pour ya a cuppa?"

He smiled. Molly believed a good cuppa could fix anything. "Thanks. I think I'll just have some quiet time. Would you check to see if they're here yet?"

She wrinkled her forehead and squinted at him. "Sure thing. If you don't mind me sayin', them being here, after all this time, well, that'll surely put the flint in the tinder box."

The woman had a phrase for everything. Just one more reason he was so thankful for her.

Frolic rifled through the program and the Scripture readings one last time then settled into his favorite chair. From the dark leather wingback he could see out the window to the continuing flow of his fellow townspeople.

Oh, Sam, how this town will miss you.

An ache pierced him. He'd said those same words to Sam less than two weeks ago. The last time they were together. They'd talked for almost three hours that night at Colfax County Memorial.

Frolic closed his eyes…and remembered….

Sam lay in his hospital bed under a standard white sheet, his head propped halfway up and his knees bent. Machines beeped and gurgled on both sides, and tubes ran around and into him like some unfinished cobweb. A small translucent green tube fed oxygen to his nostrils.

Frolic wanted Sam to leave this world with his mind and heart filled with the wonderful memories of a life lived so richly for others. He wanted to see Sam smile and relive the happy times that marked his life. He pulled the stiff-backed chair up alongside Sam's bed and leaned in close to his dear friend. "Sam, tell me about the best moments, the things that come back easily to you now and bring you happiness. It's been an incredible life. Tell me what's on your heart."

Sam opened his eyes, and Frolic could swear he saw a hint of eternity in them.

"God is so good." Sam managed the short sentence then breathed deep from the air tube.

Frolic could sense he wasn't in pain, but the heavy medication for a failing heart made it hard for him to keep a clear line of thought. So as they talked and told old stories, Frolic filled in the gaps.

He relished every moment.

This may well be the last time he would see Sam alive. Sam knew it too, although neither of them mentioned it. It was a reverent understanding between old friends. "Do you remember what you thought when you first laid eyes on this town?"

Energy seemed to fill Sam, and he pushed with his elbows to sit up a little straighter. "Sure can. I was just a sophomore in high school when my folks decided to move here. I think I yelled, 'This is the sticks,' when we drove in."

They both laughed—Sam through coughing and wheezing. He calmed his breathing and continued. "Dad worked hard to help us get along…repairing grain threshers. 'Bout worked himself to death during harvest. He had time off in winter…he and Mom never got used to the winters…it was hard on his asthma."

Frolic pressed his hands together, anguishing as he watched Sam struggle to create short, choppy sentences. This dear man had always been so articulate, a master storyteller. Yet despite the struggle the tone of his voice still carried the same amazing sense of peace and gracefulness. Frolic poured some water into Sam's plastic hospital cup, put a straw in it, bent it at an angle and handed it to him. "I can't remember—how old were you when he died?"

Sam finished a long sip and took another deep draw on the oxygen. "Seventeen, just starting my senior year at Harvest High. Mom never got over losing him…every shop and sidewalk reminded her of him. I've never seen two people more in love…I guess that's why she finally moved away. I can't blame her, Frolly…some people criticized her for leaving and moving back East to be with her sister. But they're wrong…it was the best thing she could've done."

"I can't believe you moved into that little room above Bob Poole's old garage. How did you ever keep warm?"

"Back then, I lived pretty much my whole day…between Dickersons' and the bowling alley. I'd get to my job at the shoe store at 8:00 a.m. and get warm…I'd work until 5:00 p.m. then go grab something to eat at the bowling alley." He took another pull on the oxygen and waited a bit. "I'd hang out there until 10:00 p.m. some days. I was only at the little room long enough to shower, sleep, and do my devotions…. Still, I like to have froze some nights."

"Old man Poole never turned the heat on for you?"

Sam leaned forward with a twinkle in his eye. "Frolly, that *was* with the heat on." Sam laughed hard, which made him grab his chest and cough. The nurse came in and told them both to go easy. That only brought more laughter.

When they calmed down, Sam got a faraway look in his eyes. "It was so lonely after Mom left…and it about killed me. Would have driven me from Harvest" —he met Frolic's eyes and smiled—"had it not been for that one, sweet April morning."

Frolic inched forward in his seat, hanging on every familiar word.

Sam looked ahead to where the ceiling met the wall, as if looking to a horizon at sunrise. "She was a vision, Frolly, a true vision. This little Lori Evans comes prancing into Dickersons' looking for some kitten heels—they'd just come into fashion, as I remember." He took his time, borrowing energy from the oxygen. "She's eyeing a new pair on the shelf, and the sun is dancing off her skin like it was delighted just to touch her…. Of course, I'd seen her before in school, but you know how there is that moment in a girl's life…when one day she's a plain ol' tomboy in jeans and a ponytail, and the next she's turned into a woman, almost like she doesn't know it?…Well, it was like that. That day in Dickersons'…she was a woman, all right."

Sam picked up a Kleenex and wiped his nose and mouth. He adjusted the oxygen back in place and sat up a little straighter. His bright eyes and joyful smile bore testimony to his delight in telling the story.

"We fell in love as fast as two people ever could. Don't have any idea what she ever saw in me, but there was plenty to see in her. Dear Lord, Frolly, she was beautiful. She was smart, happy, and I loved her so." Tears welled up in his eyes.

Frolic smiled, and his heart was breaking.

Remember, Sam. Remember and be at peace.

"Sam, I know you miss her—"

"Frolly, I'm not crying because I miss her." He leaned a little forward and pointed to the sky. "It's because I know how close I am to seeing her again. These are tears of joy."

Now Frolic had to fight tears. He listened as Sam retold stories about the days he and Lori dated, as enthralled as the first time he'd heard them. Sam talked in detail about their long walks along Orchard Avenue admiring the graceful houses with deep, cool porches that looked out on sweeping lawns.

"Lori loved those old homes. It was on one of those walks that we first stood and admired the mayor's house.… Oh, Lori got such a twinkle in her eye when she looked at that old, abandoned home. I can still hear her saying, 'One day I can see myself on that porch, rocking my children to sleep and watching the town go by.' I told her she better marry a rich man. You know what she said to me, Frolly?"

Frolic did, but he was happy to hear it again, so he shook his head.

"She said, 'No, I just need a hard-working man with a great heart.' She had such faith in me. Huh, a lot more than her father did, that's for sure."

Sam winced then shifted a bit in the bed, struggling to rearrange his pillow. Frolic reached over to adjust it for him. "Oh, yes, I remember. I had just gotten to know the Evans family in my first year at Resurrection. I think Jack had started his first term as state senator, and Margie was teaching ninth grade—"

"—and singing the national anthem at about every event in the county," Sam said with a laugh. "Old Jack didn't think much of me…'a loner with little ambition and even fewer skills,' I think is what he told Lori he thought of me. Man, he was a tough old bird."

Frolic had had his own battles with Jack. "Yes, he was, but he came around. I'm not sure anyone in this town admired you more, Sam."

Jack and Margie both came to love Sam. His unmistakable love for their daughter touched her parents deeply. "So do you remember when we first met, Sam? That day you were trying to replace the gutters on that old mansion?"

"Oh, yes, dear friend. I certainly do. You were there just in time to watch me fall.… It's by the grace of God I didn't break my neck falling off that ladder. That was one of many times that house nearly killed me."

"I remember. Scared me to death. But we had such a great talk on the porch while you iced your shoulder. I knew then I'd found a real friend. That's what you've been to me, Sam, the dearest friend a man, and a pastor, could ever have. I want you to know that."

For the first time Sam's gaze fixed on Frolic, and his countenance conveyed a depth of gratitude only a dying man can offer. That was enough for Frolic. That's all he wanted; contentment and peace to sing in Sam's heart in these last hours.

Time was slipping away, and Frolic wanted to fill each second.

"And you did finally get those gutters up."

"Yup…with about every nail and coat of paint I would say to myself, 'Sam, how is it that a nobody like you…is living in the mansion built by the wheat baron Clarence Fuller?' You know, every mayor of Harvest lived in that house until Bill Hightower. He bought a new place out by the golf course…that beautiful old house sat empty for three years before we bought it, and it showed it. Everything needed to be replaced. Everything."

"It took you both what, eighteen years, to restore it?"

"Twenty years! I can still remember the day Lori and I applied the last brushstroke of paint…I was just telling Walter about it the other day. You remember the ceremony the town put on for us, don't you?"

Frolic nodded. He'd been on the board of the Chamber of Commerce when they voted to declare the manor a regional landmark. The house became a source of pride for the entire town and a monument to Sam and Lori's patience, persistence, and loving care.

"You bought that house about the same time you started at the mission, is that right?"

"Yes, yes, it is. Two years after Lori and I were married, they called me to see if I would be interested in running the mission…. That was the start of over thirty years at that wonderful old place. How I loved every minute of it."

"How many lives did you save over those years, Sam? Gotta be tens of thousands."

Sam shook his head, his graying face mustering a frown. "Not one. You know as well as anyone, we don't save a soul…. But I take a lotta joy in believing that God saved a bunch. We just did what we could…served a hot meal, offered a shower and prayed with those that would let us. We saw a lot of folks set the bottle aside or fight through the withdrawals from meth or other awful things. We saw some healed, some saved, some even transformed…. But so many others came and went and came back again. So much pain out there, Frolly, but I don't have to tell you that."

Sam paused, and Frolic saw his expression shift from calm to consternation.

"Do you think we made a difference?"

Frolic's eyes widened. "Yes, of course you made a difference. More than you'll ever know." He laid his hand on Sam's arm. "You may be the most beloved man in this county. I know you've always been a humble man, but I want you to hear me. You are leaving behind a legacy of lives changed forever because of you and the work of that mission. Are you hearing me?"

Sam's breathing grew heavy, and Frolic jumped up and called for the nurse. She came into the room and checked one of the many tubes connected to Sam's arms.

Frolic glanced at the doorway. *Please, God…let Sam's children show up soon.* He couldn't bear the thought of leaving Sam alone. Walter was on his way, too, but wouldn't be there for a couple of hours.

The nurse finished her inspection, made a few adjustments, straightened Sam's pillow and handed him his water.

"Keep drinking, Sam. As long as you feel up to it, you and the Reverend can keep talking."

Thank heaven. Frolic let loose a breath he hadn't realized he was holding. "Do you want to go on?"

Sam took a long drink through the little straw then set the cup down and struggled to take a deep breath. His words were more labored, and he worked to form each one.

"Remember…when Alex was born?"

"Yes, Sam. It's one of my favorite memories. And I remember when Anna was born, and Merideth and Reed. They were all great days."

Frolic sat back down and drew close to Sam. "They're great kids. You and Lori did a wonderful job raising them. I know they've gone down paths that have caused you a lot of pain, but they'll find their way back. I want you to have peace in your heart regarding 'em, Sam."

Sam struggled to turn toward Frolic.

"I want that, too. Frolly…. There's something I want you to do for me." Sam reached out and grabbed Frolic's hand as his began to shake. "I want you to pray for Walter…I have left him with a great burden, and he could use your prayers."

"Of course I'll pray, Sam. And if I can be of any help—"

"Just pray…that will be enough." Sam lay back and looked to the ceiling. "That's all that's needed now."

Sam patted Frolic's hand and leaned back. Then he closed his eyes and drifted off to sleep. Frolic put his hands on Sam's head and said a prayer. He adjusted the sheet, more in reverence than necessity, walked to the door and stopped for one last look. It wouldn't be long now. Sam would open his eyes…

And he'd be with Lori.

The sound of voices outside his window pulled Frolic back to the present. He opened his eyes to see the last of the few faithful make their way up the sidewalk to the front door of the church.

Molly poked her head into his office. "Reverend, it's time. And just so ya know, our four guests are here, all seated in the front row. It's a sight, I'll tell ya."

Frolic took a few moments to collect himself then put on his suit coat, took one last look through his papers, and followed Molly to the sanctuary.

CHAPTER
Jour

lex looked down the aisle of Resurrection Christian Church. His face was hot. *Smile, just walk and smile.*

He stiffened his spine and kept his gaze focused straight ahead, making his way to the first pew. He caught glimpses of familiar faces. And he smiled.

He took his seat next to the aisle and let a lung full of air escape through his lips. This was even harder than he'd expected.

Reverend Hastings emerged from the side of the altar and came down the three steps to the first pew. Alex stood, and Frolic offered his hand.

"Alex, it's so good to have you back here. I'm sorry for your loss. I hope we can honor your father today as he would have wanted."

Honor Dad, yes. Please keep the focus on him.

Alex accepted the handshake. "Dad probably wouldn't have wanted a service at all, but I'm glad you're here to help us through this." He watched the pastor work his way down the pew to greet Anna. She remained seated, shoulders hunched, gazing at the ground. When Frolic offered his hand, she could only muster a weak, half-handed response. She struggled to look Frolic in the eye.

Anna, be strong. We'll get through this.

Next, Frolic greeted Merideth who stood and gave her usual performance: a half-smile, overdone handshake, and an authoritarian tone to her greeting. Alex forced himself not to let his disapproval show.

When Reed stood and received the pastor's greeting, his gaudy Rolex emerged from under Reed's cuff-linked, tailored shirt. Alex stifled a sigh. His brother did love his clothes and gadgets.

As Alex sat down, he took a quick glance behind him. The church was filled to capacity, and deacons were scrambling to set up folding chairs in the aisle for the overflow.

This town really did love his dad. And his mom.

Alex managed to remain composed throughout the service, focusing on the hymns and readings. Three people got up to give short testimonials to his father's influence in their lives. Alex fidgeted. Maybe he should've agreed to say something. He'd agreed to do so during a conference call with Frolic just a few days ago.

Merideth had wanted no part of it. "With all due respect, Reverend, I'm not standing up there and looking out on a church full of people who will be more interested in judging me than listening to what I might say about Dad."

Anna had offered to speak for all of them, but Alex insisted if anyone should do so, it should be he, seeing as he was the oldest.

"I know your father would've been pleased to know you spoke for your siblings at the service," Frolic said.

Merideth and Reed agreed.

He still didn't know what happened. Fear, guilt, despair? Whatever it was, he hated the memory of his call to Frolic backing out.

I should've kept to the plan. I can't believe none of us is going to say anything at Dad's funeral.

He looked at Anna, and she returned the glance, disappointment flashing from her eyes. Alex shifted in his seat. Maybe he should just stand up and speak, even if it wasn't on the schedule.

He tensed to stand—but then Frolic was at the pulpit, telling one of the familiar stories that marked Dad's life.

"It was one of the most amazing sights these old eyes have seen in their sixty-seven years of life. There stood my dear friend, Sam Roberts—burgundy red paint dripping off his head and onto his shoulders, his face half-covered with smeared paint that had been rubbed off with a towel, his white teeth smiling and his blue eyes twinkling as he held his firstborn son in his arms. Oh, my goodness, what a sight it was."

Laughter echoed through the sanctuary.

Dad had told that story a merciless number of times. How he'd been painting the molding in their dining room from the top rung of a ladder when his neighbor rushed in with the news that his wife had gone into labor while at a friend's house and they had taken her to the hospital. Dad scurried down the ladder, kicking the last rung and tipping over an entire can of Sherwin Williams' Mellow Merlot from its perch on the tray. The can missed his head. The paint did not. Doused in burgundy latex, Alex's dad ran out of the house. But Alex's mom had their only car, so he ran all seven blocks to St. John's

Hospital. He arrived, dripping in paint and sweat. Wiping latex from his face, he asked for his wife....

Alex could still see the way his dad's eyes shone when he got to this part of the tale.

"Moments later, a nurse handed me a bundle of blankets that enfolded my firstborn son." At that point, he'd beam a smile at Alex as he said, "Alex Daniel Roberts."

Dad loved that story. He'd always stop there, get a big silly grin on his face and say, "My tears mixed with the paint, and my smiles turned to laughter. That's a moment to remember."

The paint stain on the dining room floor had never faded. Looking back now, Alex wasn't sure his mom and dad really wanted it to.

Frolic went on to talk about their dad's work at the mission, his civic spirit, and how much he missed their mom. Alex could hear the sounds of muffled crying all around him.

Anna broke into sobs off and on. Alex put his arm around her and drew her near. He glanced over at Merideth in time to see her steely exterior give way to a few tears that worked their way over her high cheekbones down to the corner of her mouth. She dabbed them away.

He shifted again. These pews were about as comfortable as a bed of nails! He hung his right arm down over the side, letting his fingers rest and then move along the face of the dark mahogany. They stopped at a gouge cut deep into the otherwise smooth surface.

Suddenly, a smile. He knew this mark. It was his. He'd chased Tracy Kolb through the sanctuary with a shovel. Tracy had thrown dirt on Alex's head, so, of course, he'd had to get even. They were *supposed* to be digging weeds in the front flowerbed.

Dad had been roaring mad.

That memory stirred his heart. For the first time on this visit he began to look, really look, at the church that had been so much a part of his younger years.

Memories sparked and flooded back. Christmas pageants, potlucks, Vacation Bible School, his first communion...the memories brought a warmth to his face. As he glanced around, he saw something else. Eyes staring back at him.

Disapproving eyes.

His siblings probably saw and felt it as well. Quite the contrast to the warmth being poured out for their dad. His memories faded.

Soured.

Tears threatened again, but for an entirely different reason. He grew up in this church. It used to be his favorite place in town. Now...

He couldn't wait to get out of there.

Merideth refused to look anywhere but straight ahead. No way would she make eye contact with anyone unless she had to.

Just stay calm and focused. That was the key.

Good thing she chose the business suit and not the green dress—although that dress looked stunning beneath her flowing red hair. But this was not the time to look feminine or frail. A power suit. Definitely the right choice.

Her stomach tightened. Dad wouldn't have liked the suit…but then, he hadn't liked much of her adult life. Well, at least she was consistent.

She waited for that to make her feel better. It didn't.

Her gaze rested on the coffin at the front of the church.

I'm sorry, Dad. I guess I'll never win this.

Pleasing him while pursuing a life contrary to his worldview had been impossible. But she never stopped wishing, hoping, even praying that somehow they could be closer. Like they once were.

Now you're gone. Dad…I'm so sorry we ended this way. I'll miss you….

She dabbed the wet spot near the corner of her mouth and followed the tear's trail from her eye, trying to be inconspicuous.

Reed leaned close. "Steady, sis. Don't break the image. Anna will cry enough for all of us."

Nice. Why did he have to be such a jerk? She gave Anna's arm a gentle squeeze. What would it feel like to grieve so openly, to be so free, so uninhibited—?

Good night, what was she *thinking?*

How would it feel? *Weak,* that's how.

She pulled away from her sister and left Anna to her mourning.

Throughout the service, Walt's focus shifted between his grief and a study of the four people seated in front of him. He'd greeted them when they arrived just a few minutes before the service began. Alex was cordial but distracted. Walter could see the pain in his eyes. Anna gave him a warm hug, but she looked so frail. Merideth was polite but cool. Walt had hoped the history he'd had with her would be just that, history. Even so, her demeanor didn't surprise him. Reed…was Reed, laid-back and friendly, but serious enough for the setting.

Sam's children. They were finally here, all together. Too bad it took Sam's death to make it happen.

He'd known them all from the time they were born. Now he would be with them on what he prayed would be the most important day of their lives.

The service lasted only an hour. It ended with the entire assembly standing and singing "Amazing Grace." When the song was finished, Frolic left the altar and invited Sam's four children to accompany him down the aisle. Alex led the way, and Walter followed them out. He was pleased to hear whispers from both sides of the aisle as Sam's children passed.

"Bless you, children."

"Glad you're here."

"Welcome back."

Too bad the warm words mixed with disapproving looks and side comments as those assembled shook hands with the kids. Walter watched the four smile, trying to look as though they didn't even notice people's disapproval.

Walter walked outside and held open the door to the black limo rented for the occasion. The four siblings climbed in, and Walter joined them. The door closed with a click, and Merideth exploded.

"I can't *take* these people! They look at us like we're some sort of pariahs. How long will the graveside service take?"

"I think we can give Dad all the time he needs, Merideth," Reed shot back.

"Look—this is not about Dad. I loved him as much as any of you, and I'll miss him every day, but I mean, really, the stares and the disapproving sighs...I don't have to take this."

Apparently, Alex had had enough. "I don't like it either, but this is Dad's funeral. We will take whatever we must and sit there and pay our deepest respects to him."

Anna began to cry again. Reed held her hand, and his voice softened. "Hang in there, sis. I know how much you'll miss him. I'll miss him, too."

Merideth stared out the window. Alex looked straight ahead, his features emotionless. "So will I...more than you know."

Walter remained silent. He would have his moment, but not now.

The graveside service was brief. Molly had provided four long-stemmed red roses, one for each of the children to place on the casket. A picture of their mother nestled amidst the flowers.

Walter watched as the simple casket was lowered into the ground while the church soloist sang "Be Thou My Vision."

Sam's favorite song.

Walter pulled a handkerchief from his suit pocket and dabbed at his eyes. Cathy Blake moved next to him and hooked her arm in his, patting his arm. Together they watched as Sam and Lori's four children stood, their arms around each other, watching their father being laid to rest. At least now they allowed themselves tears.

Cleansing tears. A good place to start, given what awaited them.

The February sky gave up one short burst of late-afternoon sun before turning to dusk as the graveside service ended. Alex stood with his three siblings in a last tribute. Then they joined the procession of the fifty or so gathered for the burial. Alex lagged behind, lost in his conflicting emotions.

Walter caught up with him. "Alex, how are you doing, son?"

How was he supposed to answer that? *I'm sad. I'm confused. I'm angry. I'm filled with guilt.* How did one say all that? "I'll be okay. Just a lot to deal with."

"Why don't the four of you go back to the house and get comfortable? Some women from the church brought dinner by. It should be warming in the oven when you arrive. I'll be there around seven."

They walked on in silence; then Alex turned to the man he'd known all his life. "Walter, I don't know what to expect. None of us do. I mean, is there something we should...? Do we need to be prepared to...?"

"Nothing at all. Your father has prepared everything. He just wanted you to be together, and you are. That's all he asked for. Oh, and we'll meet in the living room. That's important."

Alex nodded, shook hands with Walt, and watched him go to join Frolic. How was he supposed to prepare for this? He kept pushing his guilt down so it wouldn't overwhelm him. The return to the church, the house, even the smells of Harvest churned up in him both deep longing and searing pain. He longed to jump in his car and drive away. Yet the thought of leaving this place behind haunted him even more.

I feel like I'm balancing on the wall between devastation and salvation. God help me.

The thoughts tore at him as he joined the others in the limo for the ride back to the house.

Merideth leaned toward him. "Did Walt say anything about what happens now?"

"He told us to get comfortable and have dinner. He'll be by around seven." No help there.

Reed rubbed his hand on the window to clear a hole in the glaze of moisture.

Through the hole his brother created, Alex watched the town pass by.

"I can't figure why we had to stay through to tomorrow evening," Reed muttered. "How can an estate settlement take so long? I'm not critical, just wondering."

Anna had regained her composure. "Do you think Dad's secret is for real? I mean, it sounds so incredible. I know he wouldn't mislead us, but, well, it's just incredible."

"Frankly, I'm skeptical." Merideth crossed her arms, hugging herself. "I'm not doubting Dad or his sincerity, but I just think we shouldn't get our hopes up."

Reed's brows arched. "Hopes up for what? All we know is that Dad called each one of us, told us that when he died there would be an inheritance for each of us, that it would be life-changing and that we had to promise not to say anything to anyone. Who knows what he meant by that? I mean…you know Dad. It could mean anything."

Anna frowned. "But, Reed, Dad wouldn't have said *life-changing* unless it was, you know, something extraordinary. Dad didn't throw words like that around lightly."

Alex resisted shaking his head. She was almost pleading for them to agree with her.

"Alex, what do you think he meant?"

He tried not to let his frustration show. "Honestly, Anna, I have no idea. But we're here, and you can bet Walter will be on time, so we'll know in an hour or so."

An hour. An hour until he found out how his life was going to change. Whatever his dad meant, it was something he looked forward to. If there was one thing he needed…

It was a change.

Alex cracked the front door, and the aroma of roasted chicken and fresh baked bread rolled over him. He heard cupboards shutting and silverware rattling, and he was the first down the hall and into the kitchen.

"Hello?"

A tall, rather plump older lady looked up and threw her hands into the air. "Alex, oh, and all of you. Come in, come in. I'm just leaving, but I'm glad to have caught you." It was Bernice Baxter, head of the Lady's Auxiliary at Resurrection. She was known countywide for her cooking.

"Hello, Bernice. Wow, that smells amazing."

His siblings joined them in the kitchen, peering at the food.

Bernice fidgeted with the top of the honey pot and then placed it on the table. "Oh, I'm so glad. We just wanted you all to have a nice meal tonight. Well, hello, Anna, Merideth, Reed. It was a lovely service. Didn't you think so?"

They all nodded, but Alex could tell their focus right now was the wonderful fragrances filling the kitchen.

Alex took off his topcoat and lay it on a chair. "Bernice, this is very gracious of you. Thank you so much. What can we help you with?"

"Oh, nothing at all, dear. The table is set; the bread is cooling on the counter. There's fresh salad in the fridge, all ready to serve. And my honey mustard chicken is just finished in the oven. There's a stir-fry of fresh veggies on the stove. They just need a stir. Let's see, chocolate coconut pie is also in the fridge, and, oh, yes, Gladys Merton sent along a couple dozen of her chocolate delight cookies. You know, for bedtime."

A couple dozen?

Everyone thanked her, but before they could say more she grabbed her coat and was headed out the door. She stopped short and turned back. "It's so wonderful to have you kids all back here at the house. Just so wonderful."

With that, she turned and hurried out.

It was wonderful, not that Alex could figure out why. He just allowed himself to enjoy it for the moment.

Reed opened the oven door and let the smell burst into the kitchen. "This is awesome, and I'm starving. Let's get to it."

A half-hour later they'd feasted on the food and even managed to keep the conversation skimming along the surface of their lives.

Reed talked about his growing business, but that was fine with Alex. It was good to get caught up on his brother's life. "So you have five coffee stands now? That must be giving you a strong cash flow."

Reed grimaced and let out a short grunt. "Well, let's just say cash is certainly flowing. I need more of it to stick around."

Merideth turned to Reed. "You've got to control your spending, business and personal. You're still a startup, even after three years."

Alex shook his head. She sounded like she was giving some kind of business lecture.

To his credit, Reed didn't call her on it. He just shrugged. "I know, I know. But I do love what I'm doing. Next month I'm going down to the Virgin Islands on a sailboat cruise."

A *cruise?* Alex caught his sisters' glances. Yes, they caught the irony as well.

Reed grinned. "Hey, it's research for coffee beans."

They all burst out laughing.

Merideth talked about her marketing work. If there was one thing his sister relished, it was the opportunity to tout her success.

"We're setting records almost every month. In April I'll be in Paris to land a new fashion design client, then Hong Kong in July. We're really on a roll."

And on and on it went. She'd climbed the ladder in such a short time that she was now a vice president of Seattle's premier marketing firm.

How many bodies did you leave in your wake as you advanced, Mer?

Anna looked across at her sister. "So how are *you* doing?"

Merideth's expression grew even more distant. "To be honest, it's taking all I can give it. It's such a cutthroat business."

Reed grinned. "Sounds perfect for you."

Alex tensed, waiting for Merideth's response. But she let it pass. Almost.

"I'll admit, I do enjoy it. You don't have to be mean"—she shot a look at Reed—"just shrewd…and a little brash."

Alex nodded. "It sounds a lot like the real estate business. Shrewd and brash, yup, that pretty much nails it."

Anna scooped up wedges of pie and slid them onto four plates. "So, Alex, how is the market? Are you doing well?"

His turn on the hot seat, apparently. "Well enough. Holding our own and waiting for real estate to turn around. But I've had a good quarter, so I can't complain." With any luck, that would satisfy them.

Reed leaned close. "Any women in your life?"

Or not. Leave it to Reed to ask something like that. "No. A few dates here and there, but nothing serious. I'm too busy for relationships. You know how it is. How about you, Mr. Playboy?"

Reed put both hands out. "Hey, you know I'm not the serious relationship kind. I'm a happy bachelor, and I intend to keep it that way, at least until I get this business off the ground." He turned to Merideth and Anna, waggling his brows. "Sooo…how about you two? Any men in your life that your brothers need to know about?"

Anna put her fork down, wiped her mouth with her napkin, and looked up with a slight gleam in her eye.

Alex blinked. It was the first time since they'd arrived that Anna didn't look…burdened.

"Well, actually, I was dating a man for several months. Kevin and I were getting somewhat serious—." She looked down, and Alex's heart hurt as he watched whatever weight his sister was carrying settle over her again. When she spoke again, her tone was subdued.

"But then he took a job in Alaska. We tried the long-distance thing, but we just finally drifted apart."

Alex smiled his encouragement. "Anna, I'm so glad you're dating. You'll find the right guy."

"Darned lucky guy, too."

Alex nodded at Reed's comment, and Anna smiled. "Thank you, Reed. Well, I'll just trust God and see what happens. For now, I'm fiddling away at the restaurant until something else comes along."

Alex resisted every urge in his body to challenge her choices. What had happened to his slender, beautiful sister? What changed her into this sad, fragile creature? Why did she let herself go like this? Whatever happened, her physical appearance now matched her mental state.

Reed pushed on Merideth's arm. "How about you, Mer. Any men in your life?"

Merideth shot him a comical half-smile. "Hundreds, just not any romantic ones." She gathered up her dishes as if to brush away any seriousness to the question. "I'm like you, way too busy to think about a relationship. It may come, and it may not. I'm not losing any sleep over it."

As the conversation went on, Alex leaned back in his chair, watching his brother and sisters.

It was sad, really.

Their parents gave them such a great model for a healthy marriage, and yet…none of them was in a serious relationship. They were all so busy, finding…

What, exactly?

Success?

Alex got up to refill his coffee, half listening as the stories his siblings were sharing shifted to their years growing up together. There was the usual posturing, mixed with occasional teasing and even laughter.

He returned to his seat and sipped his coffee. When was the last time they were all together, eating and laughing around this wonderful old table? When was the last time he'd seen his siblings this relaxed? A pang struck deep, and Alex had to look down.

Had they missed more than they knew? Had they turned their backs on so much of what made them who they were?

The mantel clock chimed 6:30 p.m., and Alex looked up. Walter. He'd be here soon. "Hey, troops, we need to clean up and get changed before seven."

Everyone assumed a duty. Anna washed, Reed dried, Merideth put things away, and Alex assembled the prodigious leftovers and found places for everything in the refrigerator.

"The last time I had Bernice's honey mustard chicken"—soapsuds flew around as Anna gestured—"was at Grace Graffenberger's funeral. It must be the official funeral food."

"I'd forgotten that Grace died," Merideth said. "That's been what, six years ago?"

Anna looked up at the ceiling, probably doing the math in her head. "Seven, I think. It was breast cancer. Poor Walter. He's been such a friend to this family. Did you know that he and Dad worked out at the YMCA every Saturday? I mean they golfed together, fished together, and had a men's Bible study every time Walt came to town. First he lost Grace, now Dad. I wonder how he's doing."

Good question. Alex looked at his watch. "We'll find out soon. We've got about twenty minutes. Let's finish up and get ready. I don't know if this will be a quick deal or take all evening, so let's get comfortable."

Five

Walter pulled his topcoat tight around his neck as a north wind picked up and blew snow flurries up Orchard Avenue. He stopped to check his watch.

6:58 p.m.

He turned up the walkway to the Roberts home. As he approached the front door the sound of the children's voices, the glow of lights from almost every window, and the fragrance of Bernice Baxter's honey chicken brought a smile.

How great to see life back in the house.

Lord, we have prepared for this moment for months. I have no idea how they'll respond. But I pray that You honor Sam and Lori's heart tonight. Fill this house with Your Spirit, and help me carry out this task as Your servant.

He heard the mantel clock in the house begin to chime seven times.

This is for you, Sam.

Walter no sooner knocked at the door than Reed opened it.

"Hello, Walter, come in and get out of that weather. Is it snowing?"

Walter smiled at Sam's youngest son as he shook light flakes off his topcoat. "Just started. It's not supposed to turn into much, so your flight back tomorrow shouldn't be a problem. And the roads should be fine as well."

Reed hung Walter's coat up, and they walked together down the hall.

"We're all in here. We just finished the feast that Bernice Baxter made for us. What a spread! You should've joined us."

"Thanks. I had a meal with some friends, but I always hate missing one of Bernice's dinners."

Walter followed Reed into the living room and surveyed the scene. This had always been Lori's favorite room. She and Sam worked hard to make it a place that drew people in. Every chair beckoned you to lose yourself in its arms. The walls were textured and painted in rich greens and rusts. The lighting was warm and relaxing. The main wall boasted an oversized rock fireplace fixed with a dark cherry wood mantel. And everywhere there were quilts. Lori was a master quilter. Small, framed, ornate quilt squares hung on walls and stood on bookshelves and end tables. The large leather couch had no less than three large quilts spread out on it, including one that had been Merideth's favorite since she was a child. The two rockers next to the fireplace each had one rolled up neatly on the seat.

And then there were pictures. Too many to count. Family vacations, reunions, sports events, proms, Christmases, Thanksgivings, and so on. Walter could still see Sam walking along peering at each one then telling a story he was sure Walt had never heard.

Alex was tending a reluctant fire. Anna had settled into one of the rockers, unrolling her mother's quilt and wrapping herself in it. Merideth was on the couch under her comforter, sipping a glass of red wine.

She held up the glass. "You don't mind, do you, Walter? I know Dad never had alcohol in the house, but we thought a little wine might not be a bad thing for a night like this."

Walter smiled and nodded. "Actually, I would like something to drink as well. Tea, if you have it. With honey?"

Merideth left the room and a few minutes later returned with a steaming cup of Earl Grey accompanied by the honey pot and a spoon.

Reed settled into the other rocker, and with the fire starting to crackle to life, Alex joined Merideth on the couch. Two chairs remained empty.

Lori's and Sam's.

Walter chose Lori's chair, a deep burgundy La-Z-Boy that sat between the couch and the fireplace. Straight across from it was Sam's worn leather recliner.

The empty chair filled the room with an eerie sense of Sam's continued presence. Walter gave the quiet moment space to breathe.

This is perfect. Absolutely perfect. Now for the Spirit to move.

Walter sipped his tea. None of the children spoke. They just waited. He could feel their tension and anticipation mixed with anxiety. He paused, looked at each one and then sipped again.

Finally, Walter set his tea down and opened his briefcase to pull out a fat envelope. He closed the briefcase and eased open the envelope with a bit of dramatic flair. Fishing a set of reading glasses from his breast pocket, he laid the document on the table at enough of an angle so that no one but he could read it. He cleared his throat and began.

To my beloved children, Alex, Anna, Merideth, and Reed, I have asked my dear friend, Walter Graffenberger, to read this letter to you. He will read my will at the proper time, but this letter must come first. Let me begin by telling you that your mother and I love each of you so dearly. It gives my heart peace as I write this to know that you will be hearing this while sitting in our home, where we all shared so many years of laughter and tears. Look around. How many memories rush to your mind? I hope this house will always be a special place for all of you. It was one of the most profoundly wonderful gifts God gave to your mother and me.

There is so much I would like to say, but that must wait for later. For now, I must tell you the story involving a Mr. Melvin K. Sidek. Mr. Sidek came to the mission two years before your mother died. He was homeless, addicted to cocaine, and desperate for help. He had once been a successful attorney, but several setbacks and many bad decisions cost him his practice, his license, his marriage, and nearly his life. I know you have heard me tell stories like his many times over the years.

When Mel started in our program, he was barely able to say his name or walk to the bathroom. His withdrawal from drugs was ferocious, and three times he was rushed to St. John's on the brink of death. Your mother sat by his bedside on many nights, putting cold washcloths on his forehead, reading promises to him from the Bible, and praying for him. After three months Mel stabilized and began his recovery and rehabilitation. He took on responsibilities around the mission and seemed ready to rebuild his life. But the drugs kept calling him.

Six months into his recovery, your mother and I asked Mel to live in our home and watch over it while we were away at a missions' convention. It seemed a safe thing to do, given his great progress and clear sense of responsibility and trustworthiness. We were not aware that he was secretly beginning to buy and use cocaine again. When we returned after three days, our home had been burgled. Several items of value were gone, including your mother's most precious possession—the diamond and sapphire ring her grandmother had given her. There was no sign of forced entry. Nor was there any sign of Mel. We found him the next day, strung out on cocaine, which we presumed he'd purchased with money he'd gotten for all he'd stolen from us.

We prayed for guidance and came to the conclusion that it would serve no great purpose to turn Mel in. But the pawned property was traced to him, and a week later the police arrived at the mission demanding to see Mel. He was brought into the room to face your mother and me. Bud Porter, chief of police, produced a photo of a ring and a yellow receipt and waved them in front of Mel.

"Do you recognize this? We have you on videotape pawning a diamond and sapphire ring last week. Lori, is this your ring?"

Your mother said it was.

Bud shouted at Mel. "Do you admit that you stole it from the Roberts's house?"

Mel stammered and looked at your mother and me with eyes that conveyed the full weight of his sorrow and guilt. Before he could answer, your mother did something that, to my last day, I can scarcely believe.

She walked over and took the receipt from Bud's fingers. "Steal it? Oh, no, Bud, you have it all wrong." She turned and opened Mel's hand then placed the receipt for her beloved ring on his palm and closed his fingers over it.

"Mel didn't steal it. I gave it to him as a gift." Your mother looked into Mel's stunned face and smiled. "I am sorry for all the fuss, Mel. This ring is yours, just like we agreed."

Bud was pretty irritated. He asked about the watch and silver pendant that also turned up at the pawnshop.

I stood amazed at your mother's grace. Then I turned to Bud. "Yes, they too were gifts from us."

Bud knew full well what was happening, but without complaints from your mother and me he had no grounds to arrest Mel.

"Well, I guess we will just let this man go and leave him to you two." He shook his head then looked at me. "I hope you know what you're doing, Sam."

So we took Mel back to the mission, and he spent a second hellish month trying to break free from his cocaine habit. And again Lori was at his side, tending to him like he was her own son.

Day by day, week by week, with great effort and faith, Mel recovered. His newfound freedom from drugs and self-hatred rejuvenated the drive that had taken him to the top of his profession. Within a year of coming to the mission, Mel was leading our men's Bible study, reorganizing our administrative structure, and helping us write a new strategic plan. Eighteen months after staggering into the mission, Mel left to regain his license to practice law and restart his life.

He was a changed man, and what changed him most was the love your mother showed him. They only spoke of it once, and Lori refused to ever let him mention it again. In her heart, the matter was closed. Mel later told us that her attitude gave him more freedom than anything he'd experienced in his life.

Your mother was an incredible woman. Mel could have gone to prison and, most likely, died there. Instead, he walked out of the Harvest Gospel Mission a transformed man.

Nine months later, I received a letter from Mel. He had heard of your mother's death but had been overseas working on a business deal at the time. He told me he had completed a major project he had started before his collapse. His partners had kept it on hold during his recovery. It is an amazing story, but not one that I need to tell here. Mel was distraught over your mother's death, and he vowed to make a gift to the mission in her memory. I wrote and thanked him and then heard nothing for six months.

A month or so after my doctor told me of my heart condition, I received a phone call from an attorney who had been in partnership with Mel. To my surprise and dismay, he informed me that Mel had died suddenly, while working on a project somewhere in China. His years of drug abuse had taken their toll, and he had a massive heart attack that took him in a matter of minutes. The attorney went on to say that Mel's will named only one beneficiary and that was me. I asked why it named me personally and not the mission. The attorney replied, "Mel said you and Lori saved his life, and he trusted you *to use the money in a way that would most honor God." The attorney went on to tell me that Mel's assets would likely exceed $40 million. And so they did. Two months ago Walter helped complete the transfer of $43,671,880 into a brokerage account. The entire amount remains there today.*

Walter halted when a collective gasp reverberated around the room. He looked up for a moment at the stunned faces staring at him and then turned back to the page in his hand.

When I knew I did not have long to live, I shared with each of you that I had an inheritance for you that would change your life and that its disposition would be settled upon my death. I know you all have kept this secret as I asked you to. No one knows about this except the five of you in this room and Mel's partners.

Walter and I have met over the past few weeks to discuss the disposition of these funds. I have wrestled in prayer over this decision, and I have made it. Listen to me now, my children.

Walter smiled as he read the words. That request was far from necessary. All four of Sam's children leaned forward.

Walter cleared his throat and took another sip of tea.

Here we go, Sam.

My greatest wish has been to leave for each of you a legacy that will stay with you the rest of your lives. I love each of you so, and yet my heart is troubled as I write these words. Your mother and I were not perfect parents. We made many mistakes, and we know the kind of guilt that haunts every parent as they watch their children make poor decisions and venture down paths of life that lead to meaninglessness and despair. I have watched each of you with great anticipation, only to see you choose life journeys that broke my heart. Please know I am not disappointed with who you are as wonderful men and women, but rather in the choices you have made. I remain so very proud of each of you. You have given your mother and me joy that is beyond expression. But with that joy are pain and great concern. As I pondered the disposition of so great a sum of money, I had to balance my love for each of you with my concern for the journeys you have chosen.

Walter looked up, letting the weight of Sam's words sink in.

Merideth stood and walked to the window. She pressed her hand against her chest, and her shoulders arched as she seemed to struggle to draw a breath.

Alex sat back into the couch. His hand covered his mouth, and his eyes searched for a place to focus.

Reed stared down at the floor, rubbing his hands together, shaking his head.

Anna's eyes were wide, and her mouth dropped half-open, as if she were begging for an explanation, but no sound came out.

Walter set the letter down, eased himself back in his chair and sipped on his tea.

Alex shifted to the edge of the couch. "Please continue, Walter. This is unbearable."

But he did not respond immediately. *Oh, Alex…your mother and father have waited so many years for you…you can wait a moment longer for this.*

After a few moments passed, he picked up the letter and read on.

After much fervent prayer and many sleepless nights, I have reached a conclusion. I have decided to trust the good that your mother and I know resides in each of you. Therefore, I will leave $5 million in an endowment to the mission, and I will divide the remaining inheritance among you equally.

"Dear *God!*" Reed stared at Walter wide-eyed.

Alex dropped his head back and looked up to the ceiling. "Dear God, indeed."

Merideth's reserved exterior eroded for a moment as she looked at her father's empty chair. "Dad, God bless you."

Anna laid her face in her hands and wept.

Walt gave them a moment to gather themselves. "Please, may I continue? There is more, perhaps the most important part."

Alex and Reed nodded, and Anna regained her composure.

Walter read on.

There are, however, two stipulations. The first is that you must, together, read the story I have written for you. Walter will give it to you after he finishes reading this letter. Then you must receive the gift I have selected for each of you. Once you have read the story and received the gift that is yours, Walter will make the arrangements to have the money transferred to your accounts. If you are willing to accept these terms, Walter will have you sign accordingly.

The story I wrote contains my last words to you. Please read it with an open heart. It is, far more than any money could be, my legacy to you. And that of your mother as well. We love you all dearly.

Your father,

Samuel Roland Roberts

Walter paused for a moment then folded the letter and returned it to the envelope.

Alex opened his hands and gestured to Walter. "I am not sure I understand, Walter. Dad wants us to read a story and open a present? Is that all?"

Walter met his gaze. "That's all. Just sign here, indicating your agreement with the terms your father established, and we can move on. And, by the way, these papers were my idea. Sam was not happy about it, but I insisted we have everything legal. So I will need a signature from each of you."

One by one, the four moved to the table and signed on the line that had been prepared for them. Walter placed the papers in the original envelope and returned them to his briefcase. He set the briefcase on the floor, stood and walked to the library bookcase bordering the right side of the fireplace. He reached up to the third shelf and took down an ornate box. He carried the box back to the table as if it were a priceless vase and set it down with great care in front of Sam's children. The reflection of the fire danced across its polished exterior.

Walter reached inside a small pocket of his vest and produced a silver key. He worked the key in the lock and opened the box. Inside lay a leather-bound book. It was not professionally bound but held together by long strands of thin leather strips woven through the holes at the edge of the pages. Walter lifted the book from the box and set it on the table. He paused for a moment then looked up and gazed at all four of Sam and Lori's children.

"This is your father's and mother's legacy to you. In my opinion, it is far more precious than the money sitting in Sam's bank account. But that's for you each to decide. You've made a promise to read this with an open heart. I trust you will do so in honor of your parents. When you have finished the book, I will give you each the gift your father has chosen for you. Then my work here will be complete."

He stood and walked to a chair that sat back away from the main living area.

Well, Sam, it's up to them now.

Alex was struggling.

What is this all about? A story? About what? And what does it have to do with the inheritance?

He stood, walked over and took Walter's seat in front of the book. His siblings drew in closer to see the book for themselves.

Alex ran his fingers across the cover. "Well, I gotta say it's a beautiful book. Dad always loved leather." He eased the cover open. Printed in clear, neat script on the inside page was the title.

Merideth looked over Alex's shoulder and read it out loud: "*Steward of Aiden Glenn.*"

Reed frowned. "How long is it?"

Alex paged through, careful not to bend any of the pages. "Looks to be a couple hundred pages."

Anna followed by fingering the pages. "I never knew Dad could write something like this."

Walter spoke from behind them. "Sometimes things are easier to write than to say in person. And sometimes they're also more readily received that way."

Anna looked at Alex. "Alex, you should start."

Merideth walked to the couch and grabbed her glass of wine from the end table. "I'll need another drink for this."

Alex moved to add another log on the fire as Reed took off his shoes and put his feet up on the ottoman. Anna returned to her chair and wrapped herself up in her mother's quilt.

In a few moments, Merideth had returned. The fire's cheerful crackle filled the room. Alex looked at his brother and sisters…they looked like kids at a slumber party waiting to hear a good ghost story.

He took a deep breath, picked up the book, turned to the first page and began to read.

CHAPTER
Six

Steward of Aiden Glenn

On a cool autumn morning, Logan picked his way around rocks and holes that cluttered the narrow path leading through the rugged hillside north from the village of Aiden Glenn. His aging knees ached as they bent and flexed to pull him along the steep ascent. His fellow hiker was ahead of him, bouncing up the trail as if gravity had no hold on his energy and youth. Logan's heart pounded as he struggled to keep up. He paused to catch his breath and study his young companion.

The boy was slight of build, healthy and strong. His head was held high, his gait was sure, but Logan sensed the lad's caution.

Eighteen years we have prepared for this journey. Now it is upon us. Steward, my son, you are about to unlock the secret of your birth and discover the true meaning of your life.

Logan pressed on. Steward waited for him now, and when Logan reached his son's side, the two stood at an outcropping of rock. Logan looked ahead to the ascending trail that would take them to the high pass through the mountains surrounding their village.

Steward took in a chest full of mountain air. "I love it out here. Father, do you remember all the games of King's Castle we've played here? Erik always thought he was the fastest, but I beat him four times summer before last."

Logan smiled, his heart vacillating between joy and heartache. "I remember. And how many sunsets have your mother and I watched from this very place. It is magical, up here, just below the mist."

The smile disappeared from Steward's young face. He turned, and his eyes followed the trail as it continued up through a saddle between two ridges, disappearing into the gray bank of vapor suspended above Aiden Glenn.

Logan sensed his boy's fear. This was as far as most people dared travel. Steward's journey, if he chose to continue it, would lead him through the pass to where no one since his ancient ancestors had traveled. "Are you ready to continue on, son?"

Steward paused then turned back to him. "I am."

They climbed on. With each step Logan's chest tightened, and anxiety clawed at him. His son's journey would require a step of faith to go beyond the pass. A step he had to take alone.

Sooner than expected, the trail crested the hillside, and ahead of them lay the ridge marking the way through Callater Pass. Logan watched as his son paused to look around and take it all in.

Steward's gaze came back to Logan. "I know this place. I remember what happened here. We were just having a prank, pretending we were so brave and daring each other to go farther. We came up here, five of us, and went back only four."

The terror on Steward's face when he rushed into their house that fateful day was still fresh in Logan's memory. "Where was it you last saw him?"

Steward studied the pass ahead. "There, right where the mist meets the pass. We dared Trevor to step through it, even though we knew no one had ever returned from the mist. We never thought he'd do it. Then suddenly, he was gone through the vapor. Just a step...."

Steward looked back at Logan, confusion and grief contorting his features. "Just a step, that's all he took. We could almost still see the back of his anorak. Then he was gone. I yelled at him to stop fooling around and tell us what he saw. But he never answered. I was ready to run into the mist and bring him back, but Erik and Malcolm grabbed me. We ran all the way back to the town screaming and crying...and that was it. He never came out...never came back... never...."

Steward sat down. "Father, I don't think I can go on. Not alone." He turned and looked back down into the valley. "I want to go back home. I want to be back in Aiden Glenn. I'm not ready for this." He looked at his father, eyes pleading. "Please, Father, let's turn back."

Logan's heart ached for his son, but...

There was no turning back.

He sat beside him. "Steward, do you remember your sixteenth birthday, when I first told you the story of your birth?"

Steward nodded. "Yes, very well. You told me how you and mother wanted a son, but you weren't able to have children. You asked the advice of every doctor and healer in the land. You even considered traveling beyond the pass to seek help, for you'd heard that the king could help you. You never made the journey, but you believed that somehow the king would know of our plight and come to your aid."

Logan smiled and nodded. "Yes, yes, that's just as I told you. And I know you remember the rest. How one day a man came to Aiden Glenn from beyond the pass. He stopped at our house and asked for a drink of water for himself and his horse. I gave it to him, and as he drank, he asked me about my children. I told him I had none, despite our deepest longing to have a son. He finished his drink, looked up at me and said, 'You will have a son, and he will be strong and wise and will make you proud all of your days. But he will be born to you only if you make an oath with me today that you will send him on a journey on his nineteenth birthday. This journey will take him beyond the pass and along the path that will lead him to the very throne room of the king. There he will learn the meaning of his name.'

"'His name?' I inquired—"

"'—you are to name your son Steward.'" A smile lifted Steward's lips. "Yes, father, I remember."

Logan continued. "'And only the king can tell him his name's true meaning and the true meaning of your son's life.'" Logan's speech quickened as he stared at his son. "Your mother and I made the oath with that man that very day. Ten months later you were born. And now, at the age of nineteen, you must keep our oath and journey to meet the king. Today, my son, you embark on that journey."

A spark of confidence returned to Steward's countenance. He stood and paced as he talked. "For three years I've prepared for this journey. At first, it was thrilling. Such a grand adventure awaited me at such a young age. I used to stand in front of the mirror and say to myself, 'I will see the king. I will stand in his throne room, and he will tell me the meaning of my name and my life.' I dreamed of it and counted the days."

Steward stopped, rubbed his face, lowered his hands, and stared back at his father. "But as the time grew nearer it became a burden. I didn't want to leave you and Mom. I wanted to be back with my friends, back in Aiden Glenn, and forget this talk of the journey. Please, Father, can we go back?"

Steward's plea hung in the air, thicker than the mist over their heads. Neither spoke. This was the most critical moment in his son's life. Logan reached out and offered him a hand. "Take a walk with me, son."

He led them back a short distance down the path; then he turned to follow a tiny, almost imperceptible trail. It led them through a wooded thicket and out onto a large area of flat rock that jutted into the open air above Aiden Glenn.

Logan stopped and took in the view. "Do you recognize this place?"

Steward stood next to him and gazed down into the valley. "No. But why does it matter? This event happened nineteen years ago. Why do you think it is still my calling?"

Logan turned to him. "My dear son, every year on your birthday, the stranger with whom we made the oath appears on this spot atop his horse. He waits for your mother and me to come to this place and bow to him, indicating that we remember and continue to be faithful to our vow. It is our oath, it is your destiny, and you must embrace it with passion and expect great things from it."

He grasped his son by the shoulders. "You will see the king! No one since our ancestors has ever seen the king. I am so proud of you—and envious. Please do not rebel against your destiny. It's a wonderful gift. Embrace it. Embrace it with all of your heart!"

Logan pulled Steward into his arms, held him close for a moment, let him go, and turned to walk back through the trees.

Steward followed him to where the two trails intersected. "Father, I know this is the journey I was born to take. I want to see the king. I want to know the meaning of my name and the purpose of my life. But I'm scared."

Logan straightened the satchel that hung over Steward's shoulder.

My son, this is your moment to turn from a boy to a man.

"Trust the king. He will protect you. I must leave you now. This decision is yours. I love you, and so does your mother. Whichever way you choose, we will be proud of you."

Steward watched as his father walked away, working his way down the trail, his crooked gait testifying to his failing knees.

Steward ran his hands along his satchel and thought back to earlier in the day. His father had stood, staunch and proud, as he produced the satchel that contained a loaf of bread, a small cask of apple cider, and a fine new set of clothes "to wear in the presence of the king." His mother had kissed him on the cheek and hugged him as her tears wet his shirt.

Now, as his father disappeared around a far bend, an unwelcome silence hung in the air, broken only by the rustling of the breeze through evergreen needles. Steward was alone, staring at an empty trail that vanished into the ever-present mist.

He searched his heart for the courage to continue. He couldn't let his father and mother down, not after nineteen years of waiting and preparing.

I vow this day that I will not walk back down that trail to my home until I have met the king.

A flicker of confidence sparked within him. It was enough. After all, he'd be back home soon, and things would return to normal. He rose to his feet, fixed his satchel on his shoulder, and turned to face the crest of Callater Pass.

It was time.

He took a deep breath and willed his feet to move ahead. Each step was calculated. Heel. Toe. Careful. Steady.

He could feel the cool mist on his face. He remembered the last time he'd felt it, the last time he'd approached the pass—and the fear. But this was different. This was *his* journey. This time, he would trust the king.

He looked down and watched as one foot stepped past the crest. Then the other. One more step…and the mist enveloped him. He could only see far enough on the path for one step at a time. He struggled to breathe in the dense, humid air. Step after painstaking step, he eased his way along the path, never knowing where the next few feet would take him.

Then, just as the mist had enveloped him, it began to thin. Everything around him grew brighter, and ahead a brilliant light waited. Two more steps, and the brightness washed over him. It felt like fire on his skin.

This will consume me!

He fought the terror, but he couldn't go back. Not now. He stepped farther, and farther, each cautious stride bringing him deeper into the light. And then…

…wonderful…brilliant…warm, like ten fireplaces roaring at once.

He loved it. It was the brightest sun he'd ever seen. So bright he shaded his eyes with his hands, squinting. As his eyes adjusted, he opened them a bit more until he could take his first full look around. He stood atop a high plateau, with mountains towering up on two sides. The path continued ahead, curving back near the pass. He followed it, and to his surprise it rounded at a point where he could look back down on Aiden Glenn.

How could this be? Aiden Glenn was so…gray…so dreary…so cold. The mist's hazy dullness engulfed the town. The colors of the houses were lifeless, the air looked heavy and oppressive, and even in the afternoon sun the town appeared nestled in the shade of some unwanted umbrella.

All those days he'd spent thinking he was enjoying the warm summer sun.

I've never seen the sun…never really seen it before today. No one in Aiden Glenn has.

All his life he'd been looking up through a cloudy, gray sky thinking he was seeing the bright sun shining down from a cloudless heaven. He'd spent hours gazing up at the sun and wondering what it would be like to travel to it and walk around on it. He'd wondered what the world looked like to those who live on the sun, for it didn't look much different from his own world.

Now he knew—he'd been deceived. He couldn't look at the sun—the true unshielded sun—without burning his eyes! And the warmth. In Aiden Glenn, even in the midst of summer, the sun was never able to overcome the perpetual gray and persistent chill of the village. Coolness and dampness were a part of life. But here, above the mist, the warmth enfolded him, soaking through his skin to his very bones.

As he looked down on his village, he wanted to shout and wave and—

But wait. Why hadn't he ever seen this place from Aiden Glenn? He'd looked up to these mountains all his life, but he'd never seen the place where he now stood.

Of course.

Nothing could get past the mist. No smoke from the chimneys, no sounds or voices, no smells of Mother's cooking—nothing made its way to this point on the mountain.

The mist was like a seal. Nothing got out, and very little got in. The little town looked so sad, so lost, and no one down there knew. Life went on as if their sun was bright and the skies were clear.

I will return and tell them. They must all come up here…after I see the king.

Steward turned and looked to the path ahead. It wound away from the cliffside and through a beautiful meadow filled with—

And Steward made his second discovery of this new land!

Color!

Flowers dressed in shades and tones he had never seen before in a dazzling display of vibrancy. He picked a few flowers as he walked along and held them up to let the full rays of the sun explode the yellows, reds, and pinks against the azure blue sky. Even their fragrance seemed more powerful and more delicate than the flowers in Aiden Glenn.

Mother would love these.

Steward looked around him, taking it all in—the sun, the warmth, the colors, the smells, the warm afternoon breeze that brushed against him. He closed his eyes, put his arms high into the air, and just soaked it in. He could hear the sounds of birds chirping as they flew from tree to tree. He could hear a distant goose honk, and then more and more birds. He opened his eyes, and in the far meadow a herd of deer meandered out to eat the grass that rose to their shoulders. The scent of wildflowers filled the air with a soft, clean sweetness.

This is bliss! I wish Mother could see this. How she would love the warmth and flowers and the birds and…all of it.

Callater Pass was already a distant memory. The most dreadful part of the journey had turned out to be a source of wonder, and now he was ready to face whatever lay ahead.

Steward had walked for over an hour beyond the crest of Callater Pass. How far would he have to go to reach the throne room of the king? Even as he wondered, his pace slowed, his stomach tightened, and a chill ran down his chest.

He was not alone.

A figure appeared next to him.

Steward caught sight of it out of the corner of his eye. He took two more steps then stopped, spun around, and confronted the stranger—

Relief escaped on a sigh. "Oh…you gave me a fright. I'm glad it's you. Hello, good Phaedra."

The hooded figure was shorter than Steward and wore a simple cloak that folded at the waist and continued up, covering the man's head as a hood. Steward could see part of Phaedra's face, but not all of it, even in the bright afternoon sun.

The Phaedra lived among the people of Aiden Glenn, but never *with* them. In fact, they held an odd place in the social structure of the village, as they seemed to have in every village Steward ever visited across the land. This place and role stemmed from their history, which itself was rife with intrigue and mystery.

Steward had long been told of a time when the king's empire was in direct conflict with the empire of the Phaedra'im. The two powers were in constant war for land and power and people. Great battles were waged, and many of the heroes of Steward's upbringing were those warriors who won victories over the dreaded Phaedra'im.

The long strife between the two great empires finally came to an end at the Battle of Kildrachan Plain, a strategic region, where three great rivers converged to form the headwaters of the Golden River. On that plain the king's army defeated the Phaedra'im and then exiled them to the region beyond his kingdom, forbidding them from ever entering his lands.

It was in the great and awful battle of Kildrachan Plain that the king's son had fallen.

As the years passed, however, the Phaedra'im eased their way into the outer villages of the king's empire. There they kept a low profile, wearing hoods to hide their faces and taking on servants' roles. Some tolerated them at first, although many villages refused them any entrance. As generations came and went, however, people forgot how powerful and evil the Phaedra'im once were. They forgot all the blood shed to defeat them at Kildrachan Plain.

And so the Phaedra'im grew in numbers and presence.

Though never the focus of any attention, they were always…there. Their reputation for wisdom began to grow, and they were often advice-givers to people of power and wealth. Steward seldom saw a prominent person in any town or village without a Phaedra nearby, whispering to him. They served almost as a conscience to people of distinction. They seemed less interested in serving the more common people, many of whom remained suspicious of their motives.

Some of the more powerful people of the empire began to accept the Phaedra, and most events held by the wealthy of the land included Phaedra, though always in the background. This created for them a humble and mysterious presence that unnerved some and fascinated others. They were gentle, soft spoken, and reserved. Yet their influence was powerful, and their presence commanded respect.

Steward's parents had little positive to say about the Phaedra. They cautioned their children to treat them with respect, but to keep their distance and never seek their advice. Yet Steward had seen many leaders in the village listen to them, and he had seldom heard a negative word come from any Phaedra whom he had happened to overhear. So, on this first day of his new journey, he was thankful for the company of one so familiar, wise, and humble.

"I didn't expect to find you here above Callater Pass, good Phaedra." They were always addressed as "good Phaedra," although Steward was never sure why.

"Good day, Master Steward. This is the first day of your great journey, is it not? And how do you find this land beyond Aiden Glenn?"

Steward looked around as the two continued down the path. "It's remarkable, incredible. It is so warm and bright and—"

"—fresh?"

"Yes, clean and fresh and clear. I have never seen such colors or smelled the air so sweet or heard birds sing so loudly or seen trees stand so tall."

The Phaedra looked ahead and slowed his pace. "It is a remarkable place, but do you know where you are going?"

Steward considered the question. "I assume the path I am on will take me to the king. So I plan to follow it until I reach the throne room." He did his best to sound confident, but it was hard since he didn't really have any idea where he was headed.

The Phaedra continued his slow and steady pace. "And why do you want to see the king?"

Steward fought to find an inner strength. He could hear his father's voice assuring him of the importance of his journey. But was his father's faith enough for him? "Why? The king will tell me the meaning of my name and the purpose of my life."

"And then you will return to Aiden Glenn?"

Was the Phaedra joking? "Of course I will return to Aiden Glenn. It's my home, and my parents will be waiting for me and watching for my return."

The Phaedra continued walking, as if he took no account of Steward's exasperation. "Perhaps, or perhaps they expect that you will find your destiny beyond Callater Pass and never return."

Steward stopped. He stared at his companion as his heart raced. Never return to Aiden Glenn? Never see his parents or friends or home again? Why would the Phaedra say such a terrible thing? It wasn't right! "I shall return to Aiden Glenn, good Phaedra. I will certainly return."

The Phaedra halted, motionless—then gave a brief nod. "Of course you shall. But tell me, Master Steward, how do you know the king wishes to see you?"

Steward shared the story of his birth and the oath handed down to him by his parents. "So it is my destiny to see the king and learn the meaning of my name."

The Phaedra walked on. "Dear Steward, you have done well to travel beyond Callater Pass. Few would have had the courage to do so. You are indeed brave, and for that you will be rewarded. Let me ask you, did the stranger on the horse tell your parents that *only* the king knew the meaning of your name?"

Why this question? Steward searched for confidence in his reply. "Not exactly. I believe he said that I would find the meaning of my name as I journeyed to see the king."

"So it is *on the journey* that you will find your answer, but it doesn't have to be in the throne room of the king?"

"Yes, I suppose that is right. I guess the king can tell me what I need to know at any point. But I do so look forward to seeing his throne room. Our ancestors spoke of its glory and brightness and splendor. One tale says that all of Aiden Glenn could be built just in its outer court. Another says there are more jewels in the floor than in all the rest of the kingdom. It must be glorious, and I can't wait to see it."

"It is indeed a glorious place. But tell me, if you find the true meaning of your name and the purpose for your life before you reach the throne room, what will you do?"

Some other place? Where…and why? The journey was to lead to the king. If it does not, what does this journey mean?

Play along. Confidence, Steward.

"I guess I will accept the words of the king wherever I hear them. Why do you ask such questions?" His tone bordered on impudence.

"Why, my dear Steward, it is because *I* know the meaning of your name *and* the purpose for which you were born."

"You…you do?" Steward stopped and stared at the hooded figure. He could make out only a few features of his face, like the curve of his chin, part of his mouth, the end of his nose, and the white glare of his eyes.

The Phaedra peered back at him from the shadows of his hooded retreat. "Of course. And I can speak for the king and tell you here and now."

Steward's heart raced. His breathing came short and fast. "Oh, then, please do, at once." Was he about to learn what he had been seeking all his life? And this was only the first day of his journey?

I will be back in Aiden Glenn by suppertime.

The Phaedra sat down on a large rock just where the meadow ended and the path entered an area of deep woods. The afternoon sun cast long, golden shadows across the ground. Steward sat opposite him and listened intently for the words that would unlock his destiny.

"Your name, dear Master Steward, means 'one who takes care of all he has.' That is your calling—to take care of what you have in service of the king. Do you understand this?"

He didn't, at least not fully. "I'm not sure. It seems so simple. What does it mean to take care of what I have?"

"What does it mean? My dear young Steward, it means that you must acquire all you can, and as you do you must put it to good use. You must invest it, build great things with it, enjoy it for your own, and, from time to time, be generous with it."

Steward thought of his small satchel and simple clothes. His heart sank. "But I have nothing. How can I take care of what I do not have?"

The Phaedra leaned toward him. "That is precisely why you must *not* go to the throne room of the king. How foolish you would look if you were to learn of this meaning of your name and have nothing to show for it. How would you bear the scorn of the king if you were to appear before him empty-handed, only to learn that your very name means what it does?"

The scene unfolded in his mind.

Him standing before the king with nothing to show. He could imagine the magnificent face of the king, and he watched his countenance grow sullen and angry. Steward felt the humiliation and shame. The king glowering at him as he stood empty-handed.

Save me from this!

"Oh, dear, good Phaedra, you have kept me from a great embarrassment. How foolish I would have looked! But what must I do now? I can't go back to Aiden Glenn empty-handed. Without anything acquired for which I can care. And yet, where am I to acquire things so I may care for them?"

"Very good questions, dear Steward. Very good questions indeed. And now I must leave you." The Phaedra rose to his feet and adjusted his robe.

"Leave me! Where are you going, and what am I to do? How can you leave me here without helping me know what to do?"

"Oh, but you are very near to your answers. They all lie farther down this path just through these woods. Travel for one hour and you will find a crest overlooking the first land beyond here. It is called Petitzaros. There you will find the answers you seek. Stay there and do not venture any farther, for all you need to know from this journey can be found there. It is the most wonderful, magical place in the kingdom, and the king would have you seek all the answers to your questions there. Do not worry about journeying beyond, for after Petitzaros are only death and sorrow. No, my young Steward, hear my words. The answers you seek are all to be found in Petitzaros. And now you must continue on your own."

Steward had little time to ponder these words before the Phaedra was gone. The evening sun was close to the horizon, and Steward wanted to get through the woods and find the vista before dark. So, with his satchel over his shoulder and a fresh drink of cider on his lips, he set his face toward the woods.

The terrain was not difficult, but as the light faded, each step became one of increasing faith as Steward struggled to make out the contours of the path. As dusk gave way to night, the woods seemed to close in on him. The once beautiful sounds of birds now took on an eeriness, and it made his skin crawl. He pressed ahead as fast as he could, and soon, to his great relief, he could see the path emerge from the forest.

Not far beyond the forest edge, the path climbed a short hill and rounded at a crest that offered the view promised by the Phaedra. Steward climbed with great enthusiasm until he was standing at the edge of the precipice.

He gazed down into the wide valley below, stunned by what lay before him. In the last glimmer of evening light, he could make out ten, no, twenty—no, wait!—it must be more than a *hundred* castles filling the valley floor. Each one displayed a flag of different color and shape, and no two castles were alike.

A kingdom of castles.

Petitzaros.

As the light faded and the castles below disappeared into the darkness, Steward found a smooth area on the forest floor and stretched out on it. Exhaustion from the emotions and physical work of the day settled over him. He opened his satchel and ate the meal his mother so lovingly prepared for him. She always provided just what he needed. He tore off a piece of the homemade bread and dipped it into the olive oil.

His first day had been a triumph. He'd learned the meaning of his name, and now he waited on the crest of his destiny.

I do wish I could have seen the king and his throne room, but I am at my destination. What more could I hope for?

Tonight he would sleep here, and tomorrow his journey would be complete. With this promise fresh in his mind, Steward lay his head on his satchel, pulled his cloak over his shoulders and fell asleep.

~~~~~~~~~

Walter watched as Alex set the book down on the coffee table and rubbed his neck. "Well, that's the first chapter."

Reed got up to put two more logs on the fire. The room remained quiet.

Merideth swished the remaining cabernet in her fish bowl glass and broke the silence. "I never knew Dad could write so well."

"And a fairy tale at that," Reed said.

Anna looked at her dad's empty chair. "Dad always loved a good illustration. I just wish he were here to tell us this story himself."

Walter rested his hands on the arms of his chair. "I think he wants you to read this story as if he is here. Listen for him and hear his voice...and your mother's."

Anna nodded. "Dad and Mom often talked about what it meant to be a steward. I guess Dad is trying to tell us something in all of this."

"Trying to tell *me* something, you mean." Reed flailed the fireplace poker in a circular gesture. "After all, I am the one that spends money as fast as I make it, right?"

Alex sat up and flipped a few pages of the book. "I'm not sure Steward is meant just for you, brother. But it is curious that the story seems to indicate that a steward is just a person who makes and spends money carefully. That doesn't seem to fit Mom and Dad's views."

Merideth leaned over and grasped the pages between her thumb and index finger. "Well, we do have nearly a couple hundred pages to go."

Alex touched her arm. "And I would like to just listen for awhile. So, sister, how about taking a turn?"

"Fine, but if I'm going to read, I need a drink, and it probably should be water." That drew a laugh from her siblings.

As Walter listened, he couldn't help wondering, why had they spent so little time together over the past ten years? Alex had told him earlier that, other than their mother's funeral, this was the only significant amount of time they had been together since Alex went off to seminary. What joy they'd missed. Maybe now...a new future could open up for each of them.

Walter looked at the book that lay open on the table. He knew what was coming, and he sat back and turned his heart toward heaven.

Dear Lord, open their eyes.

Merideth returned, took her place in front of the book and began to read.

CHAPTER
Seven

Steward shielded his eyes against the sunlight shining on his face. He felt its warmth and sat up. The first rays of morning sun flickered through the leaves of the tall birch trees and splashed all around him. The crowing of a rooster in the distance made him smile.

He gazed for several moments down on the castles of Petitzaros then looked as far as he could up and down the valley. The city and its castles filled the expanse and continued out of sight around a large ridge on the north side. The morning sun lit the roofs of the castles sitting at the westernmost edge of the city then swept its way eastward until the valley sparkled like jewels strewn out on a verdant green tapestry.

Could there be a more beautiful sight? Surely he would find the answers he was looking for in this wondrous place.

Steward prepared himself for his day of discovery. He finished the remaining food in his satchel, fixed the bag on his shoulder, and set his face toward Petitzaros. Before long, he was walking down the path that widened to a road leading to the city's enormous set of gates.

As Steward entered through the gates, the noise and activity inside caught him by surprise. The streets were crowded with hurrying people, as if everyone was preparing for some great emergency.

What was the panic about? Or was it a panic at all? After watching for several moments, Steward got the sense that this was…normal.

People scurried into and out of the shops for no reason Steward could discern. Carts were driven down the streets at alarming speeds, and shoppers were shoving and pushing their way as they walked. Elbows, sharp comments, and not a "pardon me" to be heard. The intensity of the activity was mesmerizing.

He watched and then shifted as a growing sense of panic rose within him. In all this chaos how would he make his first acquaintance? How would he find someone who could help him discover the way he could live out the meaning of his name? He watched for an opportunity, and then it grabbed him.

Or rather, a hand grabbed his shirt, jerking him forward, thrusting him out into the bright morning sun.

"Oh, my dear fellow, how horribly poor you are, my dear, poor, destitute fellow!"

Steward caught his balance and shaded his eyes from the morning sun. He turned toward the voice to find a most unusual sight—a man dressed in fine silk clothes and sporting an enormous felt hat adorned with feathers and sequins. His voice was that of a boy, but his weathered face bespoke a man well advanced in age.

"What brought you to this lowly state, young traveler?"

Steward was too distracted to answer, for the man was hunched over under the weight of a large chain of gold rings fixed to gold-colored bands on each wrist. The mass of rings was flung over his shoulder.

Should Steward lift the chains and help the man stand upright?

The man shuffled over and picked at Steward's shirt. "My dear boy, you must be starving to be dressed in this way. Come with me, and I will get you some food and proper clothes."

"Thank you, sir, but I am really quite satisfied. I only came here to seek my destiny."

"Nonsense!" The man struggled to lift his arms in the air under the burden of the chains. "Why, look at you. You have no…no…well, you have nothing to show for yourself."

Steward looked around him. Everyone had a chain fixed to both wrists. The chains were of different lengths and shimmered as though made of pure gold. Those with shorter chains stood more erect, but those with larger chains were hunched like the man before him.

Perhaps a tyrant king had enslaved the city. "Why is everyone in chains?"

"Chains? Why, my dear boy, these are golden rings. They are precious—marks of distinction and prestige. And that is exactly your problem. You have not one ring. Why—" The man came closer and carefully pulled back Steward's shirt sleeves to expose his bare wrists. "You have no Bracelets!"

A clamor erupted. Everyone seemed to be talking at once.

"No Bracelets? How could this happen?"

"A boy of his age? Imagine!"

"It's unthinkable."

"Something must be done with him."

"Throw him out of town. He's a freeloader!"

"Silence!" The man in silk struggled to lift his shoulders in what seemed an attempt to command more respect. "I will take this young man to Czartrevor. If you remember, he too came to us without the king's Bracelets. He may know this lad and what we can do for him."

"To Czartrevor!"

The crowd's chant followed Steward as the man led him along the streets of Petitzaros. He considered resisting, but—

Could the Bracelets be part of his answer? Was the king here in Petitzaros? Would Steward meet him after all?

They arrived at an enormous castle that glowed in the sun like a tower of mirrors. Steward's mouth gaped open. It was the largest castle he'd ever seen. Surely the king was in this magnificent place!

He turned to the man in silk. "Does the king live here? I have been sent to see the king. Can you take me to him?"

As soon as Steward mentioned the king, the atmosphere around him changed. Several Phaedra emerged, appearing out of nowhere. They walked among the crowd, speaking in hushed but urgent tones.

"The king is not concerned with the affairs of Petitzaros."

"You must not bother the king with trivial matters."

"Hasn't the king left these affairs up to you?"

The man in silk shuffled forward and bellowed in as strong and authoritarian a tone as he could muster: "The king is not concerned with the affairs of Petitzaros. We will not bother the king with trivial matters such as these. Besides, hasn't the king left these affairs up to us?"

Several in the crowd nodded. "Yes, he has, he certainly has. Well spoken."

Others joined in. "We must not bother the king. No, not with these trivial matters. The king expects us to deal with these matters ourselves, and so we must."

Steward watched them, shaking his head. *They're just mimicking the Phaedra. Can't they see that?*

The people around him gripped his arms and escorted him inside through a great portico with arches that seemed to reach the sky.

It was magnificent. This *had* to be the king's castle.

The stairs led the small assembly up through the outer courtyard and into an inner chamber. Wood beams stretched across the ceiling, held up by marble pillars and adorned with gold-etched murals depicting scenes of luxury and opulence.

Steward could no longer contain himself. "Who lives here? It must be the king!"

The man in silk didn't halt his labored pace. "Oh, a king does indeed live here."

A king—? Steward stopped, stiffening his back and facing his escort. "Is he the king of Petitzaros? Please answer me straight. I must know."

"King of Petitzaros? That's a rich one." The man managed a crooked grin and gave a thready, wheezing laugh. The entire assembly broke out in laughter.

What was so funny? Impatience stirred within him, and Steward was about to demand an explanation when a loud voice rang out from the far end of the great chamber: "What is all the levity about?"

The man in silk caught his breath. "Ah, Czartrevor. We have a visitor for you. One who reminded us of you when you entered this city so many years ago. Come and meet this unfortunate young traveler."

Steward watched as the figure drew closer, and his mouth gaped. *It can't be...it just can't be—*

Before him was a hunched-over, rather obese man dressed in fine clothes who, like the others, had a huge set of golden chains thrown over his shoulder.

He's old and gray, but he looks like—

The man looked back at him, studying him, then raised his hands as best he could beneath the weight of his chains. "I declare, Steward, is that you?"

"Trevor! Great Saints of Palindor, how did you...and when...and where did you get those—?"

Trevor began to laugh. Not a young boy laugh, but a wheezing, rasping laugh like an aging, tired man short on breath and hope. "I know. I know. It's incredible, isn't it? I left... what was the name of that old place?"

"Aiden Glenn! You have only been gone three years. How could you forget the name of your hometown?"

Trevor scowled. "Three years! Oh, no, you must be mistaken. I have been in Petitzaros for—my dear Czarrudolph, how long have I been here?"

The man in silk rubbed his chin for a moment. "Oh, heavens, for years...decades, I believe."

Steward shook his head and moved in front of Trevor. "No, Trevor, no! You only left Aiden Glenn three years ago, and...." He paused. "You were so young then. You were—are—the same age as me."

"Impossible! My dear Steward, you have been traveling too long. Let's not stand out here. Come in and be comfortable. Eat, drink, and relax. That is what this place is all about." He adjusted the chains on his shoulder and began shuffling his way back into his palace. "Oh, Steward, I have so much to tell you. You'll love this place. It's a magical, wonderful land. I'm so glad you are here. What fun we will have. Come in and get changed into some real clothes."

The man in silk called out. "Um, Czartrevor, if I may. We have a problem. You see, young Steward here, well, he has no...that is...he does not have...."

"Spit it out, man."

"Bracelets. He has no Bracelets."

Trevor tightened his wrinkled face, producing even more winkles. "Oh, dear. That's right. I believe when I came here I had no Bracelets either. It has been so many decades ago that I had almost forgotten."

"Three years. It has only been three years," Steward muttered. He watched as Trevor—no, *Czar*trevor—walked through the assembled crowd and spoke with one of the Phaedra who, as usual, had just...appeared.

Steward frowned. How did they *do* that? Before he could form the question, the Phaedra nodded and left the room.

Czartrevor waved a hand at him. "Soon you will have your Bracelets, and all will be well. Now, on to the feast. What a party this will be. Imagine, good old Steward from Glenn Adair."

Steward spoke through clenched teeth. "Aiden Glenn. You're from *Aiden Glenn*." His correction went unnoticed.

Most of those who had accompanied Steward to the castle of Czartrevor left with warm words of encouragement. Only about ten people, including Czarrudolph and his entourage, remained to follow Czartrevor into the banquet hall.

Steward hurried to his friend's side. "Trevor, I have so many questions. First of all, what's with the name? And Czarrudolph said something about you being a king, but not the king of Petitzaros. Is that right? And how did you get to be so...so...old?"

Czartrevor ignored him, busy as he was ordering servants to get clothes, shoes, food, and drink. Finally, he motioned to Steward to sit down. "Your clothes will be here soon, as will your Bracelets. And then the banquet. Now let me see if I can help you with some answers."

Czartrevor sat down, and before he began two Phaedra emerged from the shadows and sat down near him.

"How can I explain Petitzaros to you? This is such a wonderful place. You can have anything you want if you are willing to work for it. I came here with nothing, and by working hard and looking out for myself I have amassed, well" —he looked to the immense ceiling and raised his hands in the air—"all of this. Pretty incredible, huh?"

"It is, yes. But, Trevor—"

"Please, Steward, my name here is Czartrevor."

"Yes, that's what I mean. Why the name and the chains and the Bracelets?"

"Okay, okay, one thing at a time." Czartrevor's smile reminded Steward of the way adults smiled at children who were trying to understand something too difficult for them.

He didn't like it much.

Czartrevor leaned back in his seat. "First, you need to know that in Petitzaros every person can build his own kingdom. That is what the king put us here to do."

As soon as Czartrevor mentioned the name of the king, the two Phaedra began to whisper:

"The king does not bother himself with the affairs of Petitzaros."

"The king is not concerned with what happens here."

"The king has more important things to do."

*Czar*trevor didn't even seem to hear them. He just went on with his explanation. "You see, my dear Steward, the king has left this place to us to build lives for ourselves. He has given us all we need, and now we are to work hard and prosper and enjoy life."

"Does the king visit here?"

"Oh, no. You see, the king does not bother himself with the affairs of Petitzaros. He is not very concerned about what happens here. He has more important things to do, after all."

Of course. Just as the Phaedra said. Over and over and....

Steward shook his head. "And the name and chains?"

"Ahh, the Bracelets." His friend lifted one hand, letting the chains clang against each other. "Yes, let's get to that. First, you must know that every person here is capable of building his or her own castle. That is our calling. To acquire and build and care for what we have."

The words grabbed him. He leaned toward his old friend. "Yes, that's my calling, my destiny. Why, it's the very meaning of my name. One of the Phaedra told me that very thing just yesterday after I made it past Callater Pass."

"Oh...yes. I remember now. Your journey! This is your journey! I had forgotten after all these years. You have come to find the meaning of your name and the purpose of your life. And it is here in Petitzaros. I am sure of it."

Steward nodded. "I think you're right. My name means 'one who takes care of all he has.' That's what the Phaedra told me. And he also told me that in order to care for things I must acquire them."

Czartrevor slapped his hand on the table. "And this is the place to acquire all you ever wanted. And I will show you how."

From the corner of the room a Phaedra appeared holding an ornate, carved stone box. He set it before Czartrevor and backed away.

Czartrevor opened the box and held up its contents. Two large, heavy, golden Bracelets. "Here they are, Steward. Your ticket to abundance beyond your wildest dreams. They are a gift to you from the king."

"From the king? They are from the king? How do you know?"

Czartrevor didn't answer. Instead, one of the Phaedra stood, walked closer to the two and whispered, "Dear Steward, millennia ago when the king established this land, he wanted all of its inhabitants to prosper. So he created these golden Bracelets and commanded that all citizens of Petitzaros wear them. No one knew why at first, but the magic of the Bracelets soon became known."

A second Phaedra joined the other and continued the story. "All who wear the Bracelets are allowed to use the Elixir of Mah Manon to gain wealth, power, and position."

Elixir of Mah Manon. What was that?

"And be generous," Steward interjected. "The Phaedra told me that I must also be generous."

Czartrevor shrugged and looked at his hooded companions. "Oh, yes, of course. There is always room for a little generosity."

The Phaedra took the two Bracelets and handed them to Steward. "And these are for you. With them you can complete your journey and live out your destiny as a citizen of Petitzaros. You can amass great wealth and care for it." He glanced at the Phaedra next to him, and with a slight nod he went on. "And, of course, be generous with what you have." The Phaedra placed the bands around Steward's wrists and, with a quick twist, secured them in place with a sound like the locking of a clasp.

Steward ran his hands over them, feeling their weight. They were heavier than he expected, and they pressed tightly to his wrists. "How do I get them off?"

The Phaedra rose. "You must never take them off. They are yours for life. They now mark you as a citizen of Petitzaros."

Citizen? But this is not my home. Steward sat up and studied Czartrevor, looking at his gnarled hands and shriveled face…and a chill ran through him. "What if I want to return to Aiden Glenn?"

Soft whispers broke out in the room. Steward glanced to the side and saw they came from the other two Phaedra. The whispers echoed all around him.

"This is your home now."

"You need never return to Aiden Glenn."

"There is nothing for you there."

"Your destiny is here."

The Phaedra who had placed the Bracelets on Steward's wrists raised his hand, and the room grew silent. "Young Steward, you must seek your destiny here. This is the goal of your journey. Here you will find the purpose for your life. You need venture no farther down the road or return the way you came."

Czartrevor nodded. "The Phaedra is right. Stay with me here, and I will show you how to acquire all you ever wanted. Then you can truly be Steward. Isn't that what you have been seeking?"

Steward's stomach churned, and his hands began to tremble. His spirit was wrestling with conflicting emotions. He wanted to run, to run back home and leave all this behind. Yet the words made sense. They were true, weren't they? He was just tired from the journey. Best to listen to the Phaedra and his friend. "Yes, yes, it is." But he couldn't help adding, "I just thought I was supposed to complete my journey and find my true answers in the throne room of the king."

The whispers of the Phaedra sounded again.

"You don't need to see the king."

"This is not a matter for the king."

"Your destiny is here."

Then one Phaedra's words increased above a whisper and were delivered with a venomous hiss: "The king does not care about you."

Steward froze. The words cut him. For the first time in his life a Phaedra frightened him. He glared at the hooded figure in front of him.

As though sensing Steward's reaction, another Phaedra continued in a more consoling tone. "The king wants you to be happy, young Steward, and so he has sent you on this journey to Petitzaros to fulfill your destiny. That is wonderful news, is it not?"

Steward held his stare then looked away. "Yes, I guess it is."

Czartrevor let out a sigh. "Great, it's settled then. Tonight we shall party, and tomorrow we shall help young Steward begin his work. Call to the people of my kingdom and tell them there shall be a great feast tonight in Steward's honor. Go, and I will begin preparations."

As the Phaedra left the room, Steward adjusted the bands on his wrists. They may be blessings, but did they have to be so tight and heavy?

Czartrevor rose and managed a feeble wave. "Come, let me show you the banquet hall." Steward followed his friend into a huge dining room, which held enough tables and chairs for a hundred people or more.

"Where will you get all of the food and wine for so many guests?"

"Ah, now is the time for your first lesson in the magic that is Petitzaros." Czartrevor walked to a large safe and began to turn dials until the clicks of the tumblers fell into place. He pulled open the heavy door and took out an ornate bottle with a stopper fitted in the top. He closed the safe behind him and walked to the empty banquet table in the center of the room. His eyes gleamed as he looked at the vial, holding it up to the light to measure the volume of its precious contents.

Steward was mesmerized. "What is it?"

"This, my dear friend, is the Elixir of Mah Manon. It is the lifeblood of Petitzaros. Watch, dear Steward, and see the magic that can be yours."

Czartrevor opened the bottle with great care and leaned over the table. A single drop made its way out of the top and, after clinging for a moment to the edge of the spout, fell from the bottle. It dropped onto the tabletop and exploded into a staggering array of fruits, vegetables, meats, cheeses, breads, flasks of wine, and more delicious, sweet desserts than Steward had ever seen in one place.

This was incredible!

Czartrevor placed the delicate stopper back into the neck of the bottle. "That, my friend, is the power of the Elixir of Mah Manon. Now aren't you glad you have come to Petitzaros?"

Perhaps his friend and the Phaedra were right. Maybe he should trust them. This was, after all, the most amazing thing he'd ever seen.

Soon, Steward was the honored guest at Czartrevor's great banquet. Hundreds of chain-laden guests were there; but, despite the lavish food, drink, and music, they all bore the countenance of somber resignation. How could they look so burdened with this abundance before them? Though he heard laughter and even merriment, the whole party felt like a sad facade, as if the people's fun was forced to hide a deep despair.

Steward rubbed a hand over his eyes. He must be tired—probably just imagining it all.

Later that night, after the last guests had left, as Steward prepared for bed, he thanked his friend for such a grand welcome. "I do still have two questions, Tre…I mean Czartrevor. Why the new name, and what about the rings?"

Czartrevor sat back in his overstuffed chair, his belly sticking out a bit from underneath his waistcoat. "Two answers and then to bed. We have much to do tomorrow. First, the name. When someone in Petitzaros gains a high level of wealth and prestige, they are given the title of *czar*, which is added to their given name. It is a sign of respect, marking one as a complete citizen of this land. It means your kingdom is large, and your power and influence are substantial. It is everyone's goal to reach this place of honor."

"Everyone's?" Steward had seen a few people with no chains when he entered the city.

"Well, not exactly everyone. There is a sect of rather crazy people who live alone out in the northern country and believe an old superstition about the Bracelets. But that is not important. No, you must set your face toward nothing less than the day you will be called Czarsteward. After all, according to the Phaedra, that is the true meaning of your name—and your destiny."

"Yes, I guess it is. Czarsteward." Steward smiled at the sound of the name. "And the rings?"

"They are the great mystery of this land. No one knows how they appear or exactly why, except that they seem to increase with one's wealth and prestige. One day you will have two, and the next time you look, there will be three. The Phaedra say they are part of the blessing on this land. You get the Elixir of Mah Manon, the golden bands, and gold rings in abundance."

"But aren't they heavy?"

"Oh, no, not at all. And we can take them off whenever we want. It is just that they are such a wonderful sign of our blessings that we never do. The more rings, the more honor in the land. Don't worry. Soon you will have rings of your own."

Steward wasn't so sure.

The evening was over, and Steward was led to a massive suite with a four-poster bed as large as his entire room back in Aiden Glenn. He was exhausted and full and…confused. As he crawled in between sheets more luxurious than he had ever felt, he thought back on the day.

Surely this is my destiny, the purpose of my journey.

His momentary concern over the Phaedra probably stemmed from his fatigue, nothing more. They were wise, and he would do well to believe them when they said this was the completion of his journey. Still…

I will *return to Aiden Glenn one day. As soon as I've acquired enough to prove my name and fulfill my purpose.*

With that thought cheering his heart, he drifted off to sleep.

From the corner of Steward's room, a Phaedra slipped out of the shadows and came over to his bed. Leaning down, he whispered in Steward's ear.

"You never need to return to Aiden Glenn. Your destiny is in Petitzaros. You will stay here and become Czarsteward. The Phaedra are right. They are always right."

~~~~~~~~~

Walter's heart rate quickened. He watched as Merideth set the book down and took a deep drink of water. She looked at no one.

Reed rubbed his wrist under his Rolex. "Golden Bracelets…pretty clever."

Alex stood and walked to the fireplace, grabbed a poker, and jabbed at the dying fire. Sparks erupted and crackled at him. "I know some of those gray people. Lots of money, but no real happiness. Obviously, that's what Dad is getting at."

Merideth finally looked up. "They're not all gray. I know wealthy people who seem pretty happy to me. Money doesn't always have to come with chains."

"Oh, they're there." Reed leaned forward. "They're always there. I mean, I'm not filthy rich or anything, but those chains Dad's talking about? Stress, fear, jealousy, all the stuff that comes with having money. Fear that you'll lose it, envy against others who have more. Trying to protect it and grow it, keeping the government from taxing it and others from stealing it. Oh, yeah, trust me, sister. The chains are there. And they're heavy."

Merideth's face tightened. She stood and pushed past Reed to walk to the kitchen. Her irritated words drifted back to them. "I'm not buying it. Not for everyone. I get the point, but there are exceptions."

Walter waited until she disappeared into the kitchen. "What do you think, Alex?"

He was still trying to stir life into the fire. He added two logs and pushed them into place. "I'm not sure. Still processing it, I guess. I'd like to think Mer is right. Seems an odd notion that money always brings burdens. I've done well and made good money. I've put some away, and it looks like a lot more could be coming. Will it come with chains?" Alex returned to his seat, his unanswered question hanging in the air.

Merideth returned and sent an arch look at Walter. "So what do you think? Does it?"

He didn't expect that from her. He recoiled from the idea of being thrust into the discussion, *their* discussion.

Help me, Lord.

"I think Sam wants you to wrestle with those kinds of questions. But from my own experience, for myself and the people I've known and worked with, I'd have to say—"

They all turned to look at him.

"—the chains are there for most everyone. I know only a handful of people who handle great wealth without it becoming a burden. And they have one thing in common. They gave most of it away."

Merideth rolled her eyes and sat down next to Alex, leaving her mom's chair vacant. Reed moved over in front of the book.

"I'm anxious to see where Dad takes this. Mind if I read?"

 Eight

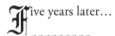 ive years later...

Reed stopped. "Five years? That can't be right."

Anna drew back in her chair and frowned. "No, it can't be. Are you sure we didn't miss something?"

Reed shook his head. "Nope, that's what it says."

Merideth smiled and raised an eyebrow. "Well, this ought to be interesting."

Reed picked the book up and set it in his lap and continued.

Five years later the Black Knight galloped his horse along the broad road leading through the gates of Petitzaros. He pressed his powerful steed along, its untamed mane sparkling in the morning sun as it rose and fell with the motion of the canter. He stopped to adjust his helmet, letting the rigid neck shield fall back on his shoulders and wiping some sweat from his face through the narrow front opening. The weight of his chainmail coat pressed down on his shoulders. Good thing he was near the end of his ride.

Petitzaros.

He had waited five years to enter these gates.

The warrior rode beneath the stone and timber gates, and his senses sharpened. All around him were stares...

And fear.

Good.

He reached down and pulled at the crimson, hammered metal sheathing covering his legs so the onlookers would take notice. He positioned the large sword at his side so everyone could see its cross-shaped hilt. Strapped to the back of the saddle was his small shield bearing the image of a crown. His horse pranced and neighed. They had everyone's attention.

The knight spoke to no one but paced his horse along the streets. He gazed back and forth as he rode along, returning the stares from the mass of people who scurried in and out of shops. A few people edged toward them, but most backed away.

He had heard tales of this place, but the opulence was beyond his expectations. He made his way down the long streets lined with towering palm trees and countless shops and places to eat and drink. He continued past the bathhouses, banquet rooms, parks, and palaces. The palm trees were strung with lights, and everywhere the rich and powerful filled the sidewalks in their fine silk clothes, great sequined hats, and the ever-present gold chains thrown over one shoulder.

His stomach churned. *This is not as it was meant to be.*

As he reached one end of the city, he turned his horse down a road that led them to a different part of Petitzaros. This, too, he had come to see.

"C'mon, boy." He patted his horse on the neck. "Let's see the rest of this place."

As he rode, the customary, fine, brown paving stones ended, replaced by coarse, dusty gravel. These streets boasted no fine stores, palm trees, or bathhouses. Instead, there were simple houses, older stores with faded and tattered awnings, and a tiny, unkempt park where a few children played. Gone were the bright colors, lavish fountains, and street vendor carts overflowing with flowers, food, and trinkets. The air hung heavy with the smell of a place where people scraped and sweated to survive. The people here wore plain clothes—rags, really. They had no bands or gold rings. But they stood tall, and their faces were bright.

The knight paused to take it in. How could such a place exist right next to the garish opulence of the rest of Petitzaros?

The knight turned his steed back onto a main corridor, returning to the affluence of the city, with its streets filled with hunchbacked figures and their sad, gray faces squinting in the sun as they hurried from store to bathhouse to banquet hall.

It's as if they're rushing to avoid the reality of their existence, hoping that the next experience will bring some happiness into their lives. This was far worse than he'd anticipated.

As he made his journey through the streets, he sensed another presence. His horse reared up, and the knight fought to calm him. He peered at the shadowed corners and secluded alleyways.

The Phaedra were there…lurking, watching. None of the scurrying people seemed to notice them. The Phaedra withdrew as he went by, and when he glanced back they reappeared behind him.

He ran his hand along the hilt of his sword. Its time would come.

He found his way to the entrance of the castle he sought. It was small compared to most other castles he had passed. The gatekeeper's eyes widened as he approached, and the knight restrained a smile at the man's alarm.

"May I h-h-help you?" The gatekeeper's eyes were fixed on the knight's sword.

"I am looking for a young man named Steward."

"Steward?" The gatekeeper looked around as if he had never heard of him. The warrior dismounted and took a step toward him.

The man scrambled backward. "Steward? Oh, *Steward!* Yes, of course, you must mean Czarsteward. Yes, he lives here. This is his palace. Is…is he, uh…expecting you?"

"No, not anymore. But I am here to see him nonetheless."

The gatekeeper wrung his hands and wrinkled his brow. "Oh, well, I see. I mean, I am not sure I do see, you see."

The warrior scowled down on the quivering man. "Is Steward here in this…*palace?*" His derogatory tone was not lost on the frightened doorman.

"Why, yes, he is home. But if he is not expecting you I will need to go and ask if it is all right for you to be seen."

The knight drew his sword. "I'll ask him myself."

He turned the hilt end forward and lunged past the gatekeeper, smashing into the doors. Wood sprayed everywhere, and the doors flew open. The knight turned to the gaping man. "It appears it's all right for me to be seen."

The gatekeeper ran around a side passage and hurried out of sight. The knight walked into the courtyard and through to the main hall. He stopped to take in the surroundings. Marble pillars, heavy wood paneling, and thick tapestries.

Pitiable. So gaudy, tawdry…and worthless.

The sound of shuffling footsteps caught him.

Ah. His quarry approach—

He frowned. *That can't be Steward!*

"May I help you? What is the meaning of this intrusion?"

The knight looked the man over. His face had some of the same gray sadness he had seen in the people on the street, but it lacked the deep etching and vacuous eyes of so many others. He stood a little more erect than most, but then only a small number of gold rings were linked to each wrist. So few that they didn't even touch the ground when his hands were at his sides.

The knight smiled. There might still be time.

"You are Steward of Aiden Glenn?"

"No. Well, actually, yes, I guess I am. I have not heard that name in decades."

The warrior ignored the comment. "It has been five years since you entered Petitzaros. I have been sent by the king to ask why you are still here."

Steward started to respond then stopped.

Dozens of Phaedra emerged out of the shadows. Their sheer number created a heavy tension in the room. Most kept their distance, but six came forward to stand at Steward's side and face the knight.

The first one stepped forward and offered a slight bow. "Good day to you, stranger. If your intent here is peaceful, then you are welcome."

The second joined him. "We are a peaceful people, and there is no need for swords or armor here."

A third spoke from behind them. "There is no battle to be fought here. We are a peaceful people."

Steward seemed to regain his composure. "Yes, of course. Please lay your sword aside. It must be heavy and cumbersome. There is no need for a fighting weapon in Petitzaros. And it does make some people nervous, as I am sure you can understand."

The knight drew closer to Steward. "I was sent by the king to ask why you are still in Petitzaros."

The Phaedra moved to encircle the knight.

The first Phaedra confronted him, speaking now in a more authoritarian tone. "The king has no concern for what happens in Petitzaros. He has more important matters to attend to. He has left us to our own to prosper and take pleasure in the fruit of our work, which is according to his own good wishes." He circled the knight, taking him in from all sides. "And you know that to be true, don't you, good knight?"

The knight ignored the Phaedra, his eyes locked on Steward. "Young Steward, you were sent on a journey to see the king. Why have you stopped here?"

Another Phaedra started to reply, but Steward interrupted. "This is where I was supposed to stop. This is my destiny." He raised his hands toward the ceiling, his rings clanking as he looked up at the ornamentation that filled the room. "This is the meaning of my name and the purpose for my life."

The warrior tensed. Anger washed over him. His hands clenched as he came to Steward. His tone was sharp. "Who told you this was your destiny? Who told you this was the meaning of your name?"

Silence. All eyes fixed on Steward as he pondered the knight's question. Then Steward turned and pointed toward the figures standing beside him. "They did."

Of course they did. When Steward turned back to him, the knight held his gaze. "Only the king can tell you the meaning of your name. And only in the throne room of the king will you learn your destiny."

Steward stood frozen and silent. Could this strange knight be telling the truth? Did he really know the king? Could the Phaedra have been wrong?

A Phaedra moved closer and whispered to him, "Who is this knight that he knows the mind of the king?"

A second Phaedra circled him. "How do you know he is even from the king? Perhaps it is a trap, Czarsteward, to lure you from this place."

A third Phaedra joined in. "Do not listen to him. He is a deceiver. His voice is darkness. Even his skin is blackness."

Then, in hushed whispers that grew in volume, all the Phaedra began to chant, "Liar, liar, liar."

The knight didn't seem to care what the Phaedra said, although the chant forced him to raise his voice almost to a shout. "Steward, you were born for a reason. The journey does not stop here. Your destiny lies far beyond Petitzaros. You must leave with me at once."

The Phaedra closed rank around Steward. They spoke in turn, their voices sharp and accusatory.

"Do not go with him."

"He will kill you."

"He is not from the king."

"Throw him out, Czarsteward. Make him leave. You are only safe in Petitzaros."

Steward stared at the knight. Had the warrior come to kill him? Did he want Steward's kingdom? How could Steward be sure the knight really knew the king?

All around him the Phaedra kept up their chant: "Liar, liar, liar."

And then two of the Phaedra spoke, and their comments shot through Steward.

"The king does not speak through darkness nor use blackness as his voice."

"This knight is from the *Tohu Wa-Bohu*."

There was a sudden, chilling silence. Energy, like an electrical shock, pulsated through the room. Everyone froze.

Tohu Wa-Bohu. The forbidden name.

That settled it. Steward met the knight's hard gaze. "I will *not* go with you. Now leave my house at once. If you try to take me by force, I will fight you with all my strength."

The Phaedra entourage closed ranks around Steward. They each reached into the hidden folds of their robes and pulled out a short sword crafted with a unique series of curves that gave the weapons the appearance of glistening silver snakes.

The knight stared back at Steward one last time, and with a powerful turn his chain-mail coat swinging around him, he strode out of the room. As the sound of his heavy boots and clanging chainmail faded, Steward gave a sigh.

The Phaedra sheathed their weapons. One drew close to Steward. "Well done, Czarsteward. Today you have fulfilled your destiny."

The moment he finished speaking, Steward felt a heaviness in his arms. He looked down to see that six new rings had appeared on his chain. For the first time, it was connected in one chain linking wrist to wrist. Steward smiled.

This was surely his reward.

He grasped the chain of rings in both hands and, with a great tug, flung it up over his shoulder. "Now I am truly *Czar*steward." He hunched his back to bear the weight of the new rings and shuffled out of the room.

Behind him the Phaedra whispered, "Indeed you are, our young Steward. Indeed you are."

~~~~~~~~

Reed paused and looked around the room. He raised his eyebrows. "Next chapter?"

Alex waved to him. "Carry on."

Nine

A shaft of sunlight worked its way along the floor and up onto the face of a sleeping Czarsteward. As he rolled over to avoid the brightness he could feel a weight tugging at his wrists. He sat up, pulling his arms out from underneath the comforter and examining his Bracelets. Then he counted his links.

One, two, three.

Four. FIVE.

"Excellent!"

His shout brought a servant into the room. "Is everything all right, sir?"

"Oh yes, much more than all right." He jumped out of bed and examined the chains in the sunlight. "Look at these new rings. They're fantastic. I will surely receive more Elixir. You know what that means? Bigger parties, nicer clothes, and status...*status,* my little friend."

The servant nodded and shuffled over to straighten the sheets. "Today is the Feast of Nines. Is it not a good opportunity to display your new blessings?"

Steward smiled in delight, rubbing his hands across his new rings. "Yes, I'd forgotten. Wonderful. I will get ready and leave at once."

Steward left for his walk to the banquet hall and strode along the path, bearing with joy the weight of the chain over his shoulder. With this larger chain, he could acquire more of the Elixir of Mah Manon, with which he could build a greater palace, throw more splendid banquets, and become more powerful and famous. This was a great day. Surely, this proved that his destiny was here in Petitzaros.

As Steward passed an orchard, he heard a commotion just behind him. He looked back and his heart raced. Galloping out from the rows of apple trees was a huge figure driving his horse toward Steward at full speed. Steward screamed and began to run, but his heavy chains made each step a struggle. Before he could escape, the man grabbed him by the back of his robe and flung him up onto the back of the massive horse.

"Hold on to my armor or you will be thrown off and killed!" shouted the rider. Steward looked, and the ground was passing underneath him at such speed that he grasped the armor of his kidnapper with both arms to keep himself on the back of the galloping horse.

Steward looked up. To his horror, he recognized the armor and mail coat of the Black Knight. If he did not fall to his death from the horse, he would be killed by the sword that flapped alongside the great warrior, who drove them forward at breakneck speed through the streets of Petitzaros.

"I will not harm you," the knight shouted as they came to a sharp turn. "Now hold on tight!"

Whatever fate awaited him at this journey's end, being flung from a horse was *not* the way he wanted to die. So he held tightly as they rode through the city, out of the great gates, and up into the hill country. As the mighty horse climbed a steep path along the edge of a forest, it struggled for breath. The knight pulled the exhausted beast to a stop and jumped off. Steward jumped off as well and ran for the forest edge, but the knight caught him and pulled him to the ground.

"Do not fear me, Steward. I will not harm you. I was sent to help you find your way to the king."

With that, he let Steward go, backing away.

Steward examined his options. He couldn't outrun the knight. Even in full chain mail, the man was far faster than he. Even if he could, the great black horse had enough left in him to run Steward down. Besides, they were miles from Petitzaros with only a forest on one side and a cliff on the other. And so, for better or worse, Steward was a captive.

The knight pulled off his helmet and coat. His hair was black—as black as his horse's mane. Steward thought of the warning about the *Tohu Wa-Bohu*.

The knight turned and looked at Steward, examining his face. "You're afraid of me because I am black."

Steward dropped his gaze then looked back up, his eyes fixed on his captor. "Are you really from the king? How can you prove that to me? Why should I believe you?"

The knight sat down on a rock and stretched out his legs. He motioned to Steward to sit as well. As the knight rubbed his neck he began to speak.

"Twenty-four years ago, I was sent by the king to a small village just beyond the edge of the upper kingdom. I was told that the village was to be the birthplace of an important man. I was never told what he was to accomplish or why the king was so interested in this man, but my mission was set, and I was not to fail at any cost. I rode to the village, dropping down into the lower kingdom and through the gray veil. There I met a young man grieving over his wife's inability to have a child. As we spoke, I knew that this man's wife was to be the mother of the promised one. So I pledged to him that the king would grant him a son if he and his wife would give him to the service of the king."

Steward's chest pounded. He had all but forgotten the story handed down to him by his parents, just as he had forgotten about the journey. Could it be…? Was this the knight his father spoke of?

The knight leaned forward, his gaze locked onto Steward's. "The name of the village was Aiden Glenn. It was your father who received my promise. And every year I returned to be sure that your mother and father affirmed their pledge. Now do you believe I was sent by the king?"

What could he say? No one else could have known that story, not in that detail. Steward jumped to his feet. "You…you are the knight? My parents never told me you were black."

"I don't think it mattered to them." The knight paused, and the comment hung in the air. The knight stood and came close to Steward. "Young Steward, the evil of the *Tohu Wa-Bohu* is not seen in color but in the difference between truth and deception. Watch for deception in any form or color."

Steward nodded but his mind was racing between faith and fear. He wanted to believe, but the Phaedra, the Bracelets, the castles…they all called to him. He stepped away to collect his thoughts. He took off his coat and looked down at the chain that dragged on the ground and rubbed his wrists where they had become red and irritated under the increased burden of the six new rings. As he worked to get his coat off around the rings, the knight said, "I see you have new rings. That was a result of your rejection of my help."

Steward stopped and turned toward him. "Why was I blessed for refusing to go with you, if you are really from the king?"

"*Blessed?*" The knight bellowed the word. "Why do you call the rings blessings?"

"They're gifts from the king for those who prosper in Petitzaros." Steward refused to be intimidated.

"Tell me, Steward, why do you have so few when you have been in Petitzaros for so long?"

Steward shifted where he sat. The last thing he wanted to talk about was the most painful time during his five years in Petitzaros. But he knew the knight would press him, so he might as well get it over with. "Two years ago, I was among the most affluent of the younger men of Petitzaros. I had built a large palace, and my kingdom was growing daily. At one point I had so many rings I had to drape them over both shoulders. Oh, I was so very wealthy." Steward sighed.

"One day, I was on a hunt with five of my friends. Czartrevor led the party. We hunted farther out than we had ever gone, and as the hunt progressed we became separated in unfamiliar territory. I was close on the heels of the fox when my horse stumbled and threw me to the ground. I was stunned for a time, and when I woke a young woman the likes of whom I had never seen in all my years in Petitzaros was tending me. She wore plain clothes. She had no oil in her hair or makeup on her face. I saw too that she had a very different kind of bracelet on her wrist. It was not wide and ornate like ours, but very simple, small, and light—but gold nonetheless."

Steward stood and paced. "She was joined by others, and soon I learned that I was in the village of Remonant. I had been warned that there was such a village inhabited by a sect of crazy people who believed, among other things, that our gold rings were a curse and not a blessing. I learned from them that they used their Elixir of Mah Manon to be sure everyone had their needs met, but no more. If they had Elixir left over, they went to other villages and gave it to people who needed food or shelter or clothes. No one had a lot, but no one had a little either."

"What happened to your many chains?"

His chains? Ah, the knight meant his rings. "The people there helped me take some of them off, which was hard to do. They told me that the rings were signs that I had chosen to love things instead of people. They said that only those who are not generous, who want to get rich and become powerful, get these rings. They told me that they were a curse."

The knight studied him. "Did you believe them?"

"Yes, at first. They helped me get almost all of them off. And as they came off, my back grew straighter, my face got warmer, and it filled with color. It felt wonderful."

"What did they do with the rings?"

He turned to face the knight. "That was a most remarkable thing. They seemed not to care about them at all. Here they had these rings of gold, and they just left them there."

"Go on."

"I spent a week at Remonant. It was a glorious week—until near the end. They told me the time had come to remove my bands. I asked them why. They said the king did not desire that we wear such ornate bands, but simple ones. I didn't see why there was a difference. They all wore golden Bracelets. Mine were just larger and clearly worth more. But they insisted. It was then that I realized all they really wanted were the bands and the rest of my rings."

His hand fisted. The memory of their betrayal was as painful now as it had been back then. "I saw through their deception. They would wait until I had no bands or rings at all, then sell me as a slave. So that night I snuck out of the village with as many rings as I could carry. I ran all night, and only by great luck did I encounter a traveler on the road who took me back to Petitzaros."

"What happened when you got back?"

What happened? Rejection. Humiliation. Did he need to relive this?

"It was terrible. My friends saw my damaged rings and ridiculed me. Without my rings, I had no power to keep my palace or my place in the order of things in Petitzaros. I had to start over with what little I had and build my kingdom all over again." Steward bit his lip and looked at his feet as the memory washed over him.

The knight put a hand on Steward's shoulder. "Have you forgotten how wonderful it felt to take off the chains?"

Steward pulled away and sat down on a rock outcropping near the edge of the clearing. How could he explain this to a stranger? He couldn't even sort it out himself.

"Almost, yes, but not entirely. I mean, it still haunts me. I don't understand how blessings like these rings can make one feel so good when they are discarded." He was pleading now. His heart begged for some answers.

"Do you know the answer to that? Tell me, Black Knight, can you really help me?"

The man came and sat next to him. Neither spoke for several minutes. Then the knight turned toward him.

"I have many answers for you, young Steward. But you must believe who I am and who sent me. First of all, my name is Zedekai. I know you are searching for the true meaning of your name. Here is mine. It means 'the justice of the king.' That is my calling, to see the king's justice reign throughout his kingdom. Your journey is part of his plan. He claimed you from birth and sent me to see that your journey will not fail."

The knight leaned in toward Steward and pierced his soul with his gaze.

"Now will you believe my words to you?"

What else could he do? He'd come to see the king, and the king was not in Petitzaros. Questions were still pulsing through his head, but his heart found a moment of peace that he never knew in his little castle in the valley.

Mother, Father, if this was the one to whom you pledged your word all those years, I must trust him.

Steward met his gaze. "Yes, I will, good knight."

The knight smiled. It was the first time Steward had seen him do that.

"Good."

Leaning back, Zedekai gave a nod. "Then here is the answer to your question. The rings are not blessings but curses. They weigh down those who seek to use the Elixir of Mah Manon only for themselves. Didn't the Phaedra tell you that part of the meaning of your name was to be generous with what you have acquired?"

How could the knight know of the conversation Steward had had with the Phaedra on the first day of his journey? "Yes, that's what he said."

"Then why have you done so little for the poor and those in need? I rode through the area where they live. You had so much. Why did you share so little?"

Heat filled Steward's face as the answer came to him. "I...forgot about them, I guess. They were easy to forget about."

Zedekai pointed to Steward. "Steward, your chains were burdens, punishment for choosing not to ease the burdens of others. The more you spent on yourself, the greater the burden of the chains became."

Steward ran his hands along the rings making up the chain between his wrists. For the first time, they did feel more like links of a chain than rings of gold. Their weight had drawn Steward's shoulders down and made his back ache.

His friends' voices echoed in his mind. *"That is the ache of power."* But as he thought about it now, Steward knew they were wrong. It was just an ache.

"I have spent every day in Petitzaros trying to acquire these rings, and now you tell me they are a curse, a sign of my lack of generosity and a mark of my guilt. How can I ever hope to see the king now?" Steward hung his head between his hands, and his face was buried in the fine silk of his tunic. How could he have been so wrong?

Suddenly, he felt a movement. He looked up to see the knight standing— and picking up his scabbard! Zedekai pulled the sword out.

What was he doing? Before Steward could pull away, the knight grabbed the chain, draped it over a rock, and lifted the giant sword high above his head. Steward closed his eyes and turned his head just as the knight brought his sword down in a mighty crash, sending bits of rock and rings flying into the evening sky. The sound was deafening, and pieces of the rings pelted Steward's face. When he opened his eyes, he saw several rings lying in pieces on the ground.

His once long chain had been broken into two shorter chains hanging from each wrist and reaching to about his ankles. Steward rubbed his wrists where the large bands continued to irritate his skin. "Can you take these off for me as well?"

"That is all I can do for you." Zedekai returned his sword to its sheath. "Only the king can remove the bands."

Steward leapt to his feet. "So I will see the king?"

Zedekai tied a band over the hilt of his sword and secured it back on his saddle. "That's up to you. I'll put you back on the path, but you must make the journey yourself. Now come and take a last look."

The knight motioned Steward over to the edge of a cliff. As Steward approached the precipice, he frowned. This place looked familiar. Had he been here before?

Of course! This was the very place he had slept the night before entering Petitzaros. And there it was beneath him—Petitzaros, bathed in the late afternoon sun. How amazing it all had looked to him that first night. Now, as the broken chains dangled from his wrists, all he felt was sorrow.

Zedekai stood next to him. "How does it look to you now?"

"Empty."

Steward turned and walked away.

Zedekai followed him and pulled a bundle of clothes from a satchel. Steward changed out of his silk tunic and put on the simple clothes, clothes such as he'd worn in Aiden Glenn. Comfortable clothes.

The knight wrapped the chains around each of Steward's forearms, tied a lace of leather to the top ring, then fastened each in a loop just above the elbow. The long sleeves of his shirt covered the chains completely.

"They're heavy." Steward lifted each arm above his head.

"They will remind you every day of the decisions you have made. Now, climb on and let's ride a ways before it gets dark."

Steward climbed on the great black horse behind Zedekai, and they rode for three hours until the sun disappeared from the sky. They stopped and made camp. The knight produced a large satchel of meats, bread, oils, and wine, and they feasted together by the fire. After a long silence, as the fire and wine warmed Steward, Zedekai began to speak.

"Tomorrow you will continue your journey. This path will take you through three more lands before you reach the throne room of the king. Listen now, young Steward. Each land holds a key to your destiny. There is much for you to experience and learn, but you must always be ready to continue your journey when the time comes to leave."

Steward raised a hand toward Zedekai. "How will I know when that time has come?"

"There will be no doubt. You must trust me in this. It will not be like Petitzaros. The lure of Petitzaros is unique to that land. The other lands will not so entice you."

"Will you go with me?" Even as he asked, Steward surmised the answer.

"I was sent by the king as one of your guardians. I will be watching, but this must be your journey. I can't always be there to help you. But the king has more allies in the land. If you have trouble, look for his messengers. Remember, they'll often come in unexpected forms."

"And colors." Steward offered a repentant smile.

The knight smiled back.

Steward worked up the courage to ask the question that had been troubling him the most. "And what of the Phaedra? Are they evil or good?"

Zedekai's face tightened. "That is for you to decide. The king will likely ask you the same question, so seek the answer on your journey. It must come from you and no one else. Tomorrow, the path will be long and often steep. There'll be water along the way and fruit trees to sustain you. Always keep to the path. You will have a full day's journey to reach Ascendia by nightfall."

"Ascendia? Is that the next land on my journey?"

"Yes, and when you arrive you are to go to the house of Bendor and announce yourself to the three sisters. They are expecting you and will give you food and lodging during your stay."

Zedekai laid a hand on Steward's shoulder. "You've learned a great deal today, but much more awaits you. Now get your rest."

More what? Danger? Lies? Phaedra?

Despite the questions that pressed on him, the thought of returning to his journey danced in Steward's mind. *I'm ready for this. I'm ready to see the king.*

Steward drew his cloak over him and fell into a deep sleep.

~~~~~~~~~~

Reed laid the book down on the coffee table, leaned back, and gave a long sigh. Walter remembered when Sam wrote that last scene.

"Will they hear the message?" he'd asked Walter.

Walter was about to learn the answer.

After several moments of silence, Anna reached over and pressed her hand on the book. "There's a lot to digest here."

Alex looked at Merideth. "A land of kingdom builders. That's pretty descriptive of the world I live in."

Merideth stood, stretching her arms and rubbing her neck. "I suppose that's one way to depict greed. But there are a lot of questions the story leaves unanswered."

Anna shot a look at Reed. "Well, as you said, we have a long way to go with our friend Steward."

Walter watched as Reed walked over to his briefcase, opened it, and removed a large stack of papers.

"You want a modern-day version of what Dad is talking about? Here they are: financial statements, parts of a business plan for a new restaurant, bills, invoices, and investment prospectuses."

Reed took the stack in one hand and lifted it up and down, measuring its weight. He spoke, mostly to himself. "Chains. Golden chains."

Alex reached down and patted his briefcase. "My stack is bigger than yours."

Reed gave him a slight grin. "The more you keep for yourself, the heavier the burden. The larger your own kingdom, the grayer life becomes. Dad couldn't have been more clear."

Thank God for their honesty...but Walter worried about Merideth. She stood and placed herself between her brothers. "I don't know. Steward seemed pretty happy in that palace. Mom and Dad never cared much for the finer things of life. I'm not yet convinced that golden chains are worse than no chains at all."

How did Merideth's heart grow so hard? *Dear God, open her heart to her father's message. And to what is yet to come.*

Sam and Lori had struggled with understanding Merideth. For all the love they had lavished on her, they couldn't understand why, almost from birth, she fought them at every turn.

Watching Merideth now, a memory swept over Walter. Sam and Lori had been sitting at their kitchen table, rereading a letter Merideth sent them. She'd laid out her career plans and asked that they not speak to her again about what they thought of her choices.

"Why is Merideth the last one to accept anything we say?" Lori shook her head. "She meets every blessing with skepticism, as if there's a shield around her heart that keeps anything from getting in."

Sam had sat down beside her. "I don't know, dear. But somehow we've failed her. We've prayed for her to find meaning and purpose in life, but she has become so driven by success that nothing tender ever seems to touch her."

Lori grasped his hand. "We can't give up. God hasn't! I pray she will find her way to real happiness, apart from the power that seems to pull at her. I want her to find peace and love."

Sam had nodded. "Lord, soften her heart toward others, and You."

Walter echoed Sam's prayer now.

As he watched Merideth's defensiveness, he realized that, except for the moment when the four of them watched Sam's casket lowered into the ground, he had never seen her cry. Even then, Walter wondered if her tears were more for show than from real emotion.

Lord, soften her heart.

He rose from his chair and walked toward the kitchen. "Perhaps we'll find that young Steward has a third option. I've carried my share of chains in my life, and I was more than happy to lay them down."

"Oh, Walter, you're just too good." Merideth's tone made it clear she didn't wish to argue with him.

Walter smiled and continued into the kitchen. When he returned, no one was talking. Silence seemed an acceptable refuge from the hazards of reflection and engagement. So be it. There was plenty more ahead. Plenty of time for serious soul searching.

"Alex, I think the reading duties are back to you," Anna said.

Alex nodded and took his place in the seat in front of the open book. He waited for his siblings to settle then turned to the next chapter and read on.

CHAPTER

Ten

Steward awoke, alone and cold. He jumped to his feet.

"Zedekai, where are you? Hello?" There was food left for him, enough for a full breakfast. But the knight was gone.

Steward folded his bedding and ate part of the provisions. On the ground next to him lay a shattered gold ring. He picked it up and examined it, and deep inside the struggle started.

Should I return?

No! Leave now and don't look back.

He dropped the ring, bundled up his few belongings, and took to the path as though running for his life. And he was.

He slowed to a walk as the worn trail wound through a thinly wooded area. Steward could hear water falling over rocks ahead, and when he reached the brook he filled his water pouch and took a long drink. The day was bright, with occasional billows of clouds giving respite from the warming sun.

By midmorning, Steward came to a section where the path climbed and became steep. He looked ahead—it ascended to a high pass between two ridges. He worked his way up the hillside, and by noon he reached the pass. He was panting and sweating and much relieved to feel the ground level out under his feet. His legs ached, and he sat to catch his breath, thankful for a large cloud overhead that provided a few moments of cooling shade. As he regained his strength, Steward sensed a presence on the path. He turned—

A Phaedra approached.

Steward's stomach tightened, and his pulse quickened. He'd never had this reaction to a Phaedra before.

"Good day to you, young Steward. You have accomplished quite a climb."

"Hello…good Phaedra." Why was it difficult now to call him that? "Yes, I am glad to be at the top."

Steward stood and resumed his walk. The path now meandered through a high meadow. The Phaedra walked along with him. Neither said anything for several moments, but as they continued Steward's palms turned moist and his chest tightened. It was fear.

I wonder if the Phaedra senses it.

"Young Steward, may I ask you a question?"

"Of course." *I will be courteous but cautious.*

"Were you happy in Petitzaros?"

Careful. How to answer?

"Yes, somewhat. Although I am happier now to be back on my journey. I don't believe I was meant to stay there after all." Steward let his tone register a hint of accusation.

The Phaedra seemed unmoved by the response. His voice remained steady. "Did the knight tell you what you would do after you saw the king?"

Zedekai's words rang in Steward's mind: *"You will have to decide for yourself if the Phaedra are good or evil…and the king will ask you the same question."*

He chose his words with caution. "No, but I expect the king will tell me."

The Phaedra was silent for a moment. "Will you do whatever the king asks and go wherever the king sends you?"

Why would he ask that? Stay cautious. "Why, yes, of course. He's the king, and I'll obey him whatever he tells me to do."

He'd heard this line of questioning before, and it led him to Petitzaros. Not again. This began to feel like a trap.

"Young Steward, do you know anyone who has ever *seen* the king?"

Steward slowed his pace. "I only know the stories of the ancestors in Aiden Glenn. No one I know has ever been sent on such a journey as this."

"No one indeed. And do you wonder why?"

Steward hadn't considered the thought until now. His mind raced, looking for a suitable answer. None came. And now that he was thinking it over, it did seem strange that no one in Aiden Glenn had ever actually seen the king.

When a word of proclamation reached the village through one of the king's messengers, it was treated as a major event, and the instructions were always followed word for word. The stories of the ancestors who visited the throne room and spoke to the king were legendary and never questioned. But now…

Why would Steward be the first since his ancestors to see the king? "I don't know why, but I am honored. I will fulfill my calling and carry back to Aiden Glenn the words of the king himself."

If only he felt as confident as he sounded.

"Young Steward, I must ask you a very serious question. I beg of you not to be angry with me, but do consider the question."

Steward stopped and studied the vague contours of the hooded figure's veiled face. The Phaedra's urgent and hushed voice was strange, as though what he was saying bordered on the sacrilegio—

"What if there is no king?"

"No king?" Steward stared at him. "Of *course* there's a king!" Steward paced as he spoke. "Our ancestors saw him. And what of the messengers? They come from him. And he keeps the land safe from invaders and heals the sick and—"

Steward stopped, frozen by his next thought.

This is all true, but can I really prove that the king exists? No, this is a trick. It's a deception!

Steward glared at the Phaedra. "Let me ask you a question. Who told me the wrong meaning of my name, and who wanted me to stay in Petitzaros and not continue on my journey? And who turned me against the Black Knight when he was only there to help me? It was *you*. And the others like you. So why should I listen to you now?"

Anger now mixed with confusion at the idea that there might be no king.

The Phaedra turned and continued the walk. Steward fell into step beside him, and they continued in silence until Steward could not bear his guilt. "I'm sorry, good Phaedra. I'm confused, and I had no right to accuse you of such things. I know you are wise, but I have questions about what has happened to me."

The Phaedra's tone remained steady. "I understand, young Steward, and no apology is necessary. My question came too soon in your journey. And you are right to question my previous words to you. So let me explain myself."

The Phaedra explaining himself to me? Who am I to ask such a thing?

"We are all on our own journeys to discover who we are. We seek some greater power to answer our questions for us. I found you on the path poor and alone, seeking answers. I gave you the meaning of your name as you approached Petitzaros, hoping that you would find peace and happiness there. And you did, before the knight stole you away. We hoped to keep him from stealing the rings from you. Now you are poor and alone once again. And you are still seeking answers that you may have already found. Why would the king ask you to pursue him in this way? And why a black knight as a messenger? Are these not questions to ponder carefully, young Steward? And am I wrong to raise them?"

Steward would not answer. He saw Zedekai's face, and the image gave him courage.

Just then, the path came to an abrupt edge and started downhill, descending into a valley. The path led through the valley, and on the far edge of the valley lay a city.

"Ascendia?"

The Phaedra nodded. "Yes. Is that your destination?"

"Yes, for now. I am to stay at the House of Bendor with the three sisters."

The Phaedra shrugged. "And what do you expect to find there?"

He had no idea. What could possibly await him in this place? Why did he have to go there? Just questions and no answers.

"I don't know. The Black Knight did not say. Only that I would know when I had stayed long enough and when it was time to leave." Steward turned to the Phaedra. "What do you think I will find there?"

"I think that you will not like it nearly as much as Petitzaros and that you will wish you could go back."

"And can I go back...to Petitzaros?"

"Petitzaros will always be there for you, young Steward, any time you wish to return."

Return to Petitzaros...the chains, the emptiness? What was he thinking? "Phaedra, if you would not be offended, I wish to walk alone for a while."

"Certainly."

And before Steward could look back at the Phaedra, he was alone.

Steward steadied himself as he started down the steep slope. What answers would he find in Ascendia? Would Zedekai be there? He hoped.

Regardless, I am not turning back. I have to find the king. But what do I do with the Phaedra? No king? That's absurd.

He continued on, and it was early evening when the path merged into the road that led into the city of Ascendia. As Steward drew closer, his eyes widened. Ascendia sat at the transition between a huge valley plain and a steep-faced mountain range. It looked as if the city had been crowded up against the foot of the mountain, almost repelling the open space of the fertile valley that lay to its side. But there was more. Shooting out from the city were stone bridges—ramps really—all arching their way up toward some point on the face of the distant mountainside. And yet only a very few were completed and connected to the face of the peak, while almost all the others went only partway and hung in the sky like great pathways to nowhere.

Steward passed a man traveling into the city. "Sir, this is Ascendia, is that right?"

The man raised his eyebrows. "Yes, of course."

"Can you tell me why there are so many bridges? Where are they going, and why are so many not finished?"

"Look, son, I am in a hurry. You'll find your answers in Ascendia. Ask any of the ramp builders."

Steward thanked him. Then as he hurried off he called out, "Oh, and can you tell me where I can find the House of Bendor?"

The man kept walking but pointed and shouted over his shoulder: "Left at the main street, six blocks down, yellow fence."

Steward glanced at the bridges as he walked. Each one was teeming with builders working to extend their ramp. Indeed, it looked as if everyone in Ascendia wanted to get out of the city and climb the ramps up to the mountain.

He passed through the gates and into the city. Ascendia was nothing like Petitzaros. There were few shops, and those he saw were plain and sparse. There were no grand avenues lined with palm trees, parks, and banquet halls. Instead, serious-faced people moved along the streets, anxiety in their eyes as they darted around in and out of shops and alleyways.

Why is everyone so nervous?

The people of Ascendia were dressed in simple clothes, and each one carried what looked to be a large brass bowl with handles on each side. Attached to the handles was a long piece of cloth that served as a sling. Some people had the sling over their shoulder, some around their neck, and some in a combination of the two. But everyone had the brass bowls hanging down in front of them, suspended by a cloth sling.

Steward walked the six blocks to the house and found himself right underneath one of the great ramps that hung suspended in the sky above him. He arched his neck to look up at it and squinted in the late afternoon sun. Dozens of people were hard at work, some laying stones, others carrying loads of some mixture and pouring it to form the ramp. Many of the workers were using the brass vessels to carry rocks, stones, and the paving mixture.

So that's it. The vessels must be tools for building the ramps. But why were the bowls of so many people so clean?

People were starting to look at Steward with suspicion, and they held their vessels close to their chest. Were they afraid he might try to take them away from them?

Steward walked on and found himself passing the yellow fence and standing at the gates of the House of Bendor. He knocked on the gates and was confronted at once by a huge man with a booming voice.

"And who are you?"

Steward studied his massive frame and gruff expression. Was he a friend or not? "My name is Steward. I'm on a journey to see the king. I was sent here by Zedekai to stay with the three sisters. Are they here?"

Please tell me they know I am coming. Otherwise I'm lost.

"Here? Now? Of course not. It is daylight and they are working. But if the Black Knight sent you, I will give you passage and let you discuss this directly with them when they return."

So Zedekai's words are trustworthy. I must remember that.

The gatekeeper opened the gates and waved Steward in. The courtyard of the House of Bendor had trees, bushes, and flowerbeds all showing signs of neglect. The great house that rose up at the edge of the sweeping lawn was in need of paint and repair. Steward walked up to the front door and opened it.

The gatekeeper bowed to him. "Please make yourself comfortable. The sisters will be home soon." With that, he left. Steward went inside and found more evidence of inattention. While well-furnished, the rooms were untidy and musty and begged for open windows and a good dusting.

Steward found his way to a sitting room where he could look out on the lawns. He sat by an open window to get some fresh air.

What was that?

In the distance there was a rumbling, grinding sound. He listened for a minute but couldn't detect the source. He'd ask about it when the sisters arrived....

Voices...and footsteps coming up the walk.

Steward rose to his feet as the front door flew open and in stepped three women, chatting and looking around, searching for their guest.

The first sister to greet him was a pleasant-looking young woman about Steward's age. "There you are! You must be young Steward. The gatekeeper said you would be here." Her blonde hair hung to her shoulders, and her brilliant blue eyes looked Steward over as she approached. "My name is Elopia. It's a pleasure to meet you."

Elopia's simple tunic was draped over her shoulders and hung to her ankles. It was tied at the waist and had the look of a work garment that had not seen much work. Around her neck was the sling that held her brass bowl at both ends. The bowl's edges were sharp, but the bowl was scratched and slightly dented.

Before he could return Elopia's greeting, the second sister barged forward and thrust out her hand.

"I'm Cassandra, Steward, and you are welcome here at the House of Bendor." She spoke in a deep and authoritarian voice. Cassandra was very tall, taller than Steward. She had strong features, fire red hair, and deep hazel eyes. She wore a bright white tunic edged in gold that looked like a uniform. Her brass bowl had been reshaped into a breastplate held in place by the cloth sling that ran across both shoulders and crossed in the back.

She looks like a warrior-goddess. Impressive...and intimidating.

"Thank you, Cassandra, and it is my great pleasure to meet you both."

The three waited in an awkward silence for the third sister to greet him. She approached him.

"It is nice to have you as our guest. My name is Astrid." She was quieter than her siblings, but Steward's heart was stirred.

There was a strength there. He could sense it.

Astrid's worn tunic had no sash. Around her neck a sling held a brass bowl, but hers was battered and dented almost beyond recognition. It even had a gash in it, and Steward could see right through the hole that was left.

Cassandra removed her breastplate and laid it on a chair. "Is this your first time in Ascendia? If so, you are probably wondering about these Quashes we wear."

Quashes? So that's what the bowls were called. "Well, yes, I was wondering what they are and why they are so different. What do you use them for, and where do you get them?"

Elopia laughed. "So many questions. And we must answer them all, but over supper. I'm starving." She left for the kitchen.

Astrid followed her, commenting as she departed, "Yes, Cassandra, let our guest wash up, and let's change for supper. We have plenty of time to talk."

Cassandra relented. "Very well. Fresh clothes and food, and then we will tell you all of the secrets of Ascendia."

The gatekeeper had arrived and led Steward to a guest room that bore witness to a long period of disuse. Still, Steward was happy to be there. He changed, washed up, and returned some time later to the kitchen, where all three sisters were busy making dinner.

They enjoyed a wonderful meal together, and after wine and sweets they sat in the dining room where tapestries and musty drapes hung around them and the lamps were struggling to win the battle against the darkness. The sisters took no notice.

This disarray and dust would drive Mother crazy!

Elopia looked at Steward and, when she had his attention, gave him a wry little smile. "Now, Steward, about those questions. First, it was the king who gave to our ancestors the Quash with its sash." She handed hers to Steward. It was heavier than he'd expected.

He examined it as she continued. "Every citizen of Ascendia has worn one ever since. It's a symbol of our land, and the most precious thing you can ever own. If you want, we can get you one of your own."

Steward held it up and ran his fingers along its wide brim. "I would like that. But what would I use it for, and why does everyone's look different?"

"Good question!" Cassandra regained control. "The Quash is a tool used to help each person achieve what they desire in life. But it must be *used*"—she curled her lip at Elopia—"to be useful. Too many people want to keep their Quash spotless, thus rendering it nothing more than a heavy necklace. It is a disgrace."

Astrid picked hers up and set it on the table. "Not everyone thinks it is a tool, sister."

Cassandra pounced. "No, my dear little misguided sister. People like you waste their Quash on losers and slackers, and what do you have to show for it? A deformed Quash and a miserable life. When will you come to your senses and put that thing to good use?"

Astrid shot back. "I try to use mine to help others, and for that I will never be sorry." She collected her Quash, excused herself, and left the room.

Steward was sorry to see her go.

She is so strong…and beautiful.

Elopia huffed in disgust. "Cassandra, did you have to be so hard on her? After all, we can't all be the great Cassandra." Sarcasm dripped from her words.

"You're one to talk. You have no more to show for your use of your Quash than your sister, except for those dents you have inflicted on others."

Elopia turned to Steward but continued to shoot glances at Cassandra as she spoke. "You see, Steward, in Ascendia you either attack or get attacked. Everyone wants to outdo everyone else. So if your Quash is dented, you must inflict greater dents on others. It is wound or be wounded. My younger sister cannot dish it out, so she has been assaulted all her life. Then there is my older sister, who has so overpowered everyone that she now carries her Quash like an ornament and bosses everyone around."

Steward was feeling caught in the middle of the sibling dispute.

Change the subject.

"So what about the ramps?"

Cassandra broke away from glaring at Elopia. "Ramps? Oh, you mean the Ascenders. Well, we discovered long ago that life is much better up on the mountain than down here in the valley, so we work to build Ascenders from the city up to the mountainside. Smart people use their Quash to build these ramps." Cassandra motioned toward Elopia. "Others, however, are content to spend their days inflicting dents on others, with no vision for a better life on the mountain. It is a waste and a shame."

Elopia stood and took her Quash back from Steward. "Perhaps so, big sister, but at least I am not so absorbed with my work that I miss out on the fun of life."

Steward shifted in his seat. If only he could disappear and escape this bickering.

Cassandra must have noticed his discomfort. "Oh, how inhospitable of us. Do forgive us, Steward, for our sparring. Tomorrow I will take you to the Ascender I'm building, and you will see for yourself how important and useful this work really is. And I will get you your own Quash. For now, I am exhausted."

As Steward stood and walked to the stairs, the grinding noise again reached his ears. He turned to the sisters. "One last question, if I may? What is that noise in the distance? It sounds like a great grinder of some sort."

Cassandra looked at Elopia. They seemed unsettled by the question.

"It is a grinder," Cassandra replied. "We need a great deal of paving mixture to pro- duce the streets on the Ascenders. We grind rocks and sand to create the mixture."

Elopia looked past Steward and out through the window. "Among other things."

Cassandra shot her a steel-hard look and then continued. "We do add other ingredi- ents to create the paving mixture, but that is not important now. Tomorrow I will show you the whole process. Now, please, to bed."

At that, they departed for their rooms. Steward hated to admit it, but he agreed with the Phaedra: he did not like this place nearly as much as Petitzaros.

As he headed to his room, the image of Astrid and her worn and beaten Quash drifted into his mind. *How does someone so tender survive in this harsh place?*

As he readied for bed, he cocked his head and listened. Was that Astrid's soft voice coming through the walls of his room? He smiled and slid into bed, ready for sleep.

Next door to Steward's room, Astrid lay on her bed, her eyes closed, trying to coax herself to sleep. But she couldn't. She had the same unsettling feeling she had every night, as though she were not alone. And indeed she was not.

Standing next to her bed, unseen by her, was a Phaedra bent over her bed, hands clasped together in front of him, whispering in her ear, "The king does not care about you. He has forgotten about you. You must not fight back. It is time to give up, Astrid. It is time to stop fighting back."

~~~~~~~~~~

Alex set the book down, stretched his arms, and took a drink of herbal tea that Anna had just brewed. Merideth was building walls.

She watched her brother. Was he going to state the obvious? That this part of the story was aimed at her. Well, fine. She'd beat him to it. She crossed her arms over her chest. "Well, Reed, if Petitzaros was for you, then Dad clearly meant Ascendia for me." She forced a smile. "I'll sit here and endure this for Dad's sake, but Alex and Anna, be prepared, your time's coming."

That was the ticket. Make light of it, and perhaps they'd just move on.

Alex didn't. "Mer, I gotta tell you, I'm really struggling. At first I was going along with this to honor Dad. But, man, don't you hear him? Dad's voice, his heart…and Mom's? He may be gone, but his spirit is here. I mean, I feel Dad in this story."

Reed jumped in. "I have to admit it's getting under my skin too. I'm not sure what I'll do with it, but—"

"C'mon, you guys." Enough was enough. Merideth punched the pillow she'd been leaning on. "It's a great story, but really, let's not kid ourselves. We came here entrenched in our lives, and we will leave here the same way. Oh, maybe we'll try to be a little more generous or love stuff a little less, but nothing's really going to change. I'm sorry that sounds harsh…"

"*Sounds* harsh?" Anna exploded. "It's way beyond harsh. If that's how you feel, why don't you grab a book or play on your iPhone while we finish reading the story. You certainly don't intend to listen to it anyway. Cripes, Mer, can you build your walls any higher?"

Steady, stay calm. Breathe. Don't give way.

She tightened her hold on the pillow. "Okay, I apologize for the way that came across. But I, for one, will listen to a great story without letting it drag me into some self-psychoanalysis. I'll give Dad his due, but if there's an altar call at the end, don't expect me to come down the aisle singing 'Amazing Grace.' That's all I'm saying."

Merideth turned and her eye caught Walter's. She looked away.

He already thinks I'm a lost cause…there's his validation.

Anna shook her head, got up, and took Alex's place. "If it's okay, I'd like to read from here for a bit."

She didn't wait for approval.

leven

"Keep up, Steward, we have a long walk." Cassandra trudged up the long, sweeping walkway of her Ascender. Wind blew dust everywhere, and Steward was almost running to keep pace. The Ascender had started just a few blocks from the House of Bendor. There were two guards at its entrance, and from what Steward saw, only those known by the sentries were allowed to pass by. Once on the Ascender, the slope steepened. On each side were four-foot-high walls running the length of the pathway.

Steward caught up with Cassandra. Ahead he could see only open sky and other Ascenders under construction, each heading toward the same mountainside.

"It's getting narrower." Maybe she'd slow down to respond.

The walkway was broad at first, at least fifty feet from wall to wall, Steward guessed. But now it was half that. And, several hundred yards up at the place where the construction was still underway, it looked no more than twenty feet wide.

Cassandra slowed her pace as they were nearing its end. "The farther out we build, the less width we need. By the time we connect to the mountain, it will only be six feet wide. Just enough for a horse and cart."

Steward froze, looking out over the edge. It was a long way down! "Um, Cassandra, I'm a little nervous about heights. Do you mind if I stay back a bit?"

She walked to the very edge of the pathway hanging several hundred feet up in midair, with nothing but sky and open space ahead. "Blast those workers! There should be a barricade here. Someone might get distracted and fall."

The thought made Steward dizzier. "Does that ever happen?"

"Not often, but it only takes once."

Cassandra walked back to Steward and pointed down the ramp. "Here come my workers. Now you will see the importance of hard work and using the Quash in the right way."

Steward looked back. A small army of workers of different ages and sizes plodded their way up the Ascender. When they arrived, they started hauling loads of rocks to the edge, where masons were preparing to lay a new line of wall. The whole process seemed well organized, and yet the workers were sullen, with an underlying anger that was not hard to sense. Suddenly, one worker dumped out his rocks and swung his Quash at a coworker who, apparently anticipating the attack, threw up his Quash and caught the blow before it could injure him. The sound of the clang rang out across the work area, but no one even looked up.

"Theodorus! Anthresis! Get back to work!" Cassandra demanded.

They exchanged two somewhat lesser blows and then picked up their rocks and continued their work.

"What's that about?"

"Just short tempers. We're all under a lot of stress." She looked across to another Ascender and scowled. "And there's why. Curse them! They're beating us. They'll get to the mountain before we do. We have to work harder and faster."

Steward looked out at the impressive face of the distant mountain that jutted up from the valley floor. "What's on the mountain that's so important?"

"What's on the mountain?" She sighed and spoke as if she were lost in a dream. "My dear Steward, everything you could ever want is on the mountain. There's security, peace, contentment, and power. You have control of life up on the mountain. No one can tell you how to live. You are completely your own person up there. No more toiling every day in the hot sun. The rewards for hard labor are there. It is *all* up there, Steward, and I will be up there to get it. All the way at the top. That's where the rewards are the greatest."

Steward scratched his head. This valley was beautiful. There were streams, orchards, stands of aspens. What more could anyone want? And could all this work and anger be worth it?

Steward was still intimidated by Cassandra, so he chose his words with care. "Respectfully, Cassandra, it seems that most everything you describe is available here in the valley. Do you really need to go to the mountain to find it?"

Cassandra scowled and faced Steward. "Of course you do! Are you out of your mind? *None* of these things are available down here. Do you think I would be investing my whole life in attaining something I could get just as easily here in the valley? How dare you even imply such a thing!"

He stepped back, surprised by the look of anger that filled her face. "I...I'm sorry, Cassandra."

She gave no pause to hear his apology. Turning to one of her lieutenants, she shouted, "Markus, we need more workers! And where is the paving mixture?"

As the man turned to run down the path, Cassandra continued yelling at her workers and demanding that they work faster.

And they did.

Are they all working this hard to get to the mountain? Or are they just afraid of Cassandra?

Markus returned with another small army of workers, most of them carrying Quashes full of a dull, reddish-brown liquid that had the texture of smooth cement. One by one they poured the contents onto the ground that had been prepared for the paving mixture, and other workers smoothed it out with large trowels. The mixture dried in moments in the warm morning sun.

They were there for most of the morning hours, and the Ascender grew by several meters under Cassandra's watchful eye. By midday, Steward had had his fill of the building process. The sun was hot on his neck.

How do Elopia and Astrid occupy their days? Not out here in the hot sun, I'll bet.

He waited until Cassandra paused between shouting orders and cursing the slow progress of competing building teams. "I am very grateful for your hospitality. However, I would like to return to the house and rest. My journey has been long, and I am afraid my stamina isn't what it should be."

Cassandra flipped her hands in the air as if to dismiss him. "Of course. Perhaps tomorrow you may join us in the construction work. All who work will be rewarded when we reach the mountain. But before you go, I have something for you."

Cassandra walked over, picked up a used Quash and a clean tan sash, and handed them to Steward. "There. Now you are a real citizen of Ascendia."

What a nice gesture, especially after the way I offended her with my questioning. "Thank you, Cassandra. This is most generous. I will wear it with pride. And tomorrow I will come and help you build."

She smiled at him. Steward suspected she was just relishing the thought of one more worker on her Ascender.

Steward placed the sash over his shoulder and settled the bowl into place, wincing a bit from the weight hanging from his shoulders. When combined with the chains from Petitzaros that were still wrapped around his forearms, it made his legs ache as he walked down the steep slope of the Ascender.

Once at the bottom, Steward searched for Elopia and Astrid. It didn't take long to hear Elopia's voice raised in an angry shout, the bellow competing with the clang of Quashes colliding with each other.

He hurried over and found Elopia and two other women hurling insults at each other.

"You're crazy. Anyone who thinks like that should be locked up!" a lady screeched.

Elopia shot back. "Perhaps it's narrow-minded fools like *you* who need to be put away."

Is that really Elopia? It's one thing to do this in private, but out here?

Elopia picked up her heavy Quash and swung it at the woman, who raised her own Quash just in time to block the attack. A deafening clang rang out as the two metal objects collided.

And as suddenly as it started, it was over. Not only did the two women sit down and continue normal conversations, but no one else at the table took any notice of the confrontation. A few people on the street had stopped for a moment to watch, but they turned and went on their way, as if nothing out of the ordinary had happened.

Elopia caught sight of Steward and squealed. "Steward, how nice to see you! I am glad you got away from Cassandra and her mutant army so you could see how life is really lived here in Ascendia."

She ran to him and took him by the arm, leading him to a table where several of her friends were seated—including the women she had just attacked. They were enjoying delightful-looking sandwiches, tarts and fruits, and several kinds of drinks made from things Steward had never seen before. Everyone at the table was laughing and talking.

Elopia waved her hand. "Attention, everyone. This is my new friend, Steward. He is visiting Ascendia for just a few short days. Please greet him."

How could everyone be so nice after what just happened?

The people at the table gave courteous replies, and Steward sat and ate and drank with them well into the afternoon. The conversation was delightful, ranging across a whole spectrum of fascinating topics, punctuated with jokes and uproarious laughter.

Steward studied the Quashes hanging from most everyone's sashes. They were different from Steward's—they all seemed to have sharp edges and more than a few dents. None of these had ever carried a rock or paving mixture up Cassandra's Ascender.

From time to time harsh words broke out, followed by a collision of Quashes swung to injure or maybe even kill. These learned, mature people responded as if summoned up by some deep internal demon. Only a few moments later, it happened again. One of the diners rose up and thrust his or her Quash at someone else at the table.

When an attack was not averted in time, the blow landed on the side of someone's head or across his or her arm. Steward winced at how painful the blow must be, and yet any howl of protest was kept inside, and a counterattack was launched. These skirmishes lasted only a few seconds, but they were so sudden and vicious that Steward remained on edge.

He leaned toward Elopia. "Elopia, why is everyone fighting? Someone will be killed! I don't understand."

Her eyes opened wide. "Steward, whatever are you talking about? If you mean the teasing and occasional sarcastic jab, then we're guilty as charged. But fighting? Killing? You have quite an imagination."

He was not imagining this. Something was wrong with these people, and he would rather leave than stay and try to dodge the blows.

"Thank you ever so much for your hospitality. I have enjoyed the afternoon; however, my journey has been long, and I would like to return to the house and rest for a while."

Elopia looked surprised but nodded in agreement. "Of course, certainly. We will see you there later this evening then?"

Steward thanked her then rose to say his farewells and left the strange company to continue their eating, drinking, and attacking one another. As he walked back to the house, he grew anxious. He did not like Ascendia at all.

Why is this place part of my journey? What could possibly be here that will help me see the king?

Back at the House of Bendor, he held his Quash in his hands and examined it. *What are these things? Tools? Weapons? Ornaments?*

As he thought back to the events of the day, there it was again.

That noise! The machines seemed louder now, as if they were creeping closer.

What did Elopia mean by "other things" added to the mortar?

He'd love to see them, but that would have to wait. He stretched his sore shoulders. Enough time to ask about all that later. For now, he needed rest.

For the next two weeks, Steward worked for Cassandra on the Ascender. He didn't mind the hard work in the warm sun, and he liked hearing about the great reward that awaited them all as he worked.

He carried rocks to the workers, glancing at Cassandra as he did so. "Tell us again what awaits us once we get to the top."

As always, Cassandra was happy to oblige, looking up to the top of the great peak as she spoke. "They say the mountainside is the most peaceful place on earth. There are fewer cares there. You have control of your time and the power to do as you please. The closer you get to the top, the less anyone can tell you what to do. You can create your own destiny and have the power to do whatever your heart desires. There, people respect you and fear you. On the top of the mountain, every need is met, every desire fulfilled, every dream achieved. There are only a few who make it—but for those who do, the spoils are endless."

Her vision was wondrous indeed. "Do you know anyone who has lived there?" Steward asked.

That brought her gaze back to the work at hand. "No, not directly, but the stories of those who have made it to the top are legendary. Seldom if ever does anyone return to the valley once they have made it to the mountainside, so we only have secondhand reports to go by. But last year my uncle met a man who returned. The stories he told…" She shook her head and closed her eyes as her voice trailed off.

She opened her eyes and looked at Steward. There was a wildness to them now. "I listened through a keyhole night after night as they talked about the riches and power and happiness at the top."

"Why did he return?"

Cassandra was lost in the memory, and it took a long time before Steward's question registered.

"What? Oh, well, I'm not sure I ever knew why. Not that it matters. The mountainside is not for everyone. Only those who are gifted and work hard enough will ever achieve it."

She looked down toward the valley and saw her sisters walking along the promenade. "I am afraid neither Elopia nor Astrid will ever experience the happiness of the mountain."

Steward saw them as well.

Surely you will all go together. "Won't you take them with you when the Ascender is complete?"

"Why should I? *I* did the work, sacrificing my life and career to build this thing. I organized the workers, took the risk, gave up the leisure life, and dedicated myself to this task. If I did all that, why should they enjoy the benefits of the reward when they have done nothing?"

"But they're your sisters. They're family. Doesn't that matter?"

A sneer curled Cassandra's lips. "To the weak, maybe. But not to me."

Steward looked up to the mountain and across at the dozens of Ascenders covered with workers. Their frenzy to reach the mountain was amazing, but…

What if it wasn't as wonderful as Cassandra hoped and believed?

Steward whispered under his breath, "What a shame it would be if the mountain turned out to be less joyful and peaceful than it is here in the valley."

Not quiet enough. Cassandra heard it and turned to Steward, her nostrils flaring. "Steward, I have tried to be hospitable to you, but if you are not committed to the construction, then I must ask you to leave. There are many who desire to work alongside me. Our schools prepare our young people to invest their lives in this work. If you do not have the passion to do this, then it is time for you to leave and give your place to someone who does."

Steward studied her. Every action and angry word demonstrated the stress that drove her—just like the people of Petitzaros. They just exchanged chains for Quashes.

He stood. "I'm sorry, Cassandra, but you're right. I don't share your passion. I hope the mountaintop fulfills all your dreams. But for me, I have a journey to make, and it is time for me to prepare to continue. Thank you for the chance to work with you and for the Quash. I will go back to the house and prepare to leave tomorrow."

With that, Steward walked back down the Ascender. *Why did I need to stop in this place on my way to see the king? What's here for me?* He shook his head. *Zedekai, I don't understand.*

In the distance, the rock-grinding machines rumbled.

I guess I'll leave without ever seeing them.

Suddenly, there was a tug on his shirtsleeve, and he turned around to see Elopia signaling him to follow her as she scurried out of the sunlight and into a shaded archway.

Steward followed.

Elopia was breathless. She looked around as she spoke, her eyes wild with excitement. "Steward, you must come and see Ascendia for what it really is. Cassandra hasn't told you the entire story. There's more here you must know. That's why Zedekai sent you. You must not be deceived. Please, stay close to me and stay low. I will show you the real secret of Ascendia."

She took Steward's hand, looked in all directions, then led him out into the woods through a small opening between two great trees. They followed a path that led them deeper into a wooded area, and soon they were alone. But Elopia didn't stop. She scurried along a path that wound through heavy underbrush and up a steep trail. By the time they reached the top, Steward was out of breath and begging to stop. They sat down next to a large tree and rested against it to catch their breath.

"Good heavens, Elopia. Where are you taking me?"

"Up there." She pointed to a small ledge that stuck out from the face of the hillside not far from where they sat. "Listen, Steward."

He slowed his breathing, and as he did so he noticed that the sound of the grinding machines had gotten louder and closer. Unless he missed his guess, he should be able to see the source of the sound from the ledge where Elopia was leading them. With newfound strength, Steward climbed to his feet and grabbed Elopia's hand.

"Come on."

They eased their way to the ledge, being careful not to be seen. As they approached the edge, Steward could hear the grinding sound increase in intensity. On hands and knees, he inched his way out onto the outcropping of rock. The sound of the grinders was right beneath them—along with another sound.

Voices.

But these voices…

Steward had never heard anything like them before. Some were stern, some angry... and some crying out.

What was happening?

Steward crept out just far enough to look over the edge to the scene below.

On his right was one of the huge machines, the source of the grinding noise. It was an enormous rock crusher, and above it was a chute where workers dumped in cartful's of rocks. The machine gobbled up the rocks and crushed them into gravel and sand, spewing out dust and a sound that was deafening. Steward could feel the entire ground shake as boulders the size of horses got crushed in its huge jaws.

Once crushed, the gravel and sand poured from the machine into a chute and straight into a second machine, smaller and quieter than the first. Here, the sand and gravel were crushed again and mixed with a liquid that flowed from a third machine on Steward's left. It was the combination of the sand and gravel from the rock crusher and the liquid from this other machine that created the reddish-brown paving mixture for the pathways of the Ascenders.

Then Steward saw it.

No.

His heart pounded and his stomach churned.

Impossible! This is not happening!

A line of people, like those he had seen walking the streets of Ascendia, were being brought by guards, one by one, onto a platform that reached up to the edge of the liquefying machine.

Why don't they struggle? No, I see it. They don't know what's about to happen.

Once there, the guards took their Quash, and before they could fight back they were hurled into the mouth of the machine! Their screams were drowned out by the relentless sound of crushing rocks and—now Steward realized—the sound of the crushing of human bones.

He put his hand over his mouth to keep himself from vomiting and scrambled back off the ledge.

"Oh my God, I can't believe it. It's...it's horrible!"

He grabbed Elopia and shook her. "I've never seen anything so horrible in my life! Why are you killing your own people? Who is doing this? Why doesn't anyone stop them? Elopia, why is this happening?"

He struggled to catch his breath and slow his pounding heart.

Elopia's countenance didn't change. Her tone was even and cold. "I think you need to ask Cassandra."

"Cassandra? Yes, she has to be told about this. If she knew what she was pouring right there beneath her feet—"

He stopped and looked down at his sandals, still covered with the dust and mud from the Ascender.

"Oh…*oh*…!*" He barely made it into the woods before he emptied his stomach.

The workers on Cassandra's Ascender continued at their frenzied pace. The sidewalls of her Ascender moved ahead more quickly now—several meters an hour—and the constant flow of paving mixture from the Quashes of beaten-down workers kept the pathway growing at a steady pace.

It wasn't enough.

Cassandra stood near the end of the Ascender and looked out across the sky at the other construction projects racing toward the mountain. Next to her were two Phaedra, each whispering, but just loud enough for her to hear it above the din of the construction work behind her.

"It appears that Lassiter, Phileus, and Amanda are all ahead of you, Cassandra. If they reach the mountain before you, they will keep the best places for themselves."

The second Phaedra moved closer and pointed a spiny white finger at the mountain. "And there are already several who have made it to the top. You must not fall behind or you will not have the place you so deserve high up on the mountain."

The first continued. "Cassandra, this is up to you. You do want to get there first and live at the top of the peak, do you not?"

Cassandra ran her hands back through her hair then grasped it between her fingers and pulled.

No matter how fast I work or how hard I push my crew, I can't build fast enough to beat the others.

Her heart ached for a place at the top of the peak. It was so close she could almost touch it, yet there remained so much work to close the gap between where she stood and the final meter that would connect her with her prize. And even then she would need to trek up the mountain and claim her space before anyone else could get it.

She dropped her hands and began to pace, each step kicking up dust as she stomped.

"I won't let others beat me to the mountain." She looked at the two Phaedra tormenting her. "I *will* be first up to the summit and claim what I have worked so hard to attain. Nothing will keep me from this goal. Nothing and no one!"

Steward came running up the path toward her. His face was red and covered with sweat, and he was gasping to find his breath.

"Cassandra! Cassandra, do you know what you are standing on? Do you know what this paving mixture is made of? Dear God, Cassandra, do you know what they are doing at the crushing site?"

Everyone within earshot paused, and the Phaedra stepped closer.

Cassandra came close to him and signaled for him to quiet his voice. "Steward, if you have information for me about the construction work, then please tell me. However, let's walk back to the house where we can sit in private, and I will hear you out there."

He would have none of it. His voice trembled as he shot out the words. "People, they are using people—"

"Steward! We will discuss this at the house. Do you understand?"

Five large men closed in around him. Cassandra's guard now encircled him. He knew he was in danger. And now it was clear.

She knows!

Steward nodded and replied in a hushed voice. "Yes, at the house, of course, Cassandra."

Elopia was right. Cassandra was well aware of the atrocity. How could she stand there each day and watch workers pour the hideous mixture onto the pathways? She knew. She approved. But it was worse. She drove the project so hard that more and more people would need to be abducted and…

A wave of nausea welled up in him again.

The guarded procession neared the end of the Ascender, but instead of turning right toward the House of Bendor, they turned north toward the sounds of the distant crushing machines.

Steward stopped to turn the other way, but the guards obstructed him. "Where are we going? This isn't the way to the house!"

Cassandra took him aside. Her eyes narrowed to a sinister glare. "Yes, of course I know what is in the mixture, but none of the workers know. It is a well-kept secret between the Ascender builders and the operators of the crushers. You see, naïve little Steward, most people in the city are not pulling their weight. They're freeloaders, spending their time on unproductive tasks and enjoying—actually *enjoying*—their life in the valley. These valley lovers are, shall we say, expendable. If it makes construction progress more quickly and the mountain more accessible, then what happens to the nameless citizens of Ascendia is really no one's concern."

Before he could protest, the guards seized him by the arms. As they carried him away, Cassandra glowered at him. "Dear young Steward, today you will have the honor of becoming a permanent part of Ascendia."

No! This can't be happening!

The guards began to force him down the road toward the crushing site. He struggled with all his might but could not break free. The chains from Petitzaros and the weight of his Quash were so heavy that he was exhausted after several attempts to escape.

Was this how his journey would end? Hurled into the jaws of the machine? Where was Zedekai? As he struggled, he heard a crash of Quashes—

Guards were falling around him. He was free!

He turned to see a small figure with a veiled face racing away from the scene where Cassandra's guards lay dazed on the ground.

"Come on, *run!*"

Steward ran with everything he had, trying to keep up with the fleeing figure in front of him. He heard yelling behind them, and then more yells ahead of him as workers dumped their rocks and came toward them.

"This way!" The veiled rescuer grabbed Steward's hand and jerked him past the guards and back up the Ascender.

"Where are we going?" This was the last place he wanted to go. Once on the Ascender, there was no way of escape.

"Trust me!"

What other options did he have?

They ran up the Ascender, men in pursuit. They ran past the masons working on the walls, then around lines of men with Quashes full of paving mixture, waiting their turn to dump their gory loads onto the pathway. Finally, Steward and his guide reached the end, where the ramp ended.

Only open air lay ahead.

With the men closing in from behind, Steward prepared to be captured again and thrown into the crusher for sure.

"Grab my hand! Now!"

Steward didn't hesitate. He grabbed the hand held out to him just as the first guard came running at them.

"Jump, Steward!"

And before he knew it, he was being pulled over the edge.

They fell together through the air, Steward grasping the arms of the rescuer with all his strength. The figure grabbed a hook from beneath its tunic. It was fixed to a rope tied at the waist. With a quick flick of a wrist, the hook wound around a beam in the scaffolding that undergirded the ramp. As the rope snapped taut, they swung together around the scaffolding and came crashing down on a crossbeam just out of sight.

Steward lay there on the large beam of wood. "We're...we're alive. I can't believe it!"

Groaning, he struggled to his feet. His shoulder ached, but the pain was lost in his miracle of being rescued. "Who are you?"

His liberator pulled back the veil. Steward stood frozen, stunned.

"Astrid!"

Her eyes gleamed and her face was filled with color and life. Where was the pale, timid girl he met at the House of Bendor? She was...

Beautiful.

"Astrid, how did you do that, and why and...who *are* you?"

Astrid removed the rope from her waist and smiled at Steward. "I'm the reason Zedekai sent you to the House of Bendor. You needed to see what is happening in Ascendia before you see the king. Elopia saw to that. Now that you've seen it, I'll make sure you leave here safely."

Astrid brushed by him and began working her way down the crisscross of beams that made up the huge scaffolding. She led Steward down through the maze, halting and hiding when people underneath passed by. Finally, when the street was empty, they jumped down from the lowest beam and scurried out of sight into a small side street.

Soon they reached the gates of the city. Astrid waited for the right moment, then she grabbed Steward's hand and ran through the gates and into the woods far beyond the city walls. She didn't stop until they reached a small clearing. Finally, Astrid turned and sat under a large tree, resting her back against it.

"We're safe here." She wiped the perspiration from her face.

Steward sat down against a rock where he could face her. He had so many questions. "Astrid, why? I mean, if you know what's happening, why do you stay in Ascendia? And if you're this strong, why don't you rise up against your sister and stop this madness?"

Astrid ignored the questions for the moment. She took a drink from a flask that she'd worked loose from a leather waist belt. She offered the flask to Steward, but he wanted answers, not a drink.

Astrid obliged. "First of all, you're welcome." She let the words sit for a moment then smiled.

Steward hung his head. "I apologize, Astrid. Yes, thank you for saving my life. I can never repay you for what you've done."

"No need. It is what I was appointed to do."

"Appointed by whom?"

"By the king, of course."

Steward came to her. He turned her face toward his.

"You *know* the king? You have seen him?"

"Yes, I've seen the king. And so shall you." She took off her waistcoat and rubbed her shoulders. "You ask why I stay and why I don't mount a rebellion against my sister. Well, the problem is far beyond my sister. She is just one small pawn in a much larger game. It is the entire system that must be changed. It's attitudes, minds, and hearts that must be changed. Violence can't do that…although it is tempting to try. It will take a change of heart by the ramp builders to finally pull down the crushers. And so I work quietly, among the people of the valley."

She sat back down beside him and looked up at the sky as she spoke. "Many do not want to climb the mountain. They want to live at peace in the valley. I help them find refuge from the guards and encourage them to carry on."

She looked back at Steward. "That's why I stay. I warn some about the crushing machines. I help others who don't want to spend their lives toiling on the ramps. And though there are fewer and fewer people who aren't lured by the promises of living on the mountain, I wait for the day when change will come in the hearts of my fellow citizens— and my two sisters."

She was amazing. How brave and noble and…beautiful.

Steward put his hand on hers. "You are a good and brave person, Astrid." The touch sent his pulse racing. He didn't want to leave her side. "Too good for this place."

That was it!

Steward drew his hand back and jumped to his feet, his voice shrill with excitement. "Why don't you come with me to see the king? You can help show me the way. I would so much love to have the company. Do say yes. Come with me, Astrid."

She smiled, and something in her eyes…

Could the attraction be mutual?

She stood and turned away. "I can't come with you. This is your journey, and you must make it alone." She returned to his side and put her hand in his. "But know that my thoughts and prayers will be with you, and"—she gave him a playful look—"we shall see each other again."

"We will?"

Astrid nodded. "Yes, but you must go now and continue your journey." She walked over to a mound of branches and leaves. She pulled away the brush and there, to Steward's amazement, were a fresh set of clothes, a cloak, a sleeping roll, and his old satchel. He opened the flap and found it filled with food, wine, and water.

"Astrid, you are full of surprises."

"Not I." She smiled. "Zedekai is always looking after you."

Zedekai, the Phaedra, the king. An unwelcome sense of doubt caught him off-guard.

"Astrid, when did you see the king?" It startled even him to hear the words come from his mouth.

She frowned. "When? I don't remember. Not so long ago. Why do you ask?"

"I was asked by a Phaedra how I knew the king really existed. I was hoping you could assure me." He looked around, relieved they were still alone. "Do you listen to the Phaedra?"

"These are questions you must answer for yourself. All of us must decide for ourselves if the king is real and who we will listen to. I cannot answer that for you, Steward. It is part of the reason for your journey."

Steward wasn't satisfied with that answer, but he sensed it was all he was going to get. He started to take off his sling, and the Quash fell into his hands. "And what do I do with this?"

"Take it with you. It will remind you of Ascendia and of what you have seen and learned here. And perhaps it will also remind you of me." She gave him a smile. "Now you must go. It will be dark soon, and you must reach the edge of Pitcairn Moor before nightfall. You will be safe on the edge of the moor, but Steward…" She grasped his arm. "Don't stay either on the moor or in the woods. You must stay on the edge of both. Do you understand?"

He was surprised by the passion of her words. "Yes, yes I think so. But I do wish you could tell me more and even come with me. This journey is long, and I have so many questions, more than when I started. You could help me find the answers."

Astrid put her hand to Steward's cheek, gave him a tender kiss on the forehead, and stood back. "You must find them for yourself, Steward. But only at the right time. Be patient, keep your heart pure, expect to hear and learn and know, and you will. The king has promised it."

Then she took up her Quash, tied her tunic tight, and after one look back disappeared into the woods.

Steward stood for several minutes, staring after her. He rubbed his hand across his skin where she had kissed him. For the first time in his life, he had the sense of falling in love. "I will see you again." It was a promise to her—and himself.

With the day closing in toward evening, he turned his attention to the journey—and Astrid's words about Pitcairn Moor. Steward shed his shirt and put on the new tunic. The chains from Petitzaros rubbed his arms bare in places, so he unwrapped them and applied some balm that he kept inside his satchel. He then dressed, and with his satchel over one shoulder and his Quash over the other, he set off down the path for Pitcairn Moor.

~~~~~~~~~~

Anna laid the book down. Merideth stood and walked to the large window looking out over the garden at the back of the house. In the darkness, all she could see was the moonlight reflecting off the roof of the garden shed, playing in odd patterns on the side panel of the greenhouse.

Merideth's hands shook. Cassandra's voice rang in her mind. This couldn't be happening. What had happened to her well-honed defenses? This was the last place she wanted them to fail her!

How could Dad have known? This is my story. I can't let it in…can't let it overcome me.

She jumped when an arm encircled her shoulder. Anna stood there. "Mer, are you okay?"

"Anna, I'm…okay? No, not at all. I can't give in to this. There's too much at stake."

"It's all right, Mer. We're all processing the story in our own way."

Merideth continued staring out the window. It was time for her to own this. "Anna, Cassandra's story is my story, and Dad knew it. All my pushing away won't free me from the truth that my life has been dominated by the mountains that always loomed ahead of me, by my insatiable appetite for…*ramp building.*"

She closed her eyes and could see herself standing on an Ascender, building her future on the bodies of those she had always labeled as less motivated. The confession cut her. Her defenses were crumbling. She rested her forehead on the window as the tears began to flow.

Reed went to the kitchen, and Alex joined him. They needed to give Anna and Merideth some space.

Reed leaned against the counter and waited for Alex to close the door. "That was a stake to the heart. Dad couldn't have written it any better."

"You mean for Merideth?"

Reed looked at him. "Yes. What did you think I meant?"

"I thought he wrote it for me, that's all. I know Cassandra is a woman, but I've spent a lot of the last several years building my own ramp to the mountainside. How about you?"

"Geez, I thought I was done when Steward left Petitzaros. Now I have to admit to living in Ascendia as well?" Reed laughed, and he was glad Alex joined him. The laughter was a welcome reprieve from the heaviness of the night.

Alex didn't let the light moment last. "I don't think either of us can escape this. Dad's writing about us, all of us. What do you suppose drives us to be ramp builders?"

Reed shrugged. "Our culture, capitalism, pride, fear? I dunno, probably all of them."

"Fear. Fear of failure. Fear of coming to the end of life and having nothing to show for it." Alex stopped as Anna walked in.

Reed moved over so she could fill two glasses of water from the sink.

"What do you think, Anna? Is it a fear of failure that drives us to be ramp builders?"

She wiped off the outside of the glasses as she thought. "Maybe. But I wonder, was Dad a failure? I can't remember any ramps he was trying to build. Yet he left so much behind. Stuff that mattered."

Reed looked at his two siblings. Silence. Anna's words hung in the air.

She turned toward the door. "I think Mer needs this."

"Is she okay?" Alex asked.

She drew in a deep breath. "Are any of us? I don't know if I can take two more lands, and I have a feeling the next one's for me."

Reed held the door for her, commenting as she passed. "I guarantee you, if it's like the first two, it will be for all of us."

Walter strolled in, passing Anna as he entered the kitchen. Reed cocked his head and said, "Walter, how much of this story did you know before tonight?"

Walter hesitated before answering. "Sam let me read parts of it as he finished them. I gave some feedback, did some proofreading for him, but I have never heard it from beginning to end before tonight."

"And how are *you* finding it?" Alex asked.

"Convicting. I must admit I came here praying that it would speak to you, all four of you. But I am finding my own heart aching."

Merideth appeared next to Reed in the doorway, startling him. "So there's a little Cassandra in all of us?"

Alex threw his hands into the air. "Guilty as charged. How you doing, sis?"

Merideth sipped her water then set the glass down and crossed her arms. "Look, I'm struggling, okay? I'm going to need some space and time to deal with this. I'm not ready to go much further yet, but," she glanced around the room, making eye contact with each of them, "but I'm glad we're here, hearing this together."

That was the sister Reed missed. There was a time when they could talk like this, all of them, so long ago. Before life, jobs, pressure, alienation—and fear. There it was again. Maybe Alex was right.

How did Mom and Dad figure out how to live without fear?

Reed longed for the answer. It was likely they all did.

Reed followed his siblings back into the living room. "Has anyone figured out the Quash yet?"

Anna shook her head. "I was wondering the same thing. Most of the imagery makes sense, but the Quash is beyond me."

Reed raised his eyebrows, signaling his own confusion. Alex just shrugged.

"Power, control. That's what I heard." Merideth sat back in her chair. "I mean, we all have it. What matters is how we use it. To build our ramps, to attack each other, or, like Astrid, to serve each other. What do you think?"

The grandfather clock in the living room chimed out ten times.

"Wow." Anna yawned. "Does that sound bring back memories."

Reed stretched. "Agreed. But it's also reminding me it's been a long day. First, Mer, I think you're probably right. Power, makes sense. Thanks. Now, how far do we plan to read tonight?"

Alex examined the depth of the remaining pages. "Good question. By my estimate, we have at least five hours of reading left to finish the book. So what's the consensus? How far do we read before calling it a night?"

Reed looked at Walter. "Any advice?"

Walter pointed to the open book. "Why don't you get young Steward through the next two lands and then pick it up tomorrow."

Reed agreed. "That shouldn't take more than two hours. That puts us in bed by midnight. Is everyone okay with that?"

Anna walked over to the couch and slumped into it. "Fine with me, but I'm not sure I can handle reading what's coming."

Merideth nodded. "I need time to think all this through."

"No problem." Reed took the seat by the book. "My turn."

CHAPTER
Twelve

Steward stepped through the last stand of deep woods and approached Pitcairn Moor. He stopped to examine the landscape. The late day sun was casting eerie shadows across the open moor. Fog was forming and the air cooled.

He drew his cloak round him. He hated these places in the daylight, but now, at dusk, at the end of a long day, his nerves were frayed.

I wish I weren't alone. Astrid, Zedekai, anyone? He looked around. *I'd even welcome a Phaedra now.*

His legs were sore from the running and climbing in his escape from Ascendia. He looked at his arms in the fading light.

Bruises. Mementos from the guards' painful grips. And there were the ever-present chains still wound tightly against his forearms.

Petitzaros, will I ever be free of you?

He searched for a spot to sleep.

"Not in the moor and not in the woods." Astrid's warning was playing through his mind.

Why was she so passionate about where I sleep?

He would comply. In the last moments of light he found a small, flat, grassy place at the edge of the woods. It looked out to the moor but was not in the moor.

This will do nicely.

Steward flung his satchel down and took the Quash from his shoulders. He gathered wood and built a small fire, just large enough to warm his hands and heat a cup of mulled wine. Once settled in, he began to take in his surroundings as the sunlight gave way to absolute darkness. He looked one way to see towering trees that, in the fading light, looked like giants with arms extended in anger. He looked the other way out over

113

the moor to see fog forming, turning every bush and stand of reeds into something that appeared far more menacing.

Just one night, then I am away to the next city.

But then, sounds. A rustle in the leaves, a creaking across the moor. The screech of an owl caused Steward to fling half of his mulled wine up into the air.

Was that a figure? A man? A giant?

Steward's mind conjured up figures in the fog and footsteps at the edge of the woods. Within a few short moments of the first real darkness, Steward was ready to hide. He lay down and pulled his cloak over his head, trying not to listen or think. But sleep was elusive as he tossed about, praying for the light of morning.

A chill ran through him.

I'm being watched.

He sat up and looked around but saw no one.

Just your imagination. Sleep. C'mon, Steward. Just sleep.

A gathering of hooded figures gazed at Steward huddling at the edge of Pitcairn Moor. They were in no earthly place but in the ethereal existence between substance and void. In this place there was no light, no sound, no movement of air. All that existed was nonexistence. It was the *Tohu Wa-Bohu*, and it could only be called a place because, on this night, it was occupied by figures who shared in part its detached and formless nature.

There were murmurs and sneers. One of the cloaked creatures silenced them. "Young Steward is farther on his journey than I would like. I am saddened that he left Petitzaros. That was unfortunate."

Another raised his hand. "We did not anticipate the aggression of the Black Knight. It is quite clear this journey means a great deal to them…more than we may have thought."

The lead figure spat out his words. "Of course it means a great deal to them! Do you not know what's at stake in this young one's journey?"

Other voices rang out.

"Exposure."

"Confrontation."

"Exile!" He stood, shuddering with rage. "And we must not let it get to that. Not at any cost."

"But you know our limitations," hissed another. "We have done much to delay this journey. What more can we do?"

Offers were presented.

"We can cause him fear."

"We can cause him panic."

"We can cause him despair."

"No." The others fell silent. The lead Phaedra circled them, examining the assembly and considering his plan. "We will do far more harm than that. We will cause young Steward to doubt who he is. And there is no better place for that than Marikonia."

Dawn. Steward felt the warmth of the morning sun on his face.

Thank heaven the night is over.

Steward rose with one thought. *Get me out of this awful place and on to my journey.*

Still he was hungry. He'd let the sun warm the earth while he ate.

Steward enjoyed his breakfast, thanks to Astrid and Zedekai. As the sun shed full light on the moor, Steward gathered his things in his satchel. It was time to go. He took a step forward into the moor.

"Yeoww!"

The ground under his foot gave way, and the seeping mud underneath began to pull him in.

A branch. I need a branch!

Steward turned to grab the bush that had served as a windbreak for his fire. He managed to get hold of a branch to stop his descent into the mud while, with his free foot, he found firm ground. He pulled on the branch and pushed with his foot, freeing himself, falling back onto the spot where he had slept.

"This is impossible! How will I ever cross this bog?" He let loose his frustration on a scream then picked up a rock and threw it out into the moor. It hit with a sloppy thud and sank into the mud.

Great. Now what?

The moor had turned into an endless swamp of bubbling mud. Had he slept just ten feet farther out, he would have been swallowed up whole. He turned and looked back toward the woods.

Unbelievable.

The woods he'd walked through for hours just yesterday had somehow closed in and formed an impenetrable mass of trees and bushes.

That would suffocate anyone caught within it.

Steward stood on the only spot that was safe, between the woods and the moor.

"Thank God for Astrid." He threw up his hands and shouted to the open air. "But where do I go now? How do I get out of here?"

Had he been brought this far just to be abandoned to futility and despair at the edge of this disgusting bog?

A noise. Something was moving in the trees behind him.

"Astrid? Zedekai? Is that you?"

No response. Steward knelt down behind the large bush and peered out to watch the edge of the woods. The thick brush began tossing about, and out of the tangle of trees and vines and bushes emerged a most curious creature. It was only a few feet tall and appeared at first to be a child, but no, not with its hunched shoulders and slow gait. Steward looked closer. Its face was long and thin, with telltale wrinkles encroaching on the edges of its cheeks, around its eyes and up from its neck. The little creature had vibrant green eyes that danced with life, and a bit of mischievousness, Steward thought. It was dressed in a deep blue cloak and its walk was measured, relying on a well-worn walking stick.

Then Steward realized the creature was walking straight for him. He'd seen him.

Steward stood and tried to steady his voice. "He...Hello. My name is Steward. Who are you and...how did you get through the forest?"

The little man shuffled directly up to Steward, closer than he liked. He looked up at Steward with a squint and a snarl then turned and walked over to the edge of the moor. He took his staff and poked at the mud at the edge of the moor, and when the end of his stick disappeared in the soft bubbling earth, he pulled it back.

He looked again at Steward. "Are you the one doing all the shouting?"

Steward grinned. "Yes, I guess I am."

The little man looked out to the moor. "And who are you shouting to?"

"No one. I was just frustrated. In my village, we call it 'airing your ire.'"

"In my village, we call it annoying!" he snapped back. He poked his stick at the place where Steward had slept and then again into the small fire pit he had created.

"You slept here last night?"

Steward kept his distance, although he felt no fear. "Yes, but not well."

"No doubt. You are either very lucky or very well-informed to have survived a night between these two curses."

Steward took a few steps toward him. "I have a friend who warned me not to sleep in either the woods or the moor, but at a place in between."

The man peered up at Steward. "A good friend indeed. And where is this friend?"

Steward sighed. "She remained in Ascendia. You see, I'm on a journey, and, well, it's one I must continue on my own."

He thought of Astrid; the touch, the kiss. He missed her.

"Ascendia, huh? Wicked place. Filled with anger and hatred." The man paused. "And where will this journey of yours take you?"

"I am going to see the king." Steward regretted blurting that out.

The man made no response. He didn't even flinch. He sat down on the spot where Steward had slept and poked at the ashes in the little fire pit.

Steward looked out to where the path disappeared into the moor's bubbling mud and sighed. "But that is my path, so it looks like my journey may end right here."

Steward turned back to the little man stirring up ashes with his stick. "May I ask, who are you and where do you come from?"

He didn't look up. He just kept poking at the remnants of Steward's fire. "My name is Dunston. I am an Interpreter."

"An interpreter? An interpreter of what?"

"Of life, of course."

Steward came closer and sat near him. "And for whom do you interpret?"

"Oh, I interpret for kings and rulers, queens and lords, generals and marshals, barons and emperors and sovereigns. And today"—he stopped stirring and looked straight at Steward—"for you."

So. This was not a chance encounter. "Did Zedekai send you?"

"That doesn't matter. What does matter is you, that path, and your journey. You are ready to give up your quest because the path disappears into the moor?"

Steward raised his hands, exasperated. Of course he wanted to go on, but how?

"What else can I do? The path is impassable. If I try to walk on it, I will be sucked down into the mud and die. And I can't go back through the woods. They've become too thick. Do you have a way through all of this?"

"No." The little man stood and poked Steward in the chest with his walking stick. "But you do."

"I do? What do you mean by that? I have no idea how to get through that bog!"

Steward was in no mood for word games. Was this little man really from the king? Who could he trust? He would proceed with caution.

The little creature motioned for Steward to come to the edge of the moor. "Come here and tell me what you see."

Steward looked out again across the field of shifting mud and sighed. "I see a great bog, a swamp filled with bubbling mud and reeds and mosquitoes. And I see my path disappearing into the middle of it."

"Young Steward, you will find that what your eyes see and what is real may be two different things. How do you know what you are seeing is real?"

I can see it right there. What is this man talking about? "How else can I know if something is real than to see it...and touch it? My foot was sucked into the mud, so it seems real enough to me."

The man shook his head and held a fist in the air. "No, no, no. You must learn to see things as the king would have you see them."

Steward spun around and stumbled toward him in his excitement. "You've...you've been sent by the king?"

The creature nodded. "Calmly now. Yes, he sent me to you. He wants you to understand that the world you think you see may not be the real world at all. You need to have new eyes—lenses, if you will—to see the world as the king would have you see it."

Steward was enthralled by the image. "How do I get these lenses?"

Dunston fished around inside his tunic and produced a set of spectacles. He handed them to Steward. "Here, for now you can borrow mine. They will help you discern what is real from what is illusion. Put these on and look back to your moor."

Steward did as he was told, but when he turned again to look out over the moor, it was gone! In its place, Steward saw a meadow filled with wildflowers. His path ran through the flowers. He reached up and lifted the glasses from his face, and the moor with its foreboding fog and bubbling mud was there. Then he rested the glasses back onto his nose, and the meadow and wildflowers returned.

Frustrated, he took them off. "This is a trick, some sort of illusion."

"Yes, yes, you are right. It is an illusion." The little man poked his stick again into Steward's chest. "Only which of the two views is the illusion, and which one is real?"

Steward walked again to the edge of the moor. He placed his foot on the mud and pressed down until the mud oozed around his shoe and he felt the ground give way. He jerked it back.

"This is reality!"

"Is it? Put the spectacles back on."

Steward placed the little glasses back on his face and again the beautiful meadow appeared. He watched as Dunston shuffled up to the path and began to walk through the wildflowers. He stopped and picked a bunch and held them to his nose. Then he continued strolling along in the warm sunshine.

"Dunston, how can you walk through the moor like that? I don't understand!"

The creature looked back at him. "Leave the glasses on and walk out here with me."

Okay, steady now. Just don't lift them up.

Steward took a deep breath and placed his foot on the path. Where seconds before the sucking mud threatened to pull him in, the path was now firm and sure. He stepped again and the ground was solid. He continued to look through the glasses and made his way out to Dunston, who waited for him, tapping one of his small feet.

"Come on, come on. You walk like an old lady."

Steward looked in every direction. Beauty. "I don't understand. How can these glasses change the ground?"

Dunston tapped the path with his stick. "Oh, they have changed nothing, young Steward. They have only allowed you to see what is truly real. Lift them up and look around you."

"No, I can't or I'll be pulled into the muddy bog."

Dunston struck him on the shoulder with his stick.

"Ouch. What was that for?"

"For acting like a faithless old man. Now take them off...*and learn.*"

Steward hesitated then raised the spectacles from his eyes.

Amazing.

All around him were fields of wildflowers. He looked back to the edge of the meadow and saw the place where he had slept. The woods behind it were bright and green. No sign of the tangle of brush that he had feared. He held the glasses up, examining them with care.

"So, let me ask you again, young Steward. What is real and what is illusion?"

How could he know for sure? The moor was just here. Now this?

"I guess the meadow is real and the moor is an illusion. But I felt the mud beneath my feet."

"You *believed* you felt what your eyes thought they saw. Illusion plays tricks on the body as well as the mind."

"Are these glasses the only way I can ever see what is real?"

Dunston nodded and turned, shuffling his way down the path as he spoke. "Yes, for now. But you must develop your eyes to see what is real. Everything the king has created is real. All that stands against the king is illusion. When you learn to discern one from the other, you will not need the lenses. But now you must continue on to Marikonia."

Steward hurried to catch up with him. He held up the glasses. "May I keep these?"

Dunston stopped, took the glasses from Steward, folded them up, and placed them in Steward's satchel. "Yes, but only put them on when you absolutely must. Do not depend on them. You must train your eyes to see what is real without the lenses. Look to what is good and right, and you will begin to see the king's kingdom as it really is."

Train my eyes to see the king's kingdom? How?

Steward kept his questions to himself as the two walked through the meadow and came to the edge of a steep descent on the path. Dunston gathered up his tunic and turned to Steward.

"This is where our paths diverge. You must continue, and I must go my way through the woods. Your path will take you to Marikonia, and for that land you will need this." Dunston reached in his satchel and produced a pouch containing something flat and rectangular. He handed it to Steward. "Don't bother with it now, but look at it when you reach the house of Abner the Blacksmith. His is the first house you will come to on the road to Marikonia. Stay with Abner and his family, and they will unveil the secrets of Marikonia to you. Stay only as long as you must and leave when you know the time is right."

If Steward had learned anything in Ascendia, he'd learned that it would be easy to tell when the time was right to leave. "Will I like it any better than Ascendia?"

Dunston looked back at Steward from the edge of the trees. "Doubtful, very doubtful. But always remember, young Steward, look to what is real—what is of the king—and you will see new things you have never seen before."

With that, the little creature disappeared into the deep woods.

Alone once again, Steward tucked the strange gift into his satchel and started the descent down the path. As he walked, he picked up momentum until he was in a full run. He fought to keep himself in control, but as he neared the bottom he was running so hard he feared he might vault himself forward at any misstep.

Just then, around the bend, a distinguished-looking man in fine attire came strolling along the path. Steward ran into him full tilt, sending both of them rolling head over heels down the path. They came to rest on the edge of the path with dust, satchels, and walking sticks flying in every direction.

Steward sat for a minute, shaking his head and examining his limbs. Nothing seemed broken. Only some bruises and a scraped knee. Then he looked at the man, who was just beginning to come around from a hard knock on the head. Steward crawled over to him.

"Are you all right? I am dreadfully sorry. I didn't see you, and I was coming quite fast down the hill and…I do hope you are all right. Is anything broken?"

The man came to his senses and sat up and looked at Steward. "You foolish boy, what do you mean by running down the hill so fast that you cannot avoid an old man out for his morning walk? You might have killed me."

"I am so very sorry. Here, let me help you up."

Steward tried to help the man to his feet, but he pushed Steward's hands away and leaned on his walking stick—once he had retrieved it from a bush—and made his way to his feet. He dusted himself off, massaged his legs and shoulders, and finally stood up straight.

He seemed to have come through the tumble without serious injury. "Well, I guess I have survived. But where are you going in such a rush?"

Steward was brushing himself off and fixing his satchel. "I am on a journey to see the king, and my path takes me through Marikonia."

"Marikonia? Wonderful place. But what is this about seeing the king? Why would the king wish to see you?"

Steward didn't appreciate the question.

"I've been sent to see him. It's a promise my parents made before I was born. I will see the king, and he will tell me the meaning of my name and my destiny."

The man reached down and picked up the bag containing the gift that Dunston had given Steward. "And what is this?"

"That must've fallen out of my satchel. I'm not sure what it is. It is a gift from a friend."

The man opened the bag and produced a flat, smooth object that appeared to be a mirror. He held it up to look at it, and then, in a quick motion, he waved his hand across the face of it.

"So, you are prepared for Marikonia, but I don't think you are prepared for the king."

Steward shifted. How could this stranger make such a comment, and why didn't the man give him his mirror back? "What do you mean?"

"You are not fit to come before the king. Who are you but a sorry farm boy from the outer reaches of the far south? You expect the king to see the likes of you? I know men who have seen the king. Nobles, aristocrats, gentry, the finest in the land, and even they were humbled before the king. Who are you to think the king would want to see the likes of you?"

Not fit? Why? This was growing irritating.

This man doesn't know me. Who is he to tell me I'm not fit to see the king?

Steward's words were sharp. "It is my destiny, my calling. I have been told to make this journey."

The man waved him off. "You will look a fool to stand before the king. You have been lied to, deceived. The king will not want to look on someone like you. You are unworthy, you are unfit, you are...*repugnant*."

How dare he say such things! This man was insane.

"What do you mean I am unfit and repugnant? Who are you to say such things to me?"

The man snorted a derisive laugh. "Oh, it's not me. Just look for yourself." He turned the mirror around and positioned it in front of Steward.

Looking back at him from the mirror was a disfigured image that looked enough like Steward to let him know it was indeed him, but he had bulging eyes, reddish skin, and a crooked smile.

"That…that is not me!"

"Not you? Well, my dear boy, who else is it?"

Steward grabbed the mirror and looked closer. "No, I mean it *is* me, but I don't look like that. What's happened to me?"

The man sneered. "Perhaps the light is bad. But you must admit, the king would have no interest or business with the likes of someone who looks like you, now would he?"

Steward's heart pounded. He looked again. How had his face turned so ugly? Perhaps the man was right. He couldn't possibly appear before the king looking like this.

The man patted Steward on the shoulder. "I think Marikonia is just the place for you. People there know that the Reflector never lies. So off you go now. And mind your speed." The man doddered off down the path.

Steward picked the mirror up and looked again, but he couldn't bear to gaze for long at the hideous image staring back at him. He tucked the mirror back into its pouch and walked on to the outskirts of Marikonia.

Behind him, the dapper man looked back to see that Steward was out of sight. Then the man's neat tweed jacket, vest, and well-tied ascot melted into a single cloth garment—a robe. His bearded face changed shape and disappeared into the shadows of a hood. And the Phaedra smiled and walked away.

As Steward drew near the village, he heard loud voices and sounds before he even saw a house.

"Troy, move that iron rail so we can finish the gate."

"Trek, don't blow so much air. The coals won't last."

The shouting and clanging metal rang out. Steward approached a large, open building, where a searing fire raged in a furnace surrounded by anvils, metal bars, and iron plates of all shapes and sizes. Behind one anvil was an enormous man with a hammer in one hand and a set of long pliers in the other.

Abner the Blacksmith, no doubt.

"C'mon, yield to me, you brute." He beat a piece of metal that lay across the anvil and, between blows, continued yelling orders to two younger men toiling away at their own stations.

"There, done. Now for the hinges."

The blacksmith grabbed the cool end of a long spear thrust into the furnace and withdrew a white-hot tip of molten metal from the fire. He laid it on his anvil and continued his merciless pounding.

Steward stood and took it all in: the sounds, sights, and smells of a busy blacksmith shop. Finally, the blacksmith noticed him.

"Hello, and who is this? Are you here for the garden gate for Mrs. Blackstone?" The two boys looked up for a moment then went back to their work.

Steward stepped a bit farther into the shop. "No, sir. My name is Steward and I am on a journey to see the king. I was sent here to stay with you…"

"Stay with us? Can't be. We have no room or extra food. Go find lodging elsewhere. We have work to do."

The blacksmith went back to his pounding.

"But sir…Mr. Abner…Dunston told me that—"

"Dunston? Dunston, you say?" The blacksmith shop came to a halt. Abner laid down his hammer, wiped his hands on his apron, and came over to Steward. "Well, why didn't you say so? Boys, this is our visitor from Dunston. Come around and introduce yourselves."

Thank God for Dunston.

"Hello, my name is Troy. You are welcome here."

"Thank you." Steward shook the hand of the young man who stood half again as tall and twice as broad as he.

"And I'm Trek, the younger brother." He was even taller and broader than his older brother.

"Very nice to meet you both. Thank you for the welcome. I am most anxious to learn more about Marikonia."

Abner shot back. "Why? There is not much good to learn about this place. But you're welcome to stay with us as long as you like. Going to see the king, huh?"

Steward noted the skeptical tone.

"No one around here has ever seen the king. What makes you think you will see him?"

No one has seen the king? Steward felt pangs of doubt returning.

"It's a long story, one I will be happy to tell you when we can sit and talk. For now, may I wash up?"

"Yes, certainly. Where are my manners? Trek, take young Stewy here up to the house and introduce him to Claire and Edith."

Stewy? Steward wasn't sure he liked that, but he went along with Trek without comment. They walked to the door and entered the simple thatched-roof house. Inside was a large room dominated by an ornate wrought-iron fireplace—most likely Abner's handiwork. Beyond the fireplace, two women were working away in the kitchen.

Trek shouted out. "Mom! Claire! We have a visitor. It is the lad that Dunston told us would be coming. His name is Screwit."

"Steward, actually, and it is very nice to meet you both." Steward extended his hand to a heavyset older woman with beautiful black hair and deep brown eyes.

"Steward, is it? Well, it is nice to have you here. I'm Edith." Steward liked her happy, sing-song voice. "And this is our daughter, Claire." A young girl came around Edith, shyness clear in her expression and posture. She greeted him.

As she did so, Steward tried not to stare. Claire was close to his own age, and although she showed every sign of self-neglect, she was stunningly beautiful. She had her mother's black hair, but it shone with a brilliance that reflected countless shades and tones as the sun caught it. Her eyes were a color of hazel Steward had never seen, sparkling and dazzling amid her soft eyelashes and smooth cheeks.

I've never seen a more beautiful woman.

"Nice to meet you, Claire. And thank you both for the hospitality. Dunston said you are gracious people."

"And how is the little varmint?" Trek asked with a wry smile.

"I only had a short time with him, so I am not sure how to respond."

Trek threw his hands in the air. "That's Dunston. Here one minute and then, *phoosh,* he's gone. Strange little dude, but awfully nice, and a friend of the king, so they say."

Steward made his way to his room where he was most pleased to bathe and change clothes. In the evening, the family sat around a large round table that was the centerpiece of the only main room in the house. As the four men gulped down massive helpings of meat, squash, potatoes, fried corn, pickled eggs, and beans, the women scurried about trying to keep the men's plates and glasses full and to grab a bite or two for themselves. Once the carnage was over, the men sat back and, between the belching and laughing, began to talk about Marikonia.

"So, Stewy, what can we tell you about Marikonia?" Abner grinned at him.

Steward reached down to his satchel and pulled out the mirror. "I was told that this was very important here. But I must say that the image it shows is somehow distorted. I don't look like the image I see in the mirror. What's its purpose?"

They looked around at each other, uneasy. Had he misspoken and offended his hosts?

Troy spoke first. "That's a Reflector. We all have one…have since we were five years old. It shows us who we are. Whatever your reflection, that's who you are. Reflectors don't lie."

Steward put his hands up in protest. "Oh, but this one does. Surely you can see that I don't look as hideous as this mirror…Reflector…makes me look." Steward held it up to show his face in its smooth surface. They all looked at Steward and looked at the reflection coming back at them.

"Well, Steward, how can I say this?" Edith was searching for words. "It is actually what you look like."

"What? No! I don't look like this at all. Why would you say that?"

What's wrong with these people?

Without saying a word, all five of his hosts went and brought back to the table their own Reflectors. Some were square and some were round, but all were scratched and dirty. Each of the Abner family held up his or her own Reflector, first to see in it for themselves and then to turn it so Steward could see.

No, that's impossible!

Steward didn't know what to say. The Reflectors returned images that bore little resemblance to the five members of the Abner family.

When he just looked at them, Trek and Troy had rugged, handsome features, and Edith, despite her plumpness, had a lovely round, soft face. Even Abner had a strong jaw and thick, curly hair. And yet none of those features were caught in the images displayed by their Reflectors.

The most shocking was Claire's image. Her Reflector turned her stunning beauty into a disfigured, sullen woman with sunken eyes and dull, thin brown hair.

Steward was frantic. Someone had to declare the deception.

"Claire, that's not you! Not even close. These aren't accurate reflections of any of you! What's wrong with these things?"

Abner's stern voice caught Steward off guard. "These Reflectors only give back what they see, Steward. There is nothing wrong with them. This is what we see in each other and, frankly, what we see in you. From the time we are young, these Reflectors show us who we are, and our lives are patterned accordingly. The beautiful, the graceful, and the strong live their lives in the Light District. The rest of us are simple servants who live on the edges of town and do our work quietly. It is our place, our lot in life, and we accept that."

Edith, Troy, Trek, and Claire all nodded.

I need to be polite, but this is crazy. "So…your whole life is determined by the image you see in your Reflector? Why does it matter so?"

Edith began to clear dishes from the table. "It is *all* that matters, dear. Everyone has his or her place. It is how we maintain order. And for people like us…and you…our place is in the shadows of the world. We don't stand out. We are not supposed to. If everyone plays his part, then we all get along."

Steward picked up his Reflector again and took one last hard look at his image. He tossed the device across the room. "I will not accept that I look this way. And none of you should either. This is a lie, a deception. Don't you see it?"

Abner rose from his chair. His large frame added import to his sharp tone. "Now look here, Steward, you are our guest. But if you are to stay with us, you must never talk like this again. This is the way of life in Marikonia. You may not like it or agree with it, but it is our destiny. And we must ask that you respect it. Do you understand?"

He didn't, but this was not the time to argue. He needed to get away. To think and try to figure this all out. "Yes, of course. I apologize. I think I just need some rest. If you will excuse me, I will turn in for the night."

They all said their polite goodnights, and Steward was glad to be alone to think through the affairs of the day. His heart was unsettled as he lay in bed, but his short night on the edge of the moor caught up to him, and he was soon fast asleep.

Steward spent several days with Abner and his family. He tried his hand at swinging the large hammers in the blacksmith shop, making Troy and Trek bellow with laughter. He worked in the kitchen with Edith and Claire, doing his best to pull his weight in this working-class family. The evening conversations around the great table in the dining room never returned to the Reflectors, but Steward noticed that, every once in a while, one of the kids would take a look at themselves in their own device. Each time, Steward could catch a glimpse of despair on their faces as they were again reminded of the disfigured reflection that stared back at them.

When he was alone, Steward studied his own Reflector. He looked it over from every angle.

I can't explain this. It's not right, I know it. But how do I…what do I…

As hard as he tried to find some way to explain the distortion, the same image was returned to him each time he looked at it. No bending or cleaning of the mirror helped, but Steward still refused to believe that the image in the smooth surface of his Reflector was a true representation of his face.

One afternoon, Steward accompanied Claire on a walk to pick berries for Edith's cobbler.

"Careful, you two, and be back before supper," Edith called out as they walked away, each swinging an empty bucket. Not far down the path they found an enormous stand of wild berries.

Claire laughed. "We'll be here for hours. I'm glad we only brought two buckets."

Steward began grabbing berries as fast as he could. "Let's see who fills their bucket first. The winner gets an extra egg for dinner."

Claire's eyes lit up. "You're on."

Despite the competition, Steward couldn't help but stop and stare at Claire when she was distracted with her picking. He was overwhelmed by her beauty. Just to look at her in the sunshine was a delight to his eyes.

"Ouch!" Steward drew his hand back from a berry. He'd been so distracted by Claire he grabbed right on to a bee.

"Quick, come with me." Claire grabbed his good hand and ran with him down the path to a small pool of ice-cold water nestled in a rock-encircled basin. It was fed by a spring that trickled through the rocks on the far side.

"This comes right out of the mountain snows. Here, give me your hand." Claire thrust his throbbing hand into the water and held it tightly.

The pain subsided as the frigid water began its numbing work. Steward kept his hand still in the water, and as he did, the ripples died down. Soon, the surface of the pool turned to glass-like calm. Steward looked down to check if the redness in his hand was fading— and then he saw it.

"Look, Claire! My face! Look at the reflection in the pool. *That* is me. That is how I look." But before Claire could look, he moved his arm in his excitement, causing ripples to distort his image. Claire let go of his hand and stepped back. Her face showed her fear.

"No, wait, Claire! You must see this. Wait until the water calms again, and then you will see."

She turned to leave. Steward pulled his hand from the water and ran to her, stopping her and turning her toward him.

"Claire, where are you going? You can't leave. You must see my reflection in the pool— and yours!"

"No, I won't. It's not real. Don't you understand? Only what we see in the Reflector is real."

"No, Claire, it is just the opposite. What I just saw in the pool is me, really me. That's what I look like. I don't know what's wrong with these Reflectors, but they are lying. C'mon, Claire, you have to look. Please, just see yourself as you really are."

She was shaking, but she followed him back to the pool. Steward had a firm grasp on her shoulders and turned her toward the pool. At the edge, he saw that the surface had calmed and was once again like glass. He tugged Claire to the edge, turning her face toward the pool, and together they looked straight into the reflections that glistened from its mirror-like surface.

Claire stood motionless as she gazed at her image. She moved her hands to her face and ran her fingers across her cheeks, as if to verify that it was really her own face she was seeing. She ran her fingers back through her hair, mesmerized by the reflected image of a young woman she had never seen before.

Steward whispered to her. "Claire, you're beautiful. Don't you see it?"

She paused to take it in—then her face grew angry. "No, this cannot be! This is a bewitched pool to fool me like this." She splashed her hand into the pool, and the reflection disappeared. "Why did you make me look into it? Why are you tormenting me this way? Father was right. You must never talk like this again. I am who I am and that will not change."

She saw the truth. Why won't she believe it?

"No, Claire. What you saw in the pool is really you."

She turned to run, her hands motioning back in despair. "Stop it, Steward! Stop it at once! I am going home."

She ran away, leaving Steward to follow after her in silence. They never spoke of the pool again, but Steward knew the truth. He would no longer trust the image he saw in his Reflector. And somehow he would find out what was causing everyone's Reflectors to lie.

Thirteen

On the eighth day of Steward's stay, Abner announced that he needed to see the Light District. "You did not come to Marikonia to sit around the Abner Blacksmith Shop."

So they made plans to visit the center of town that afternoon.

It would be good to get away and see more of this strange land. Somewhere lay the secret behind the Reflectors, and the deception they reflected.

After a hearty lunch, Abner, Trek, Troy, and Steward set off for the main streets of Marikonia. The women did not go.

"Too much temptation," Abner said with a smile.

Marikonia was a city of contrasts. Most of the outlying areas were inhabited with simple houses and shops. People moved about without much fuss, but as you got near the center of town, things changed.

There were lights everywhere as well as the sounds of horse carriages, music, and shouting. The Light District was electric. The energy was incredible. Everywhere groups of people looked around, trying to see someone famous or powerful. Steward watched as a person with a small entourage emerged from a large building. People ran screaming after him, asking for autographs and clamoring to get closer.

Steward looked to Abner. "Who are these people?"

He pointed to another group surrounded by gawkers. "These are the beautiful people of Marikonia. They have power and wealth, and most everyone wants to be like them or at least near them."

Beautiful people? More beautiful than Claire? What do their Reflectors show?

"May I take a closer look?"

"Yes, surely. Go see for yourself."

Trek stepped in front of him. "I'll part the sea for you." He had no trouble clearing a path through the crowd.

Steward followed him and finally worked his way to get close enough to see a woman from the little elite group walk right by him. He watched amid the screaming crowd and blinked. Looked again. Then shook his head.

The woman was…plain.

He and Trek found their way back to Abner, but Steward was even more confused than before. "I don't think I understand. The woman I saw was nothing special. She was quite plain. Why is everyone so envious of her? She is certainly not as beautiful as Claire."

Abner stopped him short. "Now, Steward, I told you we will have no such talk as that. Don't be filling poor Claire's mind with fanciful talk and lies like that. The woman you are speaking of is famous for her beauty. I know you saw it. And my dear Claire is…well…so very homely. So, please, don't taunt her like this."

"You should have been at the pool!" Steward wanted to scream, but he held himself back. Instead, he fell into step beside Abner, seeking to understand. "Do you think that the image we see in our Reflectors shows us who we are, Abner, or does our *belief* in who we are cause us to see what we do in our Reflectors?" He eyed the brawny blacksmith, hoping he hadn't crossed a line.

Abner didn't answer right away. Trek and Troy just looked at each other and shrugged. Abner paused, then spoke. "When I was young, I used to see a quite handsome young man in my Reflector. I believed I was destined to live in the Light District and go on to fame and fortune."

Trek and Troy's eyes grew wide. Troy leaned in. "Father, you've never told us this before."

Abner returned a stern look. "And I never will again, do you understand? But young Steward here has the right to know the truth. Now sit and listen."

They both locked their eyes on their father.

"I made several trips here and began to make friends. I fit in, I was indeed worthy of this place, and my future looked bright."

Trek couldn't contain himself. "Father, what happened?"

"One day I was on my way to visit the Light District when a man joined me in my walk. He began to ask me questions about where I was going, and when I told him he laughed at me and nearly shouted that I was not the kind of person who should be seen in the Light District. I pulled out my Reflector to show it to him, but when he held it and pointed it back at me, I was not nearly as confident and handsome-looking as I had thought I was. I stopped and looked into it again and again. The Reflector does not lie. I was devastated, but I decided to continue on. I came across a second person, a young woman who was walking the same way I was. When she saw me, she began to laugh. I asked her what she was laughing at, and she said it was…"

Steward was stunned. Were those tears welling up in the blacksmith's eyes?

Abner tried to wipe them away without his sons noticing, but with little success. Trek and Troy sat motionless, as though not knowing what to do.

Abner regained his composure and continued. "She was laughing at me for thinking I was worthy of the Light District. She turned her Reflector toward me, and this time I was homelier than the last. In less than one hour, I had changed from attractive and strong to plain and broken. I might have given in to total despair if not for one of the Phaedra."

Steward straightened. The Phaedra? What did they have to do with this?

Abner looked down. "He was passing by and saw the whole thing transpire. I was miserable, but the Phaedra sat next to me and told me how important it was that we affirm who we are according to what we see in our Reflector. It is not up to us to judge but to accept our image and live accordingly. 'Not everyone can be a child of the king,' he said to me. That is what they used to call everyone who lived in the Light District—children of the king. And I was certainly not one of them."

Hearing the king mentioned gave Steward new hope.

"Why were they called children of the king?"

Abner looked at Steward. "There is a legend that the king once sent his own children here to populate this land. But after many generations they intermarried with commoners, and now there is a curse on the land. I…*we* are part of that curse." Abner's tone sharpened, and the words were barbed. "We are the people who dwell on the edge of town, forced to live out our lives according to the image that reflects how unworthy we are to be called children of the king."

Unworthy? Says who? The Phaedra. Again.

"So you never saw your original image again?"

For a moment Steward feared his question angered Abner, but the blacksmith finally just shook his head. "No, because it was a lie. I was never meant to see myself that way. The image I see now is the real Abner. So, you see, Steward, we must never doubt the Reflector. If we do, we just set ourselves up for heartache. That's why I am so protective of Claire. She has been taunted all her life, and her only hope is to accept who she is."

But it wasn't! It was all a lie. The reflections people saw were nothing more than the image they had already formed of themselves. Why couldn't they see that?

Steward thought for a moment then met his friend's eyes. "Would you mind if I asked you to go on ahead without me, Abner? I need to think things through on my own for a while."

"Of course."

As Abner and his sons walked away, Steward found a place where he could sit and watch the world fly by in the Light District—and turn things over in his head.

If he was right, it was each person's own self-perception that caused the corresponding image to appear in the Reflector. So a person's true image could be seen only if it was first believed, but it couldn't be believed if the Reflector kept producing a distorted image.

It was a cycle of distortion meant to ensure that no one would ever see who they really were.

What about me? Am I seeing a distortion or the truth?

Could he even tell the difference any longer?

"Good evening, young Steward."

He jumped. A Phaedra was sitting beside him.

Steward calmed himself. "Good evening, good Phaedra."

"What do you think of Marikonia?"

Steward hesitated. His trust in the Phaedra had all but vanished. He needed help, wisdom…but he dare not trust another Phaedra.

Be wary. Find out what you can, but be on guard.

"I am confused, good Phaedra. What people see in their Reflector is not the same thing I see in them when I look at them with my own eyes. I see confident, attractive people, but in their Reflectors they see homeliness and lowliness. And when I see plain, insecure people, their Reflectors show them beauty and confidence. Why are the Reflectors' images so different from reality?"

"What is reality, Steward? Perhaps the image you think you see in people is the illusion, and the Reflector is reality."

"Perhaps." But even as he said that, Steward doubted it.

The Phaedra looked at him. "And what about your own Reflector? What does it show you?"

"My own Reflector? It is horrible. I can't believe what I see."

The sudden sound of a screaming crowd made Steward spin to look behind him. A group pressed in around a young man dressed in fine clothes as he strolled from a hotel to a waiting carriage. How plain he was! There was nothing special about him at all. Yet people almost climbed over each other to get near him, and he walked with an air of arrogance, dismissing most of the signature-seekers and barking orders at doormen and drivers.

Steward pointed. "That's what I mean. That man is so plain, yet people see him as a star."

The Phaedra looked at Steward. "Would you like to know what it is like to be one of them?"

"A citizen of the Light District? Me? How is that even possible?"

"Give me your Reflector."

Steward fished the rectangular sheet of metal from its bag in his satchel and handed it to the Phaedra, who passed his hand over it then looked into it and smiled. He handed it to Steward.

"Tell me what you see."

Steward raised the Reflector—and stared into it. The image was as much of a distortion as the disfigured face he'd seen when he first looked into the mirror—only this time the distortion was beautiful. Staring back at him was a more handsome face than Steward had ever seen, and again it looked just enough like Steward that it was easy to believe it was his face. It was as if there were a painted image over the face of the Reflector, and Steward's own eyes and mouth appeared through the image, wearing it like a mask.

"What do you think?"

Steward looked at the Phaedra. "It's…it's amazing. I look incredible. How did…?" His question was interrupted by the sound of shrieks coming from a small group of people who had left the larger crowd. They came running to Steward.

"Who are you? You must be someone very famous. You're gorgeous!" one girl gushed.

Another begged, "Oh please, tell us who you are. And can we have an autograph?"

The Phaedra smiled and, before Steward could ask him how this happened, was gone. Steward was caught up in a sea of humanity, and the focus had shifted to him. The other "star" had just reached his carriage when he seemed to notice his fans were being pulled away by this new discovery. He called Steward to come over, and Steward made his way to him through the throng.

The man opened the door of his carriage and shouted, "Come quick and get in." Steward jumped in, and the man pushed in beside him and slammed the door. The driver took off, leaving the crowd as they pressed in on the carriage windows.

"Whew, it's a relief to get out of there. And who exactly are you?"

"My name is Steward. I am visiting Marikonia."

"I'm Tristin. Welcome to the Light District. It is the *only* place to live in this dreadful country. You must stay with me and tell me of your life. Driver, let's get home."

Tristin was a bit shorter than Steward, very slender and quite pale. It looked as if a stiff wind would knock him over. His cheeks were pointed and his lips were thin. He did not look healthy or handsome, and again Steward wondered what attracted the admiration from the adoring crowd now disappearing in their back window.

"Finally, we are free. So, Steward, what brings you to a place like Marikonia?"

How much should he say? How safe was this new companion?

Just be honest. Let's see where this goes.

"I am on a journey to see the king. I come from the land of Aiden Glenn, and I have been sent on this journey to learn the meaning of my name and my destiny."

"Sounds wonderful! A journey to see the king. How exciting! You must tell everyone. They will be so interested to hear your story."

"Everyone?"

"Yes, there's always a party going on in the Light District."

And indeed there was. The carriage turned in to the entrance of a palatial home, where music and voices rang from the windows and balconies. Steward followed Tristin from the carriage to be met by shouts of welcome and raised glasses from many strolling outside under the illuminated pole lights lighting the courtyard. Steward followed his host up the stairs and into the great entryway, where they left their coats and were handed glasses of wine.

Tristin raised his glass and swept his hand across the room. "Steward, welcome to my house. A bit humble, but suitable nonetheless."

He looked around. *This is anything but humble. This would fit right in in Petitzaros.*

Great chandeliers hung from the ceilings, and everywhere were ornate gold moldings, tapestries, marble, and statuary. As Steward observed the guests, he was no longer surprised to see that most were quite ordinary-looking and some were downright homely. Everything—the surroundings, the people—all had the feel of phoniness to it.

Tristin motioned to Steward. "Come meet everyone."

Steward was introduced around to dozens of the Light District's finest citizens. There were actors, artists, wealthy landowners, and garishly dressed women. There were political leaders, athletes, and religious leaders of all kinds. One by one, Steward looked at each as he was introduced.

What was so special about these people—and so ordinary about Abner and his family?

Then two peculiar things caught Steward's eye. The first was the presence of mirrors everywhere he looked. Enormous mirrors on the walls, ceilings, and backs of doors. You could not look in any direction without seeing your image. And that was the second thing Steward noticed. In the mirrors of Tristin's house, everyone's reflection was distorted in the same flattering way that his own had been after the Phaedra held his Reflector. Homely women looked ravishing, and silly-looking men appeared rugged and handsome. Steward caught a glimpse of his own reflection, and sure enough, his image was a distorted—albeit wonderful—version of his true self.

Or was it actually his true self?

As he pondered that for a moment, something else about the gathering hit him. Everywhere Steward looked…

There were Phaedra.

Dozens of them, perhaps hundreds. They emerged from the shadows and retreated so quick it was easy to miss them, but they were there in force. Every person in the room inclined at one time or another to listen to a Phaedra. Many stood and admired themselves in one of the mirrors. Laughter or a smile of deep admiration almost always followed the encounter.

The evening wore on, and Steward realized that Abner and Edith might be worrying about him. He made his way to Tristin, who was surrounded by women listening to him tell stories of his adventures. The intoxicating effect of the wine was making it hard to concentrate as Steward reached Tristin. Before Steward could speak, his host turned to him.

"Steward, there you are. I am boring these people with my silly stories, yet here you are on your noble quest to see some great king. Come and tell us about your adventures. Everyone, come and listen to our guest. He has a great tale to tell us."

Here? Now? My story? Dare I tell them?

He didn't even like these people. He'd wanted to tell them what they actually looked like, but he would be a good guest. Mother would expect as much from him.

Steward told the partygoers about Aiden Glenn, his house in Petitzaros, the daring escape from Ascendia, and the way the moor changed from bog to meadow. He left out any talk of Zedekai or Astrid or Dunston. They were too good to be mentioned in this place.

At every turn of his story, the listeners responded with sighs, gasps, and applause. When he finished, everyone gave out a great "hurrah," and many shook his hand and patted him on the back. He became aware of the time, realizing it was even later now. Steward got Tristin's attention away for a moment from two wrinkled old women.

"Tristin, I do thank you for such a wonderful party, but I must get word back to Abner the Blacksmith as to my whereabouts. I am staying with them, and they'll be worried about me. Can you help?"

One of the women snarled at Steward. "Abner the Blacksmith! Why are you staying with *them?* What a dreadful experience you must have had. Tristin, our young adventurer must stay here with you and not return to that disgusting place."

Tristin's face tightened in horror. "Yes, absolutely! You will be my guest here. Good heavens, why didn't you tell me you were being held against your will in that forsaken place? I will have the guestroom prepared for you at once."

"No, thank you, but that is not necessary. I rather like staying with them. I just need a carriage to take me there. Can you arrange that?"

"You'll do nothing of the sort!" the woman cried out. "No one from the Light District stays on the outskirts with the likes of Abner, his two horrible sons, or that mongrel daughter of theirs."

Steward's heart raced and his face grew red hot. How *dare* this woman say such a thing! Words escaped him before he could restrain them. "Good lady, I will have you know that Abner and Edith are kind and caring people. And, unlike you, with your leathery, wrinkled skin and bony nose, and unlike the rest of these fake and phony so-called beautiful people, Claire is the most beautiful woman I have seen in all of Marikonia."

A collective gasp shot across the room.

Then absolute silence.

Tristin's eyes were the size of Edith's dinner plates as he stared at Steward. Phaedra all around the room moved close to the assembled people and whispered in their ears. The awkwardness of the moment was broken by the sneering voice of the woman in front of Steward. She enunciated each word with a venomous tone. "You, my dear stupid young boy, are an imposter. You do not belong here. We have been having sport with you, and you are too naive to see it. Have you not seen your image in Tristin's mirrors tonight?"

Steward was indignant. Of course he had.

"Yes, I have seen it. What of it? My image is just as distorted as yours. You see a beautiful woman, but you're an old hag. It is a trick, an illusion to make you all think you are something special when you are not."

He should stop, but for some reason his inhibitions were gone and his anger overtook him. He spoke loud enough for everyone to hear. "It is an illusion you use to justify your own arrogance, and you lord it over others. What gives you the right to think you are better than everyone else…better than Abner and Edith and Claire? You are the fakes, the deluded, and the stupid. You cannot even see who you really are. Well, I will tell you. You are ordinary and plain and not at all worthy of the Light District!"

People began booing him, but the woman in front of him was unfazed. When Steward finished, she turned to him like a lioness ready to pounce on its prey. "Perhaps you need to take *another* look at yourself. You seem to be quite sure of what is beautiful and what is not, what is good and true and what is false. So tell us—tell us all who you see, young Steward. Take a very good look."

At her words, the crowd parted in front of Steward, allowing him to look right into the large mirror at the end of the room.

As his gaze met the mirror's surface, he was staggered by the image that shot back at him. Gone was the handsome face he had seen just moments ago, and in its place was an even more hideous image than the one he had struggled to explain since he arrived in Marikonia.

As he stared, somewhere in the room someone began to laugh. As more and more people joined in the laughter, everyone assembled produced their own Reflectors and pointed them at Steward. In each one, he saw the hideous reflection. Everywhere he turned, Reflectors were thrust in front of him so that he could not escape the image.

Steward cried out in anguish as the laughter grew louder and louder. Even Tristin joined in, looking delighted at his suffering. Steward ran out of the house with the sounds of laughter still ringing from the windows. He ran into the courtyard and down past the entrance gate of Tristin's house. He ran through the streets of Marikonia until he came to the place where he had left Abner and his sons.

His head was swirling and his heart racing. Exhausted and overcome, he collapsed under the great elm tree in the town square.

Early the next morning, something scurried across Steward's chest, waking him. His head pounded as he stood to orient himself. He splashed water on his face in the fountain at the center of the square, and then he ambled in the direction of Abner's house.

How good it would be to be back with those dear people.

The pain of the previous night returned to haunt him as he walked. He felt for the Reflector in his satchel—which image would he see?—but he was too exhausted, his emotions too worn, to look.

After two hours of walking, Steward arrived at Abner's house. He stopped in the driveway. Something was wrong. He could sense it. There were no sounds from the blacksmith shop. As he approached the front door of the house, Abner met him. His face was stern and his eyes red.

"Is Claire with you? Have you seen her?" Abner's voice echoed his anxiety.

Claire! What's happened?

"No, I haven't seen her since we left yesterday."

Steward entered the house. Inside, he saw Edith crying in Trek's arms. Troy stood by, an empty look on his face.

Steward knelt at her side. "What's wrong? Where is Claire?"

"We don't know. No one has seen her since you left for the Light District. And where have *you* been? We hoped she was with you."

"I'm sorry. I tried to get word to you. I fell asleep under the great elm in the town square. Have you looked in the meadow or up at the hillcrest? She loves it there—"

"Of *course* we have," Troy snapped. "We've looked everywhere!"

Abner picked up a brown envelope and handed it to Steward. "When we found this, we thought maybe she had run away and you would know where to find her."

The envelope had his name written across the front. Steward opened it and unfolded the letter inside. It was written in Claire's graceful handwriting. Steward read it silently to himself, his lips mouthing the words. As he absorbed the final lines, he looked up, crumpled the letter in his clenched fist, and ran from the house.

He ran with all his might past the berry fields and along a small path in the woods. "Claire! Claire!" He rounded the final corner that led to the pool. As it came into view, he stopped dead. His mouth gaped open and his heart broke.

"Claire!"

He plunged into the pool to retrieve the lifeless body floating face-down.

As he pulled Claire's body to shore, Trek and Troy arrived, and both stood frozen on the bank. Steward turned Claire's face toward him as he sat on the ground at the edge of the pool. He held her tight to his chest and sobbed. Abner arrived a moment later and sank to his knees, and the cry he let loose was that of a father's despair. He then rose and caught Edith in his arms as she arrived. Together, they came to Steward and took their daughter into their arms, losing themselves in their grief.

Steward rose and stumbled away from the scene. He walked down the path, tears streaming down his cheeks. Then he started to run. He ran past the Abner's Blacksmith Shop and back into the woods from which he had emerged a fortnight ago. He found the place where his path continued past Marikonia, and he fell to the ground and sobbed.

He collected himself and found the courage to open the envelope again. He smoothed out the letter and read it one more time.

Dear Steward,

I have been thinking a lot about your words to me and the image I saw in the pool. I want to believe that I am as beautiful as the face I saw when you were with me. However, everywhere else I look tells me I am wrong. I see only homeliness and plainness in the Reflectors of my family, my friends, and in my own Reflector. Surely, they are right. But the image I saw in the pool haunts me. And so I will return today to look into it once again. If I see only beauty, I know that I do not wish to live, knowing that I can never be who I see and believe that I am. Therefore, I will choose to have the image in the pool be the last image I see of myself, rather than live the remainder of my life with the image I see from others. And so, dear Steward, your gift to me is a peaceful death, and for that I am forever grateful.

Claire

"Why, Claire? Why didn't you wait? Why didn't you let us talk about this? Why..." Steward let the paper drop from his hands, and as he did so he also let go of his journey.

He was through.

All he could think of was finding his way back to Aiden Glenn.

~~~~~~~~~~

Alex laid the book down. He looked at Anna. She sat silent in the great stuffed chair, seeming lost in her thoughts.

How would she get through this? How would any of them?

Alex walked over and sat next to her, slipping his arm around her. "Are you all right?"

She nodded and wiped away some tears. "Mom always told me that she prayed I would someday see myself as she saw me. I wish I could have seen that image while she was still alive."

Merideth came and knelt beside her. "I think the message here is to be sure you see it now, while there is still time."

Merideth? Compassionate? Where did that come from?

Anna managed a smile.

Alex pressed in. "I wonder what exactly we are supposed to see? More than we should? Distorted images that deceive us into thinking we are better than we are? I understand Steward's confusion. Who knows what image is the right one?"

Reed rubbed his hands as he spoke. "I know for a long time I refused to let anyone shape my own self-image."

Alex looked at his brother and raised an eyebrow.

Really, brother?

Reed shrugged. "Okay, at least I thought I did. Now as I get older, I am realizing how hard that is. We're so influenced by what others think of us. It's almost impossible to be true to ourselves."

Merideth had disappeared for a moment and came back in the room with some Kleenex for Anna. "Maybe the message here is to find a reliable source for the image we see. Find a Reflector that tells the truth, if there is such a thing."

"Thanks, Mer." Anna took the tissue and wiped her cheeks. "And if there is such a reliable source, perhaps Steward will find it for us."

Alex looked back at Walter. "What do you think, Walter? What did Dad have in mind with these Reflectors?"

Walter stood and came into the center of the room to join them. "To be honest, I never read the chapter on Marikonia. Sam never showed it to me. He always referred to it as *still in process*."

Alex turned to face him. "That's curious. Why don't you think he let you see it?"

Walter smiled. "I think I know exactly why. For years I struggled with self-doubt and a poor self-image. Here I was with a lucrative law practice and all the outward appearances of success. It was a facade, mostly. I was hiding so much self-doubt. I learned the hard way that outward success doesn't equal inner peace. In your father's terms, I never liked the person I saw in my Reflector every morning. Sam and I had talked and prayed about it for years. And now…"

He paused and pursed his lips.

Anna walked to him and gave him a hug. "It's okay, Walter. Looks like we're all in this together."

He managed a smile. "It appears my dear friend has left me plenty to think about in this book that was supposed to be for his children."

Alex glanced at Merideth. Were those tears? He put a hand on her arm. "I'm not in much better shape, Reed. Can you take this one for us?"

Merideth nodded her appreciation, and Reed moved over in front of the book that now lay more than half-open on the coffee table.

Everyone shifted around to find a comfortable position for the final chapter of the night.

CHAPTER

ourteen

"Steward."

He turned at the distant, unfamiliar voice that called his name. "Who's there? Phaedra? Abner? Zedekai?"

Nothing.

Steward trudged on. For hours he'd plodded down the road leading back to Aiden Glenn. Words of doubt echoed in his mind. It was as if a Phaedra were whispering right in his ear.

"You have done your best. It is no shame in going home. The king asked too much of you, of anyone. Look at all you have given up for this journey. You deserved better. Go home, Steward, and forget about this journey."

Happy to oblige.

Gone were his hopes and desires to meet the king. It was never going to happen. Why did he even start this journey?

I don't care how disappointed Mom and Dad will be. I'm through. I can't go on. There is nothing for me here.

It was all he could do to put one foot in front of the other, and only the thought of collapsing into his own bed after so many years away kept him pressing on.

"Steward."

The same voice, but this time louder, stronger.

He shook his head. "Don't play with me! Tell me who you are, what you want."

Again, nothing.

I am losing my mind. It's like the deceptions at Pitcairn Moor. It's just the wind.

He'd listened to enough voices and been proven a fool. The Phaedra had fooled him. Had Zedekai? Dunston?

Heartbroken. Confused. Exhausted.

Listen to your heart, Steward. It wants to go home. Mother is waiting for me. I'm going home where I can be at peace.

"Steward."

Steward stopped and listened, craning his neck toward the voice. Oh, how he wished it were Astrid—but this was a deep and commanding male voice.

He turned back, listening.

"Follow my voice, Steward. Follow my voice."

Steward took one step in the direction of the voice, which led him back down the path from where he had come. As if out of nowhere, there were other voices. Familiar and unwelcome voices. Urgent, pressing, pleading with him, almost shouting at him.

"No, Steward, turn around. It is the voice of deception."

"Go home, Steward. Your journey is over."

"The king does not want to see you."

"The king does not care about you."

"The king has given up on you."

"You cannot trust the king."

"Go home, Steward. Go home now!"

He put his hands over his ears. "Stop! I don't know who you are. I don't know what to do."

Then the powerful voice rang out once more.

"Be *still!* Leave him alone."

All the other voices stopped. All but the distant caller.

"Steward, follow my voice."

Something in that voice lifted Steward's despair and strengthened his spirit. Despite his exhaustion, he walked toward it. It led him off the path and through a thick stand of willows and thistles. The stickers poked through his clothes, and the willows snapped in his face. But he continued.

The voice led him across an open plain and up to the face of a very steep mountain.

What now? Was this another deception?

"I cannot climb this. This is too much to ask."

"Steward, follow my voice."

He leaned against the cliff face and cried out. "I'm exhausted! My strength is gone."

"Trust me, Steward."

There was an unmistakable power in those words. They resonated deep within him. "I will. I will try."

Steward fixed the satchel and Quash close to his side and began scaling the mountain. Every time he lost faith or sensed fear, the voice came again.

"Steward, follow my voice. Trust me."

On and on he climbed. His hands bled from the shale rocks and pine needles as he worked his way through steep, forested hills and up rock faces. His energy was almost depleted, but the voice grew louder with each footstep. He dared not falter. He looked up ahead and saw the sheer face of the mountain open into a cleft that offered shelter and a place to rest.

I can make it that far. C'mon, Steward. Dig deep.

He pushed with the last bit of strength to crest the ridge and go through a small opening at the entrance to the cleft, onto level ground. He collapsed, lying in the dirt, sweating and panting.

"I...I can go no farther. I am spent. Whoever you are, don't ask me to continue. I cannot. I cannot."

The voice spoke again. Only this time, it was square in front of him. Steward sat up with a start and looked around.

No one.

It is my mind. I have climbed all this way for an illusion. Wind through the trees.

Wait. He looked again. On a flat-topped rock, across from the little opening, Steward saw a small object gleaming in the sunlight, sending off rays of light in every direction. He pushed to his feet. Every muscle in his body protested, but with careful, deliberate steps he moved toward the strange object.

The voice came again—from the object in front of him. "Steward, you have heeded my voice. Your journey has not been in vain."

"Who...who are you?"

"Steward, I am your king."

Was this some trick? One more illusion? There was no king here, just this device that produced a strange voice. Had he come all this way for this?

"Forgive me, but I see no king."

"Steward, listen to my voice. It is the voice of your king. You have sought me since you crested Callater Pass. I have been waiting for you and watching over you. I sent you Zedekai when you were lost in Petitzaros. I sent you Astrid when you were being led to the crushing machines of Ascendia. I sent you the Interpreter when your path was lost in Pitcairn Moor. And now I call to you with my own voice."

Could this be true? The king, speaking to him? Why here? Why not in person? Desperate hope mixed with confusion and doubt.

"If it's you, why can't I see you? This is not the great throne room."

Am I really asking this? If this is the king, who am I…

"For now, it is enough for you to hear my voice. But I am waiting for you. Do not give up hope. Your journey is not yet complete. Come to me, Steward."

He wanted to come. With every ounce of his being he wanted to kneel before the king. To end the journey. To have everything make sense. And to go home. But the king was not here!

"But where are you? How do I get there?"

"Pick up the Transmitter."

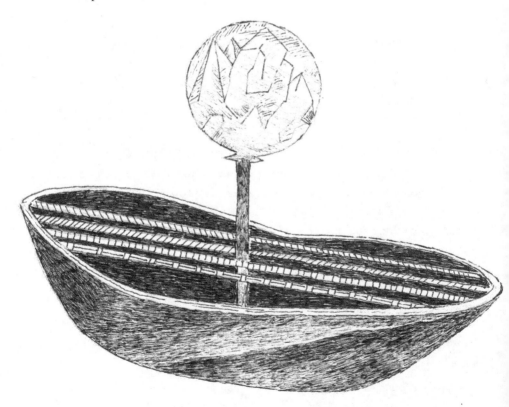

Steward picked up the device and examined it. It appeared to be a small bowl shaped like a boat. Stretched along the rim from one pointed end to the other were four golden strands made of some unusual material. Steward let his finger just rest on them.

Metal? Wound horsehair? I don't know this material.

From the inside bottom of the vessel, between the second and third strands, right in the middle of it, there emerged an arm much like a mast. Atop the arm was a round glass-like object that swiveled in all directions. It was beautiful, crafted with exquisite precision, and calibrated for whatever purpose it was intended.

With a gentle push, Steward moved the arm. "What is this vessel? What is its purpose?"

From out of the vessel the booming voice spoke. Steward was so startled that he almost dropped it.

"With this device, you will always be able to hear my voice. I will speak to you and guide you, and you will always know where you need to go and what you need to do."

It was the king, speaking to him, right to him. He was so close. If only Mom and Dad could be here, listening to their king. His shoulders lifted and air filled his lungs, giving him strength.

"Will you guide me to your palace?"

"Yes, just follow my voice. But you must leave this Transmitter here. Go to the City of Seudomartus. It is the last land you must visit before you come to me. Look for the Transmitter there, and when you find it I will speak. Follow my voice. I will lead you to me."

No, please, not another city. Not more trouble and pain.

"Why can't I keep this one? And how will I find such a small thing in such a large city?"

Why? I'm so close. Why can't my journey end now? Here?

"You must trust me, Steward. This is part of your journey. In Seudomartus, find the five wisest and most religious people in the city and ask them to show you the Transmitter. Go now, Steward. You will see me soon, and I will tell you the true meaning of your name and the purpose of your life."

The Transmitter went silent.

The king's last words calmed him. One more step. One more land, then the throne room.

He was going to see the king.

It was real. All of it. Zedekai, Astrid, Dunston, the castles of Petitzaros, the ramps of Ascendia, the Reflectors of Marikonia...and Claire. All part of my journey.

And now it would end with his last stop in Seudomartus.

His strength and courage returned. He scaled his way down the rock face and soon was in the valley below, where he picked up the trail to Seudomartus.

The five wisest and most religious people in the city. How will I find them?

As the evening robbed the sky of its last light, Steward made camp for the night. He drifted off to sleep. The voices of the Phaedra were gone now. What remained in his spirit was the painful memory of Claire's lifeless body, and the hope of seeing Astrid again. Even they were silenced by another voice that played in his mind. He listened to it over and over again.

"Trust me."

Deep in the blackness of the *Tohu Wa-Bohu*, the assembly of hooded figures considered the scene that played out before them.

The lead Phaedra stood above the rest, and his voice crackled with menacing authority.

"The king is a fool. He had Steward in his very presence, and he let him go. That gives us the chance we need to stop this nonsense once and for all."

A second Phaedra stood. "Seudomartus was our most strategic victory, and it is the place of our greatest strength. His confusion and doubt will return there. Only this time, when he is most vulnerable, we must end it."

The leader nodded. "Yes, we must end it there. And we will use the place that is closest to the king's very throne room to exact on him his greatest defeat."

He looked at the assembled figures and pointed toward them. "Let nothing hinder us from this victory! The future of the kingdom depends upon it."

In a moment they were gone, each making his way to his assigned position inside the walls of Seudomartus.

By midmorning the following day, Steward was standing on the outskirts of the great city of Seudomartus. He walked through its impressive gates, much grander than those of Petitzaros or Ascendia. This city was famous throughout the land for its Halls of Wisdom and the Sacred Mount.

I read about this place in school, but I thought it was a fable.

Now here it was, rising up in front of him.

Straight ahead was the majestic assembly hall. According to legend, the wisest men and women in the kingdom gathered there to discuss important issues and make decisions that influenced everything that happened throughout the land.

His eyes grew wide. Was he really standing in this place?

To his right, high atop a hill, was the Sacred Mount.

It's real. The mount, the cathedrals. It's all real.

Cathedrals and temples with massive spires and immense stained-glass windows towered all around him.

The grandest religious buildings in the entire world.

The wisest religious thinkers in the kingdom came here to teach and study.

He must find a way to see it before he left. For now, he needed to find the Transmitter.

He stopped. But how was he to find the five wisest and most religious people in the city? He looked all around. Whom could he ask to help him find these people?

The king has always prepared helpers for me. I will trust in that help again.

A strange new emotion welled up inside him. Could it be…*courage?*

Shouts rang out behind him. "No, you are wrong, Matthew. Truth cannot be limited to one sphere of knowledge or even one divine teaching."

"Of course it can, and it must, dear Obed. How else can truth be preserved and taught and followed?"

Steward halted, turning to see five people seated around a café table talking. Arguing, actually.

He drew close to eavesdrop, but he was soon discovered.

"We have a guest among us." A young woman smiled at him and gestured. "Perhaps you can enlighten us, good sir. We were just discussing the idea that all created things are either good or evil, and yet there is no such thing as all good or all evil. So what is the composition of, say, that satchel you are carrying?"

Steward hesitated.

How do I get out of this? Think, Steward. Say something.

"Well, when it is full of bread and wine, it certainly produces good things. But when it is too heavy on a hot day, it certainly feels like evil to my aching back."

There was a moment of silence, and then the whole assembly burst into laughter and applause.

"Well said, young traveler, well said!"

They invited Steward to join them, and he was happy to rest his tired legs. They introduced themselves and went back to their conversation. As he listened, Steward studied the participants.

There was the student from one of the cathedrals on the Sacred Mount; the two sisters from a wealthy family whose father spoke often in the Halls of Wisdom; an itinerant Teacher named Obed whose reputation was well known and admired; a poet; and a shopkeeper.

At one point when the discussion became quite complex, the shopkeeper leaned over and whispered to Steward. "I'm here to keep their heads level."

He and Steward enjoyed a brief laugh.

The day went on, and after lunch the subject turned to knowledge.

The student took the lead. "I do not believe that we can know anything for certain. For where is the true source of knowledge? Can any of us say that we have heard straight from the king?" Everyone smiled and chuckled at the idea.

"Why, yes, I have." Steward couldn't believe he'd said that!

"My dear friends, we have a prophet among us," roared the poet. "And what did the king say to you, oh most honored one?"

Despite their mocking, he was in this far, so he might as well continue. "He told me to come to Seudomartus and find the five wisest and most religious people of the city to ask the whereabouts of the Transmitter. The king will use it to speak to me and show me the way to his palace."

Silence, then laughter. Mocking again.

One of the sisters leaned toward him. "Come now, young Steward. Do you really expect us to believe that you have seen a Transmitter and spoken directly to the king?"

There was nothing left to lose. If he was to be the whipping boy, so be it.

"I don't care what you believe. It's true."

And there it was again, courage...*and confidence.*

The other sister jumped in. "Careful now, or you will be mistaken for one of the Starr Hill fanatics."

Steward's eyes narrowed. "I...don't understand. Who?"

She continued. "There is a small group of narrow-minded fanatics who believe that the king still talks to people, like in the story you just made up. They claim to have a direct line to him, and they gather under cover of dark up on Starr Hill to chant and wail and listen for the king's voice. It's quite amusing."

The student slapped his hand on the table. "It's embarrassing, in this day and age. They are all fools!"

Obed leaned forward, speaking in a lower tone. "And you run the risk of being numbered with them if you keep on with your stories about Transmitters and strange voices. So guard what you say."

"And to whom you say it," the second sister continued in a half-whisper. "It is dangerous to be counted among the Starr Hill fanatics. Many wish them harm."

Obed raised his glass. His lighthearted tone returned. "Enough of this. Let us have no more talk of heretics and old fables. The afternoon is upon us, and we must make for the Halls to hear the day's debate. Steward, will you join us?"

What? Him? Now? He wasn't ready.

"The Halls of Wisdom? I don't think so, not like this." He held out his dirty tunic. "May I inquire about a place to stay and bathe?"

Obed picked up his satchel and rose from his seat. "My place, and there will be no discussion. You will be my guest. Here are the keys. It is the mustard-colored house on the corner, just three blocks down. Take your satchel and rest there, and I will come for you just before dinner."

Deep relief poured over him. He knew he was to face much here in Seudomartus, but he needed rest and time to think.

"Thank you so much. That is most gracious."

The small band was off for the Halls, their energetic chatting continuing on until they disappeared out of sight.

Steward gathered his things and headed for the teacher's house. But soon he was not alone. A man began walking beside him, far too close for it to be a chance meeting.

"Keep walking and don't look at me." The man spoke while looking straight ahead. "I overheard your conversation with the others. I am a member of the Starr Hill Faithful. If you want to hear the voice of the king, I must take you to meet our teacher. He will help you, I promise."

Before Steward could reply, or even look at him, people on the street called out to the man with him.

"I know you. You're one of those loonies. What are you doing here? Go back to your hill and stay out of here."

"Go back and crawl under the rock you came from," another shouted.

The yelling grew louder. "You hate-mongers are not welcome here. Go away and stay away."

A rock flew through the air, just missing Steward's head.

The man turned and ran up a narrow street. Steward froze. Should he follow him?

Another voice yelled. "Hey, are you one of them? You were with him, talking to him, and I haven't seen you around here before."

"No!" Steward ducked as the man hurled the stone toward him. He lifted his hands up toward the crowd. "No! I am new here in Seudomartus. I am staying in the house of Obed the Teacher."

The name of the Teacher calmed the crowd. The man who'd thrown the rock walked to Steward and snarled beneath his breath, "You best stay clear of any of the Starr Hill crowd. They're a menace."

Steward tried to collect himself and made his way straight to Obed's house.

Who were these Starr Hill people? And what did the man mean by saying he could help Steward find a Transmitter? That was supposed to come from the five wisest and most religious people in the city, not some fanatic.

That's not the way to go. I'll stay clear of them.

Later that evening, Steward enjoyed dinner and an animated discussion with a new set of Obed's friends. After the group dispersed, Steward and Obed sat and talked.

Obed paced as he talked. "So you say you are to meet the five wisest and most religious people in Seudomartus? That will not be easy."

Steward sighed. "I know. There must be so many."

The Teacher smiled. "Oh no, young Steward, it is not that. I can tell you right now who they are. Everyone knows the five wisest and most religious people in the city. It will be gaining an audience with them that will be the challenge."

"You know who they are?" This might be easier than he expected.

"Of course. There is Melodora, the keeper of the Archives. She will be the easiest to find. Then there is Mattox the Wise, chief elder of the great Cathedral. He is elusive but may be intrigued by your journey. There is also Hambry the Pious from the Temple of Temperance. You can see that Temple from anywhere in Seudomartus. He will be more reticent, but I think we can get you in to see him. Then it gets harder." Obed's pace quickened, and he talked as if he were drawing up a plan for a great battle.

"There is Nagas the Skeptic. He won't be lured by any talk of the king or your journey. He sees all things as purely material and practical. He will give you little of his time and none of his patience, of which he has little to start with."

"But he will see me?" He had to!

Obed thought for a moment, then nodded. "He might. But then we come to the last and most difficult—Philanthra. If she agrees to see you, she will test you to your limit."

His limit? What did that mean? Physical? Intellectual? Emotional? He'd been to the end of most of those already on this journey.

"What...what do you mean?"

Obed pulled up a chair and sat next to Steward. His eyes were fixed on him. "If she sees you, it will be on her terms. And she will not give you leave until she has made her point. Do you understand what you will be facing, my young friend?"

He didn't. And he wasn't sure he wanted to.

"No. I mean, I'm not sure. I just need to ask each of them about the Transmitter. That is what I was told…"

"I know, I know, by some voice that you thought was the king's." Obed drew close to Steward, speaking now in an urgent voice.

"Steward, you are putting yourself in great danger by asking such questions of these five people. Are you sure you want to go on with this? Think it through carefully. There's a great risk in this for you."

"Trust me, Steward."

The memory of the words of the king's voice echoed through him. He looked up at the worried expression on the Teacher's face. "Yes, I am quite sure."

Obed sighed. "Very well then. Tomorrow we begin."

⁓⁓⁓⁓⁓⁓⁓⁓⁓

Walter watched and listened as the four agreed to end the reading for the night.

Reed closed the book and got up to leave. "I think we'll find Steward right where we left him in the morning. I'm up for a long rest."

Walter rose from his chair and began gathering his things. "I agree. We have a good way to go, and we need to be rested to finish this journey."

After they left, he turned off the lights, leaving one lamp burning as he paused to look around the room. He glanced out, making sure everyone was out of earshot, then, as if Sam were standing beside him, he whispered into the dimness. "I know what it means to you to see all four of them back here in your home again. They know, Sam. They know they have all missed a great deal of joy that this place could have provided when you and Lori were here. This is such a special place, and I can begin to sense that somewhere, somehow, in Steward's journey they're finding their own. Be at peace, Sam, your prayers are being answered."

He turned to the door and disappeared through it into the night.

Fifteen

Reed woke early and made his way down the staircase to the kitchen, following the aroma of fresh brewed coffee. He stopped to look out at the morning landscape. The drizzle of Saturday had given way to a glorious winter Sunday morning. He entered the kitchen and saw a cup had already been poured. He stirred in some cream and went searching for the early riser. On a couch, looking out at the back lawn, he found Merideth curled up under her favorite lap blanket. She had both hands wrapped around a large green coffee mug.

"Good morning, Mer."

"Good morning. You're up early too. I heard you stirring so I set out a cup for you."

Reed lifted his cup. "Got it, thanks. Trouble sleeping?"

"Yes, a little."

He took a seat next to her.

She gave a wry grin. "It's not the excitement over the money, if that is what you're thinking."

"Wow, where did that come from?" He wouldn't tell her, but the thought of the inheritance had kept him awake.

She looked down and sighed. "I'm sorry. That sounded nasty. I'm just having a hard time with a lot of this."

They sipped coffee and stared out the window. It was nice to be together like this. He couldn't remember the last time they had been.

Merideth looked around the room. "You know, I loved this old house. I guess I never let Mom and Dad know that, but I did. I used to sneak down here on Sunday mornings and curl up right here. I could hear Dad upstairs getting ready for church. He was always

155

singing some old hymn. Mom would be in the kitchen making cinnamon rolls." She paused then put her hand on his arm. "You know, Reed, the smell of her baking and Dad's quiet singing was one of my favorite moments of the week. It made me feel so…secure, so warm and settled." She took her hand back and rubbed her neck. "And now I am back here, sitting in the same place, but there's no one singing upstairs, and the kitchen is so quiet…"

Merideth closed her eyes and bit her lip. Reed put his arm around her, holding her close.

"I know. You can't look at a chair, hear a door creak, or smell a familiar scent in here without a memory right behind it. And too many were filled with my own brand of rebellion." He glanced at the picture of Sam holding a stringer of fish, alone. "Dad wanted to teach me to fish. He tried everything to get me to like it." Reed walked to the picture and examined it. "You know, Mer, I think he just wanted to be with me, but somehow I always pushed him away."

Something caught his eye. "Oh, my gosh." Reed laid the picture down and walked across the room. Resting in the corner was an old cane-shafted seven-iron. Reed picked it up with care, even reverence. He placed his hands on the grip and eased it back and forth.

"Dad's seven-iron. It's the first club he taught me to swing. We'd practice in the yard, digging up big chunks of grass. Mom got so mad at us." Reed laughed and kept moving the club back and forth.

Dad, I wish you were here. How I'd love to have you teach me that swing again.

Merideth watched him. "This house…it's so full of things that brought Mom and Dad such happiness."

Reed held the club up in front of him. "Too bad we weren't more a part of that, huh?"

"C'mon, Reed. We were who we were. We are who we are. I don't think they wanted us to apologize for being true to ourselves. Do you?"

He continued chipping imaginary golf balls. "No, I guess not. But, Mer…" He stopped and looked at her. "Do you ever wish you had made different choices? I mean, what if their life—you know, simplicity, generosity, service—what if they were right? What if that's really where you find happiness? Is that so strange?"

Merideth stood and walked over to the book that lay closed on the table. She rubbed her hand on the cover. "Strange? No. But it's totally foreign to my way of thinking. Still, being here, listening to Dad's story, wrestling with Cassandra and her ramp building… it's unsettling." She pulled back and walked over to Reed. "Maybe there's a compromise. Maybe we can pull back a little, slow down, and broaden our definition of success. I don't know. Like I said, I'm having trouble with all of this."

"There you are! I thought I might find you here." Alex came in, speaking to Merideth. Apparently, he hadn't noticed Reed where he stood across the room.

Merideth looked up at Alex. "Why did you expect to find me here?"

"It's Sunday morning. This was your favorite place to be, wasn't it?"

Merideth grinned. "Now how did you know that? I always thought that I snuck down here with nobody noticing it."

Alex chuckled. "Merideth, not much happened here that escaped Mom and Dad's notice. On Sundays Mom always left the lap blanket right there for you, and Dad always sang a hymn he knew you liked. They told me once that even though you were in a different room, they looked forward to this Sunday morning ritual all week."

Reed studied Merideth's face from across the room. Her eyes grew wide and soft.

"I...I can't believe it. I thought I was so clever."

"Nope." Alex came to her and took her arm. "And, Mer, when they sensed you were drifting away from them, they told me it made them feel close to you—Dad singing hymns for you and Mom working in the kitchen, knowing you were sitting in the next room enjoying being there."

Merideth sat back in her chair and pulled the comforter over her. She put her fingers to her lips and tears flowed. Reed started toward her, and Alex finally noticed him.

"So you found Dad's seven-iron?"

"You mean *my* seven-iron."

Alex recoiled. "Yours? What do you mean?"

Reed shook his head.

This will be painful, but it's a day for that.

"I guess you don't remember, or maybe you never knew."

Merideth collected herself. "Knew what, Reed?"

"In my senior year of high school, Dad took me out to the driving range one day. We hit a bucket of balls. I used this seven-iron and hit some great shots. When we were done, Dad handed it to me and said it was mine. I couldn't believe it. It was Dad's prized club, and he just handed it to me."

"So why is it still here?" Merideth asked.

Reed tried to respond, but his voice broke. He set the club back in its place in the corner of the room. He drew a deep breath and looked at them. "When I went away to college, I wanted to leave all of this behind. So I left the club on the back lawn. Dad found it there after I left."

Reed plopped down on the sofa, shaking his head. "It probably broke his heart."

Anna entered the room, a steaming cup of coffee in her hands. She took one look at them and frowned. "Why is everyone so glum? Hey, Reed, are you okay?"

No…no, he wasn't. But he couldn't say anything. He got up and walked past her, squeezing her shoulder as he left the room.

Alex came to give Anna a hug. "Don't mind Reed, sis. It seems this house is filled with reminders of what we've lost."

Anna kept watching where Reed left the room. "Yeah, I feel that too." Then she turned back and saw her sister. "At least Merideth found her Sunday morning chair."

Merideth threw her hands into the air. "Did everyone know about this?"

Anna laughed. "No, just Mom and Dad and Alex and me. I used to sneak into the kitchen and join Mom as she baked. We would use potholders to push the scent of the cinnamon rolls toward the door to make sure you got a good smell. Sometimes we started laughing and had to hold dishtowels over our mouths to keep you from hearing. It was my little part of the Sunday morning ritual."

Merideth gave her a warm smile. "You little sneak."

"There's more." Anna put one hand in the air and turned away. "But perhaps I shouldn't say anything."

Merideth stood and came to her. "No, please, Anna, I want to know."

Anna paused for a moment, then she sat down on the couch and motioned for Merideth to join her. "After Mom died, I used to come over on Sunday mornings and fix Dad breakfast, and we would just sit and talk. The house was so quiet. One Sunday I came in and looked all over the place for him. I finally found Dad sitting there in your Sunday place, under that quilt, staring out the window. I asked him what he was doing, and he said… he said…" She looked at Merideth through tears streaming down her face. "He just wanted to feel close to you again…and, and he was afraid that this was as close as he might ever get."

Anna tried to continue. "He loved you so much, Mer."

"Oh, Anna." Merideth hugged her.

Alex wiped his eyes. He had no idea this weekend would unfold like this.

Learn Dad's secret and be back to Seattle by Saturday evening. I wasn't ready for this. I'm still not. Too many pages left. Too many emotions to deal with. I can't hide anymore. None of us can. Where will this all end up? And Reed…?

Alex left his sisters to themselves and went to find Reed. He found him staring out the front windows onto the snow-covered lawn that led to the street. Alex put his hand on Reed's shoulder. "We all have painful memories of things we said and did here. Don't be too hard on yourself."

Reed was quiet for a moment. "Alex, why did we all give so little back to Mom and Dad when they gave us so much? Why did we act that way? We missed so much, and we can't go back. I can't sit with Dad in his study and talk baseball. I can't help Mom plant her petunias in the front bed and laugh at the memories of me picking and eating them when I was two. Those were such important moments." He turned and stared at his brother, his eyes filled with grief. "But they're so few, so distant. I'd give anything to go back, but that chance is gone." He walked over to a family picture hung just off-center on the wall. "And so are they."

Alex joined him at the picture. "I don't know, brother. Maybe we never understood Dad's commitment to the poor or Mom's love of simple things. I used to get angry when they wouldn't buy something I knew they could afford and would enjoy. I remember I even yelled at them once, 'If you want it, buy it!' Mom just smiled and said, 'But I don't need it, and others can use the money more than we can.'"

"Ouch."

"Yeah." Alex grimaced. "Ouch indeed. But even then I didn't understand. I mean, they sacrificed everything to send me to seminary, and when I dropped out Dad should have disowned me. He was hugely disappointed, but he still would write and encourage me in my business ventures. Sometimes I just wanted him to scream at me and throw something at me."

"Well, actually, Alex, he did."

Alex looked at his brother. "Did what? What are you talking about?"

"Dad. He did scream and throw something."

Dad threw something, in anger?

"What? When?"

"C'mere." Reed led them into their dad's study. He leaned against the mantel of the fireplace and continued. "The day he read your letter, when you told him you were dropping out, I was upstairs and heard yelling. I looked down from the top of the stairs and heard Dad and Walter talking. Walter was trying to calm Dad down, but Dad was like I'd never seen him before. He was pacing and yelling, and just as I got to a place where I could see them both, Dad picked up his Redeemer Theological Seminary paperweight and threw it across the room. It hit the corner of the fireplace mantel. He just stood there looking at the chipped mantel and the cracked paperweight. He seemed so lost. He and Walter sat and talked for hours that night."

"So that's what happened."

Reed stood straight. "You knew?"

Alex frowned. "Huh? Oh, no, not about that. But I was sitting at Dad's desk after Mom's funeral and I picked up the paperweight. I noticed it was cracked so I asked Dad what happened. He said it got knocked off his desk."

Reed ran his hand over a chip in the end brick of the mantel. "Nope. Here is the culprit."

Alex couldn't believe it—and then again he could. His dad was human. And knowing that helped. He went and rubbed his hand over the chip. "This may sound strange, but somehow that makes me feel a little better. I don't know why, but I guess knowing that Dad was really angry and got it out gives me some closure. Pretty stupid?"

"Yes, but I think I understand," Reed responded with a smile.

Walter came up the front walkway and knocked on the door. Before anyone could answer, he let himself in. He placed his coat on a rack hook and made his way to Sam's study.

Reed and Alex were there.

"Good morning, you two." Alex turned, Sam's cracked paperweight in his hand. Reed stood by the fireplace mantel.

Ah.

Walter grinned. "So you've discovered your father's angry side? I'm just glad I wasn't in the way of that thing or it would have been *my* funeral that we were attending."

The three laughed, and Walter set his briefcase down and joined Reed at the fireplace. He examined the chip and chuckled to himself.

Alex rubbed the paperweight in his hands. "Walter, what did you and Dad talk about that night?"

Walter sat in Sam's chair. "Oh, lots of things. We talked about your mom, we talked about each of you kids, we talked about legacy, and we talked about mistakes we had made and regrets that we had."

Reed sat on the hearth and leaned against the fireplace's smooth rock face. "Regrets? Like what?"

"Your dad had a lot of regrets about how he was as a father."

Alex set the paperweight back on the desk. "Dad? I find that hard to believe. What regrets could he possibly have?"

Walter leaned forward. "Your dad felt he failed as a father, especially with you two boys."

Reed looked at Alex. "I don't understand."

"In some ways, it's what all fathers do. We blame ourselves for the errors we see lived out in our children. But more specifically for Sam, he felt he pushed too hard and expected too much from you two." Walter leaned back in the desk chair as he continued. "He blamed himself for the distance that developed between him and the two of you. And, Alex, he hurled that paperweight not because he was angry at you, but at himself."

Reed opened his hands and lifted them in the air. "Dad had nothing to regret."

Alex shook his head. "Yes, but it's too late to tell him that now."

"Well, not really," Walter said. "You can't tell him face-to-face, but you can reflect on your mom and dad and all they taught you in the decisions you make in your life from today on. If you want to right the regrets you have from your past, then live your life in a way that demonstrates what you've learned in this house. That's the greatest gift you could give them now."

Anna and Merideth came in the room just in time to hear Walter's last remarks.

"That's a good word, Walter. Thanks." Anna's appreciation seasoned her tone.

Merideth walked over to the main wooden post that ran from the staircase railing to the high ceiling just outside Sam's office. The oak column bore the notches of twenty years of the Roberts children's growth.

"Look here, *Merideth, 8th birthday, 4 feet 4 inches.*"

The others joined her and began retelling stories memorialized by the dozens of notches and inscriptions. The Roberts family history could be read off that post.

Walter sat back and drank it in. *Oh, Sam and Lori, if only you could be here to see this.*

Sixteen

Anna returned to the place in front of the open book, as by midmorning the focus had returned to the story of Steward. The five had reassembled in the living room, and a new fire was blazing in the fireplace. Anna relished the renewed connection she had to her past and her three siblings. She managed a wink at Walter as the others settled in for the final chapters of the story of Steward from Aiden Glenn.

~~~~~~~~~

The Archives of Seudomartus were kept in a formidable building across the plaza from the Halls of Wisdom. Steward stumbled over the pavement as he gazed at the great hall.

Obed caught him. "Careful, these are only the first steps of a very long day."

Obed and Steward climbed the staircase leading up to the front doors of the Archives. It took both of them to pull open just one of its great entry doors.

Steward wrinkled his nose at the smell of stale air circulating around all the old, musty books.

Obed waved his hand by his nose. "Whew!"

They walked into the foyer, where the dim lighting and massive tapestries clinging to the walls added to the heavy scent, giving the place an eerie, lifeless feel.

"Good morning, Teacher."

Steward looked at the pale, stern-looking woman dressed in a high-necked blouse and tailored suit.

"Your message arrived earlier, and Melodora is expecting you. Please follow me."

Obed pulled a lot of weight in Seudomartus.

She led them through canyons of massive shelves that reached up to enormous heights on every side. Each shelf was packed tight with books and bound papers.

How could anyone find anything in this place?

Toward the middle of the great room, the famous Melodora, Keeper of the Archives, greeted them. She was a tall slender woman with straight brown hair and an expressionless face.

Is this the right person to be asking about the location of the Transmitter that will lead me to the throne room of the king?

Obed greeted her. "Melodora, how good of you to see us." He placed an awkward kiss on her cheek.

"Good Teacher, it is always a privilege to have you as a guest of the great Archives of Seudomartus. And this must be the young traveler you mentioned to me."

Obed pulled Steward in front of him. "Yes, allow me to introduce to you Steward from Aiden Glenn."

What now? Would he be expected to give her a similar kiss? To his relief, Melodora offered her hand, and Steward shook it. "It is my pleasure to meet you. I am so grateful for your time."

"Aiden Glenn." She studied Steward through her dark-rimmed glasses. "That is at the far edge of the kingdom, just below the edge of the high country. Is it true that the sun never shines there?"

"The sun does shine in Aiden Glenn, but not like it does here in the high country. And it is not as warm as here either."

Melodora nodded. "It is also a great distance through several lands. Why would a young man like you embark on such a perilous and exhausting journey?"

Finally, Steward could tell his story. "Thank you for your inquiry. Since my birth, I have been promised to make this journey to see the king and learn from him the meaning of my name and my destiny."

Obed drew a heavy sigh, but Steward ignored him. "Upon my nineteenth birthday, I set out on this quest, and I am now very near its end. In fact, Seudomartus is my final destination before seeing the king and completing my journey."

Melodora raised her eyebrows and looked at Obed.

The last land, the last assignment before standing in the throne room. No need to hold anything back.

Steward pushed on. "All I need to do is locate the Transmitter in Seudomartus. Through it, the king will speak to me and lead me to him. That is my purpose for this visit to the great Archives."

Steward had spoken so fast he was almost out of breath. "Can you help me?"

She was silent for several moments then turned to stare at the great skyscrapers of books before her. "Please, come this way."

She led them through a maze of shelves holding every kind of book, periodical, and loose-bound collection imaginable. The deeper they went into the bowels of the Archives, the stronger the musty smell became.

Can there possibly be a Transmitter hidden in here?

Melodora stopped near an ornate bookcase sealed with heavy, leaded-glass doors. They were held closed by a massive brass clasp. She worked the clasp free, and the great glass doors swung open. Behind the doors, Steward could see books that seemed to be bound in metal covers—some covered with gold and silver, and some even with jewels.

"Magnificent."

Melodora nodded. "Indeed they are. Obed, Teacher, have you seen this collection before?"

"I have not. This is a rare treat."

Melodora stood for several minutes staring up into the shelves, as if to conjure up some memory of the location of just the book she was looking for. Finally, she rolled a ladder over to the shelves and climbed up, more nimble than Steward would have thought possible. From two-thirds up the enormous shelf, she worked to free a large volume encased in a bright gold metal cover.

Obed looked up at her. "May we help you?"

"No, no." She somehow maneuvered the book and herself down the ladder. Once down, she inspected the clasp on the selected volume.

"Over here." She led them to a reading table and placed the book under a soft light. She pulled two white gloves onto her hands.

"For protection of the sacred pages." Then she opened the latch that held the tome shut and began to read through the table of contents. Her finger stopped at a strange inscription that Steward did not recognize. She leafed through the pages, turning each one with care and never at the edge.

"There it is. Is that what you are looking for?"

Steward looked at the ornate drawing depicting in almost exact detail the Transmitter he had seen in the cleft of the rock-faced wall. "Yes, that is it. I am so thankful to you, Melodora."

"I thought it might be. This is from one of our most sacred and revered texts. It tells the story of the king's first visit to this land, and it records how he promised to speak to his people for all eternity through the use of this transmitting device. According to the legend, everyone was given one, and they could speak straight to the king at any time they wished.

They only had to position the small stone on the receiver arm in a direction toward the west and listen for the king's voice."

Obed slapped Steward on the back. "Well, my young Steward, you have found your transmitting device! Now your journey is complete."

Steward stepped back and put a hand out. "No, Teacher. I am sorry, but this is only a picture of the Transmitter. Now I just need to find one of the Transmitters themselves." He turned to Melodora. "Do you have one here?"

The Keeper's eyes narrowed and her lips were pursed. "My dear friend, don't be absurd. Obed, surely he is not serious." She closed the book and took off her gloves then turned to look down at Steward. "This is a picture of an old legend. It does not represent reality. It is a fable, a fairy tale passed on by unlearned people to keep the king-myth alive. Dear boy, you must be able to separate fact from fable, and this"—she placed her hand on the closed book—"is definitely fable."

No, she can't believe that. I'm so close. She has a picture. She must know a way.

Steward's countenance fell as he looked at Obed, pleading. Obed looked back at the Keeper. "Don't you know anyone who has seen a Transmitter or heard the king's voice through one? In all these books, is there not one story about it?"

She shrugged. "Of course. There are hundreds, perhaps thousands of stories of the old king-myth. We have kept them all." She opened her hands and gestured to the endless shelves. "You can spend years in here reading those old stories. Young people still study the lives and teachings of these people. It is a rich part of our history and heritage. Many of our laws are based on some of the wisdom they spoke. Their words are even engraved on the walls of the Halls of Wisdom."

She looked to Obed, and Steward had the sense it was for support. Obed took the cue.

"You see, Steward, it's not that we don't hold as sacred the testimonies and experiences of so many who claimed to hear the voice of the king. It's just that we have no direct proof that it ever actually happened. And today, with our greater wisdom and knowledge, we believe it was not really the king they heard. But since these men and women had important things to say, we still take them seriously."

Melodora added, "Them, not the myth."

Melodora took the book and worked her way up the ladder to return it to its resting place, continuing the discussion as she went. "Although there are over a thousand books written about your Transmitter, no one for centuries, or more likely ever, has actually seen one."

"Nor has anyone heard the voice of the king," Obed added.

Steward fought his emotions. They were denying his experience and calling what he knew to be true a myth. This was wrong! He gathered up all the courage he could muster. "I have."

Melodora was back down the ladder now. "You have what?"

"I have seen a Transmitter and I have heard the king's voice. I myself. With my own eyes and my own ears. And I tell you the king is not a myth or legend, but a reality."

Obed stepped in. "I'm sorry, Keeper, I—"

She put her hand out and stopped him. Looking at Steward, she punctuated every word. "Well, I see. Young Steward, if you want some advice, I would keep that assertion to yourself. That is not only foolishness here in Seudomartus, it is dangerous."

Dangerous to speak the truth? How could that be?

She turned, and her tone changed from serious to nonchalant. "But please do not be disappointed. We all want to hear the voice of the king. Do keep hoping and searching and testing your experiences. Who knows, you may one day actually hear something that is real." She turned and glared at him. "At least, real for you."

She brushed something from her sleeve, giving the impression she was no longer interested in the conversation. "Now, if you will excuse me, I have Archives business to attend to. Obed, it's always good to have you as a guest of the Archives."

Steward watched the great Melodora walk away.

Obed let out a sigh. "I warned you, Steward, that this was going to be difficult. And this was your easiest audience. Are you sure you want to continue?"

He looked up at where the book with the Transmitter had been placed. "I have no choice. The king called me to this. He gave clear instructions, and he asked me to trust him. So I will."

He fixed his gaze back on Obed. "There *is* a Transmitter here in Seudomartus. And I must find it."

"Very well. We have an audience with Mattox the Great, but first to lunch."

As they emerged from the Archives and their eyes adjusted to the bright morning sun, Steward took another look at the Halls of Wisdom. "I'm sad to be leaving here, but it was a great privilege just to see this place. And the Halls of Wisdom, even if only across the plaza."

Obed laughed. "Oh, my young friend, you will be back. Your final two audiences are in the heart of the Halls of Wisdom themselves. But for now we must climb to the Sacred Mount."

After a short stop for lunch, Steward walked with the Teacher along an extraordinary promenade that ran a full mile from the plaza of the Halls of Wisdom to the base of the

Sacred Mount. The broad walkway was made up of close-fitted paving stones of various colors that sparkled in the sun. Each side of the promenade was lined with tall, slender cedar trees, and between them were flowers of every imaginable color and size. Every hundred yards or so the promenade divided, allowing walkers to enjoy the fountains that gushed crystal blue water from the center of the walkway. Some fountains were sculpted in the form of sea creatures, and others were beasts that Steward had never seen.

Along the path, Steward and his companion met impressive-looking men and women, all busy talking about things that sounded witty, sophisticated, and wise.

If ever a place was close to the throne room of the king, it is this place.

The promenade ended at the base of an enormous staircase running up the side of the Sacred Mount.

Steward looked up the formidable climb. "How far is it?"

"Not far, just one thousand steps." Obed laughed as he started up.

They made their way up the steps. At various places a road would lead off to one side of the staircase or the other, and Steward could see great churches and cathedrals at the end of each one. As he and Obed climbed higher and higher, the edifices became more palatial at every turn.

The staircase ended near the top of the hill, widening out into a grand plaza much like the one in front of the Halls of Wisdom and the great Archives of Seudomartus.

Steward stood to catch his breath and take it all in. "Is...is that the Temple of Temperance? And there, the Ivory Cathedral, right?"

Obed nodded. "And beyond them over one hundred temples and cathedrals, more than you could visit in a month."

In the grandeur, Steward felt very small. *Maybe I should call this whole thing off. I'm not ready for this.*

As he worked to steel his nerves, a voice rang out behind them.

"Obed, my dear friend!"

Steward looked up to see a man with gracious features and flowing white hair hurrying toward them. He met them with a big smile and outstretched arms. He and Obed embraced as old friends. "It has been a long time since we have seen you on the Sacred Mount. What has brought you up here to us?"

Obed turned to Steward. "Steward, this is Brauchus, my teacher. I owe to him everything I know and the skills with which I teach it."

Steward liked him right off. He had a gentle but serious face, and his smile warmed Steward's spirit.

"It is a great honor to meet you, sir."

"And I return the honor to you, young friend. If Obed has become your teacher, you are a most fortunate fellow. He is the wisest teacher in the land!"

Obed protested, arms high in the air. "Far from that, I'm afraid. But not on your account, my dear teacher. You taught me well, and it looks as though you are thriving in the thin and clean air of the Sacred Mount."

Brauchus took a deep breath of air and exhaled. "Indeed I am, Obed, indeed I am. This is near-paradise for me. The teaching is profound, the libraries are extraordinary, the conversations are robust, and the view...well, see for yourself."

Brauchus turned the two of them around.

Steward looked back down along the promenade that lay far below and led his eye into the heart of the great city. He could see the plaza of the Halls of Wisdom, and all across the city were parks and fountains. The mountains to the north were capped in snow, and the valley to the east was carpeted in a rich green as the spring planting was making its presence known through the black soil.

It was a glorious sight.

As Steward stood gawking at the scene, Brauchus continued. "So I ask you again, what brings you up here to the Sacred Mount?"

Obed turned back to his friend and mentor. "My friend Steward is on a journey all the way from the edge of the upper kingdom. He seeks..." Obed lowered his voice as several men passed by. He put his arm around Brauchus's shoulders and leaned close to him. "He seeks to locate a Transmitter, believing that the king will speak to him and lead him to the throne room. That is the purpose of his quest."

Brauchus looked up at his protégé. "Obed, why have you become involved in this matter?" He looked at Steward. "No offense to you, lad, but your request has placed my dearest student in grave danger." He looked back at Obed. "This request will lead you to nothing but ridicule and rebuke...and perhaps even worse. Please, go back down and rethink this entire matter. I cannot stand the thought of my greatest student becoming ensnared in such a ruse."

There it was again: warnings, alarm. And now from Brauchus, this learned and caring man.

Maybe I haven't taken the risk and danger seriously. Help me, king. Courage, confidence!

Obed kept close as he replied. "Dear teacher, you taught me to be open-minded, to seek the truth wherever it may be found. You taught me that the king may be found in many ways through myriad avenues and voices. You described to me a rich tapestry of truth and challenged me to follow every thread so that I might one day see the larger fabric. Why do you now warn me to shrink back from this particular thread?"

The old teacher wrinkled up his brow then walked away from them and stood looking out over the plaza, his hand to his mouth. Obed shot Steward a confident glance that settled Steward's nerves.

Brauchus spun around as if he had received a revelation and joined the two in the hushed conversation. "You have spoken wisely, Obed. You must indeed seek the truth wherever you think it may be found. Only hear this from me, and then we will speak of this subject no more. There is a growing sense of unease toward those in this land who claim to possess a Transmitter and have direct access to the voice of the king."

"The Starr Hill fanatics?"

At Steward's quiet question, Brauchus nodded. "Yes, and others, though they are not so well organized or visible. The others are mostly underground. Because of their outrageous and heretical claims, they are being pursued and persecuted—*severely* persecuted."

He turned to Steward. "Young Steward, if you had made this journey ten years ago, your questions would have been debated in the open with acceptance and tolerance. Your experiences would have been met with profound interest mixed with the requisite skepticism of this place. But today there is less and less room for such talk. A pall has settled on this city, and it is suffocating all ideas that would call us back to the teachings and guidance of our ancestors. Everything from our heritage is coming under great scrutiny…"

"…and attack, if we would be straight with it," Obed added.

"Yes, yes, actual attack. And those who purport to hold to the old ways are being marginalized. Talk of the king-myth is written off as pure fable…"

"…or fairy tale," Steward added, recalling Melodora's biting words.

Brauchus nodded. "Precisely. And so this is a dangerous time to be marching into Seudomartus announcing that you have seen a Transmitter and, even worse, that you have heard the voice of the king. Be careful, you two, and do not underestimate what you are up against."

Obed put his hands on Brauchus's shoulders. "Thank you, my good teacher and dear friend. Now to answer your question more directly. You will not be pleased to know that we have come to the Sacred Mount to meet with Mattox the Great and Hamby the Pious. Still, we will heed your words and proceed with as much caution as we can. Yet for young Steward here to complete this journey, we must pursue the truth of his words, whatever the cost."

For the first time, Steward understood why Obed had taken him under his wing and given him such help despite the risk. Obed too was searching to hear the voice of the king.

Brauchus hugged them, though his smile held sadness. Then he walked away, disappearing into the growing crowd that filled the plaza on the Sacred Mount.

Steward turned to Obed, whose gaze was still fixed on the spot where Brauchus vanished amid the throng. "Thank you, my dear friend. I could not have done any of this without you."

Obed's gaze came back to Steward. "Don't thank me yet. We have a great deal of treacherous road ahead. And now we are almost late for our audience with Mattox the Great."

It was late in the afternoon and the sun hung low in the sky before Obed and Steward made the trek back down the grand staircase from the Sacred Mount. They had held audiences with both Mattox the Great in the famous Ivory Cathedral and Hamby the Pious in the spire-festooned Temple of Temperance. In neither place did Steward find his Transmitter. Only more questions.

Obed shook his head. "I'm sorry, Steward. We did not find your Transmitter. I had thought perhaps Mattox…"

"I knew the moment I met Mattox the Great that he would not have a Transmitter." Steward didn't even try to hide his disdain for the man.

Obed cast him a sideways glance. "And how is that?"

"It was his spirit. There was a sense about him that no voice, no matter how clear, would ever pierce his skepticism. I have never met anyone who could speak so eloquently about being open and liberal-minded, yet who was so closed and bitter in spirit."

Obed cocked his head and smiled. "Well, my dear and wise friend, you have said a mouthful. How did you find his teaching?"

Steward replayed the lecture they had been given upon mention of the encounter with the Transmitter. The stern yet unimposing Mattox had paced around the room as he unpacked reason after reason to explain away Steward's experience…

"Steward, we often hear our own deepest longings through the voice of other beings… or objects. This journey is your entire life. You have been led to believe in it since you were young. You naturally have accepted the beliefs of your parents, and now your mind will go to all lengths to validate those beliefs, even if it means a hallucination of voices through ancient vessels. Do not be discouraged. This is actually a great gift. Few people can rely on such dramatic experiences to shape their lives. This, for you, is an epiphany. It does not matter if the voice was real or not. The important thing is that you believe it was, and that it will lead you to live a better life. Continue to seek the truth, as we all must."

"So, sir, if you don't mind me asking, have you ever heard the voice of the king yourself?"

At Steward's question, Mattox had reached the end of his patience. "We hear our own truth today, as we have in the past, through all religions, all cultures, and all faith traditions. None is a perfect and exclusive avenue to truth, but all can learn from each other. If you are to hear the voice of truth, you must listen for it in everything, for it has no single location. Truth is in all things and all things are true. No one person or group has the right to believe they have a unique access to truth through any voice or any vessel. That, my misguided friend, is the most detestable and damnable quality of the human race, and you must rid yourself of every ounce of it."

With that, the audience ended.

Steward let loose his own sigh. "I found Mattox's teaching hypocritical. He teaches that we are to seek passionately for the truth, but then he tells me it is a detestable asset when it is finally found. What value is there in searching for the truth if, in discovering it, you are condemned?"

Obed nodded. "It's a good and troubling question, Steward. Let me try to explain. We are taught that the journey is its own reward. We also know the dark history of some in our past who claim to have found the truth. Theirs is a history of persecution and hatred against those whom Mattox believes were still seeking the truth. Much evil has been done by those who claim, as you do, to have heard the voice of the king."

"But that doesn't mean the king doesn't speak or that we shouldn't seek to hear him! If he doesn't speak to us, then all this searching and seeking is folly, isn't it?"

Obed inclined his head. "Perhaps. But for many, the searching itself gives them a sense that they are on more solid footing in a world filled with questions."

Obed's comments took Steward straight back to the edge of Pitcairn Moor, to Dunston's appeal to him to see things the way the king would have him see them. "If the search is in vain, if there is no truth, then the path any seekers are on is a shifting foothold in a bubbling bog of mud that will eventually pull them under."

Obed put his arm around Steward's shoulder. "You sound as if you speak from experience."

The two continued their descent in silence for several minutes before Obed spoke again. "And what of Hambry the Pious? You seemed more taken by him and the Saints of Temperance."

"Yes. At first I was very hopeful."

The rotund, balding man dressed in the finest of clothes had seemed more congenial and welcoming than Mattox the Great. The Temple of Temperance was a grand building with huge spires on every corner. It was not as ornate inside as Steward had expected, but its sheer size made it a spectacle to see.

Hambry's eyes had sparkled as he listened to Steward. "Oh yes, my young friend, you have certainly heard the voice of the king. It is the same voice our ancestors heard, and the voice we follow carefully in all we do."

Steward's heart soared. Someone in this place believed him and even agreed with him that the king did indeed speak! "And do you have a Transmitter?"

The man brushed his questions aside. "A Transmitter? Oh no, we have no need of a Transmitter, Steward. You see, our ancestors heard from the king and wrote down his words for us. We follow these words precisely. When we hear them, we hear from the king himself."

"But why would you want to read old accounts of the king's words when he can speak to you today?"

Hambry arched a brow at him. "Everything we need to know has already been given to us. What more could the king say than what has been said and written down?"

Steward had tried a different tack. "What did the king say to your ancestors?"

"Oh, many things, books full of things. He told us how to live, what to eat and not eat, how to dress, how to worship, where to live, whom to marry, whom we accept and don't accept, and what our future will be like. Everything you need to know about life is in these books. I will give you copies, and you can study them for yourself." He turned to pull three large volumes from a shelf next to his desk. "We must honor our ancestral writings. They are sacred. Why, the Transmitter itself is sacred. These writings are our only link to the king now. He has spoken. This is his will, and we will follow it to the letter until the day of our grand transformation."

Steward's hope vanished as the truth became clear: Hambry and those like him worshipped the Transmitter and ignored the voice of the king himself.

"Steward, I asked you about Hambry the Pious."

Steward looked at Obed. "Yes, sorry, I was just thinking back to all that has happened. Why would Hambry not seek to hear the king's voice today? Why are those like him content to believe that their ancestors heard and wrote down all they need to know? It makes no sense."

"It does if you are searching for security and certainty. It's safe to believe that the only truth was written down long ago and never changes. To men such as that, it's dangerous to believe that the king still speaks."

They reached the bottom step on the grand staircase, and ahead of them lay the promenade that would lead them back to Obed's house.

"What if the books are just the words of men, and not from the king at all? What if they wrote down what they *wanted* to believe? How do they know it's true if they stop listening for the voice of the king?"

Obed considered that. "Perhaps they don't want to know. Perhaps they are so content—even comfortable—with what is written in their books that they are afraid to hear the voice of the king. What if he leads them in a new way? If you believe you have every-thing you need clearly written down for you to follow, you don't have to search, you don't have to question…"

"You don't have to think."

Obed smiled and nodded. "My young friend, you are growing wiser before my eyes."

Steward wasn't so sure. These meetings today had left him more confused and frus-trated than ever, yet something in his spirit urged him on, as if these visits were important parts to a puzzle being revealed, piece by piece.

Steward's skin crawled, and he looked around. He could swear something was… wrong. "Do you sense that? Teacher?"

Obed looked around them as well. "Yes. Careful now, something is not right."

A small group of men passed them, glaring at them. Steward heard them whispering after they passed, talking about them.

Judging them.

Steward rubbed a hand over his aching eyes. "Obed, there is a heaviness in the air. It is almost suffocating."

More people passed, and the stares and comments increased.

What was going on?

"It is the presence of the coming persecution." Obed's words were heavy. "The word is out about you. The danger to you…and now to me…is even greater now."

"I am so sorry to have involved you in this." Steward wanted to walk faster, even run, but he steadied himself to keep a normal pace and blend in.

Obed spoke, his voice low, calm. "Slowly, Steward, slowly. Show no signs of concern. And remember, you did not choose this path for me. I chose it for myself. You have noth-ing for which to apologize. If you have indeed heard from the king, then my own journey is not genuine unless I seek the answers with you."

Steward had found the ally he needed. With Obed at his side, he was confident he could complete the task.

The king has again provided exactly who I needed. I will remember to thank him.

"Thank you, Obed. Whether we intended it this way or not, our fates are now intertwined."

To Steward's great relief, the mustard-colored colonnade of Obed's house came into view as the sun gave up the last rays of the day and settled behind the massive western range. Once inside the house, they collapsed into two large chairs.

Over dinner, they talked about the two formidable visits that lay ahead of them in the Halls of Wisdom.

Steward fell to sleep that night with Obed's last words ringing in his head: "Prepare yourself, my young friend. If we felt the disdain and reticence of the populace today, what lies in store for us tomorrow will surely be far worse."

Help us, king. Courage, confidence.

~~~~~~~~~

As the last words were read, Alex could tell Merideth and Anna watched for a reaction from him. He rose and walked to the fireplace, picked up the last log in the rack, and laid it on the crimson coals. It snapped and crackled to life with flames jumping out of it, casting a dancing light across the room. He stood by the increasing warmth and then turned to his siblings.

"I heard all of those questions and studied all those false teachings and heresies while in seminary. They're the reasons why good, faithful believers go astray. In the end, it's all about being cut off from a daily audience with the king himself."

Reed agreed. "Dad always talked to us about the need for daily devotions and a personal prayer life."

"Yes, that's what Steward is after." Alex hesitated, measuring his words. "And what I walked away from."

"You still have your faith, Alex," Anna said. "You have never rejected God's presence in your life."

Alex smiled at her. "You're right, I guess. But really, I've stopped listening for the voice of the king."

Reed sat back and looked up to the ceiling. "I'm not sure I've really listened to hear God speak since Mom died. I guess I just sort of gave up on Him."

"I'm not sure I've ever heard Him."

They all looked at Merideth. She shrugged. "I mean, I've prayed and read the Bible, but I can't say I've ever really heard God speaking to me."

Anna raised her hand. "I have, but it has been a long time. And, Merideth, I think you heard God's voice in the direction and love you received in this house." She looked around at Alex and Reed. "We all have. God speaks to us through the people who love us. We heard words of guidance, support, correction, and grace. If that's not God speaking to us, then I doubt we will ever recognize His voice when He speaks."

It was a solid insight, and Alex didn't expect that kind of thing from Anna. "Well said. Maybe you should have gone to seminary."

"No, Alex. It was your calling and your passion…and I believe it still is."

The bells in the Resurrection Christian Church steeple began to peal. As Alex listened to its rendition of "Bringing in the Sheaves," an unexpected knock at the door made him jump.

Walter stood up. "I'll get that."

He was back almost as soon, bearing a large glass baking dish filled to overflowing with iced cinnamon rolls.

Now that was a welcome addition to the day!

Walter grinned. "I asked Mrs. Stratton if she would make these for you four and drop them off on her way to church. I thought it would be nice to fill this house again with the smell of cinnamon rolls on a Sunday morning."

Merideth inhaled deeply. "Bless you, Walter."

"Amen to that." Reed stood and stole some frosting on his finger.

Alex was on his feet too. "Come on, you guys. Let's try them out."

They followed Walter into the kitchen and soon were deep in gooey icing and rich cinnamon pastry.

Alex looked around. "Hey, where's Merideth?"

No one responded. They didn't have to. Alex figured he knew the answer as well. Merideth would be curled up in the chair in the next room with her cup of coffee, enjoying the smell of fresh baking on a Sunday morning.

Alex speared a bite of cinnamon roll. He had an odd feeling, one he hadn't felt for a very long time…

Peace.

All that was missing was the sound of his father's voice coming from upstairs. Though that wouldn't happen, his father's voice was with them.

"What do you say, all?"

They turned to see Merideth smiling at them from the doorway. "Ready to get back to Steward?"

They put their dishes in the sink then made their way into the room where Merideth now sat in front of the book, ready to read.

CHAPTER
Seventeen

Steward couldn't sleep. He tossed about trying to escape thoughts of the threatening day that lay ahead. At once he was jolted by the sound of a knock at the side window of the house.

Obed was already on the move, throwing his robe around him and easing his way toward the window. As he approached, the knock came again.

Steward crept up next to Obed, prepared to run for his life.

They peered out the window and eyed a figure crouching near the high hedge that surrounded Obed's property. The figure motioned for Obed to open the door.

Steward strained to see the man's face. "Who is it?"

"I'm not sure, but I don't sense he's here to harm us."

Here's hoping he's right. Steward watched as Obed unlatched the door and let the man in. Once in, he moved to the center of the room, away from the window, continuing to crouch until he knew he was out of view.

Steward and Obed stood back, but when the man lifted his hood, Steward recognized him. It was the same man who had walked with him his first day in Seudomartus.

"He's from Starr Hill," Steward whispered to Obed. "I met him on the way to your house." *Surely if we weren't in danger before, we are now.*

Obed eyed the stranger. "Speak your name and state your business, or I will sound the alarm and have you arrested."

"My name is Zanon, and I am here to tell this young man where he can find his Transmitter."

"You're from Starr Hill, is that right?"

"I am. And you are Obed the Teacher. I know you don't approve of who we are or what we believe, but I beseech you to let me speak openly to Steward about the matter that is most urgent on his heart."

Obed looked at Steward, and Steward nodded. Might as well hear the man out.

Obed's lips thinned. "You must speak clearly and leave us then as quickly as you came."

He sat on the floor in front of a couch, motioning to Obed and Steward, who joined him. "Steward, we have learned of your journey and your encounter with the king through a Transmitter. We know the king wishes you to hear his voice once again so that he may lead you to himself. We have a Transmitter, and I will take you to it so that your journey may be complete."

Steward fought to catch his breath. Was this a trap? Was he being deceived? Or was this his last chance to hear the king's voice?

This is the first person in this city who claims to have a Transmitter. I have to trust this man. It might be my only opportunity.

"When do we go?"

Obed glared at Steward and gave a quick shake of his head. "How do we know we can trust this man? He may be from the populace setting a trap for us to condemn ourselves. It is not safe, Steward."

Zanon held his hand out. "No, it is not safe. But what I am telling you is true. We meet three times a week on Starr Hill. We have to vary the dates and times because those who seek to annihilate us are watching for an opportunity to attack. I will not tell you where or when, but when I come for you, you must be ready to go. Do you understand?"

Obed and Steward both nodded, and Zanon looked at Obed. "You are going also?"

Obed smiled at Steward and then looked back at Zanon. "Yes, I am going as well. If the king's voice can really be heard, then I must hear it, if you will allow me."

Steward smiled and patted Obed on the shoulder. "If I go, Obed must come also."

Zanon paused. "The leader may not be happy with this, but we are instructed to do all we can to help you complete your journey, so I will lead you both. Just be ready whenever I come for you."

He slipped the hood over his head and was away out the back door, disappearing into the darkness.

Steward stood next to Obed as they stared out into the night, then closed the door and faced his friend. "I guess we've crossed the line. There's no going back now."

Morning came, and a sense of unease filled Steward's and Obed's breakfast conversation. Obed laid out his plan.

"We will walk straight to the plaza through the main streets at the height of the market hour. The congestion of people will make it difficult for us to be accosted. Then we'll enter the plaza and walk beside the produce carriers, who wheel their large carts across the plaza like ferries across the lake. My father worked in that trade for most of his life. I know these men, and they will not allow anything to happen to me as long as they have the power and numbers to prevent it. If we move with speed, we will make it into the Halls of Wisdom in safety."

"But won't we be arrested in the Halls?"

"No. There is no police action of any kind allowed inside the Halls, unless someone's life is in danger. We will be safe once inside, as long as we go about our business."

He hoped his friend was right. It was all about trust now.

"And what about when we are finished?"

Obed stared at him. "I have no idea. We will have to make it up from there. But one thing is for sure: if you don't find what you are looking for in the Halls today, we will need to be far from Seudomartus by nightfall."

"And what about Zanon and the Starr Hill gathering? How will they find us?"

"I don't know, but it will do no one any good if we are thrown in prison—or worse. We must first look out for ourselves and then hope to find the Starr Hill gathering."

No, I won't leave here without the Transmitter. Where would I go? Regardless of how this day goes, I have to hear the voice of the king again.

Obed paced the floor for a moment then stopped and turned. "Steward, do you really need to see these last two people? Nagas will confront you without mercy, and Philandra will not yield until your story has been left in shreds. If the Transmitter is with the Starr Hill gathering, why not go there and escape these confrontations?"

Steward wanted to agree, to skip these last two confrontations. He questioned why as well, but the king's words came to him again, "Trust me."

"Because this is the journey the king asked me to take. For what reason I don't know. But even though it may bring me pain and suffering and even lead to death, and though at this moment it makes no sense to me to do so, I'll trust him and I will obey."

Obed nodded.

Obed's plan worked just as hoped. They left the house in the middle of the busiest market hour and pushed through the center of the streets amid a throng of shoppers, vendors, and travelers. Steward watched as armed men worked their way toward them several times, but Obed was brilliant at leading Steward to slip away through the crowd.

Finally, Obed smiled. "There it is, the Great Plaza. The Halls of Wisdom are just a hundred yards away."

"Obed, more guards!"

The armed men emerged from a side street and spotted them.

"Careful, go slowly now." Obed walked into the plaza, and just as the first of the armed guards was upon them, he called out, "Albert, my dear old friend, how have you been?"

A huge man with enormous arms, who was moving a mountain of produce in a two-wheeled cart into the plaza, stopped when he heard Obed's voice. He put his cart handles down and came to Obed with a wide grin. "Obed, I haven't seen you around here for weeks. How is your father?"

The small band of guards stopped.

Steward couldn't blame them. Obed's friend was enormous.

"My father is well but misses you all greatly. May my friend and I walk with you and your companions as we talk? We are going to the Halls today."

"Of course. It would be our pleasure." Albert shouted over to three other carters, each of whom was every bit as huge as he was. "Hey, fellas! This is Obed, Troyer's boy. Mind if he walks along with us?"

No one did, and they all had greetings for Obed's father. Steward followed Obed as they worked their way to the center of the convoy of produce carts and started across the plaza. Through the lettuce and turnips, they watched as their pursuers could only follow at a distance behind them.

They were safe—for now.

Once they approached the Halls of Wisdom, Obed thanked his friends. Then he and Steward hurried up the steps and went inside. Obed straightened and assumed the posture of a regular guest inside the enormous structure.

"Welcome to the Halls of Wisdom, Steward."

With all the tension of avoiding capture, Steward forgot for a moment where he was. He caught his breath and let his gaze take it all in. "Amazing! I can't believe I'm here." He couldn't hold back a grin. "Wait until Dad hears this story."

The Halls of Wisdom were more splendid than he ever could have imagined. All the opulence of Petitzaros or Tristin's mansion couldn't compare.

Steward craned his neck as they walked. Towering ceilings suspended by cypress beams held chandeliers made of jeweled glass, which created patterns of rainbow light in every direction. Marble, ivory, and precious stones lined the floors and walls, and every detail of carved stone was gilded with gold. Paintings of great thinkers lined the hallways, and the words of the ancestors were carved across the top of every door and passageway.

Melodora was right. The kings' words are here. Everywhere. Steward's attention was broken as two men rushed toward them and summoned Obed.

"This way, quickly."

They escorted the two of them through a side door and into an inner chamber, then closed the door behind them.

"Teacher, you have risked your life to be here today. Everywhere there are men looking for you both. You have been accused of associating with the Starr Hill fanatics and of speaking heresy regarding the old king-myth. Is this true?"

Obed held a steady gaze. His tone was sharp and sure. "Since when is it against the law to speak of the king-myth? And when did it become a crime to associate with the Starr Hill fanatics? Though they have been frowned upon, how did it come to this?"

One of the two men drew closer to him, speaking now in an urgent but hushed voice. "Pressure has been mounting for months. Those who oppose all such teachings regarding the king-myth have been looking for a spark to ignite the fire that they could use to consume their enemies on Starr Hill."

The second man looked at Steward. "And they have found just the spark they needed."

Steward gasped. "Me? Are you saying I have caused all this to happen?"

The first man nodded. His expression grew pained. "I am afraid so. Your arrival here and the news of your story has generated great excitement among the Starr Hill Faithful. And it also fueled anger and resentment in their enemies. This was the rallying cry they needed, and now they have launched a full vendetta against all who speak of or believe in the king-myth. And especially you two."

The second man furrowed his brow. "How did you get to the Halls?"

Obed grinned. "Carefully, and with the help of friends. The greater question is, how shall we get out of here?"

The first man responded. "We have ways to get you out. Come, we must move at once."

Out? That's not an option!

"No." Steward stopped. "We can't go yet. We have come to have an audience with Nagas the Skeptic and Philandra the Wise. I cannot leave until we have spoken with them both."

"You can't be serious!" The second man looked like he was about to explode. "We may be able to escort you safely to the private chambers of Nagas, and perhaps, if we are most careful, we can get you through the servants' passages and near the outer reception rooms of Philandra the Wise. But either one can have you bound and handed over at their will."

Obed cocked his head. "I thought police action was forbidden in the Halls of Wisdom."

The first man raised a hand toward them. "These are not ordinary times, my friend. One who is considered an enemy of the personal quest for truth and knowledge is an enemy of everyone—both inside the Halls and out. The furor that is being raised is so great that even the sacredness of the Halls themselves may not be enough to save you."

Steward knew he was not an enemy of the quest for truth. He just knew the king was the truth.

"I don't care. We must make these audiences. I won't leave here until I have accomplished what the king asked of me."

Obed stood tall beside him. "I agree."

The two men looked at each other and shook their heads. The first looked back. "Very well. When are you scheduled for your audience with Nagas?"

"Eleven," Obed answered.

"Then let's be off."

The two escorts led Steward and Obed down a back hallway, across a small, unoccupied foyer, and through two gathering rooms. They proceeded up a short stairway, and soon they rounded a corner and disappeared into the private chambers of Nagas the Skeptic. The older man knocked and was allowed entry, followed by Obed. Steward could hear the discussion. Obed was greeted with politeness, and Steward was asked to join them in the sanctuary of private inner chambers. He was relieved to get out of sight of passersby. However, once he was in the presence of Nagas, his relief disappeared.

The renowned skeptic had piercing blue eyes that seemed never to leave Steward. "So this is the young adventurer who insisted on meeting with me to discuss the king-myth. Why are you bothering yourself, and me, with this foolishness?"

Steward's knees quivered. His mind went empty.

Think, c'mon, think!

He struggled to mumble a few words. "I…that is, my father…this journey that I am on…I need to ask five wise people about the…I came here to ask…"

Nagas snapped a look at Obed. "Obed, why have you brought this stammering young fool to me?"

Obed put his hands up, pleading. "Please, honorable Nagas, just give him a moment to organize his thoughts. We have been through a great deal today."

Nagas looked back at Steward, sized him up and down, and snorted a reply. "Very well, take your time, but answer me well. I have little time for fools."

C'mon, Steward. Think. This is your chance. Just tell him the truth. "I have come…I have come because the king spoke to me and sent me to see you."

"The king…spoke to you?" Nagas sneered and gave an indignant chuckle. "You are quite insane. Young man, listen very carefully to me." The Skeptic walked up to Steward and stood so close that his breath hit Steward's face as he spoke.

"You are an uneducated, naïve, and gullible young boy. You have been deluded into believing there is a king. That alone is nonsense. There is no proof of a king. No one has seen the king. No one has heard the voice of the king. Most everyone with any common sense lives a happy and normal life as if there were no king. Furthermore, we do not need a king, we do not want a king, and we do not and will not believe in a king. So why would a nonexistent myth suddenly speak to you and send you to me? What could you possibly want from me? Tell me, boy, *tell* me!"

Steward's heart was beating so fast he thought he would faint. He grasped his chest to help his breathing, and it was then that his hand felt the lump in his inner pocket where he kept the spectacles given him by Dunston. He could hear the little creature's words, "Only use the glasses when you need to see reality amidst illusion."

If there was ever a time, this was it.

Steward fished the small glasses out from his pocket then opened them and placed them on his nose.

Nagas stepped back. "Are those glasses to make you look wiser? Well then, let's hear your learned reply."

Steward looked up at Nagas—and gasped. The Skeptic's face had no eyes in the sockets or ears on the sides of his head. And out of his mouth came a braying sound, like a donkey. Steward lifted the glasses to see the scrunched-up face of his accuser, then let them down again and saw the blind and deaf figure before him, braying away.

What had Dunston said? *The spectacles help you see the kingdom the way the king would have you see it. Everything else is illusion.*

Steward's nerve returned and his mind cleared. He removed the glasses, placed them back in his inner vest pocket, and looked straight at the great Skeptic.

Courage, confidence, trust the king. They all flooded over him as he spoke.

"You have eyes, but you cannot see. You have ears, but you cannot hear. And when you speak, you make no more sense than a braying she-ass!"

As a dumbfounded Nagas stepped back, Steward went on. "I came here on the instructions of the king himself to ask you the whereabouts of the Transmitter. But I can see now why I was sent to see you, for you are the reason Seudomartus has become such a hostile place to the king—you and Mattox the Great and Hambry the Pious and even Melodora. You all claim such wisdom, but none of you has eyes to see the king or ears to hear his voice. And so when you speak, you all sound wonderful to each other, but in reality you are no wiser than a common donkey in the field."

"Get out! Get *out*, you impertinent, stupid little boy—!"

But before Nagas could finish his yelling, Steward turned to leave. "Come, Obed. There is nothing more for us here."

The two men who escorted them down the hall stared at them, mouths agape.

"Great lord of the sea, I have never heard anyone speak to Nagas that way," the first man said to Steward.

"And I have never seen him nearly speechless before, either," added the second, a small gleam in his eye.

Obed grabbed Steward by the shoulders. "We must surely flee this place now. Nagas will call out all the powers aligned against us. We are no longer safe here, not even in Philandra's chamber."

Steward placed his hand on his friend's arm. "Obed, you have been my friend and closest ally through this entire ordeal. Please don't fail me now. You know I must see Philandra the Wise, no matter what the cost. It's the command of the king."

Obed locked his eyes on Steward's, then he placed his hand back on Steward's. "I know, I know…and you will obey him."

Steward nodded. "And I will trust him. Will you?"

Obed looked down the halls at the commotion their presence was causing. "Right now, I have no choice." He turned to his two friends. "Can you still get us to Philandra?"

The journey took over an hour. The four figures worked their way through a basement tunnel and then walked with care through the servants' quarters, trying not to attract attention. When they reached the far side of the Halls from underneath, they walked up five staircases, being careful at each one to wait until the traffic cleared.

Still, Steward guessed they had little chance of making it all the way into Philandra's chambers. Surely by now the main Halls were filled with armed men looking for them.

As suspected, when Steward peered out from behind a storage closet door, he could see a parade of pursuers combing the Halls for them.

Obed eyed the door to the reception chamber of Philandra the Wise then turned to the two who had escorted them. "Thank you both for your help. We could not have made it this far without you. Now please go so that you won't be caught and associated with us. We'll go to our fate, but you must save yourselves while there is still time."

The two men nodded, clasped Steward's hand, and then they were gone, back down the passageway from which they'd come.

Obed turned to Steward. "Well, this is our final stop. If we wait until the hall clears, we may be able to run for it. But even if we make it, we may be taken prisoner right in Philandra's reception room. There is no certainty of refuge anywhere now."

The king had sent him such a good friend in Obed. Steward nodded. "Let's make our best effort. That is all the king has asked."

The two waited until the hallway cleared, and then they emerged from the doorway and walked as fast as they could without breaking into a full run. As Steward's hand reached for the door handle of the reception room, he was grasped by the shoulder and spun around. He could see Obed already struggling with two men who had grabbed him.

Steward fought, but he and Obed would not win against the greater number of assailants. As the stronger men gained control, they pushed Steward and Obed to their knees, and their pursuers began to bind their hands behind them.

At once the doors to the chambers of Philandra swung open, and out walked a woman of unspeakable beauty. Her long, flowing robes floated along the hallway as she approached.

"Who are these men, and why is anyone being bound in the Halls of Wisdom?"

The lead guard scrambled to his feet and looked down as he spoke. "Honorable Philandra, these are the two fugitives who are spreading the heresy regarding the king-myth and stirring up trouble among the Starr Hill fanatics."

"Obed, Teacher, are you really a fugitive as they say? And this must be Steward."

He looked up, and as his eyes met hers he lost the ability to speak. Only Claire could match her in beauty.

She smiled at him. "Do we not have an audience scheduled for today—in fact, for this very hour?" She turned to the armed men, and the fire in her eyes gave Steward hope. "And would you beat and bind my guests right outside my own chambers?"

The guard stuttered a reply. "Most honorable Philandra, we, we apologize for this skirmish. We will release them as you ask." Then his voice strengthened, and he lifted his eyes to look straight at Philandra. "But when you have finished with your audience, these two men will be arrested and tried and punished for their crimes. We will be back for them."

Steward looked around. There was no place for escape.

This is where it may end, but I will trust the king.

Steward's attackers backed away from him and Obed. Loosing the bindings on their wrists, he and Obed stood. Philandra escorted them into her chamber.

Obed bowed to her. "Thank you, Philandra, for your kindness."

She looked out her window, and from where Steward stood he saw the angry crowd outside. "I fear I have only postponed your troubles. However, I do have the power to give you safe passage out of Seudomartus. My entourage will be leaving the Halls this very afternoon on a journey to Ascendia. You may join them and receive clear passage well beyond the city gates."

Obed turned to Steward, and a smile of intense relief flashed across his lips. "That is wonderful news. Thank you for your graciousness."

Had the king known, when he sent Steward here, the effect his presence would have? "I too thank you, my lady, for your kindness. I never meant to bring such turmoil to Seudomartus when I arrived."

That brought her around, and she locked her gaze on him. "What *did* you mean to bring, young Steward? What brought you here?"

Dare I tell her? If I'm honest with her, will we lose our safe passage out of the city?

It didn't matter anymore. The fear that once held Steward in bondage was being replaced by a growing sense of the king's presence. And peace and courage accompanied it.

Before he could speak, Obed responded. "My friend Steward has come to Seudomartus at the request of the king himself. And our visit to you was also at the king's direct request."

Steward watched Philandra's face for signs of anger or repugnance.

All she did was smile. "Heard from the king? Directly, you say? How marvelous. Oh, Steward, you must be so honored, so thrilled to have been chosen to hear from the king. What was his voice like?"

He studied her as she moved closer to him. *Does she really believe me?* "His voice…it was magnificent. Deep and warm, yet powerful and reassuring. You…you believe me then?"

"Believe you? Why, yes. Why wouldn't I believe you?"

"Well, no one else has…except for Obed."

Philandra took him by the hand. "My dear Steward, everyone has a right to believe whatever they want. That is the beauty of this land. We cherish everyone's vision of truth and beauty. That is why I freed you just now. You have every right to receive your truth from the king's voice. We are committed to openness and the pursuit of truth. Every voice must be heard, and every belief must be met with tolerance and love. When we lose that, we cease being truly human."

She walked across the room, turned, and looked back at Steward. "You do believe that, don't you, Steward?"

Steady, push on but be cautious.

"Yes, I believe so. But now that you know the king does speak and wants to be heard by all his people, surely you will help me find the Transmitter and hear his voice for yourself."

Philandra gave a wave of her hand. "It is enough for me to know that *you* hear his voice. I have my own voices that I hear, that I look to for truth and guidance and a sense of the real. Would you like to hear those voices? Or what about the Cosmers, who find truth in the stars? Or the Planters, who find their truth in nature and its many gods? Do you wish to hear their voices and follow their truths? And there are the Dawners, who find truth in pursuit of suffering, or the Epists, who find truth in knowledge and understanding. Do you want to hear their voices and follow their truth?"

Philandra stopped, although Steward sensed she had countless more examples.

He wasn't sure why, but he sensed what he was about to say would mean the difference between freedom and death. "I do not know these other truths about which you speak. I only know that the king spoke to me. I heard his voice, and he has called me to this place to find the Transmitter so I may approach the throne room of the king. Will you help me?"

Philandra gazed out her window onto the long promenade and the Sacred Mount that loomed in the distance. Then she turned back to look at Steward. Her eyes had lost their glimmer. Now they were colder, calculating.

"You have a choice to make, young Steward. If you are to leave here and escape to freedom, you must leave me with the assurance that you will pledge yourself to pursue all truth wherever you find it, not just one truth in one place. There is no one truth, Steward. Do you understand that? Expand your search. The king-myth will demand your full allegiance and cut you off from all other sources of truth but itself. It has demanded such of everyone who has ever pursued it, and it will for you. For that reason, you must leave it behind. It is only in the defiance of any one great truth that we can all live together in peace. And that is my greatest desire—that we all live in unity and peace. That unity is only possible through an abandonment of the idea of any one truth and the joyful pursuit of truth at every level and in all things."

She walked to Steward, taking his face in her hands, rubbing her soft fingers across his cheeks and looking deep into his eyes. In a silky-smooth voice carried on the sweetest breath, she concluded, "You will give up your pursuit of this king, won't you, Steward? It is the only way to real freedom and peace and serenity. Give it up and I will help you find favor again here in Seudomartus. Give it up and you can live here in harmony. Give it up and you can enjoy the Halls of Wisdom whenever you want. Give it up and you can live out all your days in happiness and contentment. Give up your search, Steward, and I will set you free."

He was intoxicated with her beauty and mesmerized by her voice. Her words seemed so right and true. Perhaps his journey *was* finished. Perhaps he could stop here and enjoy this place—

"No!" Steward jumped back, pulling free of her hands. "I am sorry, Philandra, but I must be true to what I have seen and heard. I do not know where real truth may lie, but I know that I must follow the king's voice. I cannot stay here, and I cannot abandon my journey."

Philandra stood firm, staring at Steward with a fierce glare and speaking with a venom that pierced him. "Very well then, that is your choice. You shall not be free! For there is only one thing that cannot be tolerated in Seudomartus, and that is intolerance itself!"

She stormed out of the chamber and into the hallway. "Guards! Take these men away and do with them as you please. They are traitors and enemies of Seudomartus!"

Obed looked at Steward. "The table!"

He thought for a moment and then realized what Obed was asking. He reached down and picked up the heavy bronze table that sat next to his chair. He ran toward the great window that looked out on the plaza and hurled the table through it. The crash sent glass flying in every direction. He and Obed jumped through the gaping hole and plunged down onto the plaza. Bruised and shaken, Steward struggled to his feet and started running.

"Obed! Guards! Here they come!"

A band of men had been waiting for them outside the main doors and came running at the sound of breaking glass. Obed and Steward ran to the edge of the plaza. Just in time, produce carts came from everywhere, blocking the path of the pursuing guards.

Steward heard the captain of the guard shout at Albert, "We will be back for you later!" Then they pushed the carts aside and were after Steward and Obed again. But by that time they'd reached the dense forest past the edge of the plaza.

People everywhere were shouting to the guards and pointing out their position.

Obed ran at his side. "All of Seudomartus is against us now. Steward, we're out of options."

They emerged from the trees and Steward looked for an escape route, but all that was ahead of them was open parks and wide walkways. Steward glanced behind them—the guards were just yards away.

This is it. Our escape is hopeless.

"Whoa, what?" Something grabbed Steward by the ankles. He looked down to see Zanon looking out from a tunnel entrance hidden by an old tree stump.

"Quickly, in here. The time has come!"

Steward grabbed Obed's arm, and they climbed down into the tunnel. Zanon pulled the old stump over them just as the guards came into view. The three sat silent until the footsteps were gone.

Zanon lit a small torch and moved with haste down the tunnel. "This way."

They followed the tunnels for several minutes, coming to many forks that Zanon navigated with ease. Just as Steward thought his back might break from hunching over and running, they came to a long ladder that went up a shaft as far as they could see.

"Quickly, up the ladder."

Steward climbed as fast as he could, with Obed right behind him. The farther they climbed, the lighter it became until at last they saw arms thrust down to meet them and pull them to the surface.

Once Steward was out of the tunnel, a man in a gray tunic shook first his hand and then Obed's.

"Welcome, my friends. Our time is short, and we must be about our business."

Zanon emerged from the tunnel. "Good leader, this is Steward of Aiden Glenn and his companion, Obed the Teacher."

Steward cringed. Obed was not a "companion." He turned to apologize to his friend, but Obed's smile told him it was fine.

"Steward, we are honored to have you here."

Steward turned back to the man in gray.

"Unfortunately, these are now the most perilous of times for all of us."

"I am afraid I am to blame for that. My visit has brought all of this upon you."

The leader came to Steward and placed two large hands on his shoulders. "No, Steward, you are not to blame. This is the culmination of the battle that has been coming for millennia. We have prepared for it and are ready. Do not blame yourself. The king has used your visit to bring about his goodwill for this sordid place. And now we must take you to the Transmitter."

Steward and Obed followed the man across a small clearing. From there, Steward could see that Starr Hill was not far from the Sacred Mount. Indeed, a high ridge hid this part of the hill from the view of anyone on the Mount or in the plaza below. Ahead of him was a thick stand of trees, and beyond that was a tent.

The leader pointed. "There, that is the place where we keep the Transmitter."

Steward almost shouted. He was about to hear the voice of the king again!

He entered the tent, secluded as it was within a stand of large, sweeping cedar trees. Inside, sitting on a table covered in a fine silk cloth, was the Transmitter.

Steward caught his breath. *It's identical to the one I held in the mountainside.*

He walked to it and picked it up, treating it with a sense of the sacred. He turned it around in his hands. Then it came—a soft glow, followed by a light that shone with such intensity Steward had to set it down and cover his eyes. He stepped back as its warmth and brightness flooded the tent.

Then came the voice. The deep, powerful, and comforting voice of the king himself.

"Steward, you have done well, my son. I know that you have faced many obstacles and encountered great danger to complete this journey. Now it is time for you to come to me. Follow the light and enter the throne room of the king."

A shaft of light shot from the side of the vessel, marking a clear path out of the tent and across the crest of Starr Hill.

"Come, Obed, let's go."

But his friend shook his head. "No, my friend. This is your journey, and now you must complete it alone."

Before Steward could argue, shouts and screams sounded from outside. He ran from the tent, followed by the others, and saw hundreds of armed men ascending the hill.

Steward looked to the path illuminated by the shaft of light. "I'll never make it."

The Starr Hill leader pointed across the plain. "Yes, you will. You must! Follow the light, Steward, and we will do the rest. All of you, come with me."

Steward watched as the band of Starr Hill Faithful and his dearest friend, Obed the Teacher, ran toward the clearing in full sight of the pursuing mob. The sound of arrows pierced the air, filling the sky and falling to earth on top of the fleeing band.

Run, Obed. Dear friend, run for your life!

Steward watched in horror as several of the Starr Hill Faithful fell to the ground. He was paralyzed, frozen by his fear and pain. Then behind him, from the tent, the voice of the king called him.

"Come to me, Steward. Come now!"

This was his only chance.

As the angry mob moved on the fleeing band of Starr Hill Faithful, Steward spun around and ran. The shaft of light pointed him to the crest of the hill. He ran with all his energy. The shaft of light led him to the edge of the hill, well hidden by a stand of willows.

He stopped to catch his breath and crouched down as he looked back at the clearing.

Dozens of bodies lay on the ground, pierced by the arrows of the pursuing mob. And then, as he watched, Obed, the wise and kind Teacher, fell lifeless to the ground from one arrow that pierced him straight in the heart.

"No!" Steward wanted to rush the mob and avenge the murder of his dearest friend, but the pursuers heard his cry, turned at the sound, and began moving toward him.

Steward scrambled to his feet and ran for his life, following the shaft of light and nearing the edge of the hill. Then he stopped.

Where is the castle?

He could see no great castle or any entry to the king's throne room, just the shaft of light shooting out into space.

There was only an open field ahead of him now, with no cover for protection.

"Where am I to go? I don't see anything! Where are you?"

The king's voice came to him once again. "Follow the light, Steward. Come to me... and trust me."

Filled with hope, he jumped from the line of deep willows and out into the clearing, running as fast as he could toward the crest of the hill.

But the clearing was too wide. His pursuers were upon him.

Steward felt a searing pain shoot through the back of his left leg, and he fell to the ground.

He tried to pull himself up. He tried to limp ahead, but the arrow protruding from his thigh crippled him. The pain was unbearable.

"I can't make it. I can't get up. Help me! I can't see where I am to go, and I can't run."

In his fall, the small set of spectacles had been flung from their resting place in his vest pocket, and now they lay right in front of him.

"See the world as the king would have you see it..."

With the mob soon upon him, Steward grabbed the glasses. He propped himself up and put them on.

Steward looked ahead and unfolding before him was a grand staircase. At the top was a set of golden doors leading into what he was sure was the throne room of the king.

He was there. He had made it.

He pulled himself to his feet and forced himself forward through the searing pain. One step, then two, then...

A second sensation of white-hot pain exploded through his back, and Steward went down in a heap. The glasses fell off his nose. Steward couldn't breathe, and the staircase disappeared into the sky.

With his right hand he fought to reach the glasses that were just inches away. Behind him he could hear the voices of his pursuers. The world around him began to grow dim as his hand finally felt the metal frames of Dunston's spectacles. He pulled them toward him and managed to slide them on his face.

As he lay there, his face against the earth, Steward could see the steps to the throne room of the king. He was partway up them, but they were too long for him now. The shaft of light that guided his way was fading, and Steward struggled for one last breath. As he did, the image of the shining castle and the stairs faded away, and he felt the grip of death on him.

In his last moment, he saw a black arm reach out to grab him, and then Steward, the young man from Aiden Glenn, breathed his last.

And out from the depths of *Tohu Wa-Bohu* came a horrifying and delirious cry of delight.

~~~~~~~~~

Merideth's words had just left her lips when Reed cried out, "He *died*? How could he die?"

"Incredible." Alex sat there. He couldn't believe it. "How could Dad leave him to die on the steps of the king's castle?"

Reed shot back. "It doesn't make any sense. This whole journey, the lands, the king, the lessons, and now he dies?"

Alex nodded to him. "I don't get it either. There's so much here to think about, but now he's died…"

"Um, boys."

Alex turned to where Merideth held a set of pages an inch thick between her thumb and forefinger.

"We still have this much to go. I think we need to find out if the rest of the story includes our young Steward or not."

"And if not, why not," Anna added.

Alex wasn't appeased. He couldn't understand what his dad was doing and saying. He knew his dad meant this land for him, and he didn't want to let him down again. But dying? Now?

Walter stood and walked into the inner circle of the four siblings. He made his way to the fire. "Before you read on, let me ask you what you each think your father may have been saying in letting Steward die right there on the king's own steps."

Alex sat silent. What was he supposed to say?

After a moment of silence, Anna spoke. "There's pain and suffering involved in following the voice of the king?"

"And mystery," Merideth added.

Reed joined in. "The king's directions are always clear but not always logical."

Walter nodded. "And the king never asks us to understand, just to obey."

An awkward silence followed. They were waiting for Alex. They knew, as well as he did, that their father was speaking to him. What would the wiser, seminary-trained brother have to say?

Walter considered him. "Alex?"

He looked out over the top of them as he spoke. "I really don't know. I guess maybe Dad wanted me to hear in this story that being faithful means following God's voice, even when it doesn't make sense. Even when it involves pain. Even when the way seems hopeless and the journey seems futile." He paused, fighting against a constricting throat.

He thought about his struggle at seminary. The questions that plagued him and the pain in the decision to leave.

It was clearer now.

"Those arrows are the doubts that the garbage of this world constantly shoots at us. Karl's brother's death in seminary was one. My migraines that wouldn't go away were another. And Mom's death…they dropped me right at the point that I was preparing to serve God with my life. Right on the steps of the goal. Steward's death is the death of faith, the death of hope, the death of calling." Alex looked at Walter. "Steward's death is *my* death."

He clasped his hand across his mouth, and tears flowed down his cheeks.

His sisters and brother stared at him, eyes wide. He couldn't blame them. They'd never seen him cry like this. Not at Mom's funeral, or at Dad's. But now…

He was falling apart.

Suddenly they were there, surrounding him, putting their arms around him, murmuring encouragement. Crying for him and with him.

Letting him know, as never before, that he wasn't alone.

Eighteen

It was nearly noon before they returned to the reading of the story of Steward from Aiden Glenn.

Walter took his usual seat back from the main living area. He watched as the four found their way to a sofa or chair and settled in for the next part of Steward's journey.

Only eighteen hours ago they'd begun this journey.

So much has changed. That's what prayer will do. Help them, Lord, for what still lies ahead.

Walter continued to study the four. Gone were the stiff exteriors and well-honed facades. In their places were openness, even vulnerability, between the siblings. He never would have thought it possible. Somehow Steward's journey and his death on the steps of the king's own castle had dismantled their defenses and reconnected them with their own deep sense of brokenness.

Walter could see that each one of them, in his or her own way, had found in Steward's journey a piece of themselves that they had lost. And they were still searching, wondering about the impact the story would have on them.

Walter could not be more pleased.

Sam, this is just what you wanted, what you and I prayed for. Now let the rest of the story find its way into their hearts.

Anna agreed to read. "It's time to find out how Dad will continue a story after killing off the main character."

She opened the book and read on.

~~~~~~~~~

Three figures walked on a long, open veranda supported by fifty magnificent columns. The air was cool and sweet, and the sun shone brightly, giving off a warmth that touched their cheeks as they strolled along. They looked out over a sweeping landscape of rich fields, towering cedars, and orchards resplendent with fruit. They descended a short stair-case that led them to a courtyard, where a tent stood. Great flags flew from each corner, and the tent itself was made of the finest gold and crimson material. There were no sides on the tent, and underneath it they could see a large bed surrounded by attendants. As they drew near, one of the attendants came to them.

"The preparations have been made. We have done all we can. Now we will wait for the king."

Their wait was not long.

Trumpets blared from atop the colonnade, and from a distant part of the palace came an entourage following the king. As he approached, everyone bowed and smiled, their allegiance to him mixed with the joy of just being in his presence.

The king smiled back and stopped to embrace the three visitors. In his rich and mag-nificent voice, he said to them, "You have done well, all I could ask for. Thank you. How-ever, as you know, your service has just begun."

Then the king turned and walked under the tent to the bed at the center. Attendants stepped back, and the king looked at the body that lay in the silk sheets. The king placed his hand on the still forehead. "Young Steward, you have done well. You were much deserving of this deep, cleansing rest. But now your slumber must end, and your final journey must begin."

With those words, the king drew a breath and blew onto Steward's face.

Steward gasped and opened his eyes wide.

Where was he? What happened—?

He looked up, and a face looked down into his. Joy flooded him, and he knew that this was the face of the king. He had never seen such a countenance. The king's face was both compassionate and commanding. It gave the immediate sense of deep grace and absolute authority.

Steward looked into the king's eyes, so full of love. "I…I'm alive. And you are the king. I must have passed through to the other side. Am I in heaven?"

The king smiled. "No, my dear Steward, you did not die…only nearly." He took Stew-ard by the hand and sat him up so that he could look around.

Steward waited for the pain.

Nothing.

He reached down and felt where the arrows pierced his leg and back.

All that met his fingers was smooth, unmarred skin.

"How did I survive those wounds? I felt my life draining away and the grip of death upon me."

"What else did you see and feel?" the king asked.

Steward fought to remember the final moments before he lost consciousness. "An arm reached out and grabbed me, but I thought it was one of my pursuers ready to give me the final blow."

"Tell me about the arm that reached for you. What do you remember of it?"

Steward paused to rethink the memory. "It was a strong arm, a firm arm..." Steward sat up straighter. "A *black* arm. It was Zedekai who grabbed me on the stairs!"

"Yes, and he saved you from the mob."

Steward rubbed his hands again along the back of his thigh. "But what about my wounds? How did they heal so quickly?"

The king's eyes widened, and a grin crept onto his lips. "Quickly? Steward, you have been with us for months. I had you put into a deep sleep, and these healers have been attending to you until your wounds closed and your strength renewed."

Steward bowed to the attendants. "Thank you. I thank all of you."

The king signaled for them to take their leave. "And now that you are healed, we have much to do. Today you will eat and rest, and tomorrow we will talk. I have much to tell you."

Rest? He was in the presence of the king. *Finally!* He did not want to rest. He wanted to ask questions, hundreds of questions.

"I have much to ask...and learn. Can we not talk now?"

The king turned back as he exited the tent. "Patience, Steward, you have a lifetime ahead of you. Rest while there is peace in the air."

After a day of dining on the most wonderful foods he had ever tasted and continuing to rest and recover, Steward was summoned to the king's throne room.

His time had come.

This is it. I will stand in the throne room of the king.

His excitement was mixed with a deep sadness. He was at the pinnacle of his journey, of his life. But his heart broke as he thought of Astrid, left back in that dreadful Ascendia. And Abner and Edith, struggling on the outskirts of Marikonia to deal with the death of their beautiful daughter. There was Obed, who gave his life for this journey. And so many others...Trevor still in chains, Tristin deceived, Cassandra demanding more paving mixture, and the five deluded elites left to influence all of Seudomartus.

I thought this would be the happiest day of my life. But now I have more questions than joy. I pray the king can help me.

He was dressed in fine but simple robes and escorted by two female courtiers down a hallway too splendid to describe. They brought him to great golden doors. He paused; he'd seen these doors before. He looked to his right and down a long staircase that ended at the edge of a glorious sweeping lawn that disappeared into the distance. As he looked closer, he could see a stain of blood on the stairs near the bottom.

One of the courtiers acknowledged his curiosity. "Yes, Steward, that is where we found you."

He looked at the courtier beside him. "Where is Seudomartus?"

She bowed and passed her hand to summon him along. "That is a question for the king."

The courtiers pulled back the large ring that hung in the center of one of the great doors, then released it so that it pounded against the door. At once the doors swung open before them.

Steward's heart pounded just as loudly. He was struggling to keep his composure.

The beauty of the scene before him stunned him. He had been preparing all these years for this one moment.

This is beyond all I could have dreamt.

The throne room of the king was not opulent like the castles of Petitzaros or the Halls of Wisdom. Yet there was an overwhelming sense of pure glory in the room. The walls were not hung with rich tapestries, and the ceiling was not gilded in gaudy gold as at Tristin's house. The windows were not stained glass as in the Temple of Temperance, nor were there spires reaching up from each corner.

There was a simplicity about the throne room that was startling, yet the entire place was filled with power and beauty.

Then Steward saw the king.

He was not dressed in flowing robes. He did not wear a crown, not even here in his throne room. But the pure presence of his passionate love and unquestionable power flowed through the room like a torrent.

His voice echoed through the chamber. "Steward, come to me."

Familiar words. Only now, would his feet move? Steward tried to obey and urged his trembling legs along as he walked to the king.

He arrived before the throne. The king sat and studied him for a moment. He spoke now more like a father than a king.

"I know you have waited long to be in this place. Is your heart at peace here?"

Steward breathed in deeply. The peace here was unlike anything he had ever known. "Oh yes, my heart is greatly at peace here."

The king rose from the throne and walked to Steward. "Remember this feeling. It is the Deep Peace. It should go with you wherever you go and stay in your heart whatever you face. It is the feeling I wish for all my people, every day. It is my greatest gift to them, and it's why they were born into this kingdom: to know me, to trust me, and to experience the Deep Peace."

All the people of his kingdom?

Steward cocked his head. Did he dare ask a question?

"Do you mean the people of Petitzaros and Ascendia too?"

"Yes, and the people of Marikonia…and even Seudomartus. They all were brought into my kingdom to know this Deep Peace." He paused and then locked his gaze on Steward. "Did you experience this Deep Peace in any of these lands?"

Steward shook his head and frowned. "No, I certainly did not."

At that confession, the king walked away from Steward as if to think, or maybe to let Steward think. Steward wasn't sure which, but the time seemed an eternity. Finally, the king turned and came back to face Steward.

"Tell me, Steward, why did you stay so long in Petitzaros?"

No, that's not a question I want to answer. Not here.

He knew there was no escape from the truth. Steward shifted his weight. What a place for the king to begin. Steward hung his head as he spoke. "I guess I loved the wealth and power that it gave. I loved being able to use the Elixir of Mah Manon to create anything my heart desired. I loved the friends who thought so highly of me because of what I had obtained. I just fell into it all and wanted it all…and more."

"And what about the Deep Peace? Did you have it in Petitzaros when you had everything else?"

The answer was easy, but the words stuck in his throat. Five years in that place, and never a moment of the Deep Peace. "No, I did not."

The king paused again. An image flashed in Steward's mind. It was his mother kneading dough. She pressed the palms of her hands into the dough to force out the air and prepare it to become a perfect loaf. The king's silence was working the same way in Steward's spirit.

The king returned to his questions. "What did you feel in those days?"

"Anxiety. I was always anxious and never…at peace."

"Anxious about what?"

Again the words did not come easy. "That I might lose what I had. That I might fall behind and have fewer rings than my friends. That I might not be doing enough to receive my rings. That I might be missing some way to get more rings, or that my friends might find other and better friends unless I threw greater parties and built a more impressive palace. The entire time in Petitzaros was filled with worry and doubt and frenzy and...despair."

"Then let me ask you again, why did you stay so long?" There was no accusation in the king's voice.

Why? Can I tell him? Greed. Lack of trust. Can I say that here? To him?

"I guess I don't really know. I wanted all the stuff, to be...you know...happy. But I wasn't, not in my heart, not for a day. I suppose I just got...pulled into it all. And the chains..."

The chains! He'd forgotten about them.

Steward looked down and realized the two heavy gold bands were still fixed around his wrists. The chains were finally gone, but the wide bands remained. Steward reached down and rubbed the skin beneath them.

Again he looked at the king, shaking his head. "I don't think you ever wanted the people of Petitzaros to wear these heavy gold bands. Will I ever get these off?"

The king smiled with a nod. "Of course. And I will replace them with new ones."

"New ones? Then we are supposed to wear these things?"

The king waved the comment away. "No, not those." The king walked over to a large cabinet and took a wooden box from it. "These."

He opened the box, which displayed two thin, light, fine gold Bracelets. He took a key from a pocket inside his robe and, with a quick turn, unlocked the heavy bands from Steward's wrists. For the first time in what seemed like a lifetime, he was free of the chains from Petitzaros.

"That feels wonderful."

The king took the Bracelets from the box and slid them onto Steward's wrists. Compared to the heavy bands of Petitzaros, the new ones felt like air. Steward studied them for a moment. He had seen such Bracelets before.

"The people of Remonant."

"Yes, they wear such Bracelets."

Steward rubbed the fine gold bands between his fingers. "I remember them, but tell me why we wear any Bracelets at all?"

The king turned and gestured for Steward to follow him. "For that, we must take a walk." The king led Steward into the courtyard and down the colonnade walk. They turned up a staircase that led to the top of the palace. When they reached the highest point on the roof of the great palace, the king looked out over the entire kingdom.

Steward looked too, and he was startled to find that from this point he could see his entire journey. "There is Petitzaros, and I can see the ramps of Ascendia to the east."

He ran around to the other side of the roof. "And there is Marikonia, and...I can see the Sacred Mount of Seudomartus!"

The king pointed out into the distance. "And look to the south. What do you see?"

Steward squinted into the midday sun. "I see a great plain divided by a mighty river. That's Kildrachan Plain and the Golden River!" Steward walked to the edge of the palace roof to get a better look.

"I can see everything from here! There is Pitcairn Moor, where I met Dunston and the first meadow I entered after emerging from Callater Pass. There are the woods where

Zedekai and I ate after my escape from Petitzaros, and there is the cleft in the mountain-side where I first heard your voice coming from the Transmitter. I can see it all from here!"

"And even farther to the south?"

Steward shaded his eyes as he strained to see into the distance. "There is a large gray cloud covering much of the far southern kingdom…it's Aiden Glenn." He turned back to the king. "It is my home." The mixed emotions welled up in him again. Joy for knowing he may soon be going home, but sadness at the thought of his mother and father sealed beneath the veil of clouds.

The king came to his side. "Yes, I see everything that happens in my kingdom from here. And I like very little of what I see. My heart breaks every time I come up here and look at the present state of my kingdom."

Steward looked up at him. "But you are the king. Why don't you change things if you are saddened by what you see in your kingdom?"

For the first time, the king's expression grew sad. "I did, young Steward."

The king led him back around to the south end.

"Look out over Kildrachan Plain. It was there that I fought for the sake of my king-dom and every person who dwelt in it. I brought my full army to bear against the evil of the Phaedra'im. It was a horrific battle. We lost so many men. My very own son fell by my side." The king's words were grief-laden. "And we won. The Phaedra'im were driven out of the kingdom, forbidden for all time from crossing over the Golden River and exiled into the *Tohu Wa-Bohu* to live out their unearthly existence in the very midst of nonexistence."

"But I have seen the Phaedra. They're everywhere."

"Yes, it is so. The Phaedra'im would only stay in exile if the people of the kingdom refused to give them entry back across the river. So I gave four gifts to my people that they might have a rich and full life—a life of peace free from the Phaedra'im."

Four gifts, four lands, and four distinct deceptions. Steward began to put the pattern together. "What were the four gifts, and what did your people do with them?"

"You have seen for yourself, young Steward." The king paused, and when he had Stew-ard's full attention, he added, "That was the purpose of your journey."

My journey was about the four gifts? But what of my name? Surely I'll learn of that as well. Patience.

Steward looked down and rolled one of the Bracelets on his wrists.

"The golden Bracelets. They were one of the gifts, weren't they?"

The king nodded. "Yes. I gave everyone in my kingdom a set of fine golden Bracelets to remind them that the land they are in does not belong to them. They are caretakers of this kingdom. I won it back for them with the blood of my men…and my son. And now I have given it to them to tend and enjoy and share. Every time they pick up a plow, plant a seed, build a barn, tend to an animal, or trade in the market, the Bracelets are there as a joyous reminder that they are caretakers of all I have given them. I wanted them to enjoy it all, share it among themselves, and rejoice in my gift to them."

The Bracelets, signs of sharing, rejoicing, and caretaking? That hadn't been his experience.

Steward shook his head. "In Petitzaros, the bands don't remind them of any of those things…or you. They have become a curse instead of a blessing."

"Indeed they have. The people in Petitzaros forgot that the Bracelets symbolized their role as caretaker. Instead they chose to play the owner and hoard them. They thought that by having more Bracelets, they could be happier. And in the whispering deception of the Phaedra, the Bracelets came to mean power and control."

Questions were swirling in Steward's mind. "Please, tell me about the Phaedra. They are everywhere in Petitzaros. How did they get there?"

Now the king spoke as if the words were hard for him. "The richest people in Petitzaros received word that the Phaedra'im possessed an elixir that had the power to make them even richer than the golden Bracelets. They were lured into a meeting at the edge of the Golden River. There they struck a deal that changed the kingdom forever. The Phaedra'im convinced the leaders of Petitzaros that with this elixir they could become kings themselves. And so they took the elixir in exchange for allowing the Phaedra'im back into the kingdom."

Of course! "The Elixir of Mah Manon."

The king nodded. "And so the Phaedra'im became the Phaedra, and Petitzaros became their first outpost back into my kingdom."

Steward scrunched his eyebrows. "That's not much of a change in name— Phaedra'im to Phaedra. I mean, did that really fool anyone?"

The king huffed. "Fool anyone? No, and it wasn't meant to. That, young Steward, is the lesson you must learn about the hearts of men. People knew the Phaedra were direct descendants of the Phaedra'im. It was taught in our schools, and stories of the great battles were retold in most households across the kingdom. Oh no, people knew. But the hearts of men, if left unchecked, will desire those things that serve only them. If their steps are not ordered by the king's work, they will linger along the pools of temptation to the things that will offer them power. When their ears are not attuned to the king's voice, they will itch for the whispers of that which tantalizes the senses and sets greed loose in their spirit. This is the heart that is ready to be led into deception, even when all signs point to danger. So, yes, the name was not meant to hide anything. Quite the opposite. It was to signal the audacity with which the Phaedra would infiltrate and infect the minds and wills of my people."

Steward understood. "And it started here in Petitzaros."

The king nodded. "They hated the people of Petitzaros and the Bracelets I had given them, so they filled their minds with thirst for more and more things. As they did, the people exchanged my Bracelets for the heavier bands of the Phaedra. And the Phaedra cursed those bands so that they would grow and become heavier as the wealth of each citizen grew."

He knew it! Zedekai was right. "So they are curses."

"The worst kind. They are curses that are seen as blessings. The greater the curse, the more my people think they are being blessed. The Phaedra are nothing if not clever."

"And the Elixir of Mah Manon is evil also?"

The king took a few steps forward and rested his hands on the top of the stone railing. "Only if it is used for evil purposes. The Elixir itself can be used in wonderful ways. It can build a house for a poor man, provide food to a hungry man, clothing for a naked child, or medicine for a woman who is ill. It can be used to provide everything needed by everyone in my kingdom, but only if it is shared. Once it is hoarded and used to make the rich richer, it becomes an evil unto itself."

The rich became richer, an evil unto itself. It was all so true. "That's what it has become in Petitzaros." Steward thought about how many times he had delighted to pour out one drop and see the extravagance it produced, but only for the rich. Guilt welled up in him. "I would have killed to obtain more of it." The confession startled him.

"So, do you understand the true purpose of my gift of the golden Bracelets?"

Steward rubbed them again. Light, comfortable, and beautiful. "I do."

"Then let us look farther east to Ascendia." The king moved across the palace roof. "How did you find Ascendia?"

That was easy. "Horrible! Do you know they crush people in a great grinding machine to make their pavement for the Ascenders?"

The king nodded. "I know."

Steward didn't understand. His tone turned to near accusation. "Can't you stop them? You're the king!"

The king didn't answer. He looked out over the kingdom to the east. Silent.

Steward regretted the tone. This was the king. *I have no right!* But the questions remained.

The king finally turned to Steward. "Listen to me now, Steward. I know your heart is broken over what you have seen. So is mine. This is my kingdom, and these are all my people. I can do great things for them, but I will not force them to obey me or accept my ways. I have won the great battle for them. I have driven out their enemy and given them the gifts that will allow them to live in freedom and peace. But they must choose that life for themselves. If I force it upon them, I will become to them a tyrant, not a king. Do you understand this?"

He wanted to. He yearned for an explanation, some answer that made sense. He rolled it over in his mind. "I think so…but the crushing machines are so horrible. It must cause you such pain to watch this happening to your people."

The king walked a little farther toward the edge, and when Steward followed him he saw the great machines in the far distance. Steward looked away, to the king, and saw his chest heave as he breathed.

Steward knew emotional pain when he saw it. And the king's pain was profound.

Soon the king turned to a courtier who had appeared next to them. He took something from her then turned back to Steward and held it out in front of him. "This belongs to you, does it not?" The king held up the Quash Cassandra had given Steward.

Steward accepted it. "I thought I had lost it in the chase from Seudomartus. How did you get it?"

The king ignored the question. "Do you know what this is, Steward?"

Steward felt its dented edges. "I…I'm not sure. I saw it used as a vessel to carry rocks and…the paving mixture. I saw it used as a weapon against others and as a breastplate for protection. But I am not sure what it really is."

Could it be? Steward looked to the king. "Was this one of your gifts to your people?"

The king nodded. "Its use has been so distorted it's no wonder you can't recognize it for what it originally was."

Then the king took Steward's dented Quash and dirty sling. He untied the sling, separating it from the brass vessel. The king turned the vessel and placed it in Steward's hands. Then he neatly folded the cloth lengthwise and laid it over Steward's arm like a towel.

Steward looked down and it became clear.

"It's a basin and a towel." Was that all it was? The brass basin and the cloth towel were simple objects when presented this way, but Steward had never seen it.

The king looked back out toward Ascendia. "When I won back the kingdom for my people, I knew that the Phaedra'im would try to divide them and pit them against each other. Through rivalry and hatred, the Phaedra'im would have an avenue to regain access to my kingdom. So I gave to each person in my kingdom these two simple items—a brass bowl and a towel—to use to serve each other. It was a symbol of relationship, of hospitality, of care, and of compassion for one another. They could be used to wash and bind wounds, clean dirty faces, and cool thirsty mouths. When my people served one another, there was no opening for the Phaedra'im to re-enter my kingdom and kill my people."

Steward ran his fingers across the rim of the Quash. "It's not service I saw. It was anger, domination...murder."

"When my people replace love for each other with love for whatever gives them authority and power over each other, they surrender all to the Phaedra'im."

Astrid! Did the king remember her? "Not all of them have done so!"

"No, not all of them. Many still seek to use the basin and towel as they were meant to be used. And a few..." He paused to look at Steward. "A few, like Astrid, lead the people in revolt against the power of the ramp builders."

Steward's heart leapt. The king knew Astrid. Was he aware of their escape, and of his parting words and feelings for her? "Will I see her again?"

The king continued his gaze into Steward's eyes. "Astrid is among my most valued followers. When she is needed, she will be summoned."

That was all the hope he needed, but his questions continued. "Good king, how did your symbol meant for service become the tool that leads to such hatred and violence?"

The king looked back to the south. "From the south, there came news to Agapia—that was Ascendia's name when it was founded—that the people of Petitzaros were building great castles with the help of the Phaedra. The people of Agapia had forgotten their history, so they did not know that the Phaedra were the descendants of the Phaedra'im. They invited a delegation of these so-called helpers to visit Agapia to aid them in their own building projects. During that visit, the Phaedra planted in the minds of the people the idea that the best place to live was high on the mountain and not in the valley. They began whispering doubts in the ears of the weaker that they would need to look out for themselves if they were to get up to the mountain. As distrust seeped into the community, a few of my people organized themselves and began building a ramp. Panic and resentment took over from there. All the Phaedra needed was to keep sowing doubt and distrust in everyone's minds. Soon the Quash was used as a tool for carrying rocks, then for mortar...until they ran out of mortar."

Steward's stomach churned again at the thought of the crushers.

The king continued. "But not everyone wanted to build. Many were content in the valley and continued to use the basin and towel for their intended purposes. Those bent on building saw them as unproductive citizens and persecuted them. One day a fight broke out near the rock crusher. A worker fell into the machine, and the rest watched as the residue poured out. A quiet pact was made to begin rounding up the poorest and least productive of the land and use them when the mortar mix ran low. Just as a substitute, at first. Then more, as demand increased. Twice I sent an armed force to shut the crushers down, but the people opened them again as soon as my force left."

How could people become so evil? What could ever stop them?

The king continued. "As I said, Steward, I cannot, I will not, force my people to obey me. I will not play the tyrant." Then he turned and looked at Steward. "But I will also not stand by and watch them destroy themselves."

Yes, there is a plan.

"What will you do?"

"That is for tomorrow. For now, we turn to Marikonia."

Steward was anxious to know how to destroy the crushers, but the mention of Marikonia filled him with grief. Steward bowed his head. What he would give to escape reliving the pain of Claire's death—but of course he could not.

"Steward, what did you see when you looked into this?" The king held up the Reflector that had plagued Steward during his days in Marikonia.

Steward looked away. "First I saw a horrible reflection of my own image. Then later a far too generous reflection."

The king laid the Reflector aside. "Tell me of your time in the house of Tristin."

"There were mirrors…Reflectors…everywhere. And the people were so plain when I looked at them, but in the Reflectors they were handsome and beautiful. Everything was distorted. Nothing looked as it should have. It was so confusing. In the end, I didn't even know my own face."

"Do you know it now?" The king picked up the object and handed it to him.

Steward was afraid to look.

What's waiting for me in this, more pain? Distortion?

He hesitated then lifted it and looked at the image that peered back at him.

It was his own face! Steward wanted to throw out his arms and dance. "Yes, this is my face."

"It always was, Steward."

"But…" He shook his head. "I know what I saw. When I looked in the Reflector, I saw first an ogre and then a far more handsome man than I shall ever be."

"Did you believe either of those images?"

Steward recounted the emotions that seemed to push him back and forth every time he looked into it. "No, not really. I always knew each was a distortion."

The king swept his hand to the east. "Then you are far better off than those who dwell in Marikonia."

Steward studied the Reflector and looked up at the king. "This was your third gift, wasn't it?"

The king nodded. "I wanted my people to know, for all time, how much I love them. The Reflectors were to help them see the image they each bore—the image of an heir of this land and a beloved citizen of this empire. I wanted them to see and know my love for them and experience the Deep Peace as they recognized their own worth, value, and beauty. I wanted them to know joy and contentment in who they were as my children and never look elsewhere for it."

"Then how did the images get so distorted?"

"Actually, the Reflectors in Marikonia are just as they were when I first gave them to the people there. What has changed are the eyes of those who gaze upon them."

"But I saw the distortion. Were my eyes bad too?"

The king seemed to ignore his question. "Do you remember the man you encountered in the road to Marikonia?"

Steward rubbed his shoulder at the memory. "Encountered? You mean bowled over and nearly killed? Yes, I remember him. He retrieved my Reflector and gave it back to me."

"And he placed doubt in your mind that you read back into the Reflector. When we doubt our own worth, we see that doubt reflected back to us, and it's most often quite ugly. He caused you to doubt your worth, and when that was planted in your mind, you saw in the Reflector exactly what you saw in yourself."

Steward thought back to the man's cutting words. He realized that by the time he actually looked into the Reflector, he was already doubting his calling and his worth. "But what of the other experience, of seeing more than I was? I think I can see now that the distortion works both ways."

"Yes, well said. Those that see themselves more highly than they ought to also reflect an image far nobler than what is real and true. They believe it with such conviction that they cause others to believe the distortion too. So the plain and homely Tristin becomes an icon…"

"…and the beautiful and innocent Claire is doomed to believe she is plain and homely." Steward was crushed under his grief.

The king's chest rose and fell from his own grief. "That is the extent to which the deception can become a reality. So many of those in the Light District are far less deserving of honor and admiration than the simple blacksmith who has believed the lie and lived the consequences."

Steward's hands drew into fists as he spat out his words. "The Light District is a farce. It is a phony place filled with fake, self-deceived, and sad people."

"Perhaps, but as long as everyone around them believes the distortion, it becomes the reality, does it not?"

He hated the thought. But the king was right. It became reality for everyone there. "Yes, I guess it does. And if you try to unravel the deception and challenge the distortion…"

"People cannot, they *will* not, believe it. Instead, they will despair to the point of taking their own life."

Steward fought back tears. He looked up at the king. "I am so sorry. She didn't deserve to die. She…"

"She was taken too soon. But you are not to blame." The king's words brought a welcome relief to Steward's spirit. He continued. "The idea of her false image was implanted into her from childhood. It is a masterful deception of the Phaedra'im."

Masterful, and heinous.

"Can the people break free from it? As you say, it's a powerful thing."

"And so will be my response."

Before Steward could ask the king what he meant, the king placed a hand on Steward's shoulder. "Tell me about Pitcairn Moor."

"Bloody awful place!" Steward shot back. "I almost forgot about Dunston. Who is he…*what* is he?"

The king laughed, a rich, glorious sound that drew out Steward's laughter too. It felt good to laugh after so much pain.

"Dunston is one of a long line of Interpreters. They have been part of my kingdom for generations. They live far in the depths of the Fungle Woods and seldom come out." The king's face turned somber. "But during the battle at Kildrachan Plain, the Interpreters played a critical role. A small band of the very best of them gained access to the *Tohu Wa-Bohu*, and they overheard the plans of the Phaedra'im. They fled to tell our generals, but they were caught before they crossed the Golden River. The Phaedra'im tortured them without mercy, but they would not tell of our plans. Only one escaped the torture and lived to carry the Phaedra'im's plans to us. His information turned the battle for us."

"Dunston?"

The king nodded. "He still carries the scars of the torture and the pain of losing his comrades. When I needed an Interpreter to meet you at Pitcairn Moor, he was the first to volunteer."

"But why didn't I see the stairs without the spectacles? Dunston told me I would learn to see the kingdom the way you wanted me to see it, but I never did—not without the spectacles."

"It was a great deal to ask for such a short journey. The distortion is too strong. It takes time and great commitment to see through it to the truth of the kingdom. But you see it now, and from this time onward you must see it always. Do you understand?"

The king sounded so…urgent.

Steward swallowed hard. Did he? "I think so."

"Then let us complete our discussion and consider your time in Seudomartus." The king walked to the farthest northeastern corner of the palace roof.

Steward looked out at the land where so much had happened. Where should he start? "There is so much to say. I heard such stories of truths and myths, of writings and heresies. My head was spinning with questions, challenges, and debates. So many people have so many opinions and views and ideas and interpretations. Some believed in you but most did not. Some encouraged my journey, and others rebuked me for it. Some questioned the existence of truth, and others thirsted for it."

He closed his eyes, seeing again the place, the people, and the events. "So many falsehoods, so much deception, so many searching hearts—and so much uncertainty." He opened his eyes and met the king's gaze. "And all in places called the Halls of Wisdom and the Sacred Mount."

It all still amazed him. "People knew about you, but no one *knew* you. Many knew that you spoke once, but no one cared that you speak *now*. Many worshipped the Transmitter, but no one worshipped *you*!"

"Did you see any of the Phaedra in Seudomartus?"

Steward had never considered it before, but now that the king mentioned it, he realized that he hadn't. There hadn't been even one Phaedra in all Seudomartus.

"No, actually. They were nowhere." He looked to the king, his eyes wide open. "Why weren't they there?"

"Oh, they were." The king began a slow pace as he talked. "The Phaedra have realized their greatest and most compelling victory in Seudomartus. So complete is their domination of that land that they need not even appear. Every ear in the city has been filled with their lies, and every heart is wholly won over to their cause."

"Except for the Starr Hill Faithful." Obed, Zanon. Such courageous people.

"Yes, except for them. The Starr Hill Faithful have been holding out against the Phaedra for centuries, but their power was waning when you came into the city. Your presence
brought the opposition to its peak and caused the destruction of one of the last Transmitters in the land."

"After I was shot, the pursuers destroyed the Transmitter?"

"No, the Starr Hill Faithful destroyed it. They felt it was better to destroy it than to
have it taken by the mob and be subjected to the scrutiny and ridicule of the learned of
Seudomartus. They would have used it to prove that the king was a myth and the Transmitter was but a deluded superstition."

"But couldn't you speak to the people of Seudomartus through it?"

The king stopped. "Steward, the Transmitter was my fourth and greatest gift to my
people after the victory at Kildrachan Plain. It was a symbol of my heart's desire to speak
directly to my people, that they may know my will for them and never doubt my love and
devotion to their well-being. I gave a Transmitter to every person in my kingdom. They
were directed to use it whenever they wanted to hear my voice. In faith, they were to set
it on a flat surface and orient the front of it to the north. Then, moving the crystal on the
arm in a clockwise direction, they were to wait and listen for my voice. I would speak to
them when the crystal was aligned with the exact direction of my palace."

"It sounds like a lot of work."

"It was, and that was the point. You see, I would be happy to speak to my people at any
time and in any form. But I wanted them to seek my voice and believe me when they heard
it. So you see, it is the faith of the user that activates the Transmitter, not the device itself."

"Then…without faith the Transmitter remains silent."

"Like a great paperweight." The king shot Steward a smile.

Steward chuckled at the comment. And when he thought about the five people he
had met, he had to admit they each would have treated it like a paperweight if they ever
actually possessed one.

But I heard the king speak through it.

"So if the owner believes, you will speak?"

"For generations I spoke to my people through the Transmitters. Young and old, rich
and poor—everyone could hear me. Then the deceivers came, and the focus shifted from
faith to the device. They convinced the people of Seudomartus that the magic was in the
Transmitter. So people began to worship the device, and they conjured up all kinds of
stories and myths about its powers. When it stopped transmitting my voice, they began

to hear other voices from other sources. Soon the distortions became the new revelations. Distorted doctrines enshrined false teachings, and misguided devotees started following every voice that tickled their ears. False teachers and charlatans sprang up everywhere, and without my truth everyone claimed their own form of truth."

"The Halls of Wisdom were built as a place for these false teachings?"

"Not at first. The Halls were built to celebrate the open discussion of what I shared with my people. And the Sacred Mount was a place of worship and of teaching my ways and commands. But when the great distortion began, faithless men and women overtook the Halls and exchanged the truth of my words for their own cleverness. And on the Sacred Mount…" The king paused, as if in pain. He caught his breath and continued in labored speech. "On the Mount, my cathedrals were once places where my truth was taught, where justice was honored, and every voice carried my words of freedom, joy, and peace. But my cathedrals are now havens of every kind of deceptive form of truth and beauty. And, worst of all, they used my name to legitimize their shameful ways."

Steward sat silent. He recalled Philandra's chambers and his confrontations with Nagas the Skeptic, Mattox the Great, and Hambry the Pious. Supposedly the wisest and holiest people in the land. All deceived.

And Obed…dear Obed…

The king placed a hand on his head. "Obed died that you might see this day."

"I miss him."

"Many dear ones in my kingdom have died that you might see this day."

That stung. Why did people die for his journey?

Steward met the king's gaze. "You speak of people giving their lives that I might complete this journey. You speak of your own response to the evil in your kingdom, and that my work is not yet done. Can you tell me, your majesty, what all of this means?"

"Yes, it is time. Come with me." He led Steward back down the staircase and into the throne room. Once there, he turned and faced Steward.

"On the day you were promised to your mother and father in Aiden Glenn, they were told that you would stand in the throne room of the king and be given the meaning of your name and the purpose of your birth. That time has now come."

Steward's heart pounded in his chest as he awaited the words he had dreamt about his entire life.

The king walked to the enormous cabinet that ran from the floor to the ceiling of the throne room. Opening the doors, he took out an object that Steward could not quite make out. As the king turned back to him, Steward watched the throne room fill with people. Soon he was the center of attention of a great assembly.

The king stood and addressed the crowd. "Since the foundations of the new kingdom, we have awaited the coming of the one who would liberate our people from the oppression of the Phaedra'im. This is our day of celebration, for the Liberator has come."

Steward looked around.

It must be Zedekai. Or is some other great warrior about to be introduced?

But the king did not look at anyone else.

The king looked at *him*.

"Steward of Aiden Glenn, your name carries only one meaning, and with that meaning comes your one purpose in life." The king held out what he had taken from the cabinet. It was a magnificent sword and scabbard, even greater than the one worn by Zedekai. The king presented it to Steward. "The meaning of your name is *warrior*, and from this day forth you will be known as Warrior Steward, Keeper of the Truth."

The king strapped the great sword on Steward's waist, and the entire room broke out in cheers and applause. Steward had no idea what to say.

Warrior? Me?

The king spoke to Steward but also to the assembly. "Steward, when I gave my gifts to my people, they were to be used and treasured. In one sense, the Phaedra you encountered on your first day out of Aiden Glenn was correct. Your name does mean to care for everything you have. What they failed to tell you is that everything you have is a gift from me. This includes these four precious gifts. But with the return of the Phaedra, these gifts are now in peril. Your journey has introduced you to the distortions and lies of the enemy. You have seen for yourself how the gifts I have given my people have been used against them. You have experienced their wrath and known their hatred. No longer can these gifts be taken for granted, but they must be fought for and won back from the deception that has engulfed them. And you will lead the charge to restore them to my people and reclaim my kingdom. That is the purpose of your life, and your time has come."

As the crowd cheered, the king escorted Steward out of the throne room and led him down a long staircase.

"Dear king, I don't understand. I am no warrior. I cannot wield a sword or fight the Phaedra'im. You cannot place your trust in me to restore your kingdom!" He was pleading now.

The king didn't speak until they reached the stables. Then he turned to Steward. "You will not enter this battle alone. Come with me and I will tell you the plans. Do not fear, Warrior Steward."

The king mounted his horse and summoned Steward to mount the steed that had been prepared for him. The two rode toward the southwest as the afternoon sun burned bright above the distant hills. They crossed vast fields of wheat and rode into the orchards, through row after row of apple trees. They raced along ancient routes through the dense forest and galloped along the crest of a steep ridge. They rode for several hours, and it took all Steward's might to keep up with the king. As early evening came upon them, they rode out into a large clearing. Ahead lay a small village of tents set up around a roaring fire. As Steward and the king approached, several servants came out to take their mounts.

Steward climbed off his horse, tired and sore and out of breath. "Where are we?"

"Look for yourself." The king pointed out across the large clearing as the last bit of light faded into darkness.

In the distance, Steward could hear the sound of a mighty rushing river, and as he looked across the vast open space ahead of them, he knew where they were.

"Kildrachan Plain."

~~~~~~~~~

Walter checked his watch as Anna read the last words and set the book down. Three more hours is about all they had. They would have to be diligent. There was more to be done when the story was finished.

Anna stretched. "Well, that explains a lot of things. Now we know what the Quash was for."

Alex stood and joined her in a stretch. "Four gifts, four lands, and four distortions. It's all coming together."

"And four of us." Merideth leaned back. "I think Dad has us right where he wants us."

Reed turned to Walter. "This is an incredible story when you begin to see all the pieces come together. How long had Dad been thinking about it?"

Walter held back a smile. This was a discovery that he couldn't wait for them to make. "I believe he started writing the story a few days after he received word of his ailing health. It was about that time that he began to talk to me about the importance of legacies."

Merideth raised her hand. "Wait, if Dad started writing this that soon after his diagnosis, then he had not yet heard of Mel Sidek's death..."

"...or the inheritance." Alex's expression was priceless.

Walter paused for a moment to enjoy it. "That's right. Your father wrote a good part of this story before he ever knew there would be an inheritance."

He let that new realization set in.

Reed rose and walked to Walter. "Then...it really isn't about the money."

Walter shook his head.

Anna was fixated on the book. "Walter, did the story change after Dad found out about the Sidek inheritance?"

"I can't say for sure, but I doubt that it did. Your father had a clear sense of what he wanted to leave each of you. He took seriously the importance of a legacy that would live in each of you far after he…and your mother…were gone. I don't think it mattered to him if the legacy had dollars attached to it or not."

Merideth pushed her fingers through her thick red hair. "I have to say, knowing that Dad wrote this without the inheritance in mind…well, it's just amazing. It changes the way I understand it."

Alex cocked his head at her. "I agree, but I'd like to hear why it changes things for you?"

"I guess I was tying much of this to Dad's concern that we would blow the money. And he's gotten his point across about that. Okay, he's spoken to me through this story about as powerfully as anything or anyone ever has. But to know that his motivation really was about how we lived our lives and not just about how we spent the inheritance…"

"It is pretty overwhelming. Yes, that's what I was thinking too." Alex looked at Walter, his expression still bearing witness to his astonishment. "Walter, are you telling us that we would have still been reading this story if there had been no financial inheritance at all?"

There it was. Their father's heart fully exposed.

Walter nodded. "Actually, for Sam, this *was* your inheritance. The money just added urgency to the task."

"Forty million dollars adds a lot of urgency." Reed smiled.

"Indeed it does, and your father felt the weight of every penny of it. He was well into the story when the word of the inheritance came. To your question, Anna, I really don't think the story changed. But he wrote with more urgency to be sure the story was completed before his death. And it was a good thing he did. I helped him type the last ten pages when he was too weak to sit at the computer. I was terrified he would ask me to finish it for him."

Anna's eyes widened. "Did he?"

"Luckily, no. I write great briefs and can bang out a mean subpoena, but I would be lost if I had to finish such an epic. When I typed the last words, I was more thankful than Sam that it was done." Walter chuckled. "And I am anxious for you to hear those words. We aren't far now, so why don't we continue?"

Anna stood. "If you don't mind, I'd like to continue reading."

They all agreed, and after fresh drinks and new positions in the living room chairs and couch, they continued the story.

CHAPTER
Nineteen

As the sunlight disappeared, the king led Steward into the largest tent, where a dinner was set up for them. Steward counted fifteen places prepared for the banquet.

"Who is joining us?"

"Ten of my mightiest warriors and three old friends."

Steward heard the sound of approaching horses and soon the tent doors flew open. In walked ten of the largest, most terrifying-looking soldiers Steward had ever seen. They formed a semicircle around the king and Steward. Then they bowed, going down to one knee, and said in unison: "To our king and to our Liberator!"

Good heavens! They were bowing to the king—and him! Steward looked to the king. "Why do they bow to me? O king, I have told you I am not a great warrior. I cannot lead these men into battle. Please don't depend upon me. I am not worthy, and I am not able."

Before the king could respond, the tent flaps opened again and in walked three figures. Steward's eyes opened wide as he saw the first figure come into the light of the tent.

"Zedekai! My friend." He ran to embrace the majestic knight. "It was you who pulled me from the stairs and away from my pursuers."

"And nearly too late. But you are strong, Steward."

Steward slapped him on the shoulder. "You saved my life, and I will forever be in your debt."

From behind the great knight there came a whiny and angry voice. "Tell this charcoal mountain to get out of my way. The lad owes his life as much to me as anyone."

Steward would know that voice anywhere. He grinned as Dunston elbowed his way around the legs of the great knight and stood before Steward.

"Dunston, my little friend. It is good to see you again." Steward tried to find a way to embrace the little creature, but he would have nothing to do with it.

"If I am correct, I saved you two times…once at the moor and once from that nasty Nagas."

"Yes, your spectacles. They did save me from a fate worse than death." Steward laughed, then his tone grew more serious. "And, Dunston, I do thank you for your service to the kingdom and to me. The king has told me of your past. You're so brave, far braver than I will ever be."

Dunston looked back at Steward. "My people have paid a heavy price that we might see this day."

Again the expectations. Even with the sword, and the encouragement from the king, he was no Liberator. When would they see he was just a boy from Aiden Glenn?

Dunston came close, pointing his stick in Steward's chest. "You are, you certainly are."

Steward gaped at him, and Dunston gave a sniff. "We Interpreters can hear a heart as well as a voice."

Steward looked around. "I count only fourteen of us, and where is the final member for the banquet?"

The ten soldiers, Zedekai, and Dunston all moved away from the entry, revealing one more figure that now entered and came into the light of the banquet tent.

"Astrid!" Steward ran to her and embraced her, wrapping her in his arms and holding her tight. They looked for a long moment into each other's eyes, and it was as if they were the only two people in the entire kingdom.

The king cleared his throat. "The banquet is ready, and the chairs are now filled. Come and let us feast together."

Servants brought an endless stream of platters with meats and fish, vegetables and dried fruits, cheeses, puddings and cakes, and the best wine in the kingdom. They ate and drank and laughed for hours. Steward recounted many stories of his adventures in the four lands. Astrid and Steward retold their story, even standing together on the edge of the banquet table to act out their daring plunge off the end of the Ascender and their crash onto the supporting beams below. The mood was happy and festive, and in the distraction of the great feast, Steward lost his fear and began to take heart in the power and ability of the company around him.

As the night wore on, the king called for the guests' attention. He directed the discussion toward more serious business. "This is a night for the entire kingdom to rejoice. I have waited for this night for centuries, as have we all. But now we must talk of the serious matters before us. Tell us, Zedekai, what is the status of the Phaedra'im?"

They followed the great knight as he spoke.

"The Phaedra'im are still convinced that they have won a great victory. The news of Steward's death in Seudomartus brought much celebration to the land of the Phaedra. And they still believe he is dead. They are content to wait for now, but they will surely plan an offensive against those who remain loyal to the king. We have but a little time to act without their discovery of our young friend's immortality."

The king's eyes narrowed. "Then we must act with great speed and care."

Zedekai was confident and powerful. *Surely he will lead the battle.* "Please, king, tell me what we are to do. Tell me…why I am here."

Astrid placed her hand on his arm and gave him a look of reassurance.

The king stood and walked to the wall of the tent. He pulled out a large map, and two servants hung it from the tent ropes so all could see it. The king looked at it for a moment and then turned to his guests.

"We are here, in Kildrachan Plain. This is the most sacred site in my kingdom. It's the place where the Phaedra'im were conquered. It is the site from which the decree was sent out banishing them from the kingdom. It is the very place…" He paused. "It is the place where my son fell. And it will be the place from where we will launch the final great assault on the enemies of this kingdom."

He pointed to the locations on the map as he spoke. Steward could now see how the entire kingdom was laid out. The meadow into which he emerged on his first day—indeed from the very edge of Callater Pass—was actually the southernmost edge of Kildrachan Plain. In a full day's ride from where he sat, he could be home.

"The plan is this. Steward, you will lead this band back along the eastern edge of Kildrachan Plain and around the southern edge of the Fungle Woods. Here you will intersect the road near the place where your journey began. From there you can journey north and revisit all four lands."

Lead the band? Revisit the lands? Steward stiffened. "I am sorry, good king, but I do not understand. Why must I go back to the lands I visited? I have seen the gifts you have given them. I understand the distorted way each one has been used and misused. I have learned the lesson. What else can I do?"

The entire assembly watched as the king walked to Steward and placed his strong hands on the young man's shoulders. He looked him in the eyes. "You must set them free."

Set them free? Me? "How am I to do that?"

The king stepped back and looked at everyone assembled, then back at Steward. "With the truth. The truth about who they are. The truth about the gifts I have given them and how they are to be used. The truth about the Phaedra and the truth about me. That will be your greatest weapon. And with it you will carry out your destiny. You were born for this, Warrior Steward. I gave you your name. I called you to this journey. I have given you these comrades. And I will be with you in victory. Trust me, Steward."

Those words resonated deep in Steward's heart. Something welled within him as he looked to the thirteen people around the table—and to Astrid. For the first time, he knew that the task was his to do, even if he felt unprepared to carry it out.

"I do trust you, my king. And I will do my best to lead this band through the cities of the kingdom and proclaim your truth wherever it may be heard."

Strong words, but Steward's doubts lingered.

The king smiled. "Now you must know more about our adversary, the Phaedra. They started as my special legion, trusted with the secrets of the kingdom and called upon for wisdom and strategy. But one day they revolted against me and sought to create their own kingdom. They built an impenetrable encampment, and their strength grew over the decades. There existed a tense but manageable truce with the kingdom of the Phaedra'im until the birth of my son was announced."

The king paced as he talked. "The Phaedra'im had planned to wait and endure my reign, then retake the kingdom at my death. But when my son was born, they realized there would be one to carry on after I died. And so they began planning their assault. They tried to overthrow me once, upon my son's second birthday, but their attack failed and many of their ranks were lost. Twice they planned to kidnap my son, and twice, through the courage of my army, the plan failed.

The king looked at Steward. "The rest is known to you—the great battle of Kildrachan Plain, the banishment of the Phaedra'im to the *Tohu Wa-Bohu,* and the deception of the gullible leaders of Petitzaros. Once the Phaedra'im regained access to my kingdom, they weighed their options and chose against another attack. Instead, they planned to lay hold of the hearts of men, seizing on their weakness to turn them against me. To destroy my kingdom from within. They exchanged physical weapons for spiritual."

The king pointed to the map, moving his finger from place to place as he spoke. "Little by little, the Phaedra gained access to the cities of the kingdom. They not only blended well into the life of the four lands, they also ingratiated themselves to the richest and most powerful people in the kingdom, which assured them protection and access to power. In time, the Phaedra caused greater damage to the kingdom than the Phaedra'im had done through countless military attacks over centuries."

Zedekai stood. "That is why we will fight them—not with arrows or blows from the swords of mighty men, but with clear and simple truth from the mouth of a young man from Aiden Glenn."

Astrid stood with him. "And you will be heard, Steward, because your heart is right and your spirit is pure. If you speak the truth to them, they will listen."

Oh, to have her confidence! "But what if we are confronted by the Phaedra?"

Dunston struck his cane on the ground. "You mean *when* we are confronted, for they will surely stand and fight when they must."

"Then"—Zedekai drew his sword from its scabbard—"we shall deal death blows to them again."

The king stepped in between Steward and the great knight. "However, my young Liberator, we must not seek outright war with the Phaedra. Not yet. They are still a very powerful enemy. You must do all you can to complete your task while engaging them as seldom as possible. Truth and grace must be your first weapons, not swords and arrows."

Zedekai nodded and sheathed his sword.

Keep the sword close! "Can the Phaedra be killed?"

Dunston shuffled forward. "The Phaedra are more spirit than flesh. The spirit of a Phaedra is like a parasite. It uses its physical form as a means to enter and move about our world. A fatal blow to the Phaedra will send its spirit screaming out of its flesh and back to the depths of the *Tohu Wa-Bohu*. All that is left behind is an empty robe, and one more Phaedra is gone forever."

Zedekai patted his scabbard. "They are skilled and clever warriors, but they can be defeated."

Steward hoped he was right.

"And now one last thing." The king stood at the map again. "Once the Phaedra know that you are alive and leading the charge through the lands of the kingdom, I am confident many will retreat and prepare for war. I do not believe they will return to the *Tohu Wa-Bohu*, but instead they will assemble again in the Ancient Fortress of the Phaedra'im." The king pointed to an area in the south. "There they will make their plans for war. If we are to avoid such a conflict, we must not let them get there."

Steward looked at the map then moved for a closer look. "Where is the Ancient Fortress?"

The king placed his finger on the spot. It was written in old script, and Steward squinted to decipher the blood-red ink: "Ancient Fortress."

Right below was the more readable description.

Steward gasped. *Village of Aiden Glenn.*

"Aiden Glenn?" He stared at the king. "My home is the site of the Phaedra'im's fortress? How can that be? I lived there all my life. I've climbed every hill and walked through every valley and glen. I know that entire country like my own room. I've never seen any sign of a great fortress."

The king's gaze was steady, his voice calm. "The Phaedra'im's fortress is built at the top of the great mountain that looms over Aiden Glenn. The thick cloud that hangs over the countryside of Aiden Glenn was formed by the Phaedra'im to keep those who lived in the valley from seeing to the top of the mountain. My dear Steward, you and your ancestors lived innocently, never knowing that the greatest evil to beset this kingdom had its stronghold right above your housetops."

Zedekai leaned forward, his hands clasped on the table. "Every year when I came to receive the assurance from your parents that you would make this journey, I looked across to the empty fortress before descending through the clouds and across Callater Pass. I vowed each year that the man who emerged from beneath the ramparts of that evil fortress would one day return to tear them down."

Astrid was now beside him. "So, you see, Steward, the Liberator was born in the very shadow of the enemy's stronghold."

He looked from her, to the knight, to the others. "And if the Phaedra return to amass and plan for war, they will gather on the mountain above my parents' house."

"Which is why we must not let that happen." The king folded the map and returned it to its sheath. He turned and raised his hands toward Steward. "Not at any cost."

The entire company responded. "Not at any cost."

And with that the banquet was concluded.

The king took Steward aside and led him out into the cool evening air. They walked onto the expanse of Kildrachan Plain. They did not speak but just took in the beauty of the night sky, the stars, and half moon that hung low in the eastern sky. They could hear the distant sound of the Golden River as it roared through the rocky ravine before slowing to a wide, peaceful flow along the western edge of the great plain.

It seemed at first that they were walking without a purpose, but soon Steward sensed he was being led somewhere. They climbed a slight rise in the plain and emerged at the top of a small, domed hill that gave an even more impressive view in the moonlight. Far behind them were the voices of the camp and its crackling fire. Ahead was the expanse of the plain rolled out to the horizon.

The king continued a few feet and then stopped next to a stone that looked like it had been set upright and placed with great care. As Steward drew near, he saw that it was a headstone for a grave. The king knelt, grief evident in his heavy sighs. Then he stood and turned to Steward.

"Warrior Steward, this is the grave of my son. He fell at the place where we are camped, and we buried him here. I wanted you to see this place and know the price that was paid so we might see this day."

Steward's throat constricted. A painting of the king's son hung in the great throne room, and Steward had studied the man's noble features. Anyone had only to hear the king speak of his son to know the depth of his love for him. Such grief and anguish must be with the king every day.

But this new reminder of the responsibility that was being laid on Steward rekindled an anxiety that now threatened to overwhelm him. "Good king, I am overcome by the faith you and the others have put in me. I...I know the strength of your ten warriors, and I have great confidence in Zedekai, Astrid, and Dunston."

"Then what do you lack?"

"It's me. I have no confidence in me!" He spread his hands before the king. "How do I lead, and why should anyone follow me? I am not equipped for such a task. It's too great for me. Please, please, dear king, don't send me out to fail. I can't bear the thought of failing you or my colleagues or the kingdom...and your son. I can't fail him, not at the price he paid. Please tell me how I am to lead and not fail."

The king took Steward by the shoulders. "Steward, my dear Steward. You must remember that it is not whom you are leading, but who is leading *you* that determines the nature of your legacy and the success of those who will follow you. Listen to my voice. Trust me and follow me. Do that and you will have all you need to lead others."

That was the last time Steward would speak of his doubts. The die was cast. Later, as he tried to sleep, the challenge before him rolled over in his mind.

All four lands. That means Czartrevor, Cassandra, Tristin…and Abner. And it means a return to the Ascenders, the Sacred Mount, the Halls of Wisdom, and Philandra. My hope must be built on the king alone. Trust, Steward. Trust.

The dawn's first light was enough to wake Steward from a fitful sleep. He rose and dressed. He strode from his tent, aware that the time was at hand for the last great episode in his journey. The ten soldiers were already preparing their mounts. Zedekai was placing supplies in his satchel. Astrid emerged from her tent dressed for battle, which took nothing away from her beauty. Even Dunston looked like a warrior. He would ride with Astrid, since no horse small enough for the little creature could ever keep up.

Steward looked around but did not see the king anywhere. Then he noticed that the king's tent and the tents of his servants were packed and gone.

Zedekai was saddling his horse.

"Where is the king? I want to say goodbye and ask for his blessing."

"The king is already back in his palace. He asked me to give you this." He handed Steward a small round shield with the insignia of a crown on it. As Steward examined it, he found words inscribed on its rim:

it is not whom you are leading but who is leading you that will determine your legacy.

Steward smiled back at him. "It is just like yours."

"It is the signature of the king. All those who carry it do so in his name and with his blessing."

Steward placed the shield on his saddle, in full view for everyone to see. He gathered his satchel and strapped it to his horse. Then, donning his sword, he climbed aboard the great steed and waited for the others to gather.

"Today the sword of truth will be wielded throughout the kingdom until the enemy is vanquished and the people of this kingdom know again that the king reigns in splendor and power and justice and grace." Steward raised his sword to the sky and then, joined by his thirteen companions, cried out, "This is the day of liberation!"

He kneed his horse and galloped across Kildrachan Plain to the east, toward the Fungle Woods.

~~~~~~~~~~

"The adventure is on!" Reed was bouncing in his seat.

"And we are near the end, from the look of it." Merideth leafed through the remaining pages.

Walter sat forward in his chair. "Alex, why don't you read from here? There are only a few chapters left."

He would prefer to listen, but it seemed appropriate for him to read the end of the story. He prayed he could face whatever was left in his dad's message to him in these final chapters.

"I'll be happy to. Give me ten minutes and I'll be ready to go."

They stood to take a short break, and when all had gathered again, Alex was back in front of the book. "Let's see how Dad chooses to end this story." He slid a large pillow behind him then pulled them all back into Steward's battle for the kingdom.

CHAPTER

Twenty

Steward's horse scared up a flock of mourning doves that exploded into the air as the group's horses galloped along the path that led to the hillside overlooking Petitzaros. Steward arrived first and pulled his horse to a stop. The others joined him, the steaming breath of their tired horses filling the crisp morning air. Steward dismounted and walked to the edge of the crest. He watched as the morning sun glistened against the rooftops of the sea of little castles filling the valley below.

This is where it had all begun.

Astrid came to his side. "It's been a long time since I've seen Petitzaros."

"It's not been long enough for me." Steward looked down and kicked the ground. "I spent the first night of my journey right here."

Zedekai joined them as Steward continued. "And this is where you and I sat when I left. I'll bet if we look, we can find a few of the broken rings you smashed with your sword."

Zedekai pointed to him. "And you were wondering if I was evil in the flesh." A slight smile crossed his lips.

Steward nodded. "Yes, that's exactly what I was thinking." He stared at his friend for a long moment, keeping his eyes steady and his brow tight. Then they both roared with laughter.

Astrid just shook her head and grinned. "You two. C'mon, we have work to do."

As they mounted, Dunston called out. "Where do we start in this awful place?"

Steward pulled his reins and readied his horse to run. "To Trevor's house, of course."

Zedekai rode to his side. "You mean Czartrevor?"

Steward galloped off, shouting back, "No! Not after today!"

Steward led the band down through the massive gates and into the streets already crowded with anxious citizens seeking the trappings of success. The presence of Steward and his warriors sent people scurrying for cover. As the entourage moved through the city, Steward sensed a familiar tension in the air. Ahead, Steward saw Phaedra hurrying through the street. They gathered in small groups under the colonnades near the city center.

We must not engage in battle. We must keep from that for as long as possible.

He signaled to the others. "Come, let's ride!"

They galloped onto a side street that took them through the southernmost part of the city into lesser Petitzaros. In this neighborhood of the poor and forgotten, no one took much notice of the band, and the Phaedra were nowhere to be seen.

Steward reined in his horse. "Let's stop here first." He looked around at the dirt streets, rundown shops, and people clothed in simple clothes, even rags.

Quite a contrast to the opulence of the gilded corridors of the city.

"In the five years I lived in Petitzaros, I only visited here once. Early in my stay, I'd come to carry out my duty to share my wealth with the poor. That's what I thought I was supposed to do. But once I got here, I was so unnerved and uncomfortable I just left a small gift and…ran."

"You never came back?" Astrid looked around.

Steward shook his head. "Now that I'm back, I need to see these people for who they are."

Three children played in the street. Steward dismounted, seeing their eyes widen as he did so. They were surprised.

But not afraid.

He approached the boys and asked them their names.

"I am James," the first replied.

"And where do you live, James?"

"There." He pointed to a small house made of mud brick, tin, and tarps. "These are my brothers, Jesse and Jacob."

"It's a pleasure to meet you. May I meet your parents?"

The boys scanned the warriors' fine clothes and weapons. James shrugged. "Sure, I guess."

He ran to his house and soon returned with his mother and father. Astrid joined Steward, and he couldn't restrain his sorrow as he watched the parents come to them.

Tattered clothes, sickly appearance. This much poverty was unacceptable in a land so rich.

The father spoke first. "What may we do for you, good knight?"

"You can, my friend, tell me why you do not share in the wealth of this land? What keeps you here when there is so much abundance just blocks away?" He made sure there was no accusation in his voice, just curiosity.

The father folded his hands together. "Do you know the golden bands worn by the wealthy and powerful of this land?"

"I do."

The father continued. "They are earned by acts of selfishness and greed. They are multiplied when wealth is hoarded, and they are accumulated through work that is undertaken solely for that purpose. Look at my wrists." The man held out his bare wrists. "I work harder than any of the kings of Petitzaros. Yet I have no bands. My work is not rewarded with wealth and power because I have no ambition to wealth and power."

Zedekai stepped forward. "But surely you want more than this?"

"Yes, of course," the mother responded. "We want new clothes for our children, and education and a future for them. We want everything every father and mother want. But this place will not allow the poor to prosper without their commitment to greed and selfishness. You cannot care for family, share your possessions, and set aside the thirst for power without also forfeiting your access to these other things."

The man slipped his arm around his thin wife. "I am afraid it is either the way of the czar or the way of poverty. There is no room for generosity without poverty, or compassion without cost."

Steward walked up and placed his hands on the man's shoulders. "That day is now coming to an end. We will be back, and the liberation of Petitzaros will begin here."

Steward and Astrid mounted their horses and the band rode off. They returned to the wide boulevard that led past the gardens and gathering houses. Steward turned up a side road and soon arrived at the front gate of Czartrevor's castle.

The anxious gatekeeper looked past Steward and fixed his eyes on the Black Knight. He sprang from his post and disappeared into the palace.

Zedekai laughed. "Looks like he remembered me."

Steward climbed down and walked up to the large palace doors. With both hands, he pounded the enormous bronze rings against the hard oak. The sound thundered throughout the palace. A second and a third time Steward pounded the doors, until a shout came from the other side.

"Wait, wait! We will open the doors to you."

Steward stepped back, and the large doors swung open. He watched as the courtyard appeared, and standing in the middle of it was Czartrevor, surrounded by at least a hundred Phaedra.

"Well, so much for keeping a low profile," Astrid said under her breath.

The rest of the band dismounted, and they all walked together through the doors and up to the waiting army of black-robed Phaedra.

Steward walked straight to Trevor.

"Czarsteward, is that really you? Oh, dear heaven, you gave us all such a fright! Welcome to you and your friends." His supposed graciousness could not hide his nervousness and fear.

Steward was shocked by Trevor's appearance. He was disfigured by the weight of his chains and the deep wrinkles that engulfed his ashen face. He was so stooped over that he had to crane his neck to look up to talk to Steward. His eyes were lifeless, and his voice cracked as though he had to force out each word.

Steward stepped closer. "My dear friend Trevor, you look terrible. What has this place done to you?"

The wrinkled little man snorted in disdain. "Done to me? What do you mean? I am the one with the fine golden chains while you stand there with nothing to show for yourself. Do not pity me, for I pity you. When you disappeared from Petitzaros, we all expected the worst. That this demon—"

Trevor spat the word out, pointing to Zedekai—"kidnapped you and brainwashed you to join the *Tohu Wa-Bohu*. And now I see that our greatest fears are true. Tell me, Steward, have you come back thinking that you can now overthrow Petitzaros and claim its wealth for yourself? Because if you do, you are quite mistaken and misguided, my old friend."

Trevor's threatening tone grew in intensity, and the Phaedra drew in closer, preparing for the battle. From the corner of his eye, Steward saw his comrades place their hands on their swords. Though none drew their weapons, the scene grew tense as Steward looked down into his friend's eyes.

"I have not come to lay siege to Petitzaros, dear Trevor." He let the sound of Trevor's true name hang in the air. "I have come to set it free. And I shall begin with you!" With that, Steward drew his sword and lunged into the mass of Phaedra.

The battle was intense but short. Although greater in number, the Phaedra were no match for the skill of the king's finest. Empty black robes soon lay thick on the ground, and the remaining Phaedra withdrew, leaving a startled and shaken Trevor alone amid the warriors.

"Please...please...do not kill me, Steward! I will give you all my wealth. Take everything—my Elixir, my palace, even my Bracelets. But please, spare my life!" Trevor managed to get even lower to the ground as he pleaded.

Steward sheathed his sword and knelt next to his friend. He placed his hands on Trevor's shoulders and straightened him to look in his eyes. "I have not come to kill you, my friend, but to give you back your life." He drew his sword again.

Trevor cowered and screamed as Steward brought his sword crashing down into the pile of golden rings that lay on the floor in front of his friend. The blow sent shards of metal flying through the air in every direction, and the sound echoed through the empty, gilded halls of the palace. Trevor looked up to see the remnants of broken rings, and he looked down to examine the few that were still attached to his wrists.

"Look what you have done!" His voice shook with hate. "You might as well have killed me."

"No, Trevor, these rings are chains that have held your soul in bondage. Come with me and I will show you what real life looks like." Steward pulled him to his feet—

And Trevor stood.

Straighter.

He stared at the shattered golden links that lay around him and rubbed his shoulders as he stretched to straighten even more.

Steward walked to the large mahogany chest behind Trevor's throne and took from it the ornate bottle that held the Elixir of Mah Manon. He returned, mounted his horse, and pulled Trevor onto the saddle behind him.

The band rode out of the palace.

When the warriors were gone, the Phaedra emerged from hiding and began collecting the empty robes of their fallen comrades.

One Phaedra looked at the others. "That cannot be Steward of Aiden Glenn. This is a trick of the king. Steward is dead. We saw him die on the steps of the king's own throne room. This is a deception."

"Still," a second Phaedra replied, "we must report this at once."

Three Phaedra were dispatched to carry the news across the Golden River.

The riders galloped up the boulevard and turned down onto the dirt streets of lesser Petitzaros.

Trevor protested. "What are we doing in this filthy place?"

Steward was silent. He stopped again at the house of the three brothers, and he and the others dismounted. The father, mother, and three boys took cautious steps out from the doorway into the morning sun. Steward summoned them over. As they drew near, Steward pulled Trevor to his side.

"I wish to introduce you to someone. This is my friend, Trevor." Steward swept his hand toward the disgruntled, hunchbacked man.

"*Czar*trevor!" he shouted at them.

Steward ignored him. *"Trevor* is here to give you a most marvelous gift." Steward removed the bottle of Elixir from his satchel.

"No, you can't! That belongs to me." Trevor shook with anger.

Steward stilled him with a look. "Surely you will not miss one small drop."

Trevor watched as Steward unstopped the bottle and moved to an open area in front of the rows of makeshift houses. People began to emerge from among the tangle of shacks to watch what was happening. Steward looked around at the faces of the poor of lesser Petitzaros and smiled at the transformation about to take place.

He tipped the bottle on its side until a single drop of the potent Elixir fell from the rim and dropped into the dusty soil at his feet.

At once, the ground exploded with life. Steward backed away as fruits and vegetables shot up from everywhere. Then the finest breads, meats, and cheeses emerged from the empty soil. Soon the entire square was filled with food and drink of all kinds, as much as the entire region of lesser Petitzaros would need.

The people stood, mouths hanging open, staring at the banquet that had been created before them. Then all at once, like a bursting dam, delighted shouts and joyous laughter rang out so loudly Steward wagered it could be heard halfway across the valley. People came running from every direction, rejoicing as they plunged into the feast with total abandon.

Steward worked his way over to Trevor, who still stood in a stunned silence as children ran past him on every side. "What do you think, my friend? Have you ever seen this much happiness in the gaudy homes and garish meeting halls of Petitzaros? And when, dear Trevor, was the last time *you* felt such pure joy as these, the poor?"

Trevor watched the people then looked down at the few remaining links hanging from his heavy bands. He looked at the single thin Bracelet that hung from each of Steward's wrists. "Steward...what was it like when you took these off?"

"Absolutely liberating."

Trevor stood a little taller and lifted his head a little higher.

The transformation taking shape in his friend made Steward smile. He held up the bottle of Elixir. "Just one drop did all that, Trevor. Imagine what it would mean to these people if they had the whole bottle."

Astrid reached out and took the bottle to examine it for herself. "They would probably make sure everyone had enough."

Trevor continued to stare at the feast. "And they would be thankful."

Astrid handed the bottle to Trevor. "This is how the king intended the Elixir to be used. This is its true purpose. Not that a few have everything, but that everyone would have what they need."

Trevor held the bottle up to the light. "There is enough Elixir in Petitzaros for everyone to have so much. How is it that these poor people had so little right here, in front of our very eyes?" As he spoke, he straightened more, his cheeks filled with color, and his eyes started to shine. He shook his head. "Steward, what is happening? It's as though life is returning to my entire body!"

Steward smiled at him. "Tell me what you are feeling right now."

Trevor pondered the question. "Light, settled, happy...even dare I say it...content."

"My dear Trevor." Steward looked him in the eyes. "What you are feeling is the Deep Peace, and it's the greatest gift from the king."

"It's a feeling I don't ever wish to lose. How do I keep it, Steward?"

He was so proud of his friend. He was asking the right questions. He was sensing freedom. "You can only know the Deep Peace of the king when you know him and his purposes for your life. You keep the Deep Peace by setting aside everything that prevents you from hearing his voice."

"Steward, we have visitors."

At Zedekai's words, Steward looked to find dozens of men and women from Petitzaros gathering at the edge of the courtyard. A few arrived in carriages, and a few walked, but the commotion of the feast brought them out to see what was causing such celebration.

And there, throughout the growing crowd of Petitzaros's finest, the Phaedra milled about, whispering into the ears of the Petitzaros elite, who nodded then shook their heads in disgust and resentment.

"Look at their gold chains."

Steward heard Trevor's low words and turned to see his friend staring at the wealthy people who had gathered.

"How they glisten in the sun..."

He looked at Steward, who recognized in Trevor's eyes the yearning to hear the comforting whispers of the Phaedra assuring him that he was a good person, that his wealth was justified, and that his palace was nothing more than he deserved.

Trevor stroked the bands on his wrists. He shook his head. "What have I done? I've lost my rings. My reputation. Prestige. Fame." He looked back at the people feasting, and his lip curled. "Look at this mob! They don't *deserve* this banquet."

Steward watched Trevor's face begin to pale. His shoulders hunched ever so slightly. The deception of Petitzaros was calling him.

"Dunston, I think we have need of your splendid spectacles!"

At once the small figure came to Steward's side. He reached into his waistcoat and produced the set of gold-rimmed glasses, which he presented to Trevor with notable ceremony.

"What's this? Who is this child, and what am I to do with these spectacles? I can see fine, thank you. And what I see is that I have been a fool to reject the finer things of Petitzaros."

Steward kept his voice even. "Trevor, you are so close to your freedom, but you will always be in bondage until you can see the world as the king wants you to see it."

"As it *really* is, you mean." Dunston crossed his arms over his chest. "Not in the distorted way you have learned, but the way that is ordered by the king. And I am no child. I camped in these hills before the first castle was ever built, before the great lie was told to the people of this valley, and before the Phaedra began their campaign of quiet deception. Put on the glasses and see for yourself the reality of this scene."

Trevor snorted at Dunston but slid the glasses onto his nose. He looked up and caught his breath.

Steward understood. Well he remembered the first time he looked through them. "Tell me what you see, my friend."

It took a few tries before Trevor could respond. "It is most startling! The poor people of lesser Petitzaros aren't dirty or in rags. They are dressed in elegant robes that glisten like the finest silk. Their hair sparkles and their faces shine as if reflecting some wonderful warm light. Their eyes are bright, and their smiles and laughter are so sweet."

Trevor slid the glasses down and looked at the crowd without them.

"And now?" Steward smiled encouragement.

"When I look at them with just my eyes, the dirty garments of peasants return." Trevor slid the spectacles back up his nose. "And now they are beautiful people feasting on the banquet in the square." He frowned. "But if they look like this, then…"

He turned to look at the elite of Petitzaros—and jumped back.

Steward steadied him. "It is all right, Trevor. You need not fear the truth in what you see."

"But…they are horrible. Oh, Steward, their faces are so contorted that I can scarcely look at them. And their gold bands and links? They are lead-gray chains. Their eyes are so…so cold and lifeless." He looked away. "It's hideous."

Steward wished Trevor could be finished, but there was more he had to see. "Trevor, please, look again. Tell me what else you see."

Hands trembling, Trevor slid the spectacles on his nose and looked at the elite once more. It took a moment, but then Steward saw his friend's eyes widen behind the glasses.

"What is it?"

Trevor shook his head. "Walking among the twisted figures of the people…"

Steward nodded. "Yes?"

"The Phaedra. They are everywhere. But they look…horrible. Boney, ashen faces. And their smiles!" Trevor shivered. "They are the sickening kind of smile that evil men wear when they've achieved something diabolical. They look…"

"Evil?"

Trevor nodded. "They have the satisfied and gloating look of evil having its day." His voice choked, and he grabbed the glasses from his face. "Is that…the way the wealthy were…is that how…I really…look?"

Steward nodded.

Trevor fell to his knees and sobbed. He put his hands to his face then pulled them away and stared at the bands and the long chains of heavy rings hanging from them. "It's these cursed things! They are a deception, a lie. They put chains on us and tell us we are free. What fools we are!"

He struggled back to his feet. "Steward, how did you get your Bracelets off? Can you help me?" Trevor held out his arms, trembling.

Steward so wanted to help his friend, but the king hadn't given him instructions on how to remove them. He looked at the other thirteen in the party, and all shook their heads. "Trevor, I am afraid I cannot take them off."

Trevor cried out. "Surely someone can remove these Bracelets! How else can I be set free?"

A voice rang out from behind them. "I can remove the bands."

A man emerged from the crowd, and as soon as Steward saw him, he knew exactly how the king meant for freedom to sweep across Petitzaros.

The man came to Trevor. "I am Jonah. I'm one of the people of Remonant. We have been given the keys to unlock the bands of anyone who wishes to have them removed." He pulled a key from his pocket. "Do you really want to remove them?"

Trevor looked around him at the joyful throng feasting on the produce from one drop of an Elixir that had sat on his shelf for years. Steward saw his friend's anguish that so much suffering had gone on just a short ride from his palace and the ease with which *he* could have alleviated that suffering.

Trevor held his hands out to the man from Remonant and cried out, "Take these cursed things off me!"

Jonah stepped forward and with a quick flick of his wrist turned the key in the lock and the heavy bands fell to the ground. Trevor rubbed his wrists then lifted his arms in the air and danced around. "I'm free, I'm free!"

Steward waited for him to stop and then produced a small box. "Trevor, this is a gift to you from the king. It is the true way in which we are to wear Bracelets." He opened the box and produced two of the small, fine gold Bracelets.

Trevor looked from them to Steward. "Then the king does want us to wear gold Bracelets?"

Zedekai joined them. "Yes, the king created everything and called it good. He gave us the Bracelets so that every time we stretch out our hand to tend a crop, pick a piece of fruit, build a wall, polish a piece of steel, or put a kettle on the stove, we will be reminded that it all belongs to the king, and he has given it to us to enjoy…"

"And share," Astrid added with a smile.

Steward slipped the Bracelets onto Trevor's wrists and then handed him the bottle of Elixir. "This is now yours to use in whatever way you see fit. Be aware, Trevor, that these light Bracelets can grow into the heavy ones you have just taken off if you use the Elixir for your own gain while ignoring the needs of others. Use the Elixir with wisdom and care. It is the source of both blessing and curse."

Trevor took the bottle and looked up to the towering castles all around them. "I shall have a great challenge convincing the others to shed their chains and share their Elixir. I am not very optimistic about my success."

Steward patted Trevor on the shoulder. "The king is not interested in your success, just your faithfulness. Besides, the wealthy of Petitzaros are not your enemy or your cause."

As he spoke, a movement caught his attention. Phaedra had taken up position on the outskirts of the area.

Trevor saw them as well. "The Phaedra, yes. How do I handle them? They'll be after me to conform to the pattern of this place. They will haunt me and torment me with their whispers and lies until I cave in and return to my former ways. How can I stand in the face of their power and presence?"

Zedekai pointed to them. "If you have no ear to hear them, the Phaedra are powerless. Their only weapon is weakness of spirit. If you refuse to hear them, they will leave you alone."

"And we will be there for you." As Jonah spoke, dozens of the people of Remonant emerged from the crowd and encircled Trevor. As they did, the Phaedra backed away and disappeared down the streets of Petitzaros. "We stand as one against the Phaedra, and we will overcome in the name of the king."

The lead guard of the king's army stepped up. "Warrior Steward, we must be off if we are to stay ahead of the Phaedra."

Steward nodded to the warrior.

Trevor raised an eyebrow. "Warrior Steward?"

"Yes, my friend. I completed my journey and stood before the king in his throne room. He gave me this name, and now I pass it on to you. We are all warriors in this battle, and now you and all the people of Remonant are part of the fight. I commission you all, in the name of the king, to resist the Phaedra and set your people free. Will you fight with us?"

The assembly raised their hands and shouted. "We will fight with you, Warrior Steward, for the sake of the king and all that is true!"

Steward mounted his horse and prepared to leave. He looked back to Trevor, who returned his look with a broad smile.

"Thank you, my dear, dear friend. You have truly set me free."

"Not I, Trevor, but the king. Now the Deep Peace of the king to you and to everyone who is set free to know and serve the king!"

"Deep Peace, Warrior Steward," several cried back, lifting their hands to the sky.

Steward nudged his horse, and he and the warriors sped off through the streets of Petitzaros. Steward held back a grin at the way Dunston clung to the back of the lead warrior, his face shining with joy. As they rode toward the gates, Steward looked back one last time.

May this place be changed forever. Good king, give my friend Trevor the strength to set these people free.

They rode on through the gates and turned north along the road leading to Ascendia.

~~~~~~~~~

Alex held the book in his lap. "That's a great story, but in real life, in *my* world, can one person really save Petitzaros?"

Anna considered his question. "I dunno, but I want to get a pair of those glasses."

"I think I'd be too scared to even put them on." Alex gave his siblings a weak smile. "Who knows how any of us would look?"

Walter had come in to join them. "I shudder at the thought. But your father and mother had an uncanny way of seeing things in people that few others could see. It was like they *did* have a set of lenses that allowed them to see potential and good where most of us saw hopelessness. That's why your mother was able to care for Mel Sidek as she did."

"And why we're here today." Merideth's words were soft, thoughtful.

Walter nodded. "Precisely. Everything in this story and in this house is a testimony to their ability to see the world as God sees it. Through the eyes of faith."

"And with the mind of Christ." Alex smiled at Walter's look. "I did learn some things in seminary. I think Dad would say that Dunston's glasses reveal the kingdom of God that is present everywhere, even when we can't see it."

Walter showed his approval with a slow nod. "I think that's your father's intention with these spectacles. He and your mother tried to see the world as they believed God saw it, which is why they were able to do the work they did with such grace."

Merideth stood and stretched. "Back to your question, dear brother. Can one person change Petitzaros?" She walked toward the kitchen and looked back. "Not the Petitzaros I live and work in."

Reed got up to join her. "I have to agree. But somehow, don't you think Trevor has a chance?"

She shot back. "Ghost of a chance, if you ask me."

Anna joined in. "It may be more about Trevor's own change rather than how many join him. Most revolutions start with one passionate person."

Alex set the book down and looked at Walter. "Still, one convert in a world that's sold out to everything material seems pretty weak. I know Dad always told us to believe that each of us can make a difference in the world. But I just think our dear friend Trevor is in over his head."

Reed came back in from the kitchen. "Maybe that's the point. Alone, we'll drift back to our old kingdom-building ways. We need others, like the people of Remonant, to stand with us. Only where are they? Who are they?"

Walter let a couple of moments of uneasy silence go by and then replied. "Perhaps they're all around us. They're the people we don't see because they live simple and humble lives. They don't call attention to themselves, but they're there nonetheless. And in strong numbers, I believe. If we choose to follow the way of young Steward—"

"Warrior Steward." Anna smiled.

"Yes, Warrior Steward—then we'll want to search out others who live this lifestyle every day. And when we find them, we will have found our comrades and colleagues in the battle."

The room fell silent again, and Alex sensed that it was time to continue. He picked up the book and read on.

CHAPTER
Twenty-One

Five hours of riding brought the warrior band within sight of the sweeping arches over Ascendia. As they came into view, Steward slowed his powerful chestnut steed to a trot, and Astrid drew her horse next to his.

He sensed her unease. "Are you ready for this?"

"I don't know. It depends on what role you want me to play."

Steward rode on for a few moments. How should he respond, seeing as he really didn't have any great plan in mind? "How do you think we should play it?"

Astrid considered the question. "Cassandra is the key, we all know that. There's no use wasting time on Elopia. She couldn't lead a revolution, even if she were to be convinced."

Steward was relieved. He never liked Elopia. But Cassandra? Leading the revolution?

"I agree, but convincing Cassandra will be an enormous task. Trevor's conversion was far easier than any we will encounter from this point on. She already knows about the crushers. I don't think Cassandra will be won over by anything short of a shocking realization that her ramp building is all in vain. And I have no idea how to make her see that."

O king, we need your help. How do we win over such a powerful person as Cassandra?

They rode on without a decision. The path turned a corner and opened ahead of them directly into the main city gates of Ascendia. Steward brought his horse to a full stop. The band of warriors gathered around him.

C'mon, Astrid, I need a plan.

There was a moment of uncomfortable silence as Zedekai and the king's warriors awaited their instructions. Dunston peered out from around the back of the lead warrior and blurted out, "Well, what's the plan? Let's get going! What's the holdup?"

Steward opened his mouth, hoping something brilliant would tumble out. But before he could speak, and to his relief, Astrid replied.

239

"This will be a greater challenge than Petitzaros, but Warrior Steward will lead us to victory here as well. The key will be to show Cassandra what lies at the end of the ramp she is building."

Steward was still lost. *Yes, okay. But how?* "And, Astrid, tell the band just how we will accomplish this."

She smiled. "It is quite simple really. We will take Cassandra to the end of a completed ramp and show her what really lies there."

What? Steward took Astrid aside. "Astrid, even in my short time in Ascendia, I learned that there is a penalty of death for anyone who enters without permission onto another person's ramp. The entrances are well guarded, so how are we going to gain access to a ramp and then ride it all the way to the mountain? And there are only a few that have been completed, and they're the most heavily guarded. I have no idea how to pull this off."

Astrid patted his hand. "That's because you don't know my sister as well as I do." Astrid turned back to the band. "Here is how we will do this. Cassandra will be amazed when she sees me alive. I will tell her that we survived our fall, but that Steward died on the outskirts of Seudomartus."

Dunston cackled. "That will please the Phaedra, who you know will be everywhere."

Steward was hanging on every word. "Yes, that will do nicely."

Astrid was speaking at a quickened pace now. "Cassandra's greatest competitor and rival is Donturnates. I will tell her that his men found us and gave us medical attention, nursing us back to health. They knew who I was, so they cared for me so that they could learn from me all they could about my famous sister's construction plans and schemes. When the time was right, they asked for information from me in payment for their kindness. I gave them everything they asked for, but little of it was accurate. They finally let us go, and as a token of their appreciation for our cooperation, they offered us free entrance to Donturnates's completed Ascender, that we might visit him on the far mountain. This way he could gloat and revel in his victory over Cassandra."

Astrid was brilliant! This would all work. He jumped in. "If Cassandra buys the story, we'll offer to disguise her and take her with us."

Astrid beamed at his enthusiasm for her plan. "Yes, and I can assure you she will not be able to resist the offer to get to the mountain and see what awaits her there." Astrid's eyes flashed at the thought.

As Steward worked the plan in his mind, his mood changed. "I still see two problems, Astrid. First, we must keep the Phaedra away from Cassandra during the process. Second, when we ride onto Donturnates's ramp, it must appear as though we have been invited, not that we're storming past guards and jumping walls."

Zedekai rode forward. "Warrior Steward, you may leave those two issues to us." The warrior band nodded, and the plan was set.

Astrid looked at Steward. "As for you, you shall have to wear the head shroud of the Barbariq. They trade here from time to time, and the men cover their faces except for the eyes. I'll tell everyone you're my bodyguard. That way you can keep your identity from the Phaedra and Cassandra until we are on the mountain."

"And what about me?" Dunston shrieked. "Am I to stay behind and pick daffodils while you rescue Ascendia?"

"No, my little warrior friend." Astrid walked her horse over to Dunston and bent down to talk to him almost nose-to-nose. "You will have the greatest role of all. You must find a way to keep Elopia distracted. I believe we can sway Cassandra, but we will not fool them both. Keep Elopia away and you will have ensured the plan's success."

Dunston thought a moment then managed a crooked little smile. "It is appropriate that I should have the most important role, and I shall perform it flawlessly."

Steward laughed. "Indeed you will. Very well, then, the plan is at hand. We shall meet Cassandra on the ramp at first light. For now, let's camp and prepare. Tomorrow the liberation of Ascendia will begin."

A cool, gray, and breezy morning met them as Steward and Astrid rode through the gates of Ascendia. Astrid wore simple tunics and a shawl over her face. Steward wore a makeshift hood made to look like a Barbariq's. They had no trappings of war—no sword, shield, or chainmail. The plan was to call no attention to themselves. The warrior band would enter in pairs and go different directions, meeting up near the entrance to Donturnates's ramp. Dunston was hidden under Steward's cloak, looking like a lump on the saddle behind him.

All around them, people seemed oblivious to their presence, just as they'd hoped. They sauntered on through the streets of Ascendia. They passed under several partially completed ramps and past the entrance to the House of Bendor. Astrid hid her face so that the gatekeeper wouldn't notice her. Steward also looked away as well, and the two hurried past him without being detected.

Just beyond Bendor, Steward tapped Dunston on the head. "This is your spot. Time to go to work." Dunston slipped out and was down off the horse and out of sight more quickly than Steward thought possible.

As Steward and Astrid rode on, he could hear in the distance the never-ending rumble of the crushers. Steward recoiled at the thought of how many townspeople of Ascendia might end up at that horrific place by the end of the day. His resolve was strengthened, and he was more determined than ever to liberate this place from the stranglehold of Cassandra and her ramp-building colleagues.

Astrid and Steward rounded the corner and looked ahead to the entrance of Cassandra's ramp. But instead of the usual five or so guards, there were at least fifteen men. Behind them was a wall of Phaedra.

Steward pulled his horse to a gentle stop, not wanting to look frightened. "This doesn't look good."

"It's not. Someone tipped them off."

"So what's plan B?" Steward and Astrid held their horses to a slow pace as they moved closer to the massed guards.

"There is no plan B. We just have to make the plan work. All's not lost yet. Let's just follow the script." Astrid kneed her horse to pick up the pace and trotted up to the line of guards. "Good morning to you. Is Cassandra of the House of Bendor on the ramp this morning?"

The guards made no reply. Instead they parted to let a Phaedra through.

"May we help you? This is a restricted ramp, you know. Only Cassandra's men and guards may enter here. Do you have business with her?"

Astrid slid back her shawl to reveal her face, and those assembled gasped.

The Phaedra bowed his head. "I am quite pleased to see you, Astrid. We all assumed the worst when you fell from the end of Cassandra's ramp. How delightful to see that you are well. And who is this riding with you?"

"It is my bodyguard from the Barbariq people."

Two Phaedra drew closer to look at Steward.

"May I see my sister now, please?"

The Phaedra continued staring at Steward but then turned away and nodded. "Of course. Let us escort you to her."

"There's no need. I know where to find her."

"I wouldn't think of it. You are a special guest, and you shall have an entourage." The Phaedra feigned a show of respect—and the game was on.

Meanwhile, Zedekai had led the ten warriors of the king into Ascendia. He'd divided the ten into pairs, ordering them to ride in from different directions. Two warriors wasn't that unusual. All ten at once? That would cause quite the stir.

Each duo had their assignment to work their way through the labyrinth of streets, past markets, schools, parks, and palatial government buildings, until they all arrived at the end of Donturnates's ramp.

Zedekai looked ahead. While the ramp had not yet been walled up, twenty armed guards stood watch over the small opening leading to it. Out across the valley, the far end of the ramp rested against the face of the distant mountain.

He signaled to the other warriors. It was almost time to take the ramp and secure it for Astrid, Steward, and Cassandra.

Dunston had made his way on foot through the city streets. He smiled when he heard Elopia's shrill voice right where Astrid had hoped she would be—in the city market. Dunston looked across the open market square and spotted Elopia, who was, as usual, engaged in an animated conversation with a group of her friends. The group of six or so meandered across the market, stopping to pick through some fabrics or dried goods or clothing items as they chatted nonstop. Maybe they would remain occupied by the lure of the salesmen and the endless arguments that seemed to be the glue that held them together.

No such luck.

Elopia glared at her companions. "You are all just too brainless for me. I must leave you before I scream."

One of her group swung a Quash at her, and Elopia swung hers to collide with it. The sound of clashing Quashes raised no attention, not even from the others in Elopia's group. She snarled at her attacker then flashed her a sneer and stormed away.

Time to act! Dunston grabbed a large cantaloupe from a market stand and walked toward Elopia. As their paths intersected, he feigned a fall and, with a shriek, threw the cantaloupe in Elopia's direction.

As he'd intended, she darted in his direction just in time to catch the piece of fruit before it smashed to the ground.

"Bless you, oh, bless you, my darling young lady!" Dunston lay sprawled on the pavement, holding his leg for added effect.

"Are you okay, little man?" Elopia tried to help him to his feet and return to him the rescued fruit.

"Okay? *Okay?* Why, I'm certainly *not* okay. These streets of yours are treacherous indeed." He struggled to stand then limped closer to her and peered up into her eyes. "But you, my dear, are among the fairest of the women I have seen in all Ascendia. Indeed, in all the kingdom, I do so swear."

Elopia blushed. "That is very kind of you. Here, let me help you." She supported Dunston as he drew out regaining his balance and dusting himself off.

"My dear lady, you are so kind. And your kindness will not go unrewarded. Walk with me and let us talk about how I shall repay you, for I am a man not without means." He began walking in the opposite direction of Cassandra's ramp.

Elopia stopped. "Oh, I would love to talk about a reward, but I must join my sister on the ramp. She gets very cross if I don't report to her once a day. She is such a tyrant, but I really must obey."

Dunston waved her on. "Yes, yes, you must obey. But the day is young. I will leave you plenty of time to make your appointment with your sister. But if you want the reward, you must follow me now. Please, for only a little ways. Then I will set you free to return to your sisterly duties."

Elopia didn't move. Would she turn from him? Head for her sister? Dunston was about to sweeten the lure, but the thought of a reward must have been too much for her to resist.

She smiled at him. "All right, but only for a short while. When I have my reward, I must go to the ramps."

"Of course, of course. Now come, my beauty, and let us walk and talk of rewards and wishes and dreams come true." Dunston led Elopia across the market and out into the maze of streets running the opposite direction of the ramps.

Astrid and Steward rode onto Cassandra's ramp amid a large escort of Phaedra. Steward looked at the ramp—how had it progressed so much in so little time? Her workers had brought the mountainside within reach, and she had them working at an even more frenetic pace than when he was here last.

Yet as Steward caught site of her imposing figure at the ramp's end, he could see that the mountain was still far away. Cassandra was shouting orders and seemed almost hysterical as they drew near enough to hear her.

"Ten meters! That's all we made yesterday? How can we be going so slowly with all these workers?"

Her chief engineer threw his hands in the air. "You know as well as I do that at this height, each meter requires a massive support system. Your Ascender is now hundreds of feet above the ground. This is as fast as we can go."

A few workers spotted Steward and Astrid, and the small band of Phaedra with them, and stopped to watch them.

Cassandra scowled. "What are you all looking at? Get to work. We must do better than ten meters today or I will fire you all!" She turned in the direction of her workers' focus and saw Steward and the others. She squinted and watched them approach.

Then Cassandra's mouth fell open. "Sister? It cannot be. Astrid! Little sister!"

Astrid slid off her horse and embraced Cassandra. "It *is* me, back from the dead—or nearly."

Cassandra stepped back. "Astrid, why did you risk your life to rescue Steward? Is he still alive?"

The Phaedra drew near, as though listening for her reply.

Thank heaven for the mask he wore!

Astrid looked down. "I am sorry, sister. He deluded me, and I shouldn't have betrayed you. We both survived the fall, but he died later in Seudomartus."

The Phaedra seemed quite satisfied with the confirmation of what they believed.

"But there is more. I have some very exciting news for you." With a flair of emotion in her voice, Astrid told the story just as they had planned. She stopped just as she was about to unveil the idea of taking Cassandra to the end of Donturnates's completed ramp. "Sister, can we talk in private?"

They had planned this as well. Astrid needed to tell Cassandra of their plan without the Phaedra hearing her.

Cassandra looked at the Phaedra, who had moved in close to catch Astrid's every word. Cassandra inclined her head to them. "Please excuse us for a moment. We have some sister talk to do."

"Great Cassandra, we are here to serve you. But how can we serve if we do not hear and know the story that Astrid has come to tell you?" There was caution and urgency in the Phaedra's tone.

Cassandra looked at them and then at Astrid. "This is nothing to concern you. Just family talk. I assure you that nothing of importance will escape your hearing. But please give us a few moments."

"Very well. We will await your invitation to rejoin you." The Phaedra shot a glare at Astrid and backed away.

Astrid and Cassandra walked to the ramp's far edge. As any good bodyguard would do, Steward nudged his horse to follow, staying a short distance away, but close enough to hear.

When Astrid and her sister were out of earshot, Astrid made her offer.

Cassandra placed a hand on her sister's arm. "Take me to the mountain on *his* ramp? Yes, I will do it."

Astrid looked past Steward, probably back at the wall of Phaedra. "But how will we get off this ramp without the Phaedra protesting?"

Cassandra thought for a minute. "Do you remember Creaker's Tunnel?"

Creaker's Tunnel?

Astrid nodded. "Yes, of course. I think we are the only ones in Ascendia who know about it." Astrid paused then smiled. "Yes, that's perfect."

Cassandra was almost smiling. "Meet me there with my disguise on the hour. Now follow my lead."

Cassandra turned back toward the anxious Phaedra and scowled. "Why aren't we working? And where is the paving mixture we need? Enough talking. Astrid and her bodyguard will spend the night at the House of Bendor, if she so wishes, but we have nothing else to say to each other. As for the paving mixture, I will see for myself what the problem is."

With that, she mounted her horse, galloped through everyone, and disappeared down the ramp, seemingly in a rage.

Astrid looked offended and shook her head. "I don't know why I even came! Come. Let's leave this place and my deluded sister."

It took all of Steward's self-control to restrain a grin. These sisters were quite accomplished at deception.

Astrid and Steward rode off. As they did, Steward raised a long staff into the air, from which a single red flag waved. He did it as though he were required to do so as part of his duty as bodyguard, but in reality—it was a signal.

At last.

Zedekai had been waiting, watching through a looking glass for the red flag. He lowered the glass and signaled to the five pairs of warriors.

"It is time."

The warriors rode out from their hiding places, and before the guards at the end of Donturnates's ramp could react, they started the assault.

Cassandra rode through the streets until she was out of sight of the Phaedra. She turned her horse down a narrow street that passed under three successive archways then dismounted and led the horse farther on foot. She rounded a high wall and cleared away brush to reveal a small passageway from where a stream emerged. She tied her horse and walked into the darkness.

She followed the cool, flowing water and, after a short distance, spotted a beam of light shooting out to illuminate a domed cavern just large enough to stand in. She and Astrid had found this secret place long ago. It served them well as they met here to frustrate Elopia, who was never let in on the location of the hideaway.

Before long she heard footsteps, and Astrid emerged behind her. "Creaker's Tunnel. I never thought I would be back here."

Just then Cassandra heard the distant sound of a horse and cart overhead, and the cavern gave out a groan. Cassandra and Astrid looked at each other and grinned. "Creaker's!"

Enough frivolity. Cassandra straightened. "We don't have much time. Are you sure you can get me to the mountainside on the ramp?"

"Yes, it's all arranged. Here's your tunic and veil. Come, let's go."

Astrid and Cassandra emerged from the cave, right where Astrid had told Steward to wait. They mounted the horses he'd brought, working their way through backstreets toward Donturnates's ramp.

"Just a little farther, dear lady."

Dunston had said that very same thing countless times, and Elopia had gone along. But this time she stopped, planting her feet.

"You must give me my reward now, for I will go no farther. I am too far from the ramps, and I must return to my sister, who will be furious with me for taking this long. I must have my reward now, if you will."

Dunston took as much time as he could, clearing his voice and playing out the drama. Then he looked Elopia in the eye. "You foolish girl. You *have* the greatest gift right in your hands, and yet you don't even know it."

Elopia looked down at the Quash that she held in her grip. "My Quash? Yes, I know its power. This is no reward. You've tricked me and wasted my time!"

Dunston put his hand up to silence her. "My dear, if you knew for one moment the real power of the Quash, you would realize how rich you are. The power of the Quash is the power to serve, to heal, to know, and to give love. It is the essence of everything you crave and cannot attain. It's the secret of your existence, and it's the gift to you from the king. And that knowledge, my dear, is the ultimate reward, is it not?"

Elopia studied her Quash. Then her hand gripped the edge, her knuckles turned white, and when she looked at Dunston, fire sparked in her eyes. "Yes, it is powerful, as you say. And for this *great reward,* let me make sure you feel its power."

Dunston saw what was coming and tried to duck. But she swung the Quash at him with such speed and force she caught him upside the head. Stars exploded in his brain, and he hurtled back onto the street.

The last thing he saw was Elopia sprinting toward the ramps.

Astrid, Cassandra, and Steward rounded the final corner before the entrance to Donturnates's ramp.

Steward looked ahead. *Here's praying the king's warriors have cleared the way.*

As the three rode up to the entrance, guards at the gates of the ramp stepped forward—and Steward smiled. They were the king's warriors, pretending to be the guards!

Somewhere there are a bunch of guards tied up in the bushes.

"What business do you have here? This is Donturnates's ramp, and no one is allowed entrance here."

Convincing. Very convincing. Hopefully Cassandra is buying it.

Astrid straightened, looking every inch the regal woman. "I am Astrid of the House of Bendor. We have been invited by Donturnates to visit him, and we are here at that invitation."

The warrior-guard studied her. "Yes, we remember you and the invitation. But only you three may enter. Donturnates's home is near the ramp's end on the mountainside. You are free to pass."

From beneath his covering, Steward allowed himself a quick smile as they rode on past the warriors. Thank heaven they'd made it to the ramp. And without a Phaedra in sight. He looked down to see the dust flying from their horses' hooves. How many people had died to create the pavement under them?

The enormous ramp swept across the entire valley. They galloped their horses for nearly an hour before Steward saw the ramp's end coming into view.

Cassandra pulled the veil from her face and drew a deep breath. Steward saw the anticipation in her features. She thought she was about to see the goal for which she had been working all her life.

He almost felt sorry for her.

They pulled their horses to a trot as they came to the place where the ramp merged into the mountainside. A path lay ahead.

Astrid turned to her sister. "Well, this is it. What do you think?"

Cassandra looked around her, as did Steward.

The path led into a forest, where shafts of light from the brilliant midday sun streamed through. The meadow surrounding the forest entrance was filled with wildflowers, and the songs of birds were everywhere.

Cassandra drew a deep breath. "It is magnificent! Just as I had hoped and believed. But we must not stop here. Let's see where the path leads us." She took off, galloping away as though driven by some internal force.

Steward pulled the shroud from his head and looked at Astrid. "What if we're wrong? What if this is everything she thought it would be? She'll be a more voracious ramp builder than before."

Astrid looked around. "I have to admit it is beautiful here. But the king didn't call us to be ramp builders. I sense there's more here to see and learn." Astrid rode off, and Steward put his hood back on and followed.

He caught up to the sisters just as the meandering forest path emerged into another meadow. Steward knew it was time to tell Cassandra the true purpose of the trip. "Cassandra!"

The two women reined in their horses and turned toward him. He rode to their sides, reached up, and pulled the hood from his head.

Cassandra recoiled. "Steward! It can't be. I thought you died in Seudomartus!" Then her eyes narrowed and she shot a piercing look at Astrid. "So you lied to me. What else have you lied about, little sister?"

Astrid put her hands up to try to calm her sister. "Cassandra, I'm sorry. I did lie to you about, well, about everything. Donturnates's men didn't rescue us. We escaped the ramp by use of a hook and rope."

Steward lifted his chin. "Well thrown, I may add. And I didn't die on Starr Hill but recovered at the king's palace."

Cassandra threw them a sneer of disbelief. "The king's palace? You mean to tell me you have been to the palace and seen the king? Hah!"

"Yes," Astrid replied, "and we are here because the king has sent us to *you*."

Cassandra shook it off. "This is insanity! Why would the king send you...or save *you*?" She glared at Steward.

How could they convince her? Somehow she needed to see reality. But how?

"We came to help you see the horror in building ramps with the blood of your people. We came to show you the futility of it all and to help you discover the life the king would have you live."

Cassandra pulled her horse around and circled them. "You lied to me and kidnapped me to get me to stop my ramp building? You're jealous of my progress. You want my ramp for your own. That's it, isn't it? You brought me up here to kill me. Then all I have will be yours!"

Help us, king. We're about to lose her. What can we say?

Astrid pleaded. "No, Cassandra! We came to show you the *real* end of your ramp-building work. And we came to tell you the purpose of the Quash and sash that you wear. The king has shown it to us, and now he's sent us to show you."

Cassandra glowered at her. "I know all too well the best use of the Quash. And I see that you have found out the secret of the paving mixture. Well, that is fine with me because I will have you both turned over to the guards as soon as we are down the Ascender."

Steward stiffened. She had to be shown. She had to know. "You're wrong. You don't know the real purpose of the Quash and sash. And regardless of what you plan to do to me, I will fulfill the king's command and show you."

Steward climbed off his horse, untied his own Quash, and removed the sling from it. He walked over to the stream running along the path and scooped fresh water from it. Then, draping the sash over his arm, he walked to Cassandra. Before she could react, he removed her foot from the stirrup, untied her sandal, dipped the sash in water, and began to wash her foot.

She froze. But only for a moment. She kicked the Quash from Steward's hands. It went flying, just missing his head.

"Idiot! Who do you take me for? You think the Quash is nothing more than a *washbasin?* Is this more of your trickery?" She looked at Astrid—it was the look of betrayal.

"No, Cassandra, it's the truth." But before Astrid could continue, something caught Cassandra's attention.

Steward turned and saw it too. In the distance, silhouetted against the azure sky, was the roofline of a great house.

Cassandra gloated. "That must be Donturnates's house. You've lost! Your little ruse has failed. Come. Let me show you the purpose of my ramp building!" She spurred her horse to a gallop.

Steward jumped on his own horse, and they followed in rapid chase behind her.

The castle soon came into full view. At first it looked to be a magnificent structure. Towers with parapets rose on six sides, and a large road led to mighty gates. Ivy grew up the walls, and a stream of cool, clear water ran along the entire length of the front of the castle.

Steward swallowed hard. Had their plan failed? But as they turned the final corner on the approach to the impressive mansion, the reality of the situation came into full view. The castle was only partly finished. The walls on the north side were nearly complete, but the south and west walls were still under construction, and the east walls weren't even started. More surprising was the clear evidence that no construction had gone on there for years. The partly completed walls were covered in thornbushes, and the ground around the mansion was overtaken with heavy brush. This was not just an incomplete construction site…

It was an abandoned project.

The whole scene took on an eerie feel, as though someone had packed up and left right in the middle of the work. What could make someone do such a thing?

Steward guided his horse up the main path to the gates, and his eye caught the movement of a figure walking within the house's courtyard.

Cassandra must have seen it too. She called out, "Donturnates, are you there? We are here to greet you. May we come in?" She dismounted, peering toward the figure.

Steward and Astrid also dismounted and examined the ruins of the project. It was even more overgrown than Steward first thought. What could have happened to Donturnates and his grand castle home?

Just then the main gates creaked open and a thin young man walked out. He was ashen at the site of visitors.

The young man's voice shook as he spoke. "May…may I help you? And how did you get here?"

Cassandra stepped forward. "I am Cassandra of the House of Bendor. This is my sister Astrid and…her bodyguard. We are here to visit Donturnates. Is this his house?"

"Yes, this is his house, but he's not here. He's never here. He lives and works every day at the ramp. I am just a caretaker who guards the house."

Cassandra pulled her head back in disbelief. She scoffed. "We've just come up the ramp from Ascendia, and we saw no one there."

"Oh, I do not mean the ramp from Ascendia, but the *new* ramp. You'll find it just a short distance farther down the road."

Cassandra looked back at Astrid. "There's a new ramp? I must see what he is up to."

She was up on her horse and away before Steward or Astrid could say a word. They mounted and tried to catch up to her, but Cassandra arrived first at the scene. As Astrid and Steward approached, Steward was sure his eyes must be deceiving him.

Cassandra slid from her horse and stood frozen for several moments. In front of them was a massive cliff and, in the distance, a mountain higher than Steward had ever seen before.

But that was not what fixed his attention.

Near the cliff's edge, a single figure was working. He was small in stature, hunched over and frail. His face was ashen gray, and he struggled to complete even the smallest movement. As the three drew nearer, Steward could see that he had gathered two small mounds of stones fashioned into little walls about twenty feet apart. They were crude in construction, and as the bent-over man stooped, picked up a stone, and struggled to carry it to the wall and place it on top of the others, Steward surmised that even the modest piles of rocks must have taken months to complete. The hunched-over man stopped, hands on his knees, gasping for breath.

Steward had never seen a more pathetic sight.

Cassandra walked up to the man, who startled when he saw her. Then his eyes widened and his mouth formed a sinister grin. "So, the great Cassandra could not wait to see how badly she's been beaten. Well, take a good look at what you have yet to achieve. While you are still toiling in the hot Ascendia sun to reach this mountain, I have already conquered it."

Cassandra looked back down the road from where they had ridden. "But why did you stop building your castle?"

The man circled in front of her. "Why? *Why*? Can you not see what's right in front of you? Open your eyes and look at *that!*" He swept his hand across the skyline toward the mountain looming in front of them. "Imagine what must be up there. We all thought that this mountain was the goal. That here we would find the contentment and happiness we all thirst for." Then he drew close, and Steward almost stepped back, so wild were the man's eyes and distorted his face.

"But, Cassandra, it's not here. No, it's not here. It's up there. *There* is where we must go. Everything we want is up there. This is just a transitional place. We must keep building a new ramp, and when we reach that mountainside, then we will find it!"

Steward felt a lump in his throat at the man's desperation. *He's losing his mind.*

Cassandra looked around her. "But you have so much here. This is a wonderful place. Your mansion is huge. There are forests and streams and flowers and so much here. Why don't you stay here?"

Donturnates glared at her. "Stay here? Stay *here*? And I thought you were my greatest competitor. How can you be content here when there is such a great mountain calling to you? The same thirst that called you to this mountain will call you to the next one. You say the forests and meadows are fine here? My dear deluded Cassandra, the forests and streams and meadows in the lowland are every bit as grand as these. But they weren't enough for you. No, you were quick to leave them behind and give your life to ramp building so that you may stand in this place. Now that you are here, the same drive will keep you building to the next mountain—"

"And the next," Astrid said.

"Yes, and the next." Donturnates sneered. He spun on his heel and went back to his work. "Whatever it takes." He picked up a battered, dented Quash. With tired, feeble motions he began filling it with dirt.

Cassandra looked down at Donturnates's hands as he gripped the Quash. They were cut and bloody from the work. Such pain, and for what?

She looked around at all the beauty of this place and watched the figure before them struggle in the impossible task of building yet another ramp to yet another paradise.

She looked up at the mountain looming in front of her. If she did make it up her own Ascender, how long would she be content here knowing another mountain loomed? How soon would she wonder what was up there? How long before she would be just like Donturnates? Hunched over, pathetic, and never at peace. Always ramp building. Always yearning for the next mountain. And what if that wasn't the end? What if there was another mountain? And another. And...

Shock jolted through her.

I've been a fool! Her heart pounded and her hands trembled. *How could I have been so blind? Astrid is right. There will* always *be another mountain.*

As this truth struck deeply, piercing her heart and soul, Cassandra turned away. She looked to the woods, to the beauty of the meadow and the flowers…

And cried out.

Undone.

Wasted. All these years, all this energy, all her hopes…wasted. And on what? On a lie! Donturnates was right! The forest and meadows here were no more beautiful, no more wondrous than those in Ascendia. This place, her desired paradise, was just like where she'd grown up. It was beautiful and wondrous, but so was Ascendia. She'd just been too blind to see it. Too determined to reach her goal. So determined that—

Oh! The terrible things she'd done!

She looked around. What was she to do now? What could she do to make up for it all? How could she?

Of course. Steward had told her. At least he'd given her a place to start.

Fighting tears, she untied her Quash and held it in her hands. Her symbol of power and progress. She ran her fingers over its fine, smooth edges…

What would happen if she used the Quash as Steward said the king intended? She looked at Donturnates as he stumbled between the rock pile and his sad little ramp, and foreign emotions flooded her.

Pity.

Compassion.

She walked over to a small stream trickling out of the mountainside and filled her Quash with cool water. She placed the sash over her arm and walked to Donturnates.

He startled as she approached, but she didn't hesitate.

"Here, let me show you how a Quash is meant to be used."

He watched as she dipped the sash in the water, took his bleeding hand in hers, and began to wash his wounds.

Frozen. Disbelief.

Anger.

Donturnates snatched his hand back and spat at Cassandra. "Get away from me! Who do you think you are? I am the great Donturnates! I beat you and everyone else to the mountain. I am the greatest ramp builder in all the kingdom!" He backed away as if the three of them were somehow contagious. Or mad.

He continued shouting at them, and Cassandra wanted to weep. It was hopeless. He would never accept her help.

Someone touched her arm, and she turned to meet Steward's gaze.

"Come. It's time for us to leave."

Steward and the two sisters mounted their horses and trotted away. As they left the cliff's edge and entered the forest, they could still hear Donturnates shouting.

"How dare you pity me! Pity yourselves. You will never be as great as I am. You will never reach the mountainside. You have lost, and I have won. Do you hear me? I have won! You should bow down to me. Don't you understand? I have won, *I have won!*"

Finally, the bitter voice trailed off and gave way to the sound of the stream running along at the path's edge. Steward glanced at Cassandra. She looked so...lost.

They plodded on, passing the abandoned mansion, and through the forest, emerging back at the end of the ramp. The view back down into the valley was spectacular. Cassandra drew her horse to a stop and paused to take it in.

"It's beautiful." She shook her head. "What a fool I've been."

Steward wanted to comfort her, but no words came. Then he caught the sound of a distant rumble. The crushers.

Cassandra must have heard it too. She jerked at the reins of her horse. "I will stop this! No one will ever again die in the crushers. Not to build these ramps. Not for any reason. I will stop this *today!*"

Astrid grabbed the reins of her sister's horse before she could gallop off. "Cassandra, you'll face great opposition when we return. People won't believe you when you tell them about Donturnates or the next mountain."

Steward pulled up beside her. "Your heart has been changed, but how will you change the hearts of those who haven't seen what you have?"

Cassandra reached down and ran her hands along her Quash. Then she looked up at the sprawling city before her. "I will change minds and hearts by showing them how I've been changed. They may not listen to words, but they will pay attention to actions. First we must destroy the crushers. Then we'll start using the Quash and sash for the king's purposes." She met Steward's, then Astrid's, eyes. "That is how we will change Ascendia—one act of service at a time."

Astrid looked out on the city and blew a short breath through her lips. "An entire generation has been raised to think that ramp building is the only way to happiness."

Cassandra's determination was clear in the set of her jaw. "Then we'll raise up a new generation to know the joy that comes from using the Quash to serve one another, to *give* life instead of taking life." She looked back at Astrid. "And we'll begin with Elopia."

"Huh, good luck with that one!" Steward couldn't believe he'd actually said that out loud. But Cassandra and Astrid broke out in laughter.

They eased their way back onto the ramp for the ride down. Steward looked at the peace on Cassandra's face. She didn't even look like the same person. Probably because she wasn't! "Cassandra, what did you feel when you washed Donturnates's hands?"

She thought for a moment. "I guess it was a sense of certainty. A sense of rightness and completeness and...contentment."

Steward smiled. "That is what the king calls the Deep Peace. It's his gift, and he desires that you know it every day."

Astrid smiled at her sister. "That peace guides you in knowing what is truly of the king. Whenever you are doing the king's work, you will know it, even when times are hard."

"It's a wonderful gift." Cassandra looked toward the end of the ramp as it came more into view. "If only I might show them how to know it and experience it for themselves."

They arrived at the end of the ramp, where Zedekai and the ten warriors awaited them. They all smiled as they saw Cassandra's face—the peace evident in her features. The plan had worked.

Steward put a hand on Cassandra's arm. "This is our friend and fellow warrior, Zedekai, and these are the king's warriors."

As the sound of the crushers roared in the distance, Cassandra looked at the mighty warriors before her. "May I borrow them?"

Zedekai didn't hesitate. "Of course." He turned to the warriors. "Do whatever she tells you, and then meet us at Pitcairn Moor when you have completed your work here."

Steward looked around. "Now where is Dunston?"

Zedekai flipped his hand to the horizon. "He's already on his way to Pitcairn Moor. He feels he failed the mission since Elopia made it to the ramp. We didn't tell him you'd already left." A sly smile flashed across his face.

"Steward, look."

He turned to follow Cassandra's gaze. A large contingent of Phaedra was making their way toward them—with Elopia in the lead.

Cassandra put her hand on Astrid's arm. "Quickly, you all must leave at once. I will contend with the Phaedra and Elopia. Your work here is done. Now it's up to me. Please go, and hurry."

"I will miss you!" Astrid spoke through tears. "Remember, the king is always near you. Trust him, and the king's Deep Peace will be with you."

Cassandra leaned forward and kissed her sister's cheek. "Thank you. You have saved me. Please return soon and see what we've done in the king's name. Deep Peace to you. Now ride!"

The Phaedra were getting close enough to see who they were. Steward gathered his horse's reins. "Come on, Astrid, we must go!"

There was shouting and a rush of black robes as Steward, Astrid, and Zedekai rode down the side road leading past Creaker's Tunnel. They rode hard and fast to the city gates. They held tightly in a darkened alleyway, and Steward watched Zedekai for his signal. When he gave it, they galloped through the gates and up into the hills beyond. Finally, out of danger, Steward reined his horse to a halt and looked back down on Ascendia.

In the distance, he heard a great noise. "Look!" He pointed, and Astrid and Zedekai turned to Ascendia. In the fading light of day, they watched as the crushing machines came crashing down in clouds of dust and debris.

Astrid put her hand to her mouth. "Good work, sister."

Steward looked at Astrid. "You were wonderful. Your plan worked, and now the liberation of Ascendia has begun."

She returned the smile. "One day I will return and work by Cassandra's side for the full liberation of the city. But for now we have more to do than hours to do it. And we have a disheartened friend to find."

"To Pitcairn Moor then," Zedekai shouted, and the three rode off into the Fungle Woods.

~~~~~~~~~

As Alex read the last words, the bells in the steeple of St. Anne's rang out their weekly four o'clock tribute to the great hymns of the faith, starting with "The Old Rugged Cross" followed by "Amazing Grace."

The Roberts children sat and soaked it in.

All but Merideth. She muttered, "*Whatever it takes.* That's a stake to the heart."

Reed overheard her. "Why's that phrase so important?"

Merideth leaned back, shook her head, and closed her eyes. She drew a breath and pushed it out through her pursed lips. She opened her eyes and looked around at her siblings.

Might as well come clean.

"You remember Margaret Erskine-Jones?"

Alex reared back. "Whoa, yeah, the second coming of the iron lady, right?"

Reed nodded. "She was in Congress for about a hundred years. No one wanted to challenge her. She was a piece of work, as I remember."

Anna looked at her sister. "You worked on her campaign, didn't you?"

Merideth folded her hands. "Yup, for one glorious summer. I admired her and relished every chance to watch her work. She was intimidating, confident, and shrewd."

"Great character traits," Reed snorted. "Oh, sorry, Mer, I didn't mean…"

She waved him off. "That's okay. In a lot of ways you're right. But I adored her. One day I got to sit in on a policy meeting she ran. She was brutal. She all but eviscerated her biggest rival. It was painful in a delightfully triumphant way. Anyway, as we walked out I mentioned my admiration for her aggressive approach. You know what she said to me?"

Reed smiled. "I can guess."

Merideth returned the nod. "She said, 'Merideth, if you want to get what you want in this life, you must be willing to do whatever it takes.' That became my mantra. I wrote it as my screen saver and scribbled it atop the notepad for every meeting I've led."

Alex put his hands in the air. "Did Dad know that?"

Merideth shrugged. "I didn't think so, but now…"

"Wow," Anna added.

"Wow indeed," Reed replied. "Well, I guess we've all built our ramps. We've all used people at one time or another to get what we wanted. We've all done whatever it takes at one time or another. I mean, that's business. That's how you get ahead. You build ramps or you end up in the crusher."

Alex gave a thoughtful nod. "Yup, I agree. In my world, you either press forward or fall back. There is no neutral or sideways. Success comes to those who take it, and everyone else slides back. If some get caught in the slide, well…then they do. You can't change that. So it seems the lesson is to learn how to build ramps without hurting people?"

Merideth exploded. "No!"

The three siblings sat back, eyes wide.

"It's not the ramp building. Did you catch it? I mean, Reed, Alex, you're right to a point. It's my world as well. Dad knew that. But there's something deeper here that Dad's saying. It's not about better ways to build ramps or treating people better or even about the use of power for your own gains. That's all there but it's secondary."

Now she leaned forward and all three of them leaned with her.

"Don't you see? What Dad's talking about is abandoning the whole drive for ramp building in the first place. It's about *not* being driven to do whatever it takes. Cassandra's conversion is about appreciating where you are, about being satisfied, about…"

She paused, and Walter finished her thought. "Contentment?"

She opened her lips to continue then just shook her head.

Walter pushed the discussion. "I think you're right, Merideth. If Cassandra was content in the valley, there would be no ramp building. Perhaps that's the lesson of Ascendia."

Reed looked around the room. "Contentment. You know, that word feels right in here. I was trying to find the right word to express it. My feelings, I mean. I sensed it when I first walked through the door yesterday. It's hung in this room since we started the book. Walter, I think you're right."

Alex and Anna nodded their agreement. But not Merideth. She was looking at the ground. Her tension showed as her chest rose and fell, and her knuckles grew white from her grip on the armrest.

Walter pushed once more. "Merideth, what are you feeling?"

She looked up, scowling. "It's contentment, and I hate that word."

"Why?" Reed asked.

Well, here we are, at the heart of it. I can't run…can I?

Total vulnerability or more walls. This was the moment. Four sets of ears waited.

Honesty oozed at first, then ran in a torrent.

"Why? Because it contradicts everything I stand for. It means I stop being driven by what other people think of me. It means I set aside the measurement of success that the world has established and I pursue every day of my life. It means I stop comparing myself to others, envying and hating their success. It means I allow myself to enjoy today instead of believing that happiness won't come until tomorrow, until the ramps reach the mountain, until I have won. Contentment? It's like a rogue wave wiping out all the sandcastles that I've spent my life building."

She was breathless, almost shouting as she flashed her gaze from one sibling to another.

"Don't you understand? It means everything collapses around me; my defenses, my justifications, my rationale that gives me room to do…*whatever it takes*. It's impossible! It's too much. I'm a ramp builder. I can't go back, not now. I'm a lost cause."

Suddenly an image flashed through her mind. A Phaedra, whispering and smiling.

Oh…dear…God.

Lies, deception, distortion. She'd bought them all.

"Help me." She was shaking.

All three siblings ran to her side, kneeling and holding her.

"Mer, it's okay, we're here." Anna put her head on Merideth's shoulder and held tightly. Merideth felt the touch and heard the soft words of assurance from the three people in the world who loved her most.

Like a balm to an open wound, their love began her healing. Her shaking slowed, then stopped. She collected herself, but this time there was no urge to save face.

A first, small victory.

"Thank you. I—I think I'm okay. I'd like to step outside for a breath of air." She rose and walked to the hallway. There was Walter.

No more games. She stopped and embraced him.

"Thank you. You've put up with a lot from me over the years. Give me a little time, but I'd like for us to be friends."

Walter beamed. "We already are."

Once reassembled, Alex led them into the final chapters of the story.

Twenty-Two

In the emptiness of the *Tohu Wa-Bohu,* the assembly of hooded figures debated the events of the past few days.

"It cannot be Steward of Aiden Glenn. I tell you I saw him die with my own eyes on the rocks of Starr Hill. It's the king's illusion."

"I agree. And we must not be fooled. He's buying time. He knows that Steward's death would mark our great uprising. So why are we waiting? We must act now."

"I hear the ramps in Ascendia are being torn down!"

"Yes, and the poor of Petitzaros have received the Elixir of Mah Manon. The people of Remonant have emerged, and much of our work there is being undone."

"Silence!" The leader rose from his chair, his arms outstretched and his bony fingers reaching to the ceiling. "If you are all so wise, why do you not see the larger plan unfolding here? The king is luring us into a trap. If we believe that Steward is alive, we will, no doubt, pursue him again. If we worry for Marikonia, we will amass our people there. All the while, the king works to build his army for a last futile attempt to banish us again to this detestable place. No, we must not be lured into this trap."

A Phaedra stepped up. "If Steward is indeed dead, then we must gather our forces and make for war. Even if we lose Marikonia."

"And Seudomartus," another said.

The leader glared and shot back. "We shall *never* lose Seudomartus! It is our greatest victory and most important stronghold in all the kingdom. And it lies at the very foot of the throne room of the king. Seudomartus will always be ours because the hearts of the people there remain content in their delusion. They are satisfied by their own wisdom, reason, and, yes, even their own spirituality." A satisfied, hissing sneer reverberated from the hooded assembly. "The *good and wise* people of Seudomartus will remain forever beyond the grasp of the king."

The lead Phaedra walked to the map hanging on the wall. He ran his bony finger across the Golden River and down Kildrachan Plain, stopping on the place of the Ancient Fortress, just above Aiden Glenn. "We must amass our army and return to the fortress of our ancestors. From there, we will wage the final war against the king."

The leader paced then turned to the assembly. "This is our last and greatest hope for victory. We have made great progress in the hearts of the kingdom's people. Their resolve is weak. They are too easily swayed and cling too tightly to the things that gratify them. They have no stomach for real war, and we must use that advantage—and fast."

He drew in closely. "Now, take the word to every corner of the kingdom. Assemble everyone at Kildrachan Plain, across the Golden River at the site of our last great battle. From there, we will move to the Ancient Fortress, and the victory will be ours."

The king stood looking out over the land from the rooftop of his castle.

A warrior entered behind him. "Great king, I have come to announce that the crushers of Ascendia have been destroyed. There is also news that some ramps have been abandoned."

The king turned to look at the massive warrior standing before him. "Thank you for your good report."

The warrior inclined his head and continued. "The poor of Petitzaros have been reunited with the people of Remonant, and some of the people have shared their Elixir. There is a new sense of hope in the kingdom."

The king turned back to his vista and shook his head. "The liberation has begun, and Steward's work is admirable. But so many remain lost. The Phaedra have infiltrated the entire kingdom with their lies and distortions that even the Great Liberation may not be enough." He turned. "We are headed for war, and nothing can stop it now. We must prepare. Begin to amass the armies. Take word to Steward and the party that they must complete their work at once, then ride to Kildrachan Plain at the far southern end of the Fungle Woods. We must stop the Phaedra before they reach the fortress. Now ride, and the Deep Peace be with you."

The warrior bowed to the king and left. The king swept his gaze across his kingdom. *Hurry, Steward. The time is short.*

CHAPTER
Twenty-Three

Dunston sat alone. He stirred a small fire that cast early evening shadows across the bubbling bog to his left and danced up the trunks and into the branches of the massive trees looming over him.

He stared into the fire. "I am certain Elopia reached the ramps and alerted Cassandra of the plot. They seized Steward and Astrid. The Phaedra must know now that he is alive and will plan for war. All is lost, and I am to blame!"

The clamor of approaching horses sent him to his feet.

The Phaedra! They are coming for me! Well, let them have me. I will not run. What good am I to anyone now?

A horse emerged from the forest, and he stood, head down with arms straight out in front of him. "Take me. I will offer no resistance. I am your prisoner. Only treat me with dignity, as we did your ancestors."

The riders reined their horses to a halt then dismounted. They walked up to him, and the one in the back called out in a deep voice, "I think we should kill him!"

Dunston couldn't hold back a whimper as he waited for the lethal blow. One of the riders drew near, knelt down, and said in a soft voice, "I don't know. He doesn't look very tough to me."

Dunston opened his eyes wide. Not tough? He'd show them! He craned his neck up to face the foul creature and—

"Astrid!"

His friend grinned down at him.

Dunston blinked. "You're safe…and so am I!" Then he looked over at the other rider who stood near—Steward, who was laughing.

263

Dunston shook his head. "You all but killed me with such a fright. But I am so very glad to see you."

They embraced, and Steward clapped him on the back. "Come, let's sit and we'll tell you what happened."

Steward, Astrid, and Zedekai told Dunston the whole story—making sure to tell him the important role he played in distracting Elopia just long enough for their plan to work.

"So, you are a hero!" Steward said.

Dunston wouldn't have it. "No, I am no hero. But I am glad to have played a part. Now we must prepare for Marikonia as soon as the warrior band rejoins us."

Astrid stood and looked out over the swamp. "How shall we liberate Marikonia?"

"And what of Seudomartus?" Dunston added.

Steward stirred the fire with Dunston's walking stick. "The key to Marikonia lies with the sons of Abner…and Tristin."

Dunston grabbed his stick from Steward. "Tristin? I think he's hopeless."

Steward wasn't ready to agree. "I will at least take the challenge to him. The liberation of Marikonia must come from both sides, from those who see themselves as less than they ought *and* those who see themselves as more than they ought. Both must see themselves as the king sees them."

"I agree," Astrid said, "and what of Seudomartus?"

The thundering sound of hoofbeats rang through the clearing. Before they could take cover, the clearing was filled with warriors—not just their ten companions, but more than twenty of the king's warriors.

One dismounted and approached. "We have ridden directly from the palace with words from the king. The time is short. The Phaedra have begun amassing an army for the march to the Ancient Fortress. The king has called all of his people to prepare for war." He turned to Steward. "Steward, you and your party must complete your work with all haste. You must make for Marikonia at first light, and from there to Seudomartus."

"We will do so," Steward replied. He flashed a look at his companions. "But we have no plan for the liberation of Seudomartus. Did the king send any word with you?"

"The king will tell you the plan when you need to hear it. His timing is perfect. Go to Marikonia and Seudomartus with the Deep Peace of the king."

They shouted as one voice. "The Deep Peace!"

At first light, the party of liberators took off. They rode out across Pitcairn Moor, which became a broad and firm path under their feet. They charged down the steep path that had caused Steward such a fall, and they rounded the bend to the outskirts of Marikonia. In the distance, Steward could see the smoke billowing from the foundry at Abner's shop.

Steward pulled his horse to a stop. "I need to do this alone. Ride on to the edge of Seudomartus and find one of the Starr Hill Faithful. Coordinate a plan with them to take the truth to that deluded city. I will join you soon when my work here is done."

Astrid took hold of his arm. "Steward, can you do this alone? Let me come with you…"

"And me! We will not leave you to this work without proper backup," Dunston said.

Zedekai rode up next to him. "They're right, Warrior Steward. It is not safe to go alone, now that the Phaedra are amassing for war."

"Very well. Astrid, Dunston, and I will ride into Marikonia. Zedekai, lead the warrior band on to Seudomartus as planned. We will need you to be in place if we are to complete our work in such a short time."

Zedekai signaled to the king's men. They bowed their allegiance to Steward and rode away.

Steward turned his horse toward town. "Now, on to Abner's house. But once there, I will go in alone."

When they reached the edge of Abner's property, Steward dismounted and walked with well-placed steps, his approach drowned out by the sounds of clashing steel and hissing steam from hot metal thrust into the vats of cool water.

He'd left here in a sea of grief and anger. How would they react when they saw him?

Steward walked in, and Abner shot him a glance of surprise then looked back down. "What brings you back to Marikonia?" His tone was cool. "Word had it that you died in Seudomartus."

"Abner, I have seen the king." Steward waited for a response.

Abner gave none. He continued to beat the steel rod in front of him. As he thrust it into the vat of water, he looked at Steward. "You have, huh? Well, what did he say?"

Steward walked closer to Abner, catching sight of Troy and Trek toiling over a large sheet of tin. They saw him and looked back down at their work.

This will not be easy. "Abner, the king gave me a gift for you."

Abner set his hammer down and glared at Steward. "For me? I doubt that. What interest would the king have with a blacksmith living on the outskirts of Marikonia?"

"He has a great deal of interest in you." Steward turned and looked at the two boys. "And in both of you! All of you!"

Troy and Trek set their tools aside and walked over to Steward. Their steps were cautious.

Abner turned off the bellows, and for the first time the blacksmith shop fell quiet. "Go on. What did the king send?"

Steward removed his satchel and dug into it. The three men studied him as he pulled out the Reflector. Unlike those Abner and his family already had, this Reflector was gilded in gold—and shone the true reflection back to everyone who looked into it.

Abner recoiled, his face contorted. "Another Reflector? Bah! What good is that to us?"

"It is no good to you at all"—Steward paused—"unless you have the courage to look into it."

That stopped Abner in his tracks. He spun around. "Look, young Steward. We have been through this before. Our Reflectors have shown us who we are. What more would the king have for us to see?"

"Your true self, Abner." He nodded to Troy and Trek. "And yours, and your mother's. The king has sent me to show you your true nature, your undistorted image. It's right here…if you have the courage to look."

Troy and Trek watched their father. He stood motionless. Finally, Troy reached out his hand. "I will look."

Steward smiled. He held up the Reflector toward the tall, blond young man and turned it in his direction. As Troy caught sight of his reflection, his face lit up.

"Incredible! Look at me! Will you just look at me!"

Trek jumped forward and saw his brother's image. "Let me see mine!"

Steward turned it toward Abner's younger son, and the response was the same. "Sons of thunder! I can't believe that's me! Father, you must look. We both look so…so…"

"*Right?*"

Troy and Trek looked at their father. Troy stammered, "Yes—yes, that's it. I look … right, like I should look, like I always hoped I looked."

Abner walked over and reached out his hand. Steward saw that it was shaking. He placed the Reflector in the blacksmith's powerful hands. Abner took a deep breath and turned it toward himself. He gazed into its smooth surface, studying the reflection. His face remained emotionless. Then he began to smile. He looked over at his sons then turned it in their direction again. He looked at his sons as the Reflector shone back their image. His smile broadened.

"Tell me, young Steward. What did the king say about this gift?"

"He said it is a Reflector of the truth. It will show all who look into it the truth of who they are and how the king sees them. It will help those who are deluded by a distorted image—whether they think more of themselves than they ought or less of themselves than they ought. It will restore balance in their lives and help them live as authentic children of the king."

Abner held up his Reflector. "Then this is the truth, the king's truth."

Steward nodded.

Abner made a fist, but Steward sensed it was not in anger, but triumph.

"I knew it. I've known it all along. When I was younger I tried to see the truth, but time wore me down. Even though I finally gave in to the lie, deep in my spirit I've never believed it. I always sensed that the truth was different than what we were seeing...that, somehow, we were meant to see ourselves differently. And now, these Reflectors show us that truth, that we are noble in the king's eyes."

"It has done that," Trek exclaimed. "If this is how I really look, then I am no less than the people of the Light District. And they are no greater than me."

"Yes, but who will tell them that?" Troy retorted.

"You will."

At Steward's words, three stunned faces looked back at him.

"And just what do you mean by that?" Trek asked.

Troy walked to him. Fear was in his eyes. "We can't speak to the people of the Light District. They won't listen to us. If this is your plan, it won't work."

Steward looked at the blacksmith. "Abner?"

He nodded. "Go on."

Steward continued. "I've been sent by the king for no less an audacious task than the liberation of all Marikonia. This liberation will come by way of the truth, the truth as seen in this Reflector. But I cannot lead this liberation. I have neither the time nor the manpower. Even now, the Phaedra are amassing near the Golden River for war against the king. So, I must entrust this work to you. You, Troy and Trek, will lead the liberation of Marikonia. And this liberation will set right your sister's death. Claire knew the truth, but there was no place for her to live out that truth, not in the midst of so great a distortion. Now you must take this truth, in her name, into the city, through the streets, and into the hearts of the people of the Light District."

"How shall we accomplish so great a task?" Troy asked.

Steward drew a breath. They wouldn't like this. "We shall start with Tristin."

"Tristin?" Trek shook his head. "He is the *worst* of all the famous and powerful. How can we possibly change his heart?"

Abner placed a calming hand on his son's shoulder. "My dear boys, the truth will always win if it's presented with compassion and courage. Steward is right. This Reflector is the key to righting the centuries of distortion we've lived under. This distortion ruled us ever since the day my own Reflector was marred by the hand of a Phaedra. They've distorted all the Reflectors in this place by putting a warped image into our minds. It's our own self-delusion that causes some to reflect a poorer image and some to reflect a better image than the real and true image. Steward has helped us see in ourselves what the king would have us see. Now the same must be taken to the very heart of the distortion."

"Tristin's house."

Steward and Abner nodded at Troy's words.

Steward drew closer and spoke in a hushed tone. "I will accompany you to the house, but I must not be seen by the Phaedra. My death in Seudomartus must continue to be believed. On the way, we will construct a plan, but time is short. We must leave now."

Abner's sons took off their heavy leather aprons, washed their faces, and prepared to leave.

Steward helped Abner close up the shop. "What will you tell Edith?"

Abner looked toward the house. "May I borrow the king's Reflector for a moment?"

Steward handed it to him, and Abner disappeared into the house. Moments later, a shriek of delight could be heard across the lawn and out into the street. Abner soon returned, beaming.

"Edith will be just fine!"

Steward, Troy, and Trek set off, following back roads that would keep them from the gaze of the Phaedra. Steward knew that Astrid and Dunston followed them from a distance, protecting them as they moved along the corridors of Marikonia. He and the boys navigated their way from an alley to a dark road, until they stood at the circular drive that led to Tristin's house.

Steward leaned close to the boys. "Careful now. The Phaedra are everywhere."

They eased close to the house. Steward looked and listened. Why were the windows darkened? And why was the normally festive house silent?

Something was wrong.

They drew closer and Steward spotted one light flickering through a downstairs window. He made his way into the house through the open front door. The floor creaked beneath his feet as he walked through the colossal foyer with its massive, dark chandeliers.

Suddenly, a figure appeared in front of him.

"Who's that? Who's there?"

Steward held out his hands. "I mean no harm. I am here to see Tristin. Is he away?" He stayed in the shadows, hoping to conceal his identity as long as possible.

"Tristin is not seeing visitors. He is…ill."

A voice shouted from down the hall. "Castor, who is there?"

It was Tristin's voice. Steward kept his voice calm. "Tell Tristin it is an old friend here to visit."

The man squinted, trying to see Steward's face. "Do I know you?"

"No, but I once visited Tristin, and I wish to see him again. May I…may we go in and see him?"

Troy and Trek stepped out of the shadows, and the man looked at them then disappeared down the hall. He returned shortly and announced that Tristin would see them. As he escorted them down the long hallway, Steward looked around. What could have happened here? The once bright and gaudy rooms along the hall were now dark and silent. The place was in disrepair with many pieces of broken furniture.

Steward and the boys entered a room at the end of the hall, following Castor to a table where Tristin sat sipping a glass of wine. His shirt was rumpled and his hair was matted and uncombed. He was looking across the room, distracted and oblivious to their entrance.

Steward stepped forward. "Tristin, it is Steward of Aiden Glenn. Are you all right?"

He turned a bit, just enough to glance at them. "Steward? Ah yes, I remember you. You taunted my guests and nearly destroyed my party with talk of truth and distortion and visiting the king. So now you have returned to glory in my humiliation? Fine, so be it!"

"You're right, Tristin. I did talk of distortion and truth and a quest to see the king. And I am here because I *have* seen the king, and he has sent me back here with a gift for you."

Tristin turned to meet Steward's gaze. He laid his elbows on the table and hoisted himself up, almost lunging at Steward. "Liar! You heard of my fall and have come to rub it in my face. Well, I will have none of it. Castor, show this man out!"

Steward threw his hands up. "Wait! Before you throw me out, tell me where your guests are. Where is the party? Where are the mirrors that filled your rooms? Please, what has happened here?"

Tristin fell back into his chair. "Very well, have your fun. It appears that my Reflector is flawed. One day it began to show images that were not at all flattering, and my friends noticed it immediately. I thought it was some trick, or a problem with the surface, but slowly my image became marred in everyone else's Reflectors as well. Once that happened, my so-called friends turned out to be nothing of the sort. They ridiculed me and abandoned me for others with more splendid reflections."

He stood and picked up a slat from a broken chair, examining it as he spoke. "I tried everything to get them back. I threw more lavish parties, hired the best entertainers, and bought the finest food and wines, but all that mattered was the unflattering image they saw in their Reflectors every time they were around me. Soon no one came to my house. And no one invited me to theirs. I became an outcast."

He was panting now, emotions overcoming him. "I tried to change my image, reshape my Reflector, and change its surface or its curvature. I tried to increase and decrease the light around it. I covered it with thin cloth, painted the surface, decorated it, and even tried breaking it. But it just kept reflecting this same, dull image back to me."

Tristin's despair was heartbreaking. Steward shook his head. "What did you do?"

Tristin shrugged. "I quit and accepted that I would never again be welcome among the beautiful people of the Light District." Anger mixed with grief as he spoke. He stood and looked down the hallway at the darkened, empty rooms. "I tore down the mirrors and turned out the lights. Now I sit here day after day, night after night, waiting for someone to ask me to dinner or a party. And when they don't, I dull the pain with my wine." He raised his glass with a sarcastic flair and took another gulp. "So there you have it. The once glamorous and sophisticated Tristin reduced to a wine sot, a rejected, friendless wine sot. Are you happy now?"

Steward drew closer to him. "No, Tristin, I am not happy. You are miserable because you have been led from one distortion to the other. The truth is, you are neither as splendid nor as dull as your Reflector has shown you. Both are lies, and they have led you to this." Steward squeezed Tristin's shoulder. "Don't you want to know the truth?"

"And you have this truth? From the king?" Tristin's voice betrayed his disbelief.

Steward drew the king's Reflector from his satchel. He turned it toward Tristin, who peered into the glass face of the Reflector. He drew closer and looked again and again.

Steward tried to read his friend's emotions but couldn't. "What do you feel now?"

Tristin's eyes stayed on the Reflector. "I'm not sure, but there is something right about what I see. I can't explain it, but this image I see looks like...me. Like the man I always thought I might be but was afraid to be. Why have I never seen this image before?"

"Because your image has been distorted for so long."

Anger tinged Tristin's eyes. "Distorted by whom?"

"By everyone. By those who have made you into someone other than who you were created to be. By others who live in their own distortions. By the Light District that makes those who live there out to be more than they really are. By your own desire to be someone other than your true self. And by the Phaedra, who whisper falsehoods in your ear and warp your Reflector's image. It all works together to undo you, whether through a grandiose or grotesque distortion. Both are crippling to your spirit."

Tristin held his gaze on Steward. His tone was cool and sharp. "They have lied to us? All these years? They created this grand delusion? If you're right, something must be done. This must be set right. But how?"

Steward stepped back and swept his hand toward the sons of Abner. "Let me introduce you to my two friends Troy and Trek. You know them as the sons of Abner the Blacksmith."

Tristin recoiled. "Such lowlife in my house?" But as the two boys emerged from the shadows, Tristin's eyes widened.

He walked closer to study them. "I've never really looked at people from the outskirts."

Hope sparked in Steward's heart. "And what do you see?"

Tristin kept examining their features. "I see...purity and simplicity. It's like what I saw just a moment ago in this new Reflector." Red tinged his cheeks as he held out a hand to Troy and Trek. "Please, forgive me. You are most welcome here."

"Tristin, what you're feeling is what the king calls the Deep Peace. It's what he wants for everyone in his kingdom. And it's your mission to liberate the people of Marikonia that they might know this peace."

Before anyone could reply, Steward heard soft footsteps coming down the hall.

Lots of them.

"The Phaedra!" Steward looked at Tristin. "They must not know I'm here." He retreated into the shadows of the room as three Phaedra entered.

"Good evening, our dear Tristin. We see you have guests. Would these be the sons of Abner?"

Tristin glowered then walked to them. "Yes, they have come for a visit. Don't they look splendid?"

"Not at all, I am afraid," one Phaedra replied. "And I must say, neither do you. Why, I have not seen you look worse." The Phaedra circled Tristin as he spoke. "Surely you are despairing over your decline, and these misfits can only make matters worse for you. Please ask them to leave."

Steward smiled from the shadows as Tristin took on the challenge. "I am afraid you are gravely mistaken. I think these lads look wonderful. And I believe I have never looked better myself."

One Phaedra drew close and stared at him. "Who told you that you looked fine? What could possibly give you that impression?"

Tristin produced the king's Reflector. The Phaedra recoiled at the sight of it. He turned it toward himself until his image was clear for all to see.

"*This* is what tells me, thank you." Then he turned it to Troy and Trek. "And as you can see, these are quite smart fellows indeed!"

"Where did you get that horrible Reflector?" A Phaedra stepped forward to grab it, but as he reached for it, his hand was thrust back as though by some unseen force. The Phaedra grew agitated. Angry.

"You are a fool! This is a lie. Throw it away and return to your own Reflector."

It was time. Steward emerged from the shadows. "He will do no such thing. I will tell you where he got the Reflector. It is the king's own Reflector, and I brought it to him from the king. I am Warrior Steward, and your time of lies and distortions is ended!"

The Phaedra ran from the room, and Steward raced after them. He drew his sword and slew all three of them, leaving their empty robes strewn on the floor as their spirits cried out and flew away.

Tristin spoke from behind Steward. "That was a bold move. You were almost exposed. But I fear you are still in danger. The Phaedra always visit me in a great mob, twenty or more. Surely more are coming."

Steward looked out the window at the courtyard—and smiled. Astrid and Dunston were slaying the last of the Phaedra that had come to torment Tristin. He waved his thanks to them then turned back to Tristin. "There will be no more Phaedra tonight. Now, you three must prepare for the liberation of Marikonia. This Reflector will correct the distortions of all other Reflectors if people will look into it and believe that what they see in it is the truth. That is your mission. With Trek and Troy, you must take the truth to the people, let them see who they really are, and set them free."

"And let them know the Deep Peace," added Trek.

Steward smiled. "Yes, let them all come to know the Deep Peace. Now I must go. We must make Seudomartus by dawn."

Steward embraced the three and headed out into the courtyard to meet up with Astrid and Dunston.

As they left the outskirts of Marikonia, Steward slowed his horse and stopped. He looked to the path that led into the berry fields beyond Abner's house.

"I know we're in a hurry, but I need a few minutes to myself." He dismounted, handed his reins to Dunston, and walked down the path. He followed it around the hillside and through the meadow lined with berry bushes. Finally, he came to the pool. There Steward found a small memorial that Abner and Edith had made for Claire. Her name was written on a piece of wrought iron as only a master blacksmith could write it. Steward fell to his knees at the graveside and wept.

Arms slid around him, hugging him tightly.

Astrid.

"I wish I could have done something to save her."

Astrid turned his face toward her. "But you have saved her. You have honored her by bringing life to everyone in this place. Claire saw what everyone in Marikonia will soon see, but they will have each other to live according to their true image. Claire didn't have that. But because of her, everyone else will."

Steward put his hand to her cheek. How blessed he was to have her with him. He stood, but before they left, he picked a flower and laid it on Claire's grave. He took Astrid's hand and they walked away to join Dunston.

It was time to make their way to Seudomartus.

~~~~~~~~~

Alex looked up at Anna, and she smiled. "I'm okay, let's continue."

He smiled back and turned the page.

Twenty-Four

The air above Kildrachan Plain was cooler than one would expect for a sunny summer morning. Despite the clear blue sky and the brilliant sun shining above the early morning horizon, there was an unmistakable dampness hanging in the air, refusing to yield to the shafts of sunlight streaming through it. It was a foreign dampness, and its alien nature sent animals moving for shelter, as if pushed away by some great, menacing force. Soon the watery veil swallowed up the sun, reducing it to the faint glow of an autumn moon.

The grayness continued its relentless spread across the landscape. Beneath it, an ooze of blackness crept its way across the fertile fields, like oil being poured out on a green cloth.

Thousands of black-cloaked figures had crossed the Golden River and were filling the northern valleys of Kildrachan Plain.

CHAPTER
Twenty-Five

A series of cliffs ran from the bottom of Starr Hill to the edge of Blue Heron Lake, defining the western border of Seudomartus. The cliffs were inaccessible...*nearly*. At one point, they parted, creating a seam that continued to the lake's edge. The seam stopped twenty feet in the air, forming a grotto beneath it. Since the siege on Starr Hill, this had become the secret gathering place of the Faithful.

Huddled around the Transmitter, Zedekai and the king's warriors waited with Zanon and a gathering of about twenty others for directions from the king. The Transmitter began its glow, and soon the rich tones of the king's voice could be heard.

"My Faithful of Seudomartus, the time is short. Steward, Astrid, and Dunston will soon be with you, and you have only a few hours to begin to liberate Seudomartus."

Eyes darted around as heaviness hung in the air.

Zanon stepped forward. "Tell us, dear king, how we are to accomplish so great a task in so little time."

The Phaedra's greatest stronghold could not be liberated in a few years, much less hours. Even the Faithful's intense faith in the power of the king could not shake the doubt from their minds.

Zanon folded his hands in front of him. "And with so few resources. Even with Steward, Astrid, Dunston, and these mighty warriors, we are no match for the distortion and deceit that has suffocated Seudomartus for decades."

Zanon stepped back, his head hung. "Good king, forgive my lack of faith. It's just that we have tried for so long to bring your truth to this place, and I fear that we have less to show for our labor now than the day we began. To think that we can complete the liberation in a few hours seems…"

"Impossible?" The king's commanding voice rang from the Transmitter. His question hung in the air. No one dared reply.

The king went on. "The liberation of Seudomartus will not come as a tidal wave, but as a trickle through the smallest hole in the side of a dam. It will be so small no one will pay it heed. But it will grow larger and larger until it breaks the dam into pieces and truth flows again like a mighty river through the streets of Seudomartus. What we do in a few hours will start the trickle."

Zanon felt his confidence returning. "Tell us how we are to accomplish that. Are there any in the land who have not fallen under the distortions of the Phaedra?"

The assembly was quiet. Then one older lady spoke up. "Only the children."

The king's voice continued. "You are correct. And so, the liberation of Seudomartus will start with the children. Zanon, do you understand my strategy?"

"Yes, yes I think so. The youth of Seudomartus are free to attain their education however they wish until they turn eighteen. Then they all must enter the National Academy. From ages five to eighteen, many attend schools run by teachers trained in the Halls of Wisdom or the Sacred Mount, so the great distortion is instilled in them at an early age. However, some attend schools run by local communities or are taught within their families. These learn of you, dear king. These children are the hope for the future of Seudomartus."

"You have spoken well. Now, Zanon, assemble all youth from ages fifteen to eighteen years who believe in me. Bring them to this place at once. I will meet you all here within the hour."

As the king's voice faded, Zanon gave the charge. "Go now, at once."

The Faithful hurried away to carry out the king's request.

When Steward, Astrid, and Dunston arrived at the grotto, what Steward saw made him frown. *Children? What are they doing here?*

Sitting in neat rows, ten across and six deep, were all the children from fifteen to eighteen from the Starr Hill community.

Their eyes grew wide as the warrior band arrived. Steward dismounted and walked before them. Steward didn't speak but went to the Transmitter and held it in his hands. He waited.

No sound came from it.

He waited a little longer then looked up at the children and smiled. "Have faith. The king always speaks to those who believe."

Even as he spoke, the Transmitter began to glow, giving off its warmth and brightness. Steward set it down, and the king's voice rang out. "Steward, Zanon, Astrid, Dunston, and Zedekai. Look before you. This is the future of Seudomartus."

Steward studied the faces of the sixty or so young men and women seated on the ground. Their faces showed a mixture of enthusiasm and fear, confidence and caution. They looked at him through wide, admiring eyes.

The king continued. "Instruct these young warriors in the battle that lies ahead of them. Teach them how to fight using the truth as their weapon. Show them how to see the real kingdom, how to recognize the great distortion, and where to launch their campaign against the evil that has befallen this land. Teach them, Steward."

Steward stood in front of the assembly. "Do you know what is being asked of you? Do you understand the great distortion, and the power that is in place over the people of this city? Ask me questions if you do not understand."

No one moved, but Steward could see that they all had questions. Finally, a strong-looking, black-haired boy of eighteen stood up.

"Warrior Steward, why doesn't the king bring his mighty army here and run the leaders through?" He acted out the stabbing motion of a sword as he spoke. "His army could sweep across the city and reclaim it in a day. He could establish his rule here again and end the great distortion."

The boy remained standing, looking to Steward and then to the Transmitter.

Steward unsheathed his sword to the gasps of the children. "You mean a sword like this one?"

The boy nodded, a bit shaken by the display.

"Not long ago I stood in the throne room of the king, in the king's own presence. I asked him the very same question, not just about Seudomartus, but about Marikonia, Ascendia, and Petitzaros. I wondered why he allowed so much evil to take place when he had the power to end it and establish his kingdom." Steward lowered his voice. "And do you know what the king said to me?"

Every eye was on him, including those of the adults. Even Astrid and Dunston leaned forward as they waited to hear the king's response.

"The king told me that he had already won the great victory for us, a victory that cost him the life of his very son."

"Kildrachan Plain," one girl said.

Steward nodded. "Yes, the great battle of Kildrachan Plain. From that time on, the king trusted his people to choose the good way and to drive out the Phaedra from their midst. He had given his people the power to remain victorious over the Phaedra. He gave them precious gifts, including the Transmitter, that they might hear his voice and follow him. But in every land, his people chose to listen to the Phaedra and turn away from the king. And nowhere have they done so more completely than here in Seudomartus."

He met the boy's gaze. "Now to your question. The king will not force his subjects to believe in him or follow his ways. He will not play the tyrant. He will only point them to the victory on Kildrachan Plain and call them back to himself."

Astrid walked up next to Steward. "And the king will send emissaries, prophets, and warriors to tell his people that they belong to him and that he cares for them. But he will always leave the choice to them."

Steward let his gaze travel across the faces of the children. "Do you understand?"

They nodded.

A red-headed girl seated in front of Steward raised her hand.

"Why don't we set the Transmitter in the great market square so that everyone can hear the king and know that he is real and speaking to them?"

Steward smiled at her question. "Why not, indeed? It seems so simple, that if everyone heard the king speaking, they would believe in him, accept his words, and desire to seek him through the Transmitter. But sadly, that is not the case. So great is the distortion that people will cease to believe their own ears if their minds are already made up. Many who lead the distortion have heard the king speak directly to them, but their own arrogance or fear has allowed the distortion to warp that experience and fade the memories of life when the king ruled this land. No, I'm afraid it will take much more than one Transmitter to reestablish the king as the authority in Seudomartus. But remember, every heart in the land yearns to hear his voice. They just need to be set free to do so. And when they do, their hearts *will* be changed."

Another girl stood up. "Can such strong leaders as those on the Sacred Mount and in the Halls of Wisdom really have their hearts changed? Even by the truth?"

A bright child. Steward looked to Astrid. "I think this is your story to tell." He stepped aside to give her center stage.

Astrid told the children the entire story of Ascendia's liberation and Cassandra's great change of heart. By the time she had finished, the children were cheering and slapping each other on the shoulders, celebrating the victory over the crushers.

"This will be easy then!" one boy shouted.

That comment brought Dunston to his feet. He stepped forward as Steward quieted the children. "This is my dear friend Dunston. He is an Interpreter and he works for the king. He has saved my life twice, and he has something to tell you about the challenge that is ahead of you."

The children focused their attention on Dunston.

Dunston curled a lip at the children. "Easy? *Easy*, you say? Let me tell you another story. This one is about *my* people and the price they paid at Kildrachan Plain."

Dunston took the children through the horror that his people faced at the hands of the Phaedra'im. He told of his escape then showed them the scars on his hands, his side, and his feet. By the time he was finished, the place was silent. The children sat speechless, dazed.

Zedekai came to stand beside Dunston. "My friend does not tell you his story to fill you with fear, but to fill you with the awareness of the challenges you will face. Astrid has told you of the victory that can be won, and Dunston has helped you see the battle that must be fought for such a victory."

One young man of great stature stood. "How can we expect to win this battle when there is evil everywhere? How can we even hope for victory when all we can see is distortion and despair? How can we believe in victory when we can't see it anywhere?"

Most of the children nodded.

Steward looked again to Dunston. "My friend, I think our young inquisitor needs to look at the world through your very special spectacles."

Dunston fished the pair from his vest pocket. He walked over to the lad and placed them in his hands. "The world, the *real* world, is not as you have seen it. The great distortion has deceived even your eyes. You must learn to see what the king sees. You must train your eyes to look with truth and cut through the distortion. You must see the kingdom that is right in front of you." As he said this, he slid the glasses on the young boy's nose.

"Yikes!" The boy grabbed the glasses and pulled them down. He looked around, wild-eyed, then he slid them back on and cried out. "What a splendid sight! Is this for real?" He danced around and looked at everyone through the lenses.

The rest of the children ran to him, pleading for their turn to see through the magic lenses. One by one, each had their turn, until everyone saw and understood.

As the children sat back down in their places, Steward asked, "Tell me what you saw through Mr. Dunston's spectacles."

One girl started. "Everyone was so bright and happy and..." "Good. That's it!" said another. "Everyone and everything looked so good."

They all agreed, adding a host of other words to describe the wonderful world they saw through the lenses.

Dunston quieted them. "That is the world of the king. It is the way he created it, and it's the world that he is looking to us to restore. When you are in Seudomartus, you must look for this world and see it right there in the midst of the chaos and distortion, for only when you see it can you lead others to it."

"Tell me," Steward asked, "what did you feel when you were looking through the glasses?"

Again, several voices shouted out words to describe their feelings.

"Warm."

"Happy."

"Tingly."

"Restful."

"Content."

Steward smiled. "That feeling is what the king calls the Deep Peace, and it is his gift to you. As you free the people of Seudomartus from the great distortion, you will give them this gift on behalf of the king."

Again, heads nodded as the task ahead began to take shape in the minds of the children.

Then the king's voice rang out from the Transmitter. "Well said, Warrior Steward. The Deep Peace is for everyone in my kingdom, except the Phaedra. They relinquished it forever in their revolt against me. Now they wish to take it back by force."

Those words jolted Steward's mind back to the urgency of his mission. "Great king, the Phaedra are gathering. You've asked us to stop them before they reach the Ancient Fortress. But how are we to make such a journey in time if I am to lead this crusade in Seudomartus?"

"You are not to lead this crusade. That is left to another, isn't it, Zanon? You are one of the few remaining faithful from the last campaign. The success of this campaign falls to you—and it may be our last."

Steward looked at Zanon. He nodded and stepped forward.

"Yes, there was a prior campaign much like this one. At a time of widespread confusion, just before the great distortion took full hold on the leaders of Seudomartus, the king gathered the brightest youth in the land and charged us with the task of speaking truth into the chaos. It was known as The Calling. We were to be among the most learned of the land, and our voices were to win the day in the great debates on the Sacred Mount and in the Halls of Wisdom. It was through reason and faith that we were to be victorious in the name of the king and for the sake of the kingdom." Zanon paused. His breathing was labored, and he fought to find the words.

Astrid urged him on. "Zanon, tell us what happened to the others. Are you the only one left from the campaign?"

Zanon shook his head. "No, all of us who were called that day are still here in Seudomartus. But I am the only one left among the Starr Hill Faithful."

"The only one?" Steward couldn't believe it. "What happened to the others?"

"It happened in all kinds of ways, really. When we started through the National Academy, some of the weaker ones were won over by the eloquence of their teachers and soon deserted us. A few became our greatest opponents, challenging us at every turn, denying the existence of a campaign or a Calling...or a king."

"Mattox." Steward spat out the name.

Zanon nodded. "Several others kept true to the campaign, and after school they were appointed to important positions where they would have a voice and influence. We thought our campaign was well in hand. But one by one, the Phaedra whispered into their ears…and they listened. One became too distracted by her own ambitions and forgot about her calling. Three went off to start a new school, believing through the Phaedra that they had found a deeper truth than the truth of the king. Some tried to speak out, but when they were strongly challenged and their position threatened, they caved in and conformed to the more popular teachings of the day. A few left Seudomartus altogether to escape the growing oppression. In the end, even our own teacher slowly fell away, and today he walks among those on the Sacred Mount looking for truth everywhere except where it may be found."

Zanon paused. The weight of the memory overcame him. "Within ten years of the Calling and the launch of the campaign, only three of us remained faithful to the call. But we were labeled fanatics and lost our influence and voice in the community. We were forced to speak in the streets and hold meetings outside the city, and that's when we found Starr Hill."

Steward offered a hand to his shoulder. "And what of the other two?"

Zanon wiped tears from his eyes. "They paid the ultimate price for their courage, and both fell on Starr Hill to make the way for your escape."

Steward dropped his hand, stunned. His life had been bought with a great price, and as he thought of those two brave souls fighting for his freedom, he saw his dear friend Obed falling to the ground with an arrow in his back. He replayed the scene over and over in his mind.

The king's voice brought him back. "Zanon, you have fought the good fight, and now I must count on you to lead this last crusade through the lives of these young ones gathered here. You must not let what happened to your comrades happen to them."

Zanon held out his hands, his eyes flashing with despair. "But how can I do that? The great distortion was only just arising when we were called. Now it is fully entrenched and has its stranglehold on every aspect of life. If we did not triumph then, how can we do so now?"

Just then, one of the young girls seated in the second row stood and, in a strong voice, cried out, "We will not let you down!"

Then a boy in the next row stood. "We will not let you down!"

Then a third followed, and a fourth. Within moments, every one of the children was standing and shouting, "We will not let you down!"

Zanon stood wide-eyed at the display of courage and allegiance.

Steward smiled then raised his hands to quiet the children. "The campaign begins today. Each of you will be educated to lead the revolution. Remember, listen to Zanon and learn from him. Keep your Transmitter close and listen every day to the king. He will speak to you whenever you seek him in faith. Encourage each other and support the weaker ones among you. And every day, be aware of the battle you have entered. Keep your weapons sharp and your minds clear and keen. The future of Seudomartus depends upon you. Now stand and go in the name of the king whom you serve."

The children all stood straight and tall, and the king said, "You are my hands and my feet, my voice and my heart. You are the keepers of truth in a land of lies. I send you out with the power and authority of the king. And in honor of one who has been set free and who gave his life that you might see this day, I hereby commission you for this great calling and name you the Army of Obed."

Steward's heart swelled with both joy and deep grief. Astrid grabbed his hand as emotion washed over him. He whispered to the king, "Thank you, my Lord."

Zedekai called out, "Warrior Steward, if your work here is done, we must be off or the Phaedra will certainly beat us across Kildrachan Plain."

"Yes, you're right, we must be gone. But there remains one task for me to do before I leave Seudomartus. Astrid, Dunston—you and Zedekai must leave immediately and ride for the Plain. I will join you before you reach the end of the Fungle Woods."

"Not again. You're going on your own? Nonsense!" Dunston jutted out his chin.

The king spoke, "Dunston, my faithful servant, thank you for your care of young Steward. But he is right. He must do this alone. Ride ahead as he instructed you."

Dunston and Astrid nodded, and, with Zedekai and the king's warriors, the band was off, charging out along the cliffs and down the lakeshore to the path that led from Seudomartus into the heart of the Fungle Woods.

Steward embraced Zanon and gave his blessing to all the gathered. "The Deep Peace of the king to you and to all of Seudomartus!" So saying, he mounted his horse and galloped off toward the city.

Steward rode along the short road to the city. His only chance at completing his mission would be surprise and shock, so he unsheathed his sword and held it high as he rounded the corner and galloped headlong into the busy courtyard of Seudomartus.

People shrieked and jumped out of his way, some screaming for the authorities. Horses spooked by the charging rider and overturned carts. Sparks flew as the shoes of Steward's horse smashed against the stones of the courtyard. He passed the Halls of Wisdom and the Archives and soon was onto the promenade. He raced past an angry pedestrian, who darted out of his way just in time. Not far behind, a band of armed men were mounting up to give chase.

Ahead of him, Steward could see the grand staircase to the Sacred Mount. He held his breath, sheathed his sword, then grabbed the reins as he and his horse started the long gallop up the stone steps. He urged his horse on, even as it slipped on the smooth granite and marble surfaces. Up and up they charged, through the angry onlookers and past the elite of the city.

Finally, they crested the top of the Sacred Mount and fought their way past several men who had waited to seize them. Steward pressed his horse on, galloping across the open square, around the Temple of Temperance and, finally, to the row of majestic houses of the teachers of the Sacred Mount. Steward jumped from his horse, grabbed his satchel, and bolted through the door of the third house.

As he stormed into the living quarters, a white-haired man looked up then ran for the door.

"Brauchus! Wait, don't run. It's me, Steward of Aiden Glenn, Obed's companion."

The man stopped short and turned back.

"It cannot be. You died on Starr Hill, as did my dear student Obed. I don't know who you are, but if you came to kill me, do it quickly, for I have little to live for anyway."

"Brauchus, I didn't die on Starr Hill. The king saved me. I've seen him, and he has sent me back to Seudomartus with a gift for you. Please, I have only moments before they'll be at your door."

Brauchus scowled, unconvinced. "Obed died because of your stories of the king. It appears I shall do the same."

"Brauchus, I know who you are. You were chosen by the king to lead the first campaign—The Calling—to recover the city just prior to the great distortion. Zanon did not name you, but I knew it all the same."

The old man's face contorted, shame and guilt washed across it. "Yes, you are correct. The king counted on me, and I failed him. And now, I can hardly believe he exists at all."

Steward reached in his satchel and pulled the Transmitter from it. He placed it in Brauchus's hands. "If you believe, even the slightest bit, you will hear his voice again."

Brauchus held the vessel up, turning it around in his hands and handling it like an old familiar friend. "I did believe once. But this place has extinguished every last ounce of faith from me."

"I don't believe that. Obed was your best pupil, yet he believed. Before he died, he heard the king through this very vessel. Obed gave his life that I might complete my journey and return to give this gift to you. In his memory, and for the sake of the kingdom, Brauchus, you must believe!"

Angry voices echoed outside.

Please, Brauchus, please believe.

The Transmitter began to glow, just a glimmer at first, but then it brightened into a radiance that filled the room and spilled out through the windows.

"Brauchus, my old friend, I have missed you." The king's voice sounded from the Transmitter.

"My king!" Brauchus fell to his knees and sobbed.

A loud knock sounded at the door, followed by an angry voice. "Teacher Brauchus, we must search your house. We are looking for a fugitive. Please open the door or we must break it down."

Steward lifted Brauchus to his feet. "Brauchus, I must go, but know that Zanon, your young follower, is leading the second campaign. He needs your help. This is your time, this is your chance to complete your calling, this is…your salvation."

Brauchus looked up through his tears. "I will not fail the king again. Now run, Steward, down through my cellar and through the tunnel that leads under the back courtyard. It opens out beyond the garden, but from there you will be on your own. Run, and believe that we will bring the truth to Seudomartus."

As Steward ran for the cellar door, Brauchus called to him. "The Deep Peace of the king to you, young Steward!" Then the door to the teacher's home came crashing in.

Steward made his way through the damp cellar, struggling to see his way. The tunnel was dim, but the footing was firm, so Steward eased his way a step at a time.

Dear Brauchus, I hope you're all right.

Ahead he saw a glow—the evening light from the edge of the courtyard. He emerged, looking for any sign of pursuers.

Quiet.

He relished the moment of peace. All he had with him was his sword and satchel. He worked his way around the edges of the garden until he could see the Fungle Woods across an open field.

In moments, it would be dark. He waited. Then, with dusk concealing his movements, he wound his way down through the meadows along the southeastern edge of Blue Heron Lake and hurried into the Fungle Woods.

Twenty-Six

Night fell on the small camp of ten warriors, Astrid, Dunston, and Zedekai. Dunston fidgeted, trying to sleep. Then a sound.

Someone was in his tent. He shot up. "Who's there? Show yourself, coward!"

His tent flap fluttered in the breeze, and footsteps ran off into the woods.

"Dunston, are you okay?" Astrid came running up outside his tent and looked in.

"Yes, yes, just some prowler. Scared him off."

She came in and held a torch up to illumine the tent. "Did he take anything?"

"No, no…wait, the scoundrel. My cane, it was right here!" Dunston scrambled to his feet and searched through his belongings.

Zedekai ran in, breathless. "I chased them into the woods, but they disappeared in the darkness. What did they take?"

Astrid sighed. "They stole my headscarf, my mom's gift on my last birthday."

Zedekai huffed. "They stole my arm shield. Why would they take that and not my sword or satchel? It's like they just wanted that one thing."

Astrid nodded. "They didn't touch anything else of mine, either."

Dunston finished his searching. "Well, it appears all they wanted was my cane. Makes no sense. Nonetheless, in the morning I shall need to carve a new one."

Zedekai rubbed his chin. "An arm shield, a headscarf, and a cane. Not much of a robbery. Still, we must be on guard. They may be back."

Twenty-Seven

Steward trudged along in the last of the evening light, striking for the deepest part of the Fungle Woods. Petitzaros, Ascendia, Marikonia, and Seudomartus were all behind him.

But his heart was heavy.

Kildrachan Plain was miles away. Without his horse, he'd never make it by daybreak. He trudged on, and the night drew in around him.

Wait. What was that?

Footsteps.

"Astrid? Dunston? Zedekai? Is that you? Quit playing games. We must ride on to the Plain. Come out now and show yourself."

No one responded. His heart rate quickened. He picked up his pace, and again he heard the sound of moving feet.

Many of them. Just out of sight.

At once, the air grew cool and hung heavy with mist.

Something was stalking him. Sensing a menacing spirit, Steward stopped, turned, and drew his sword. The clouds parted momentarily, and the moon illuminated the area. In its somber glow, Steward watched as the woods behind him filled…with Phaedra.

Twenty. Fifty. Maybe a hundred.

He couldn't tell for sure, but he was well outnumbered. He prepared to fight to the death.

Out of the horde of hooded figures, one Phaedra emerged, walking in a line up to him. He studied Steward's face, and Steward could smell the stench of death on his breath.

"So, it is true. You have survived after all, young Steward. Well done."

Steward clenched his teeth. He'd like to shove the creature's mockery back in his face.

"And you have revisited the four lands of the kingdom, hoping to free them, isn't that right? Isn't that what the king told you? Well, well. How disappointing it must be for you to learn that forces are already moving that will bring an end to the king's rule. Soon the kingdom will be back in the hands of the Phaedra'im, where it rightfully belongs. And what will you do then, Steward of Aiden Glenn?"

Steward kept the edge of his sword between them. "Your confidence is poorly founded, *good* Phaedra." The sarcasm felt good to him. "I will fight for the king to the death, as will all of his subjects."

"Are you certain? Have you not heard the reports coming from throughout the kingdom?" The Phaedra circled Steward, like a predator stalking his prey. "Well, let me enlighten you."

He turned and summoned a Phaedra from the assembled army.

"Yes, now tell us what you have seen in Petitzaros just today."

The other Phaedra spoke. "I have just come from Petitzaros. I am pleased to report that Czartrevor has returned to his castle and even as we speak, his new chains are growing faster than his old ones. And the scoundrels from Remonant have been banished to the desert. All is back to normal, as we suspected it would be."

Lies. He knew better. He saw Trevor's eyes. He would *never* go back.

The lead Phaedra nodded. "Good, good. You see, young Steward, when left to themselves, the hearts of men will seek that which serves only them. That is what the king told you, is it not?"

How did he know that? How could he possibly have heard?

"Yes, he did. But I know what I saw at Petitzaros, and you are lying, as you *always* do."

The Phaedra said nothing. He pointed and another of the massed Phaedra came forward.

"Tell us what you have observed in Ascendia today."

The hooded figure bowed. "Gladly. The crushers are being rebuilt, as they have been in the past. And Cassandra is leading the construction. Oh, yes, she has ordered ramp building to proceed at all cost. It is as it was before this little distraction."

More lies. He would not give in to their deception.

A third figure was summoned to report.

"I'm glad to report that Tristin's old image has been restored, and he has resumed his place in the Light District. His house fills with merriment, while the Abner family has been humiliated and forced back to their squalor outside of the city. It seems their mongrel daughter—what was her name? Oh, yes, Claire. It appears she died for nothing."

"Liar! How dare you call her that!" Steward was ready to fight but the lead Phaedra raised his hand. Steward let down his guard and sneered.

"What is it you want? Enough of these lies. If it's a fight you want, then bring it on."

The lead Phaedra stepped back. "Oh, yes, Steward, it is a fight we want. But there is no need. The victory is already won."

"What do you mean by that?" Steward snapped back at him.

The Phaedra spoke in a patronizing tone. "I mean just what I said. Consider Seudomartus. There, you thought you had such a cunning plan."

The Phaedra gave a sinister laugh. "Do you think we did not expect that the king would send you to rally the youth of the pathetic Starr Hill brood? We knew of your plan. Brauchus has already abandoned you and returned to his hatred of the king-myth. Ooh, how I love that term…king-myth."

No, don't believe them. Lies, like always. But if it's true…

"And why should I believe you?"

The Phaedra stopped his circling and came as close to Steward as the sword would allow. "Because we are all you have left now. The end of the king's rule is here. And you have been so completely deceived by those you trusted."

Steward pushed the sword toward him, causing the Phaedra to take a step back. "I have been deceived only by the Phaedra, and I will not make that mistake again."

"Oh, my dear boy—and that is what you are after all, just a boy—the king will not fight with you or save you when the great battle begins. He has already retreated into his northern fortress, far north of where the two rivers merge to form the Golden River. He is there now, taking refuge while he sends you and your friends to the slaughter. Does that sound like a king worth fighting for…or dying for?"

That can't be true. The king is preparing to fight by their side. Steady, confidence.

"I do not believe you."

"I am not asking you to believe me. But only believe your eyes."

The Phaedra backed away to reveal a small area of heavy mist hanging in the air. "Come, see your king for who he is."

Steward looked into the mist. Images and then faces appeared. Soon he could see the king and his mighty warriors. They were sitting around a large banquet table laughing and eating as if in celebration.

Then Steward heard the king speaking. "Let the Phaedra have the lower kingdom. Young Steward served us well, diverting the attention of the Phaedra while we escaped to this fortress. Steward, Astrid, and Zedekai will die nobly, and we will live out our days in safety here in the north. It is a shame that they have to die to buy our escape, but after all, I am the king." His words were followed by the laughter of the warriors and courtiers as they raised their glasses.

"To the king!" they shouted. The words echoed as the images and voices faded into the fog.

Steward remained staring into the mist.

"This is a lie, a distortion. The king would never use us for his own safety. Why do you show me these false images?"

The Phaedra raised a hand, his voice feigning innocence. "We show you only what is real. We do not make up these images any more than we distorted the Reflectors of Marikonia or put the love of wealth and power into the hearts of the people of Petitzaros or the passion for ramp building into Cassandra."

Again, he drew close to Steward. Steward sheathed his sword.

That couldn't be the king. He knew the king, he trusted the king. But his eyes saw, his ears heard. He fought every inkling of doubt, but it began to wear him down.

The Phaedra smiled as the sword no longer kept him at bay. "You must understand, these are what are *true* in this kingdom. It is the desire to set them aside for some dreamy other kingdom that is the lie. And it is you, Steward, who is the voice of distortion. There is no kingdom, no other world. This is all there is. This is reality and nothing more. And it is your belief in the king's lies that will mark the end of the king's rule, as it will the lives of your companions."

Fear shot through his body. Anger boiled up in him.

Steward lifted his sword again and shot back. "What do you mean by that?"

The Phaedra backed away but continued. "When Astrid, Dunston, and the Black Knight reached Kildrachan Plain, there was a messy encounter waiting for them. It is a pity that their lives have been sacrificed for nothing."

"Now I know you are lying! Stop me if you can, but I am going to them, now! If I have to fight through all of you!"

The Phaedra seemed unmoved. "Very well, but before such a battle, you may want to examine these."

He held out an object in his bony hand. Zedekai's arm shield. Steward grabbed it, and blood smeared across his hand.

"Zedekai. No, it can't be."

Please, please don't show me more.

"And I believe this belonged to your little friend." The Phaedra handed him a cane, broken in half.

Steward held it, his hands trembling.

Please, nothing more…

The Phaedra came close. "And I believe this headscarf was from young Astrid. You were quite fond of her, I believe?"

Steward touched the blood-soaked headscarf, and his strength failed him. He fell to his knees in grief.

The massed Phaedra let out a roar of delight.

That was it. They *were* dead. And the king? Were they right about that too? The lands, the defeat? Was it all true?

The lead Phaedra stood over Steward, hissing now with a venom in his voice. "Get on your feet."

Steward rose, his mind still lost in his confusion and grief. Pain shot through his chest.

Fear, despair, heartache.

The Phaedra came up along his side. Steward felt every muscle in his body tighten.

"And the time has now come to end this journey of yours." He pulled his knife from its sheath and struck Steward across the face, sending him crashing to the ground. Blood flowed from his cheek as he lay sprawled on the cold earth. The clearing exploded with shouts and jeers from the horde of gathered Phaedra.

The lead Phaedra drew close and placed his boot across Steward's neck, pushing it against the ground. Steward was still stunned from the blow, and he fought to breathe as his blood mixed with the cold, black mud.

"Where is your king now, Steward? Now, when you are about to die, where are his warriors? If he is so caring and powerful, why has he left you to die alone and forsaken? Don't you see that this journey was all in vain? Your friends are dead. You have been used and discarded. Your whole life has been for nothing." The Phaedra pressed his boot even harder onto Steward's throat. "Are you ready to admit your failure and abandon your king?" He eased up enough to let Steward breathe.

Steward trembled, confusion and anger mixing with the fear of death. Everything he had believed and trusted was being dismantled, destroyed.

Don't believe them! But I saw the king…heard his words. Betrayal? Left alone, abandoned? Astrid, Zedekai, and Dunston gone? We are defeated. King, I believed in you…where are you?

The Phaedra removed his boot and stepped back, giving Steward room. He struggled to his feet, bleeding and reeling, and looked out across the sea of black robes.

This is hopeless. Have I been forgotten, left to die? So be it.

The lead Phaedra closed in again, whispering in Steward's ear. "Admit your failure. Abandon your journey. Renounce your loyalty to the king, and we will let you pass so that you may return to Aiden Glenn. It is over, Steward. Go home. There is the path."

The Phaedra pointed to a trail that led to the south. "Take it, Steward. Don't you want to go home? Lay down your sword and walk away. I am offering you your life. What is your choice?"

The army of hooded figures stood silent, as though waiting for their final victory in Steward's reply.

He looked at them and then down at the sword that hung at his side. He reached down and slid it from its sheath. He studied its shining blade and the ornate hilt that fit his hand as though they were one. As he did, one Phaedra drew close, putting out his hands to accept it as the sign of Steward's defeat.

Something deep inside him began to fill his limbs with energy. As the unfamiliar power surged through him, he lifted the mighty weapon and struck the Phaedra, sending the spirit screaming through the air as the empty robe collapsed to the ground.

The lead Phaedra recoiled, hunched his back, and turned to the gathering. "He has chosen! Let us enjoy every moment of the death of Steward of Aiden Glenn."

The sound of swords being unsheathed filled the woods. Steward stood his ground, raising his sword as the black mass of Phaedra streamed forward.

He slew the first wave, but there were too many. Two then three or more were upon him, knives at his throat when—the ground shook beneath them. Not like an earthquake, but as if someone were pounding on it with a mighty hammer. The pounding was rhythmic, powerful, and growing stronger. Everyone froze. Waited.

In the distance, a single horseman rode toward them. His horse was white, and his robes were crimson and purple. He wore a hood that covered his face, and in his hand was a sword that sent shafts of light like spears into the darkness. He rode as if in slow motion, and each time the horse's hooves hit the ground, it shook. It was a terrifying sight.

At first the warring Phaedra stood silent, as though mesmerized. Then they turned in full retreat.

Too late.

The horseman rode headlong into their midst. Screams rang out as robes of the fallen Phaedra were strewn across the clearing. The army turned and swarmed on the lone warrior, but his sword sent row after row to their deaths. No sooner had the horseman appeared than the Phaedra were defeated, with the last of them fleeing deep into the Fungle Woods.

Steward stood in the clearing, watching the warrior as he examined the black robes that now carpeted the forest floor. His horse snorted, as if to approve the slaughter. Then the warrior turned his horse and walked it up to Steward.

Steward struggled to speak. "Thank you. You…you have saved my life. Who are you that I may thank you properly?"

The horseman gave no reply. He circled his horse around Steward, examining him. Then they stopped.

"Who are *you?* That is the question."

Steward hung his head and dropped his sword. "I'm Steward of Aiden Glenn, or Warrior Steward. I, I'm no longer sure which one. According to the king, I am the Liberator of the kingdom. But if all my work is undone, if my companions are dead, and the battle lost, then I am just a boy lost in a dream who wants to go home."

The horseman pulled his horse aside to expose the road. "If that is who you are, then take the wide road leading south from here. It will take you to Aiden Glenn. If that is what you choose, the road awaits you. It is wide and easy, and you will be home by midday tomorrow."

Steward looked down the road.

Yes, it's time to go home.

He picked up his sword and sheathed it then turned toward the road. "Thank you, whoever you are. I am going home." Steward started down the wide road to Aiden Glenn.

"There is another choice."

Steward stopped and turned back. "What other choice?"

He pointed toward a small path that led into the darkness of the heart of the Fungle Woods. "You can walk into the night through the Fungle Woods to Kildrachan Plain. Was that not your destination?"

"It was, but all that is lost now. My companions are dead, the lands I tried to liberate have abandoned the truth, and maybe…maybe even my own king has forsaken me. I don't know, but I have no reason to go to the Plain. My journey is over, and my cause is a failure."

The warrior paced his horse again. "Steward, do you trust the king?"

Steward breathed deeply, searching for some answer that could satisfy his torn spirit. Just hours ago, his answer would have been unequivocal. Now he didn't know what…or who to believe. His face hurt, his spirit was crushed, his heart ached for his companions, and he was exhausted.

"I don't know anymore. So little is clear. So much is left unanswered. Nothing of this makes sense, and I feel alone and forsaken." He looked up. "No, I can't say that I trust the king anymore…but I do *so* want to!"

The warrior studied Steward. "Tell me about the sword that hangs at your side."

Steward ran his hand across the hilt of the wonderful sword, and his mind took him back to that glorious day when he stood in the presence of the king in his very throne room and was handed the sword.

His spirit ached. "It's a gift from the king."

"And with the sword came also your name, did it not?" The warrior's horse paced back and forth as he questioned.

"Yes, but I've certainly failed miserably as a warrior."

The horseman drew close again and stopped in front of Steward. "Why do you doubt in the darkness what was revealed to you in the light? If you truly doubt the king, then return home along the wide road. But if you know in your heart that his word to you is true, then trust him even in the darkness and take the narrow and perilous road to Kildrachan Plain."

The words were compelling, but Steward replied, "I still have so many questions. I don't have the courage or the strength left. Can't you tell me more? Tell me that what I saw in the mist was not real. Tell me the king is trustworthy. Tell me the Phaedra were wrong. Tell me why Astrid, Dunston, and Zedekai had to die. Give me some answers so I *can* journey to the Plain."

The horseman made one more circle. "Choose, Steward, which path you will take."

Steward stared into the blackness of the small path that seemed to lead to nowhere. He turned to the horseman, but he was gone! Steward examined the choice that was before him. The path back to Aiden Glenn was so inviting, so easy, and so wide. The small, dark path into the woods looked even more menacing. This was his moment. This decision would change his life forever.

~~~~~~~~~

"Choose the path into the woods, Steward," Anna blurted out. She was sitting on the edge of her overstuffed chair with her hands to her mouth, hanging on every word of the story.

Alex smiled, sharing her anticipation. He read on.

~~~~~~~~~

Steward walked down the path leading to Aiden Glenn. The horseman's question kept ringing in his ears. *"Do you trust the king?"*

He heard the king's own words: *"Trust me, Steward."*

And he saw Astrid's face. How he longed to see her again. He stopped. If he continued home, it would all be lost. Everything they'd done. All they'd fought for.

Courage. Confidence. Trust.

If my journey ends, it will not be in Aiden Glenn. It will be here, to die by my friends. This is my journey, and I won't end it as a coward. Tomorrow the entire Phaedra army will overtake me, but tonight, I will obey.

Steward turned and walked back to the edge of the narrow path—and took the first few steps into the darkness.

The path was hard to follow, and only the faint moonlight allowed him to keep from walking into the brush and overhanging branches that lined the way. As he struggled on, he could feel spider webs across his face. Terrifying sounds came from all directions. *Why did he take this path?*

But he could not turn back now.

He fought on until the brush and spider webs seemed to close in on him and clog the path ahead. It felt as if a thousand small hands were grabbing at him, and he began to twist and turn to get away. He pushed his way through the unrelenting brush and fell over a log that lay across the road, hidden beneath the vegetation. He struggled to get up. He was being suffocated by the impossible tangle of vines and branches that held him tightly to the earth. He was shaking, struggling to free himself, but getting more and more entangled.

"Help me, my king! Help me or I will die!"

At that, the vines and branches wilted around him. He sat up, and—

He was free!

He stood and took a few steps forward. Then he heard the snorting of a horse. He walked with careful steps in its direction. The path had widened in front of him. As he made a wide turn, he saw a saddled horse with its reins hanging down to the ground.

"Easy, boy. Easy now."

Steward approached the horse. "Don't run…don't run…" The horse shook its head and looked right at Steward! The animal seemed to be waiting for *him.* He reached for the reins, and the horse did not move. Steward climbed into the saddle and turned down the path.

Without any prompting, the horse began to trot, then gallop, and race faster than Steward had ever experienced. The woods flashed by, and he hung on for all his life as the mighty horse rounded turns and cleared hedges at a speed that outpaced the wind. Turn after turn, Steward gripped the reins and fought to stay on his mount, and the Fungle Woods became a blur as he and his horse were transported through the night by some great force.

As the light of dawn began to color the trees of the southernmost edge of the Fungle Woods, Steward's horse slowed to an earthly pace. It seemed as if time itself had been suspended and only moments had passed since he came upon the horse. He looked around and—

He was there, emerging from the Fungle Woods onto Kildrachan Plain.

"Good choice, Steward," Anna cried.

Alex set the book down. He walked out of the room, across the hallway, and into his father's study. He placed both hands on his dad's desk and slumped over, hanging his head.

"Are you all right?" Reed put a hand on Alex's shoulder. "I guess Dad made his point."

"And then some." Alex drew a breath. "That's me standing in that clearing, hearing the words of doubt and despair that everything I believed in might be wrong. That was *my* decision that Steward faced. But I chose the wide and easy road and abandoned the calling on my life."

Reed faced his brother. "Steward didn't make his choice out of any great insight or sense of calling. He made it out of sheer faith, even when nothing made sense. You still have that faith inside you, Alex."

Alex slumped into his Dad's office chair. "I did once. But after Mom died, I just couldn't find it anymore. I had nothing left. Nothing for myself, much less anyone else."

"Maybe that's where God wanted you."

Alex glanced toward the doorway and saw Anna there, resting her head on the door jamb.

She shrugged. "I mean, in the end it is all about trust and faith, isn't it? Maybe God wanted to get you to a place where all you had left to lean on was Him. Only faith and a scary, dark road."

Alex nodded. "Maybe, but I've gone too far down the wrong road to get back to a place like that."

Merideth peeked around the corner. "Hey, big brother. You okay?"

"I don't think I'm supposed to be okay. So, no, actually."

She walked over to him. "There's a lot of hope in the story, don't you think? I mean, Steward made it through to the Plain, right?"

"Because he was saved by the king." Alex turned in the chair. "Some of us aren't so lucky."

"Not yet," Reed said. "I think we all could use a word from the king. It's not so easy, but I do have to admit I'm thinking more now about what it takes for that to happen."

Anna arched a brow. "According to the story, just an ounce of faith."

"An ounce is more than we can muster sometimes." Alex couldn't help the bitter tinge to his words.

Anna hugged him. "You have it, Alex. We all know you do. Give yourself a break and listen to your heart. Dad believed in you."

"And so did Mom," Merideth added.

Reed looked straight into his brother's eyes. "And so do all of us."

Was it too late? Was he too far down the wrong road?

"Thanks. Thanks. I don't know what to do with all this, but we better get back to the story if we're going to get home today."

They reassembled in the living room.

"I'd like a break, if that's okay." Alex planted himself on the loveseat, away from the open book on the table.

"I'll be happy to read." Merideth took the position by the coffee table.

"We're quite near the end," Walter said. "I believe we should be able to finish and get you all on your way home before dark."

Merideth turned the page to the last chapter.

CHAPTER
Twenty-Eight

Steward led his horse along the southernmost edge of the Fungle Woods. His eyes searched across Kildrachan Plain. To the west were the treed valleys, where the Golden River flowed. To the south, the hills were a brilliant gold in the early morning sun. Beyond them, Steward could see the outline of the Ancient Fortress of the Phaedra'im. East of that, he could just make out the gray mist that hung over his hometown.

Steward prepared himself as he looked for the place where his companions fell.

They shall be given a proper burial. No matter how long it takes.

His heart broke at the thought of finding Astrid's lifeless body. His grief mixed with caution; he didn't wish to encounter the Phaedra army. Just then, he heard the snorting sound of a horse in the distance.

He dismounted, trying not to make a sound. He crept along through the underbrush until he could see a lone horse standing in a small clearing, just a few yards into the forest. He drew his sword and eased his way into the clearing toward the horse.

A figure jumped at him out of the brush and threw him to the ground. Steward scrambled back to his feet and brandished his sword.

And then he heard her laugh.

"That's what you get for taking so long to get here!" Astrid beamed a smile between her spurts of laughter. "You should've seen the look on your face."

He couldn't speak. So many emotions washed over him, and no words could express them.

Astrid looked at him and reached out a hand. "Steward, are you all right?"

He dropped his sword and smothered her in his arms. "Oh, yes! I am definitely all right!" He pulled back and looked at her. "I thought you were...they told me you were...I am so glad to see you, Astrid!"

He embraced her again, pressing her cheek next to his. Astrid blushed but closed her eyes, holding him closely.

"Hey, what's going on here?" Dunston came into the clearing. "This is a fine sight. We have a war to fight, and you two are acting like it's a night at the dances."

Behind him, Zedekai entered the clearing.

Steward closed his eyes. *What a fool I am. How could I believe them?* "You're all alive. The deception was so real, so powerful." He stepped back. "But wait, I saw your arm shield, and your headscarf. They were covered with blood."

Zedekai and Astrid looked at each other. Zedekai raised his hands. "So that's why they stole them."

"Quite a deception," Astrid added.

"My cane, what about my cane? Did you retrieve it?" Dunston shouted as he came up to Steward.

"Sorry, my friend. It was in pieces, and I thought you were too."

"Scoundrels! Today I will get my revenge!" He waved his new cane in the air.

Zedekai came near Steward and looked at the gash on his cheek. "What happened to you?"

"Let's just say I had a very dark night last night, thanks to our hooded friends."

"The Phaedra did this to you?" The anger resounded in Zedekai's tone.

Steward nodded. "They had me vastly outnumbered in the forest just after I left Seudomartus. They told me lies until my mind was so confused I couldn't tell what was real and what was distortion."

"They're good at that, the fiends!" Dunston looked at the scars on his hands.

"How did you escape such an army?" Zedekai asked.

Astrid had retrieved some water and began washing Steward's wound as he spoke. "The Phaedra were about to overwhelm me when out of the forest a great warrior came to my rescue. He was larger than any man I have ever seen. He was riding a white horse and was dressed in crimson and purple, and he carried a sword that sent out shafts of light in every direction. He had a hood on his face, so I never saw who he was. But he drove off the Phaedra as they were about to kill me."

Zedekai and Dunston looked at each other, and Steward sensed they knew something about the horseman.

"Did the warrior say anything to you?" Dunston drew closer to Steward.

"He set a choice before me. Either I could take the wide road back to Aiden Glenn, which is what the Phaedra were encouraging me to do, or I could walk into the woods to Kildrachan Plain."

Zedekai slapped his shoulder. "You made a wise choice."

Eventually. "But the Phaedra told me you three had been killed."

"They were very close to being right," Astrid replied as she washed his cheek. "We were ambushed as we cleared the forest, and also greatly outnumbered."

"How did *you* escape?"

She pulled back to look him in the face. "Does this sound familiar? A warrior came from deep in the forest…"

Steward finished Astrid's description. "Wearing crimson and purple and carrying a sword that sent out shafts of light in every direction. Yes, yes it does. So he saved you as well. Do you know who he is?"

"No," Zedekai replied, "but he was definitely sent to us from the king."

Just then, a chill descended on them. The mist billowed in and began moving across the land.

Steward's nerves prickled. "I've felt this chill before and have seen this mist. What's causing this weather?"

Zedekai walked to the edge of the clearing and looked out across the Plain. "This is not the making of weather." He turned back to his companions. "It is time. The Phaedra'im army is near. They will march for the Ancient Fortress. And we must stop them." Zedekai mounted his horse.

Dunston jumped on behind him and grasped his chainmail. "Then let's ride to our destiny."

Steward's heart raced at the thought of encountering the Phaedra again.

This time, I will not be fooled.

Soon the ten warriors of the king joined them.

The captain rode up to Steward. "It's good to see you, Warrior Steward."

Warrior Steward. He had almost forgotten. "And to see the ten of you!"

The thirteen riders and Dunston rode out from the clearing onto the vast open space of Kildrachan Plain. They raced toward its southern end and galloped along the hills that separated the plain from the lower regions of the kingdom. They crested the last hill and rode into the valley below, positioning themselves right in front of the access to the Ancient Fortress. There they turned to the north and waited.

Zedekai quieted his anxious horse. "There, there, boy. This may be a long wait, but when they come, we will be ready."

The morning drew on. The sun became more and more obscured behind the heavy mist. The fog grew so thick that soon they could see only a few hundred yards in any direction.

"They can slip right past us!" Dunston shook his head. "This blasted fog is *their* doing."

"Quiet, my little friend." Zedekai shifted in the saddle. "If we can't see them, we must hear them. To move an army to the Ancient Fortress, they must come up this valley. Fog or no fog, they will not escape us."

No sooner had the words left his lips than they began to hear the sounds of horses in the distance. In the fog, it sounded like they were right on top of them, but they knew that the sounds were still far off.

"Steady," Astrid said to her horse.

The fourteen warriors remained silent, listening as the distant sounds of movement grew louder and closer. Then, without reason, the sounds stopped. All became eerily silent.

No one dared move or speak.

Then, as if by fiat, the fog began to clear. First, it lifted high above the place where they were assembled. Then, foot by foot and yard by yard, the visibility increased. Within moments, Kildrachan Plain was bathed in sunlight, and the small band of warriors took in the sight that lay before them.

In all directions, the hills were covered in black. The Phaedra'im had descended in such numbers that they covered the ground for as far as the eye could see. The small band was surrounded on three sides and outnumbered by ten thousand to one.

Astrid's face grew ashen. "My lord!"

Steward's chest was tight. *My lord, indeed!*

Zedekai rode close to Steward. "Tell me, Warrior Steward, what do you feel?"

"What do I feel? I feel as though I am about to die."

"Look again. Look around you, Steward. Look at the enemy in all its power and might. Look at the vastness of its resources and the ferocity of its intent. Look closely at it then search your heart and tell me again…*what you feel.*"

Steward did as the knight ordered. All he could see was hooded figures ready to raise their swords and overwhelm their little band of warriors. He saw the anger and evilness of the Phaedra. He could sense their hatred and their thirst for vengeance. But when he looked into his own heart…

His eyes grew wide, and he turned to Zedekai. "The Deep Peace, that's what I feel."

Zedekai smiled. "Then let us fight in the name of the king and with the power of the Deep Peace." He drew his sword and raised it. The other warriors joined him. The band formed a line and faced the assembled mass of Phaedra with swords held high against the azure blue sky.

The show of force brought a reply from the Phaedra army. The sound of unsheathed swords was deafening as tens of thousands of hooded spirits lifted their own weapons above them. Then from their midst, five Phaedra rode forward into the empty space between the great Phaedra'im army and the small band of the king's warriors. They looked at the opposition in front of them.

"You cannot win!" one of them shouted. "Surely you know that. Save yourselves now, for we will take the Fortress of our ancestors on this very day."

Steward shouted back, "This is the king's plain, and you are trespassers. We will fight in the name of the king. You shall *not* take the Fortress but be banished back to your rightful place beyond the Golden River."

The army of Phaedra shouted and shook their swords. The lead Phaedra turned to the amassed army and quieted them. Then, in a loud voice that carried across the plain, he shouted, "As they prepare to die, let them see the true nature of the evil that is about to descend upon them."

At that command, one by one then thousands upon thousands, the Phaedra removed their hoods, revealing contorted, disfigured faces and heads, each one more gruesome than the last.

Steward had never seen the Phaedra without their hoods. He stared at the sea of bestial faces with horns and fangs, bulging eyes, and maggots in their hair.

With their true nature now exposed, the Phaedra began a slow march toward Steward and the warriors. The enemies' pace increased into a trot. Then the lead Phaedra shouted, and the charge began. Ten thousand horrific riders charged down the hills at Steward, Astrid, Zedekai, Dunston, and the ten warriors of the king.

The small band stayed fixed in their positions, swords in the air, ready for the onslaught. As Zedekai's horse reared up, he looked at Steward. "How about now?"

"What do you mean?"

"How about now? What do you feel now, Warrior Steward?"

Steward grinned. At that very moment, as death was charging upon them, all Steward felt was the Deep Peace of the king. "Yes! I feel the Deep Peace—even now!"

Zedekai smiled widely. "Then behold, Warrior Steward, your salvation is at hand!"

Instantly, as if engulfed by an avalanche, an army stormed from behind the little band, charging by them on every side and engaging the approaching Phaedra scarcely fifty feet in front of Steward. The sea of warriors wore every conceivable color and looked like a massive tapestry descending upon the blackness of the unhooded Phaedra. Amid the chaos of the battle, Steward saw that at the leading edge of the massed forces was the hooded horseman who had rescued him from the Phaedra.

Steward joined Astrid and Zedekai, and together they charged into the fray. Astrid swung her sword with skill and passion, but the Phaedra were coming at her from every direction. Twice she fell, just out of the reach of the thrust of a snake-shaped Phaedra sword. Steward watched as Dunston cut down five Phaedra horses as they galloped. Then, seeing Astrid crawling from two pursuers, Dunston leapt to her side and gave her time to find her feet. Together, they charged the two Phaedra and cut them down.

The battle raged on. Across the hills and fields, thousands of the king's warriors engaged in fierce battle with the endless flood of Phaedra. Two, three, four times, the king's army advanced through the black wall of hooded demons, each time only to be pushed back by a new, advancing wave.

Steward's arms ached as he swung his sword again and again to cut down the Phaedra that amassed around him like packs of wild dogs. The only thing that kept Steward alive was the constant presence of Zedekai, Astrid, and Dunston, who fought for him with a passion that seemed almost supernatural in its intensity. Still, Steward felt the exhaustion begin to set in as wave after wave of hooded fighters came at them without mercy. And he saw the exhaustion in the faces of his colleagues.

At the peak of the battle, Steward saw the hooded horseman ride to a hill overlooking the entire scene. Steward broke free from the fighting just long enough to watch as a second figure arrived at the hilltop to meet the horseman. It had to be the king! Steward's heart soared, extinguishing the distorted vision he had seen from the Phaedra. "It's the king! He is here!"

Astrid ran to him and looked up at the two horsemen. "Of course it is. He's been here the whole time. And he always will be."

They watched as the two horsemen looked down on the gory scene. Then the king and the hooded horseman faced the oncoming waves of Phaedra. From the two of them, Steward could see a light flash down into the valley, a light so intense that Steward couldn't bear to look at it, even from this great distance. The king and the hooded horseman, enveloped in an aura of piercing brightness, rode straight into the mass of attacking Phaedra. Without so much as a sword swinging in their direction, the Phaedra recoiled and fell in the presence of the horsemen. Screams echoed across the Plain as thousands of Phaedra spirits were sent out of their bodies and back to the *Tohu Wa-Bohu.*

The light grew and emanated in waves throughout the black army, obliterating whomever it touched. The king's army stopped and watched, untouched by the light, as thousands of Phaedra robes fell around them. Within minutes...the battle was ended.

As the last Phaedra escaped over the far horizon, quiet fell across the Plain.

Steward sheathed his sword.

Exhaustion mixed with joy and…relief. Not at winning the battle, but at the restoration of his faith.

"It's over. This is the king's victory." He embraced Astrid, and soon their companions joined them.

The four stood looking across the great open expanse before them. The landscape was littered with empty black cloaks and the bodies of fallen comrades. Despite the loss of many of their own, the victory had been convincing, and the Phaedra had suffered a devastating defeat.

On a far hillside the king rode alone, the halo of light now gone. He stopped to look back at the four and waved. Even at this great distance, his clear and powerful voice rang out to them. "Deep Peace, my faithful friends."

They watched as he rode out of sight. Then the hooded horseman in crimson and purple rode out from the battle lines and made his way up to them. As he did, hundreds of the king's army gathered around. The horseman dismounted and walked to Steward and the little entourage.

"You chose well, Warrior Steward."

"And you have saved my life again. But can you tell me who you are?"

The man studied Steward, his eyes piercing him from behind the hood. "First tell me, Warrior Steward, where did the Deep Peace come from as you faced the Phaedra'im army?"

He knew—but how? "I guess…I guess it came from the king. Somehow, when I should have been filled with fear, I was confident and at peace."

"So…you do trust the king after all."

Steward looked at the warriors assembled around him. He looked at Dunston, Zedekai, and Astrid. And he searched deep in his heart. "Yes, yes I do."

The horseman reached up and pulled the hood from his head. There was a collective gasp that reverberated across the entire expanse of Kildrachan Plain. It was as if the earth itself sighed. For standing before them was the king's own son.

"Your majesty!" Zedekai fell to his knees. "But you died on Kildrachan Plain at your father's side! I was there!"

Steward found it hard to breathe. "Yes, and the king showed us your gravesite."

The king's son smiled. "It appears that young Steward is not the only one who can return from the dead. I did die at my father's side, but there are forces in this kingdom greater than death. And now I have returned to reclaim my father's kingdom."

Steward bowed then looked up. "If I may ask, what was the light we saw that defeated the Phaedra?"

"The light is not a 'what' but a 'who'. She is Neumaterra. She is the spirit that carries out the king's will and work throughout the kingdom."

Dunston shuffled forward, pointing his cane at Steward. "Neumaterra. She called me to come and meet you at Pitcairn Moor."

The son nodded. "Yes, Steward, it was she who carried the king's voice across the miles so you could hear it when you were heading home to Aiden Glenn. And it was her energy that filled you with the strength to attack the Phaedra, even in the midst of your doubt."

Zedekai stood next to Steward. "And it was Neumaterra who sent me to the palace steps to rescue you from death on Starr Hill."

Astrid took Steward by the arm. "Neumaterra is the presence of the king throughout the kingdom. She guides, gives wisdom, and, when needed, provides us with the power we need to fight the Phaedra."

Zedekai looked into the sea of lifeless, black robes. "She is our greatest weapon against the Phaedra. She exposes all deception and drives out evil from her midst."

Steward nodded. "She's been with me all during my journey. I know now; I could sense her strength so many different times. Why didn't I know about her before now?"

The king's son smiled. "Steward, there is much that you do not yet know about this kingdom. Your journey has opened to you a whole new world, yet it has only started. As you continue to walk with the king through this kingdom, there are new discoveries and knowledge awaiting you. Remember, it is the battle as much as the victory that matters most. But be assured of this—the king will always come to the aid of his warriors, and the power of Neumaterra will always prevail."

The king's son dismounted and approached Steward and his friends. "You have been my father's most faithful warriors in battle, and your work will not go unrewarded. However, your work is not yet done."

"What can we do to serve you?" Astrid bowed to the massive horseman.

"Steward, you must return home and take the four gifts my father has given to you. Share them with your people and command them to tear down the Ancient Fortress. Then, when the time is right, I will come for you because your journeys on behalf of the king have just begun. Go now and be reunited with your family. And take Astrid with you, for your fortunes are now intertwined with hers."

Astrid slid her hand in his, and Steward's heart soared. "But what of our friends?"

"You will see them again, but the king has other work for them to do now."

"So the war with the Phaedra'im continues?"

The son mounted his horse. "Warrior Steward, there will always be battles to be fought with the Phaedra'im, but you must remember that if you trust the king and fight in his name and with the power of the Deep Peace, the war has already been won. Now it is time for you to depart."

He and Astrid embraced their colleagues and were overcome with emotion. Dunston tried to act unmoved, but tears ran down his cheeks as he said goodbye to Steward and Astrid, even stretching up to give Astrid a kiss on the cheek.

Zedekai held Steward by the shoulders and smiled as he said goodbye. "You are indeed the Liberator we have all been waiting for. It was my honor to ride at your side."

"The honor is mine." Steward laid his hand over Zedekai's. "If not for you, I would still be in prison, in my castle in Petitzaros, or lying dead on the rocks on Starr Hill. Thank you, my dear friend."

Steward and Astrid mounted their horses then turned to the king's son, Dunston, and Zedekai.

"The king's Deep Peace to you!" With that, they rode off for Aiden Glenn.

"And to you!" the army shouted back.

Steward and Astrid crossed Kildrachan Plain to the edge of the low country and rode down through the mist across Callater Pass, where Steward's journey had begun so many years ago.

Steward was reunited with his parents, who threw a celebration for the whole village in their honor. Steward and Astrid told the stories of their journey, their victories and escapes, their time with the king, and the final battle, including the good news that the king's son was alive.

With the defeat of the Phaedra'im, the mist that covered Aiden Glenn receded day by day. For the first time, the citizens of the village enjoyed the full warmth of the sun and looked up into a deep blue sky. Steward's father pledged to lead a campaign to dismantle the Ancient Fortress, which could now be seen looming over the town.

Steward told everyone about the four gifts of the king. He gave golden Bracelets to the people of Aiden Glenn, to remind them that everything belonged to the king. He gave each one a Quash and sash so that they would always serve one another. He gave them Reflectors so that they would see themselves as the king saw them. And, most importantly, he gave them each a Transmitter so that they would always hear the king.

Steward, Astrid, Dunston, and Zedekai would have many more adventures as they were sent by the king to new lands to carry the truth and set people free from the distortions of the Phaedra. And everywhere they went, they shared the four gifts of the king and the Deep Peace that he desired for all the citizens of his kingdom.

~~~~~~~~~

Merideth turned the final page then leaned back in her seat. "Thank you, father."

Reed folded his hands and looked around at everyone. "Incredible. I'm not sure what to say."

Anna let her emotions flow. "I feel like I've heard my father's voice for the last time. I don't want to let him go."

Alex sat by her and held her. "You don't have to, sis. As long as this story is in your heart, Mom and Dad will be too."

"Thanks, Alex. That's a sweet thought." Merideth smiled at her brother.

Walter watched them and knew it was time to complete his work. He stood and came into the middle of the room. "We need to conclude these affairs and get you all on your way." He took the book from Merideth, closed the leather cover, and turned the book over with its front cover facing him. He returned it to the wooden box, closed the clasp, and placed it back on the shelf.

Well, Sam, this is it. I think we did well.

He walked to a large wooden chest that had always held blankets and quilts the family pulled out on cold winter nights for times around the fire. However, Sam had emptied the chest of its usual contents. So now Walter reached in and pulled out the first of the four gifts promised to Sam and Lori's children.

He lifted out a glass case and handed it to Reed. "This is your gift from your father."

Reed looked at the glass case—it held two fine golden Bracelets standing upright, side by side. He looked down and read aloud the inscription engraved on a bronze plate across the bottom: "'Freely you have received. Freely give' (Matthew 10:8). May God grant you the Deep Peace that comes from the heart of a cheerful giver. Love, Mom and Dad."

Reed smiled as he studied the Bracelets and the inscription. "Thanks. These mean a lot. Walter, I'll confess I've been changed by Dad's story, but I don't know what it all means."

Walter set a hand on his shoulder. "For now, I think Sam and Lori would want you to be content to accept this gift and treasure the sense of closeness to them that it brings you."

Walter removed the second gift from the chest then placed it in Merideth's hands. "This is your gift from your father."

She held a fine, golden bowl with a wide rim and handles on each side. Inside it was a neatly folded cloth sash. Around the rim was an inscription. Merideth turned the Quash toward the light to read it. "'Love your neighbor as you love yourself' (Matthew 22:39).

May God grant you the Deep Peace that comes from a life lived in service to those around you. Love, Mom and Dad."

Merideth ran her fingers along the smooth edges of the Quash. "I'm sure Dad hoped and prayed that this moment would mark a great turning point in my life. It might, but I have a lot of conflicting things going on inside right now. Walter, this has been a real gift to me, but I just can't promise what it will lead to. I'm sorry."

"No need to be sorry. That's not what Sam wanted. These gifts are seeds being planted into your lives. Nothing grows overnight, so give it time. Give it time."

He returned to the chest and took the third gift, which he handed to Anna. "This is your gift from your father."

She held the heavy, ornate mirror in her hands. With some hesitation, she turned it toward her. "What reflection will I see? Probably still the distorted reflection brought on by too many years of listening to the wrong voices."

"Read the inscription."

Anna tipped the mirror to see the engraving. "'I am fearfully and wonderfully made' (Psalm 139:14). May God grant you the Deep Peace of knowing that you bear the very image of God Himself. Love, Mom and Dad."

"Fearfully and wonderfully made. Oh, Walter, I hope someday I can believe that."

The time had come for the last gift. Walter went to the chest, lifted it out, and delivered it to Alex. "This is your gift from your father."

Alex's eyes widened.

Walter knew he'd expected to receive a replica of the Transmitter. But Alex's gift was a Bible. On the rich, black leather cover, there was an inscription. Alex read it.

"'You will know the truth, and the truth will set you free' (John 8:32). May God grant you the Deep Peace that comes from the freedom of trusting the heart of God. Love, Mom and Dad."

Alex nodded. "I understand. The Word of God. God is speaking to us today. If we have faith to hear."

Walter let several minutes pass as each of them studied their gifts and pondered what it might all mean for them. "Well, my friends, your obligations are complete. The hour is late and each of you has a long journey ahead. I'll arrange for the transfer of funds, which should be complete within ten days. Please let me know if I can be of any further assistance to you."

Alex shook his head. "The money. I can't believe I'm saying this, but I'd almost forgotten about it."

One by one, they thanked Walter. Then with little conversation, they retrieved their bags and prepared to leave. Within an hour, Walter was standing on the front porch of the Roberts home saying goodbye to each of them.

He watched the last set of taillights disappear down Avenue B as the late evening turned to night.

Walter went back in the house and turned out the last of the lights. He stood in the doorway and looked back inside. The porch lights illuminated the hallway, and he could see the image of his last visit with Sam. It happened the night before Sam left this house for the last time, on his way to the hospital. Walter had known that Sam had sensed the importance of the moment, and he had watched as his old friend ran his hands up and down the post on the entryway that served as a living history of the Roberts family. Sam kissed the post and then walked out of the house he and Lori had spent a lifetime building into a home.

Walter walked over to the post and ran his hands along it, feeling the edges of the inscriptions carved on it from ceiling to floor. He breathed deeply and felt his grief well up inside him. Before it could overwhelm him, he turned and walked out the front door, pulling it closed behind him and turning the key in the deadbolt to secure it fast. He climbed into the comfort of his '99 Cadillac and drove away from the Roberts family home, down the quiet main street of the little town of Harvest, and headed north into the night.

CHAPTER
Twenty-Nine

Three Years Later

The long, silver Cadillac wound its way along the two-lane highway that caressed the hillsides of the Palouse. The late summer sun illuminated millions of heads of wheat heavy with grain. Even in the filtered rays of the early morning, the fields sparkled on every rise and in every direction until the golden horizon met the pale blue morning sky. The harvest would be starting soon, and Walter was glad that this trip was not four weeks later, or he would be dodging combines and hay trucks all the way to Harvest. Well, not Walter, exactly. Jack would do the dodging.

Sam had not left all his money to his children. He'd set up initial disbursements to his favorite charities and then an administrative fund to support anything Walter wanted or needed in the execution of his duties as executor of the estate. This included travel, legal fees, and, Sam had insisted in the will, the upgrade of Walter's mode of transportation.

And so, on this August morning, Walter sat in the back seat of his newly acquired Cadillac while Jack, his driver, negotiated the windy road from Spokane to Harvest. And Walter loved it! Age had made driving more of a chore, and employing a driver gave Walter more time to think and write his memos and briefs.

Walter's law practice was winding down, and he was moving reluctantly into early retirement, although many of his former clients still insisted on his direct involvement with a variety of legal matters. His law practice was, after all, about relationships.

Even his legal work had taken a back seat to his main focus, namely the administration of the Roberts estate through the work of the Roberts children.

It was just over three years since Sam's funeral and the two days spent in Sam and Lori's house reading the story of Steward of Aiden Glenn. During those years, Walter had crisscrossed the country giving counsel and watching over the ways the four children administered the wealth they had inherited. Walter had no legal jurisdiction over their decisions, of course, but he carried a great amount of influence. In many ways, wherever he went, he represented Sam and Lori.

As the silver land yacht passed the sign reading: Harvest 30 miles, Walter let his mind wander back to all that had transpired these last three years, beginning with the journey Reed began the moment he drove away from his father's house that cold February evening.

Walter had met with Reed on a number of occasions since the funeral, but three were fixed firmly in his memory. On his first visit, they sat in Reed's living room as he unfolded the last six months to Walter.

"The mental image of those golden rings of Petitzaros were stuck in my mind for weeks after the funeral. But with all the business pressures, you know, they just sorta faded away. Well, all that changed the day the funds from Dad's estate were transferred."

Reed's transformation began in a most unlikely place. He was going into a major negotiation session with twelve investors whom he had been cultivating for months.

Reed stood and paced as he recalled the situation to Walter. "Each person was hand-picked and vetted to be sure they had the capacity to make the investment we needed to take the business national—and soon international."

Walter raised his eyebrows. He'd underestimated Reed's ambition.

Reed grew more animated. "Oh, Walter, I'd polished my presentation until it was perfect, flawless! I was ready to sell them on the expansion of the business and wrap up the full investment right then and there. I can tell you, they had the money, and then some. My goal was to use as little of the inheritance as I had to. It was a game, a challenge, and I took it on. I mean, why not use someone else's money, right?"

Walter wasn't sure if he was looking for an answer, so he shot him a wry smile and let him continue. Reed's eyes sparkled as he relayed the story.

"I entered the room where the guests were assembled and greeted everyone. There was a hush as I moved to the podium and began the state-of-the-art multimedia presentation. As I moved through the sales pitch and nailed every point, I examined the men and women in the room to watch for their nonverbal response. This was a first-class group. They were dressed in outrageously expensive suits, and they wrote notes on slick laptops or paper pads in exquisite leather cases. I had known each of them for years, but on that day as I studied them, an image took shape in my mind. It was as clear as if the entire room had been transformed by a Hollywood costume and set designer. I saw heavy golden rings lying over their shoulders. Their faces grew dull and pale right before my eyes, and they began to hunch over under the burden of their wealth and all that it meant to them. As they asked questions, I could hear the greed behind their words, and before long I found myself standing smack-dab in the middle of Petitzaros, amid a group of hunched-over, sad, gray little kings."

Walter beamed then tipped his head. "Dunston's spectacles?"

Reed laughed. "Yes, that's exactly what came to mind when I saw that scene. I almost reached up to see if they were on my nose!"

Walter laughed with him. "That's incredible. The kingdom—you got a glimpse of the way God sees things."

Reed nodded as his tone grew more intense. "I'll say, but it gets even better. I stopped right there in the middle of my presentation. My partners were sitting to one side of the room, and they thought I had lost my mind. Maybe I had." Reed laughed. "I just shut off the projector, shook my head, and laughed to myself. The greatest moment of my business career, and there I was, standing in a fairytale land. But I couldn't shake it, and I knew it was over. So I looked out at my audience and said, 'My friends, thank you for coming. But I think I have just discovered what this business is really all about, and there will be no expansion under my watch. I'm sorry to have wasted your time, but I think my life is about to go in a very different direction.'"

Sam, you'd be so proud of this young man right now, and you always were.

"Amazing. And what will you do now?"

"I'm not sure, but if I am to be true to my father, I need to understand more about the discipline of giving. I've never been very generous, and I know that's what Dad was trying to help me learn in the story. And if every time I try to make money I find myself back in Petitzaros, I'd better learn how to give it away."

Walter arched a brow. "The Elixir of Mah Manon?"

Reed laughed. "Yes, I guess so. I know that was supposed to symbolize money and the power it has to change people's lives for better or worse. It will be completely new to me to give it away...and enjoy it!"

"Perhaps if you find some people who do enjoy it, it will rub off."

Nine months later, Walter met Reed again and he was surprised to hear how that final comment so many months earlier had started Reed on a journey of discovery. Reed had begun meeting with philanthropists and reading about stewardship. He started giving modestly, and the pure joy of changing other people's lives became infectious. Within a year of the transfer of the Roberts estate, Reed had sold his business and was a full-time philanthropist.

Walter beamed at the news. "Reed, you know how pleased Lori and Sam would be. I'm happy for you, happy you found that there is so much more beyond the money. Now, tell me about the rest of your big news." Walter sat forward, his eyes locked onto Reed's. He'd been waiting a long time to hear this from Reed's own lips.

Reed put his hands in the air. "What other news?" They both laughed, and Reed continued. "Oh, you mean that little five-foot-tall, blonde dynamo from Texas who swept me off my feet?"

Reed looked past Walter, losing himself in memory. "Katie and I met on a fundraising trip to Belize, actually on a snorkeling boat in the Hol Chan. She was so committed to her causes. I mean she gave money, time, passion. Definitely my opposite."

Walter caught his gaze. "What kind of causes was she into?"

"Oh, everything, you name it. She had a passion for caring for people in need, loving the forgotten, and taking care of 'God's gorgeous, green garden,' as she called it. And I fell hard for her at first and then, over time, for her passions."

"And Harvest, so it seems."

Reed nodded. "Surprising, huh? You remember when I took her there on a long weekend and stayed at that new bed and breakfast just outside of town. I gave her the grand tour, including a walk through the family home, the mission, and the church. She loved it. When we got back to the B&B, we sat and read the story of Steward of Aiden Glenn." Reed paused and rubbed his eyes. Walter could see the emotion of that moment welling back up in him.

He took a deep breath, looking at Walter now as he continued. "It moved her...so deeply. When we finished the book, she took my hands in hers, looked at me with those deep brown eyes, and said, 'Reed Roberts, you were created to be a steward of God's abundance, and your father knew it.'"

Thank God for Katie. Sam and Lori would have loved her so. "God's steward. Well, that seems a fitting title after what you read from your father's book."

Reed nodded. "It was. And we were off. From that moment, we started laying out our plans to build Eden Village."

"And for a wedding?"

Reed laughed. "Oh, yes, that too."

Walter leaned back against the car seat. His final memory took him back to a meeting with Reed and Katie on the site for Eden Village. The land for the village was high in the Cascade Mountains of Washington state, about three hours from the closest city. Reed and Katie had designed a state-of-the-art research and experiential center to educate and inspire leaders globally in the importance of generous giving and creation care. The plans were extensive and complex. Walter was moved by their seriousness but dubious about its ultimate success. But nothing could assuage Katie's passion.

She squeezed his hands as she spoke. "Walter, we will change the world from this quiet valley. Young men and women will come from all over the world to visit and study here. People of wealth will be invited to come and plan for how they can be more faithful stewards. The greatest minds will assemble here to pray, research, and lead our world toward greater generosity and responsible care for this wonderful planet that God gave us. This is our calling."

"That's a powerful vision, Katie."

Reed put his arm around her shoulder. "And a powerful young woman behind them."

Walter nodded. "And a pretty impressive man as well. Reed, God had you exactly where He planned so many years ago. Do you feel that?"

There was no hesitation. "I do, Walter. I see it now. From the moment I drove away after the funeral, the story, and all, I sensed changes were coming. I pushed them down for a while, but when Katie and I stood on this property with these plans in hand, I knew. I knew in my heart…I saw so much coming together."

Yes, it had come together. Amazing, given the self-centered and lost young man who sat in the Roberts house some three years ago.

My faith is so weak. I hoped and prayed for this for Reed, but did I believe it? Help me, Lord, to trust You more in the future, because this is the work of Your hand.

Walter was given the grand tour of the stunning conference center. Its architecture was so ingenious that if not for the large glass windows, the building would almost disappear completely into the wooded hillside in which it rested.

Walter just shook his head. "Amazing. It's as if the buildings are a part of the forest."

Katie pointed to three large, white structures in the distance. "We have hydroponic greenhouses that will grow all the food for the entire ministry. Our fish farm will supply food and lots of fertilizer. And over there, that windmill only needs a three-mph breeze to generate our electricity, along with the solar panels."

Reed waited a moment then asked with some hesitation, "So, Walter, what do you think?"

Walter looked out at the structures then back at Reed and Katie. "I can't think of anything that would make your parents prouder. They cared so deeply for the poor, and what you will accomplish here will make an impact around the world."

Reed gave Katie a hug. "Walter, we have two things we want you to see before you go."

They walked up the main road and stopped where two masons were working on a large pillar. Reed slid his arm through Katie's. "I know it doesn't look like much now, but here are the drawings of the finished piece." He handed Walter a large piece of architectural drawing paper.

Walter held it up, examining it. The drawing was a large post with rings of all sizes lying and leaning beside it. On the bottom was an inscription that read, "Do you want to be free?"

Steward's words to Czartrevor.

Walter looked at Reed. No expression could capture his joy.

Reed just smiled and nodded. "It will be the first thing people see when they visit the village."

"One more surprise." Katie took Walter by the hand and led him to the main conference center where men were working on the entryway. Above the two main doors was a large beam that was covered by a tarp to keep it clean. Reed asked the men to remove the tarp, and beneath it was an engraved piece of metal that read, "The Aiden Glenn Conference Center." Beneath it was inscribed, "In loving memory of Sam and Lori Roberts."

The Cadillac slowed down, and Walter was jolted back from that moment to the present as Jack pulled into a gas station for a break from the drive.

"Is this okay, Mr. Graffenberger?"

Walter knew that soon he would tell Jack to call him Walter, but he kind of liked the formality for now. "Yes, Jack, we have plenty of time."

Soon they were back on the road, and Walter let his mind take him back across the long and difficult journey that Merideth had traveled since that day at the Roberts home so many years ago. He'd seen her three times since those emotional two days in Harvest.

He'd had such a sense of despair on his first visit as he walked down the sterile, linoleum-lined corridor of the Rainier Valley Rehabilitation Center. He'd only spoken a few words to the cheerless attendant and the attending physician who had treated Merideth during her breakdown. They arrived at her room, and Walter squirmed at the memory of her with disheveled hair, ashen face, and eyes that were empty of passion and life.

It was awkward at first. Walter prayed for the right words. But without prompting, Merideth shared what happened to send her to the rehabilitation center.

"The drive home from Dad's funeral—the story, the inheritance, and all of it—that was the longest drive of my life. So much was coming to the surface. Things I'd pushed down. It was starting to change me. Stuff that drove me, it all began to look foolish…unnecessary. Okay, I know it sounds like Dad's Phaedra, but my mind kept telling me to wash it all away. I had the money. Nothing else needed to change. So it didn't. I didn't. Not at first."

She went on to tell him how she'd thrown herself into using the power of her inheritance to further her ambitions. She bought her way onto influential boards and made several risky deals as first steps at building her own empire. Some paid off and her early success bred a greater thirst for more until she became obsessed by it. She alienated her few remaining friends, leaving her with only a handful of shallow relationships that revolved almost entirely around her money.

"Did you think much about your father's story as you were involved in all that?"

Merideth continued gazing out her window at the manicured lawns. "Occasionally. I would catch myself imagining myself as Cassandra on the ramps, but I dismissed the thoughts." She turned to Walter. "I wrote it all off as father's sincere but naïve hopes for a daughter he never really understood."

Her brow furrowed. "What I couldn't shake was the gnawing image of Donturnates struggling to build his pathetic little second ramp with his bleeding hands and gray eyes. That image unnerved me every time it flashed through my mind. It worked in me like the constant pain of a pebble in your shoe. Every step I took, I knew that something was not quite as it should be."

"What happened?"

At that, she straightened and spoke in a staccato voice. "Well, Walter. One day I met him."

Walter's eyes widened. "Him? You mean Donturnates?"

She nodded. "It's quite a story, actually. A special courier arrived at my office with a personal invitation to meet with one of the most powerful people on the West Coast— Truman Helms. He'd heard of my resolve and was intrigued by my recent run of successful deals. He wanted to know if I was a 'genuine player'"—she made quotation marks with her fingers—"and if I was ready to move up into the big leagues of investments and mergers."

"And you went."

Her eyebrows shot up. "Absolutely! He flew me by personal jet to a private airstrip just south of Palm Desert. I was taken by limo, champagne in hand, up into the hills surrounding Palm Springs then through massive gates leading into a private world of waterfalls, golf courses, and, of course, mansions rising up in every direction."

Walter nodded. "I've been to a few places like that."

She leaned closer. "So have I, Walter. But *nothing* like this. It was…well, just unbelievable."

"So what happened?"

She sat back. "Near the top of the ridge surrounding the exclusive settlement, the limo stopped in front of the largest home I'd ever seen. I was escorted inside, where I was greeted by an assistant, given yet another drink, and invited to wait out by the pool."

She stood, acting out the walk. "I walked out onto a sweeping lanai that led down to a massive stone and plaster pool. The marble, granite, and alabaster went in every direction. From the edge of the pool, I could look across the entire Coachella Valley and out into the endless desert. The opulence of the place took my breath away."

Walter was caught up in the story. "What was this Mr. Helms like?"

She shrugged. "He was a short, stout man, which surprised me. I'd heard stories of him for years. He was renowned for his shrewdness, his ability to win every negotiation, his ruthless takeovers, and his brash personality. I didn't expect a squatty man, modestly dressed and, frankly, not the least bit intimidating. He greeted me, and I thanked him— and then asked him the dumbest question you could imagine." She shook her head. "I asked if he'd had his amazing home built. Then I said I'd never been in a more incredible home. And you know what he said to me?"

Walter shook his head.

"'Oh, well, you will.'"

Walter frowned. "What did he mean?"

"I asked him that, and he led me to the farthest end of the pool and down some stairs to a sculptured lawn area that opened up a splendid view to the north. I could see that, high up on a ridge, a massive field had been created. Big stands of rock and lumber were piled alongside pipes and parked machinery. I asked what was going on up there, and he said it was his new house! That they were starting construction in a month."

"'A new house? Why are you building another home?'" I asked. "He studied me, clearly not happy with my question. 'Merideth, let me ask you…what do you want from life? What do you really strive for? What's your passion? What makes you hungry?' I knew he was measuring me, so I chose my words with care. I told him I wanted what he wanted, to be on top, to win. I thought that would please him. He didn't flinch. Not a nod or a smirk. I guess I know how a swimmer feels when a shark is circling him. Then he asked me, 'Then tell me, why shouldn't I build a bigger house?' I couldn't believe my own words, but I blurted out, 'You have so much here. This place is so grand, what could you possibly want with anything more?' He turned on me like I was some kind of prey. 'No, Merideth, I'm sorry, but you do not want what I want. Having something more *is* what I want. I sell yachts to buy larger ones. I sell companies to purchase bigger ones. I sell horses to own faster ones. I buy and sell real estate, art, airplanes, commodities, and people to own what is larger, more valuable, more beautiful, more powerful, and more loyal. And when I'm done, I see that I have only begun.' And that's when I saw him."

"Donturnates?"

She nodded. "It gets worse. I blurted out, 'When do you stop? When do you have enough? When is your house big enough, your horses fast enough, your investment valuable enough, or your people powerful enough? Where does it end?' I can still hear him shouting. 'Ending is for those who are content with mediocrity. Content with winning *most* of the time. Content with a taste of power and a sip of success.' And then I said something that was more to myself than anyone. It became so obvious. I just replied, 'Perhaps, they are just content.' That was the end of it. I was out the door, well, almost. His parting words to me, Walter, and I swear this is word for word, were, 'I was the first one to build up on this mountain, and I will be the first to build on that mountain as well. There is always another mountain, and while others are scratching and clawing to get up there, I will be waiting for them at the top. You see, Miss Roberts, no matter how hard you work or how fast you build, I will have already beaten you. I have won, Miss Roberts. No matter what you try to accomplish, you will always have to live with the realization that I have already beaten you, because I am willing to do whatever it takes.'"

Walter's mouth dropped open. "You're kidding, those were his exact words?"

"Yup, his exact words. It was Donturnates. As I watched him walk away, it was as though he turned into that sad little man, hunched over by the burden of his unfulfilled desires, gray from lack of joy in his life, hands bleeding from work that would not satisfy, and eyes sunken and lifeless from a thirst that could never be quenched."

Walter focused back on Merideth. *I can't imagine that moment. Whatever it takes, he actually said that.* "How did that affect you?"

"It devastated me. It was all so…pointless. I was back in the moment when I heard Dad calling me to a life of contentment. I remember I talked about a life of sandcastles being washed away by some huge wave. Well, that wave hit me again. Everything just wiped away. A week later, I was checking in here."

She paused, her shoulders slumped. She managed a glance back at him. "Thanks, Walter, for coming all the way to Seattle so soon after I called. I needed someone who understood…who cared."

It was six months before Walter could get back to the rehabilitation center for a second visit, and when Merideth would agree to see him. This time, as Walter entered her room, Merideth looked rested and well cared for, bearing a softer countenance.

Was that humility? Soul searching?

He was delighted to see her this way. "Hello, Merideth. It's so good to see you."

Merideth looked up and smiled. "Thank you for coming, Walter. Dr. Schreck, can I spend some time alone with Walter?"

The mid-sixties psychologist obliged. "Of course, Merideth. Remember to look for the patterns from your past. Perhaps Mr. Graffenberger can help. I'll be back in a couple of hours."

Walter let the door close and put down his briefcase. "What did he mean by patterns?"

Merideth rolled her eyes. "Oh, he's convinced that my recovery is dependent upon my ability to reconnect with the past patterns in my life that created in me the thirst for success and fame. I think it's mostly psychobabble to make me think he can really help me." She drew up a grin.

Is she taking this seriously?

"You don't think he can? Then why are you here?"

Merideth folded her hands, rubbing her thumbs into each other as she spoke. "I needed a safe place to get away and think. When you were here last, I'd lost all sense of who I am and what I am supposed to do with my life. I'm still searching. I mean, if I'm to give up trying to be successful, then I abandon everything that motivates me, everything that gives me satisfaction and happiness. I give up real life, fulfilled life as I know it. Then, Walter"—she threw her hands in the air—"what do I have left? *What do I have left?* Nothing! Nothing that I care to wake up to every morning. I'm not Anna. I can't spend my life serving the poor or caring for lost kids. I have nothing to hope for. Nothing to live for. And that scares me. That's why I am here."

Walter took her hand. "My dear Merideth. You and I are not so very different, you know."

"Oh, come on, Walter, you are…well, you are Walter Graffenberger! How are you and I alike at all?"

How much should he, could he, tell her?

"Oh, Merideth, my ambitions have taken me several times to the brink of disaster. After leaving law school, I longed to be the preeminent attorney in the region. I did my own share of clawing my way through and around and over people to build my practice and reputation. But my success never satisfied me. I thought I just needed to work harder, earn more, and climb higher than my peers. I was on the fast track to absolute burnout, but I was so driven. Man, was I driven!" He stood to look out through the window, across the open landscape.

Merideth came next to him. "Walter, I'm…I'm astonished. You seem so…settled. So at peace. Your life seems to be in such balance. How did you get there?"

He turned to her. "You may not like the answer. I found out that God cared less about what I did than who I was. Everything that drove me was of no consequence to my Creator. I had to come to grips with the fact that I was doing it all for me. And, Merideth, that just wasn't enough."

She broke his gaze and shook her head. "That's great to say, but just how did you make such a huge change in your life? How do you go from your heart's desire to something else…something *less*?"

Walter put his hand to her chin and turned her face back to him. "But, Merideth, it isn't less. It's more, so much more. Saying it's less—that's the lie. Your father helped me understand that I was gifted to succeed at whatever I put my hand to. I just needed to choose battles that made a real difference. I didn't leave my law practice, I just changed the focus of what I did through it. I took on cases that mattered. Not for their prestige or financial reward, but for the impact they would have on issues of justice and fairness and equality. I decided that I would start fighting for what mattered in the bigger picture, regardless of what it meant for me personally or professionally."

He let his hand fall, but his caring gaze continued to hold her. "Merideth, your mother and father were immensely proud of your ability to accomplish whatever you put your mind to. They just prayed that you would find satisfaction in accomplishing things that had eternal value. Your father helped me understand the value of such work. And I know that, when he was dying, he hoped that you would find the same satisfaction in your own life. He left you that fortune because he had absolute faith that one day you would."

Her eyes opened wider. "Do you think I can, Walter? I'm not sure. I'm so far down the other road. I can't see my way back. It just seems so dark and hopeless…"

He turned her to face him.

"Merideth, you are Steward at the crossroads in the Fungle Woods. You have two paths. One is wide and familiar, the other is dark and threatening. But I am confident that you know in your spirit that the harder road will lead you to where you want to go. And I know"—he pressed in closer to her—"I know you have the courage and the strength to take it."

Thank you, Lord, for those words. They were yours, not mine.

Three months ago, Walter had made his third visit, this time to her new offices located in a row of quite classy but humble houses that had been converted into offices near Elliott Bay in downtown Seattle. The views were magnificent, but the décor was humble and brought a sense of calm to Walter. In the lobby, Walter got his first look at the beautiful bronze sculpture that symbolized Merideth's transformation. He ran his hands over it and admired its combination of simplicity and emotional power.

Merideth greeted him with a hug, and they stood looking at the three-foot-high sculpture.

She looked at him. "Well, what do you think?"

He just shook his head. "It's amazing. It captures the essence of the symbol. I can't imagine anyone looking at this without being moved."

"You're right. Almost everyone has an emotional response to it, and then they ask what it means. That's its beauty. It invites you in to learn more."

Walter walked around it to see it from every side. "Do only prize winners get one?"

"Only prize winners get first-run copies. But we will sell a second-run copy to anyone."

"How many prizes have you given so far?"

"Just nine. We hope to give out about twenty per year, starting next year. We just had our first in February."

Walter picked up the brochure. "The Cassandra Award for Excellence in Business Practices with Eternal Value." The brochure explained the cash award, ranging from $100,000 to $1 million, "to be given to companies with business practices reflecting eternal values that are expressed in acts of love and service to their neighbors and communities."

The brochures sat in a glass case next to the glistening sculpture of a Quash and sash. The detail was impeccable, with every fold in the sash so lifelike that many people tried at first to run their hands across the smooth cloth, only to find it was metal. The inscription that had been on Sam's gift to Merideth—"Love your neighbor as you love yourself"— was engraved on the bronze award.

Walter felt the deep engraving. "From your gift from your father."

Merideth let a broad smile beam across her face. "Yes, and that's what it's inspired people to do. Each gift has awarded amazing changes companies and their leaders have made in refocusing their goals to include helping others. I love the line 'acts of eternal value.' That's what I was missing all those years. A life focused on eternal value."

Walter decided to take a chance. "They have a word for that…"

Merideth didn't hesitate. "Yes, they do, it's called contentment."

Walter smiled in the back seat of his Cadillac as he rolled the thought of that visit over again in his mind. Then he moved his thoughts to Anna.

He'd been so disappointed when he first saw her a few months after the funeral. Despite her wealth and her insistence that she had been changed by her father's story, she remained unkempt, carrying the same melancholic countenance she had at the funeral. He'd met her over dinner at a small café near the University of Washington.

Walter noted the diversity of people streaming through the café. "This is quite an eclectic community. Are you at home here?"

She stared down at her lunch. "Walter, I can hide here, so yes, I'm fine."

Poor Anna, she hadn't found herself, her calling, or her passion.

He tried a cheery tone. "So what out there is grabbing your passion these days?"

She continued with no change in body language. "A lot of causes move me, Walter. But none of them feel like the place I want to dedicate my life. Why is it so hard to find your calling? When did you discover that law was your passion?"

Walter shifted at the question. He had asked penetrating questions of the four children over the years, always expecting them to be open and honest with him. That was his role, after all. Now he was on the other end. "I'll be honest with you. Practicing law is not my passion, it's only my vocation."

That was a confession few had heard, only Sam and Walter's wife, Grace.

"Since I can remember, I have had only one passion in life and that was to fly. I've loved airplanes all my life. My entire childhood I wanted to be a pilot, flying in the Navy and then commanding jumbo jets all around the world. It's all I thought about, all I dreamed about." Then he added, "It's what I still dream about."

Anna sat up with renewed energy. "Why didn't you pursue it? Did you ever learn to fly?"

He shook his head. "No, I never did. There was never enough money or time. I took an introductory flight when I was twenty-three. It was fabulous. When I took that yoke in my hands, I was happier than I could ever remember." He held an imaginary yoke in his hands as he spoke. Then he dropped his hands with a sigh. "But I never took the next steps. Paying for law school consumed my time and funds, and then it was marriage, kids, and building a practice. You know, life got in the way."

Anna reached out and touched his shoulder. "It's not too late, you know. I'll even kick in for the lessons," she said with a teasing smile.

He wanted to get away from the subject and pain of a passion unfulfilled.

"Thank you, my dear. But I'm more concerned about your passions than mine. You have your whole life ahead, and it's critical that you find your calling. Let's stay in close touch, and please let me know if there is anything you want to kick around with me. Really, Anna, I am there for you any time you want to talk or explore any idea, okay?"

Anna smiled back. "I'll call you when I have an idea…and you go learn to fly."

About seven months later Walter was back in Seattle, and Anna had asked him to meet for dinner. He could hear an excitement and energy in her voice he hadn't heard before. As he entered the lobby of the Lake Union Bistro, he was met for dinner by a far more confident, and significantly lighter, young woman. For the first time he could remember, he saw the soft and beautiful features in Anna's face.

"My, you look wonderful!"

Anna gave him a warm hug and then pulled back to look him in the eye. "So how are the lessons going?"

"Lessons?"

Anna scowled. "Do you mean to tell me you haven't started your flying lessons yet?"

"Oh, that," he replied laughing. "No, I'm afraid I'm too old to start now, but I appreciate your asking. That's a dream that will remain a dream, I'm afraid. Now tell me, what has you so excited? I could hear it in your voice when you called."

They sat at a table overlooking Lake Union. To his surprise, Anna's countenance was somber.

"Last month, Char, one of my closest friends, called me at midnight sobbing. She was inconsolable, but I managed to get from her that her daughter Cassie had attempted suicide. They found her in their bathtub with her wrists opened and blood everywhere. The paramedics rushed her to Harborview, and Char was waiting word on her condition. I got dressed and caught a cab and met her there. It was only a few minutes after I arrived that the emergency room doctor came in, and...well...you could tell by the look on his face. I guess they can't hide it. We all knew that she was gone. Char collapsed, and they had to sedate her for three days as she came to grips with what had happened. Peter, her husband, just sat for days and stared out the window. It was horrible. For nearly a month I met with Char every day, but she was never able to talk about it. Everyone was in a daze. No one went into Cassie's room. They left it like a shrine. Finally, after about a month a family member went in and looked around, and they found a letter Cassie wrote before she took her life..."

Anna paused and took a sip of water. She dried some tears, then collected herself and looked at Walter. "Walter, it was Claire's letter! Almost word for word. It was her cry for help, her lament, and her sense of hopelessness at knowing she was more than the world was seeing in her but not being able to escape the despair that she would never be free to live as she knew she could. It was Claire's letter!"

God, you work in ways I can hardly believe. "Incredible."

Her eyes grew wider. "Yes, incredible indeed. And it shook me to the core. But that wasn't the worst. After her funeral I was talking with her school counselor, trying to make some sense of how such a beautiful, smart, and popular girl could have become so depressed. I mean, to sit in a bathtub with a razor... Anyway, her counselor told me that over three-quarters of the girls she sees have contemplated suicide. She went on to say that there is an epidemic in her school of self-hatred and despair among the girls, but especially the most popular ones. She turned to me and said, 'It's as if they have some grossly distorted mirror that keeps reflecting images that have no basis in reality.'"

Walter almost leapt from his seat. "Anna, you're kidding! She used those words? A 'grossly distorted mirror'?"

Anna nodded. "Yes, those exact words. And that was it, Walter—that was my moment of clarity. That was when God reached down to me and said, 'Anna, are you listening?'"

That's the moment Sam and Lori had always prayed for you to experience.

"Oh, Anna, I'm so happy for you. So what are your plans?"

She spent the next two hours sharing her heart with Walter. She had vague plans and general ideas, but by the time they finished, Walter had helped her map out a series of next steps to investigate how she could use her wealth and her passion to respond.

He had talked to Anna almost every week for the two years that followed. He visited her monthly and served as her advisor and legal counsel while her plans took shape, but she never let him visit the site where her dreams were becoming reality.

A month ago, Walter received a special invitation from Anna. It read, "The time has come to share with you the culmination of my dream. Please bring Jack and be our guest." There was a map enclosed and nothing more. A five-hour drive took them to a quiet road near the little town of Yelm. Life was lived more slowly here in the shadow of Mount Rainier.

Jack eased them along a winding road until they were greeted by a large entry with a gate that opened onto a long driveway. They drove in and stopped in front of the stone sign marking the entry. In warm letters the sign read, "Welcome to Marikonia, A Place of Healing and Hope."

Walter smiled and shook his head.

Marikonia, it had to be. Well done, Anna.

They eased down the winding, tree-lined driveway and stopped at the main building. It looked like an old English Tudor mansion. Outside young girls were playing soccer in the fields that sprawled out alongside the drive. Anna emerged from the front doors to greet them. "Welcome to Marikonia, Walter. Well, what do you think?"

Walter looked around at the magnificent buildings and grounds.

Anna gushed. "We wanted to create the feel of a small village built around a beautiful center courtyard. We wanted this place filled with flowers, meandering walkways, quiet alcoves with benches, towering trees, and fountains—three fountains!"

Walter stood gawking. "Anna, I'm speechless. And that's saying a lot for an old lawyer. Tell me about the work."

She walked Walter and Jack around part of the 125-acre property as she unpacked her vision. "This is a ministry to young girls who have lost faith in themselves. Some attempted suicide or are suffering from severe depression. We have outreach programs into the schools and churches and support classes for parents and siblings of these emotionally scarred girls."

She stopped at a wrought-iron gate that led to a small exquisite garden. "This is our centerpiece. It speaks to our mission—to end teenage suicide among girls. I know it is not achievable, but it's what drives us every day."

She turned to Walter and stepped aside to allow him to read the inscription on the gate.

"Welcome to Claire's Garden." Walter breathed a deep sigh, his throat tightening. "Anna, it's…I don't know what to say."

She hugged him. "The best part is, when people ask me about Claire, it gives me a chance to tell Dad's story."

Anna, you are telling Claire's story, and your father's in everything you're doing. How proud Sam and Lori would be.

"Three miles to go, Mr. Graffenberger."

Jack's words brought Walter back to the present. In a few minutes, they would be back in Harvest. The silver Cadillac eased its way along the familiar curve that marked the descent into the town of Harvest. The warm, late-August sun beamed through the tinted windows, and Walter reached over to turn the air conditioning up a notch. Jack drove the car to the railroad stop at the edge of town, then down Main Street. Little had changed in the past three years. It was late summer, and the streets were filling with visitors, farmers, vacationers, and residents. The town had a wonderful quiet energy that Walter so dearly loved. They continued to the turn just beyond the Mill Stone that took them past the Harvest Gospel Mission.

It looked great. Carl had used the gift from Sam and Lori's estate to expand programs and reach hundreds more people.

The car moved on and Walter looked down the street to his left where the Roberts house stood at the end of Avenue B. It would soon be full of life again, just as Sam and Lori always prayed it would.

Jack parked the car in a reserved parking spot. He and Walter emerged and walked together up the long sidewalk toward the Resurrection Christian Church. Walter looked ahead as throngs of people streamed into the church as the midday sun warmed the air and a breeze carried the smell of apple blossoms across the landscape. It was a glorious scene, and Walter breathed it in.

"Walter, there you are!"

He turned. It was Katie, and Reed was close behind her as she ran up to greet him with her usual enthusiastic hug.

"Katie, you will squeeze the life out of me someday," he said laughing.

Reed shook his hand. "Walter, it's great to see you again. You know there's a room always set aside for you at the Village. Please come for a visit soon, will you?" Walter agreed to a visit, and together they walked up the walkway to the church.

Before they got to the top step of the church entrance, Merideth and Anna saw them and joined them.

"Hello, Walter." Merideth hugged him.

Anna added her own hug. "Oh, Walter, won't this be an amazing day!"

Walter relished the anticipation. "Yes it will. Here we are, all back here after three years."

Reed leaned in. "Quite a different change of mood."

They all laughed.

Walter looked around them. "Indeed. It's hard to comprehend what all has happened in those three years. More than your father and mother would ever have dreamed of."

Merideth looked out across the scene of people making their way to the church on the fine summer day. "Oh, I don't know. Somehow I think they had a lot of this figured out long before we did."

"Walter, we have a surprise for you." Anna held something behind her back. She pulled it around and handed Walter a book. He examined the thick novel that had the professional look of a *New York Times* bestseller. He read the title, *Steward of Aiden Glenn*. The front cover imagery behind the words was of battles, black knights, ramps, throne rooms, and the striking figures of Steward, Astrid, and little Dunston.

Priceless. Beyond words.

Anna beamed. "We self-published it. It's just being released today as part of the celebration."

Reed reached out a hand to Walter's shoulder. "Now everyone can read Dad's story."

The church bells began to ring, and people made their way inside to the pews. Extra chairs had been set up along the aisle, the side walkways, and as far back as they could be placed. Soon the church was packed to overflowing.

A nervous usher recognized Walter and made his way up to him. "Good afternoon, Mr. Graffenberger. I have your seats ready. Are your guests with you?"

"They will be along, but I'm ready to be seated."

The usher looked a little undone, but he led Walter up the main aisle. Walter stopped to shake hands with people as he walked, placing hands on shoulders and exchanging smiles and nods with so many dear friends.

This church has never been more electric. Everywhere huge smiles and laughter and...joy!

As he approached the front, he passed the pew where Anna, Merideth, Reed, and Katie were seated. Jack had been invited to sit with them. Walter was escorted to the row right in front of them, where three chairs waited. Walter sat in the chair next to the aisle.

Reed leaned forward and whispered. "Walter, are your guests here yet?"

Walter had asked the Roberts children if he could be seated in the front with two special guests. They were happy to oblige.

"No, not yet." He took a deep breath and then looked down at the program that had been handed to him by the nervous usher.

The Ordination Service for Alex Daniel Roberts

and his Installation as the

Sixteenth Pastor of Resurrection Christian Church

The words took Walter's breath away. As the opening music poured out of the pipe organ, Walter thought back to Alex's journey since the day of his father's funeral.

Several months after the funeral, Walter was surprised to hear from Alex that he was heading back to Harvest and wanted to meet Walter there. They found a quiet table at the back of the Golden Fields restaurant.

Alex was ashen. "I put the decision to come back here off for months, but from the moment I drove away after Dad's funeral, I knew I had to. I got here yesterday and stayed at the house." He paused to stir his coffee.

Walter tried to imagine Alex alone in the house with all that had taken place there. "How was it, being alone there?"

Alex shrugged. He shared a few details about his stay—breathing stale air from weeks of closed doors and windows, building a fire, walking around the empty house, sitting in the overstuffed chair near the fire, and reminiscing about those two days with his siblings as they read Steward's story.

"I was at peace. Kind of strange I guess, there all alone. But that's where it began."

Walter cocked his head. "Where what began?"

Alex looked up. "I walked into Dad's study and took another look at that cracked paperweight and the chip on the mantel. I got a laugh out of reliving the scene. Then I sat in Dad's chair and just looked around the room. Geez, Walter, you could still smell Dad's Old Spice. It was kind of comforting and a little unnerving. But that's when I decided to peruse Dad's library. And there it was, that first-edition copy of Karl Barth's *Epistle to the Romans* that Dad gave me."

The story was so painful for Alex, Walter was surprised to hear him mention the book. Alex continued. "I slid it out. I gotta tell you, my hands started shaking. Then the memories flooded in, you know, how I disappointed Dad by quitting seminary. But for some reason, I decided to take the book back with me to the living room and read a little of it."

"You'd never read it?"

Alex gave him a sheepish look. "Nope. Can you believe it? Maybe that's what got me curious. Well, that few minutes turned into hours and it was very late when I came across this passage. Here, I wrote it down." He unfolded a piece of stationery paper and read.

To the man under grace, righteousness is not a possibility, but a necessity; not a disposition subject to change, but the inexorable meaning of life; not a condition possessing varying degrees of healthiness, but the condition by which existence is itself determined; not that which he possesses, but that which possesses him. The freedom of the man under grace is founded upon the good pleasure of God and has no other foundation; it is the freedom of the will of God in men, and freedom of no other kind.

He looked up. "Did you hear it, Walter? Righteousness is not a possibility but a necessity? The inexorable meaning of life? That which possesses us? What does it mean to be possessed by God, where righteousness is a necessity and the true meaning of life? What does it feel like to know the freedom that is founded on the good pleasure of God?" Alex's soul thirsted for answers.

I'm no theologian. Help me, Lord.

"I'm not sure, Alex. I guess the one thing that jumps out at me is the idea that God possesses us. He loved us before we were born. And grace, how did Reverend Hastings used to say it, 'grace is the greatest expression of our freedom in Christ.'"

Alex sat forward. "And Barth said our freedom is founded on the good pleasure of God, and because of that, it is freedom of no other kind. I want that freedom, Walter, and I haven't found it anyplace else."

Walter nodded. "If freedom is from God, you should know where to find it."

Alex shifted in his place. "Yeah, but that's just the problem. To find it I need to look to the God who took it away from me in the first place."

Walter studied him, saying a silent prayer. "Perhaps, Alex, you are back in the Fungle Woods, wondering if the image in the mist is really the king or an illusion conjured up by the enemy to destroy your faith."

Alex set the paper down. "I'm not sure what you mean."

Walter leaned forward. "Was it God who took it from you, or could it be that the real thief is the enemy of your soul, and his greatest deception is stealing your most precious possession in such a way that the one who is giving you faith appears to be the one who stole it from you?"

Alex shook his head. "But I looked for God. I tried so hard to find Him when I needed Him. If He wants me so badly, why did He stay so hidden?"

How far could he go before getting in over his head?

"I don't know, Alex. But I have come to learn that trust doesn't need to search. It doesn't expect to find but to *be found*. How did Barth say it…'not a freedom we possess, but one that possesses us'? I think you need to find out how to enjoy being found by God rather than thinking you always need to be looking for Him."

Just last week, Walter received a letter from Alex. It chronicled a two-year journey from that lunch in a little Harvest restaurant to his graduation day from seminary and through his process of ordination. Alex concluded with this:

"Walter, in the end I found what I had been searching for all my life. It was there in Dad's story, in Mom's unconditional love. It was woven throughout the Bible and etched in the hearts and lives of so many people I had rejected. It was the simple truth that our lives are not meant to be anxious pursuits of God, but the joyous response of having been found by Him. I've been found, and I am ready to help others know the same truth. Thank you, dear friend."

The organ music stopped and then started again, this time playing a regal march version of "Crown Him with Many Crowns." The congregation stood as a parade of banners, flags, and a robed entourage walked in solemn procession down the aisle and up to the platform. The last three were the regional church moderator, the president of the Resurrection Christian Church board, and Alex Roberts. As he passed, Alex looked over at Walter and smiled. But his eyes narrowed in wonder at seeing the two empty chairs.

The entourage was assembled on the platform as the music hit its crescendo. Everyone was invited to sit, and for the next hour dignitaries, church leaders, and friends spoke of Alex's spiritual journey and welcomed him into the church. There were Scripture readings and more singing. Finally the moment came when Alex Daniel Roberts was installed as the new pastor of the Resurrection Christian Church. Alex repeated the vows of ordination, and then dozens of people laid hands on him while the moderator prayed for him.

When they were finished, the church president stood before the congregation. "Ladies and gentlemen, it is my sincere honor and pleasure to present to you the sixteenth pastor of the Resurrection Christian Church, the Reverend Alex Daniel Roberts."

At that, the whole assembly rose with cheers and applause that went on for several minutes. Walter applauded and looked on. He turned behind him and embraced the Roberts children and Katie and even Jack. He looked back at Alex and listened to the cheers from the pew behind him.

Dear Lord, how can I ever thank You for what You have done here? Thank You for Your faithfulness and thank You for the story of a young man from Aiden Glenn.

The congregation ended their applause and returned to their seats. The moderator stepped forward. "And now it is my honor and distinct privilege to invite the new pastor of Resurrection Christian Church to the pulpit to preach his first sermon to his congregation."

Alex stood up and walked to the pulpit. He was an impressive figure in his flowing black robe adorned by the white, red, and yellow pastoral stole, which was a gift from Anna at his seminary graduation. He stood and looked around at the assembled congregation, then his gaze moved to the two empty seats next to Walter. When his eyes widened and a smile lifted his lips, Walter knew Alex understood.

Walter smiled back at him.

Alex opened the Bible that Walter had laid in his hands that night three long years ago and began to preach.

As he did, Walter looked to his left. In his mind's eye, seated next to him was Lori Roberts. She sat up straight in her favorite blue chiffon dress with white embroidered trim. It was Sam's gift to her on their twentieth anniversary for her to wear "on high and holy days," he had said with a great burst of laughter. She looked up at her son, and her face reflected the deep sense of joy that lay inexpressible within a mother's heart. She then turned to Walter and smiled at him with an expression of overwhelming gratitude. And Walter smiled back at her through his tears.

Sitting next to Lori, Walter could envision Sam Roberts. He was dressed in his finest suit and the tie that Walter gave him to wear when he went asking for donations from wealthy donors. Sam held Lori's hand, as he had always done in church. They stared up as Alex began to preach from John 15.

Alex's voice rang out. "According to the apostle John, Jesus said, 'You did not choose me, but I chose you and appointed you to go and bear fruit.'"

Walter let his imagination have full rein. Through it, he watched Sam's face. As it beamed with joy, Sam glanced at Walter, leaned across in front of Lori, and rested his hand on Walter's forearm. Then, from his deep, throaty voice, Sam Roberts whispered, "Proudest day of my life, Walter…proudest day of my life."

-The End-

About the Author

Scott Rodin loves writing almost as much as he loves fly-fishing, long walks with his wife and dog, and spending time with his three children and their families, especially his four beautiful grandchildren.

Scott is president of The Steward's Journey, Kingdom Life Publishing and Rodin Consulting, Inc. He is a Senior Fellow of the Association of Biblical Higher Education and a former seminary president.

Over the past thirty years Scott has helped hundreds of organizations in the U.S., Canada, Middle East, Great Britain, Africa, China, India, the Philippines and Australia take a biblical approach to leadership development, strategic planning, board development and raising kingdom resources.

Scott holds an MTh and PhD in Systematic Theology from the University of Aberdeen, Scotland. Some of his books include:

- The fictional trilogy: *The Third Conversion* (Kingdom Life Publishing, 2011), *The Million-Dollar Dime* (Kingdom Life Publishing, 2012), and *The Seventh Key* (Kingdom Life Publishing, 2015)

- Books on the steward leader: *The Steward Leader* (InterVarsity Press, 2010), *Stewards in the Kingdom*, (InterVarsity Press, 2000), and *Steward Leader Meditations* (Kingdom Life Publishing, 2016)

- Books on generosity and biblical fundraising: *Christ Centered Generosity* (Kingdom Life Publishing, 2015), *Development 101* (Kingdom Life Publishing, 2015) *The Sower* (ECFA, 2009), *The Choice* (ECFA Press, 2014), and *Three Dimensional Discipleship* (Kingdom Life Publishing, 2013)

Scott is married to Linda and they reside in Spokane, Washington.

Follow Scott's blog at: www.thestewardsjourney.com

Sign up to receive Scott's daily inspirational text by texting stewards1 to 41411

Order books or request for Scott to speak at: www.kingdomlifepublishing.com

Morgan James
Speakers Group

www.TheMorganJamesSpeakersGroup.com

We connect Morgan James published
authors with live and online events
and audiences who will benefit
from their expertise.

Morgan James makes all of our titles available
through the Library for All Charity Organization.

www.LibraryForAll.org

Printed in the USA
CPSIA information can be obtained
at www.ICGtesting.com
JSHW021444290524
63998JS00006B/266

9 781683 509325